Sam Callahan:

Death of the Diamond Dolls

CAROLYN MCWHORTER

Copyright © 2024

Dedication

Yahweh, Rapha, Elohim, Shaddai, Jireh, Adonai

You are the lamb, and I am the saved.

I will never go to sleep, my eternal flame.

Mommy

June 25, 2023, at 2:32 a.m.

You went to be with Our Lord

I'll Love you forever, and I'll see you again.

Love, Susie

My Angel Codi

When I look at you, I see our Mighty Jesus. The spirit of an Angel,

The heart of a warrior - His masterpiece.

You're the best thing I've ever done, My Love. Never forget it.

I'm so proud of you, and I love you to infinity.

My Precious Little

God sent you to us on a star. You burn so brightly with

Fierce determination, but you also have the heart of Christ.

Your MiMi Loves you so much. You're my Precious

Tiny Girl

My Precious Tiny Boy

I see the Lord's presence in you so

Strongly. Your Sweet smile radiates joy and love.

You're MiMi's Tiny Precious Boy, and I love you so much.

Acknowledgment

To My El Shaddai who I adore with every cell of my being. Every breath, every step I take belongs to You. Thank You for Your Word that guides me and sustains me in Your way. Thank You that you never fail me; thank You that You are the light in the darkness and the lamp to my feet. Thank You that You are my security, my defense, and my Rock Eternal. You are the potter; I am the clay. To You I give all Glory. Everything in Jesus' Mighty Name, Amen.

To my Mommy who I adore. I love you and miss you. You taught me so much about the importance of family, love, and strength. We were always stronger together, and now that you are gone, I feel it more than ever. Because strength isn't something that is tangible. It's a spirit that lives in our hearts, and death can never sever that spirit as long as we cherish it. You were there for me my entire life, and God gave me the privilege of caring for you and being there for you. I thank God every day that I was there for your last breath before He took you in His arms. This book is for you, Mommy. I love you.

To my Codi who I adore. I love you more than you'll ever know. I want to thank you for who you are because who you are balances me. You have taught me that sometimes silence is best until it's time to speak. Thank you, my Angel. It's this quality and the embodiment of all your qualities that make me so grateful to be your

Momma. You are loving and kind, yet possess a warrior spirit. These are the qualities I saw in Sam Callahan, so she's nothing short of fabulous and strong. God Loves you! Hugs and Kisses, My Love for ever and ever. Mommy

To Charlotte and Everett, my precious Grandbabies who I adore. Never let anyone but God determine and tell you who you are, and know that I love you to infinity. I cherish every second I get to spend with you. Forever and ever, MiMi.

To all to the strong women throughout the ages, past, present and those yet to come. Never compromise the privilege of being a woman. STAND IN HOPE, STAND IN FAITH, and STAND IN RIGHTEOUSNESS!

Contents

Preface

Sister Mary Agnes has been tortured and murdered, her mutilated body discovered in the Tall Shadow Woods outside Tarrytown, New York. "The Butcher" has re-surfaced again, triggering an all too familiar chain of deadly events that force those closest to Sam to finally reveal the truth about her mother's former clandestine life as a British spy and her mission to liberate those enslaved in the diamond mines of South Africa.

Sam Callahan's a businesswoman…tough and intelligent, a highly respected rare gem. Shattering the glass ceilings that define and cage women of the age, Sam's all glamor yet commands attention. The velvet-covered iron glove in 1928 New York business and social circles, she walks the walk and talks the talk, and no one dares dispute her. The sole heir of a billion-dollar company left to her by her mother, Valentina Brandenberger Callahan, Sam's life is steady and unchanging until May 21st, 1928, when Sam is told an unbelievable story. The story reveals her mother's dangerous yet courageous past and how that past has come after her. There's no time to waste! Sam must face assassins and British spies driven by spite and greed, and revenge fueled by long-buried secrets that lead to a hidden truth and put Sam face to face with a vicious sleeper assassin known only as *"The Daughter"*.

"I crouch at the knee, stooping beside him…admiring my work. I know I should run, get out of here, but I can't resist the thrill. The urge to bask in the glory. He's not quite dead yet, and I know he can hear me. He'll die soon, but I want the last sound he hears in this world to be my voice. The one who took control of his life and death. Oh, the power! It sends tingling chills up my spine and floods my mind like a symphony! I love you, Mommy. I love you."

It's a race against the clock to save herself and Anashe - a sister she's never met. The one that holds the key. The one that can end it all.

The Daughter

Lizzy Borden Envy

The Drive to the Callahan Long Island Estate

10:45 a.m. – Friday, May 25th, 1928

"*Lizzy Borden took an ax and gave Sam Callahan forty*

whacks... Lovely thought! But yuk! An ax! I think I'll do Sam a little simpler and with a little less mess. I can't think of anything more divine!"

What a glorious day for Sam's death! I left the town of Tarrytown in rather a mess. My job there is done. Poor Captain Grayland. Dying a miserable death like that. I love it! And the collateral damage at the Mayfield Hotel – well – that just couldn't be helped. Cooley, Foster, Del Ray, and Sister Mary Agnes. So many notches in so little time. But Sam Callahan is the gold ring more important to me than any of 'em combined.

You could've knocked me over with a feather when Sam suggested we keep the interview today delivering herself right to me - her assassin. Imagine that! Hmmm, I dare to think what her obituary will say. Maybe something like this. "*Samantha Callahan, beloved daughter of Collin Callahan and Valentina Brandenberger Callahan, was found dead Friday afternoon with a bullet in her head. The hoity-toity candy empire heiress begged for her life, but it was no use. Her British spy cronies couldn't save her. She died a mess."* Well, I'd need more time to perfect it, but that's a fabulous start.

Oh!! Here it is! The Callahan Estate. My mouth is watering. It's show time! Honestly, though, I could care less about that diamond. No! She's dead because I need her to be. I live for her to die. Isn't that right, Mommy? Yes, yes. That is absolutely, positively right. Ha!

"And when she saw what she had done, she gave her mother forty-one."

****

****

Two Weeks Earlier

****

Sam and Felicity Farmer Fellows

The Lunch Meeting

Piamini's Garden Restaurant – Manhattan, New York, NY

11:30 a.m. - Monday, May 14, 1928

"Sam, Darling!" Felicity waves as she spots me waiting

for her at a table in *Piamini's Garden*, an up-scale Park Avenue restaurant. It's three blocks from my family's candy factory, *Brandenberger's Chocolates and Confections*. I walk to the restaurant, using the luncheon meeting with Felicity as an excuse to enjoy the brisk New York air. What a glorious day.

Felicity and my mother, Valentina, were best friends. Felicity was there for us when my father, Collin Cillian Callahan, was killed in WWI. Her friendship was invaluable during that dark time. Felicity's husband, Morgan Fellows, was a good friend of my father's. He also served in WWI but was fortunate to come home. He walks with canes because of injuries to his legs, but he came home alive. Felicity dotes on him…adores him.

It was Felicity who was there for me when my mother was murdered by a bomb that detonated on Wall Street in September of

1920. The blast from the bomb was immense. Thirty-eight people were killed, and 127 were wounded. She was killed instantly. Her killers were never caught. I was devastated. The guilt of her death was agony, but the fact that I was alive was worse.

You see, I was supposed to go with her to the bank that day, but I overslept because I had been out late with friends at a speakeasy the night before. I was sloppy drunk, and when I arrived home, I passed out cold. I didn't care to force myself to get up and go with her as I told her I would. I delayed her leaving. Had she not been waiting on me to get up and go, she would have been to the bank and left before the blast. That's my biggest regret. Our last words were an argument that resulted in her death.

That feeling still ambushes me, and that haunts my soul. It was Felicity that helped me deal with the pain, grow up and gain my footing at the factory so I could take my mother's place and keep her legacy going. Without Felicity, I have no doubt that my recovery would have stalled, and I really don't know what would have become of me. I'm immensely grateful to her and Malcolm for their kindness.

I stand and walk around the table to greet her – give her a long-overdue hug. Her company makes my day. She stands before me with her hands gently on my arms, and I can see the gleam in her eyes. She is gorgeously dressed as always, an ever-enduring picture of beauty and grace.

"Elegance Samantha Callahan!" She scolds. *Ugh...*other than my mother, no one ever calls me that! I prefer *Sam,* but since it's Felicity, I let it slide. "I haven't seen you in forever and a day!" We un-embrace, move toward our table and sit. I motion for the waiter to take our order. Felicity removes her gloves finger by finger and lays them on the table. Her violet–blue eyes engage my gaze.

"Now, let me look at you," she demands, gently taking my hand. "You are as beautiful as ever! Wouldn't change a thing, Darling. Always said you were kissed by heaven."

Felicity turns her attention to the handsome waiter and smiles with Cheshire Cat-like seduction. She daintily grasps the menu he's offered and, without reading it, places it on the table as I do mine. He takes this hint and leaves, allowing us time to decide.

"What looks scrumptious today?" Felicity asks dryly, scanning the menu up and down. "Okay! Ready." She slams the menu shut, falsely assuming I'm ready to order. This is typical lunch behavior for her, and I never protest. The waiter heeds his beckon and promptly returns to take our order. Felicity orders first

"I'll have the baked salmon and steamed vegetables, please. And a glass of white wine." She's fully aware that the wine is off-limits, but she delights in toying with the waiter. He smiles a playful smile, completely aware of her game. He plays along, and I'm patient. She does this every time.

"Madam, I apologize," he says coyly, "but we don't sell wine or any other alcohol. It's against the law." Felicity fakes offense at the waiter's hurling of the law in her face.

"Damn, prohibition!" she exclaims. "Can't even have a glass of wine! Disgraceful! Well, what *do you* have, young man," she demands.

"For you, Mrs. Fellows, we have our special lemonade. May I interest you in your usual?"

"Well, if that's all you have, I guess that will have to do," she says snidely. The waiter can hardly contain his laughter as he waits for me to order.

"I'll have exactly what my lovely friend is having, please."

"Yes, Miss Callahan," he joyfully replies. He nods and quickly departs.

"I never get tired of that," Felicity laughs heartily. "But really, that prohibition thing has gone on long enough, don't you think, Darling?" I nod my head in agreement. "The government's attempt to legislate morals has backfired. Prohibition hasn't stopped anything! Anyone can get alcohol, and they have no business telling me I can't consume it. Bootleg refreshments are available if you know where to look. And plenty of it!"

"How is dear Morgan doing?" I – inquire - lovingly, changing the subject away from her prohibition ranting and raving. "I haven't seen him in such a long time. Is his health alright?" Morgan Fellows is a wonderful, kind man, and he reminds me of my father.

"Oh, you know, Darling. He has good days and not-so-good days. We take what comes day by day."

"Don't we all," I reply. Our food arrives. I'm starving, and it smells divine!

"You know, Darling, I invited you to lunch today because there is something I want to discuss with you." Felicity's tone is tense and to the point.

"Really? I'm all ears," I answer, outwardly enthusiastic, but I feel a pinch in my gut like something is wrong.

She ever-so-daintily takes a bite of salmon, slowly chewing to judge the flavor, then makes the usual noises of approval indicating her appreciation of the delicious delight.

"Well," she says apologetically, taking a pause from her food. "I'm afraid I need a favor from you, Darling." This is serious. Felicity isn't one to beg for favors from anyone, so I'm concerned by her request.

"Of course! You know I will do anything for you and

Morgan. Just name it, and it shall be so." My assurance seems to relieve her, but I can tell that she's somewhat desperate.

"I knew you would, Darling. You know me, I don't like asking for favors. But! I really need your help."

"Is it Morgan? Is he alright?" I asked, concerned that there may be problems with his health.

"It's not Morgan, Darling…it's the magazine. I'm ashamed to say it's failing, and I am desperately, desperately trying to get it back on track." She's stopped eating her lunch. So much distress in her features. I put my knife and fork down, and I give her my full attention. Nothing Felicity had a hand in ever failed. She is business smart and wise in financial matters, so this news comes as quite a shock.

"What can I do, Felicity? Anything," I replied reassuringly.

"I need you…." She hesitates…seems embarrassed. "I need you…." She pauses again, then forces it out. "I need a huge favor, and I wouldn't ask if I had another choice."

"Okay. Sounds serious. What do you need me to do?" I reply, cautiously hesitant, – but delicately attempting to reassure her that I will do what I can to help.

"Alright. Here it is. I need you to let the magazine do an expose' on you." She knows from past conversations that I'm completely resistant to doing *that,* and I indicate such by slapping my napkin on the table and shooting her a look that says, "You're kidding, right?" "Darling, I know, I know. You've never agreed to put your life in the media, but I really need your help. I promise you, Darling, from the bottom of my heart that you will be in complete control from start to finish, and your every wish is our command."

She is begging me, and I feel my armor beginning to crack. I have never seen her like this, and no media is a staunch rule, but how can I say no when she's so desperate? She's always there for me. She's - Mother's dear friend. What choice do I have? And I know if I asked her about an infusion of cash, she'd just say no. I feel the pinch in my gut, but I blurt out...

"Of course, I'll do it."

I feel as if I just fed myself to the wolves.

"Oh, Sam darling!" she exclaims, grabbing my hand and squeezing it until the bones grind. "You don't know what this means to me." Felicity breathes three sighs of relief and wipes a tear from her eye. I don't know what to say to that. I've never seen her cry before. "I am certain that a story on you will put us back on track to success. You know so many depend on us for their livelihoods. I just can't bear to think of letting any of them go. Thank you, Sam darling." She says, smiling, obviously grateful!

She had me there. I have the same regard for the people who

work for me. They are family. Without them, the company would be nothing, so on that note, mixed feelings or not, there's no way I'm backing out now.

"So…what's this plan you speak of?"

Felicity places her napkin on her plate, no longer desiring her food. "Doing a story about you is the beginning, but I'll be honest with you, our problems all center around our editor. He's the real problem. And while I hate firing anyone, I don't have a choice with him."

"What?" I reply, totally surprised by that tidbit. "Fire Jazzy Jerry? I can't believe it!"

"He's a mess!" Felicity insists in a hushed tone, looking around, hoping no one in the restaurant can hear what she's saying. "He's a miserable drunk! The staff complains about him and his drunkenness! And the fact is that since he took over a year ago, the magazine has lost several important advertising accounts because he insists on covering sub-standard stories. The alcohol is affecting his judgment and his work, and he's caused the magazine to lose all credibility. So, Morgan and I made the decision to dump him. There's no choice, or we're going to go under. And while I know that your story alone will not cure everything, I do believe that your name and your influence will certainly attract major advertisers and help us regain some of the glory that this magazine always had in the past." Felicity pauses to catch her breath. "And I want our female readers back! That said, I forced Jazzy Jerry – oh, how I hate that name (she says as she shakes a fist at the air) - to hire a bright young female reporter. He has given her nothing but pure hell, and he is refusing to assign her to anything worthy of her talent. So, I would like to assign her to your story, and I will begin hiring a new editor immediately. Would you agree to talk to this great young lady and give her a chance?"

I enthusiastically agree, but clarify, "I will have complete control over the content. Agreed?" Felicity nods her head vigorously in agreement. "What's her name? The reporter."

"Her name is Fiona Mitchell, and she is an absolute go-getter. I know you'll like her. In fact, she reminds me a lot of you. And she graduated from Columbia just like you and your father."

"Well, I guess it's a go then," I confirm, wishing this meeting would come to an end. Felicity thanks me about five more times until I can't take it anymore and beg her to stop.

"I'll be in touch soon, Darling. I need to discuss our talk with Morgan. Thank you, dear friend. I shan't ever forget this."

I'd love to say that it does my heart good to do her - this favor, but that's not the case. I'm anxious about it, so much so that the inside of my mouth has shriveled so badly that I can barely speak. My mouth is dry after all that drama. I take a sip of lemonade to cure the cotton, but it's sour, and the shock of it makes my eyes water. I raise my empty water glass, summoning the waiter. He silently acknowledges my cue and immediately brings the water to the table. I don't bother to sip it daintily or mind my manners. I just gulp the whole glass down, allowing a dribble of water to make its way from the corner of my mouth down to my chin before I catch it with my napkin. It was refreshing, but it didn't kill the lemonade ache in my jaw.

Felicity smiles, her distaste apparent at my water gulping. "Thank you, Darling," Felicity says as she rises from her seat. "And Morgan will be elated with your decision. And – I hate to ask, but did you happen to bring some of your delicious candy? You know how he loves your candy."

"No, I'm ashamed to say I didn't. But please tell him that I'll send a courier around tomorrow." She blows me a kiss and walks away. And I breathe a sigh of relief.

I usually love catching up with her, but this lunch was odd. I have a feeling that the business woes weren't the only thing on her mind. I motion the waiter to the table. It seems Felicity stuck me with the bill. I tell him to keep the change and rise to leave, glad to be getting out of here. Business woes weren't all that was going on with Felicity. I've never had reason to doubt her motives for anything, but now, after today, I need to be careful with Felicity.

****

Sam

Just a Typical Monday

The Callahan Townhouse, Manhattan, New York, NY

Early Morning – Monday, May 21ˢᵗ, 1928

Monday morning. *Ugh!* I cover my ears with my pillow,
trying to drown out the sound of Warford's voice and his incessant
knocking on my bedroom door.

"It's seven o'clock, Madam," he announces, refusing to stop
until I answer. I'm so glad I decided to spend the weekend here in
Manhattan. My townhouse is so convenient to the factory, and I
don't have to suffer the Monday morning traffic. The meeting with
Felicity and Morgan at Extraordinary Woman is today - at eleven
o'clock. My schedule is full, and I must get to the office and clear
my desk of some work before I go.

"Come on in, Warford." He opens the door gracefully and
strolls to my bedside. The glorious aroma of coffee fills the air as he
sets the tray down and begins to pour. "Thank you so much,
Warford."

"Will you be having breakfast today, Madam?"

"Don't worry about bringing anything. I'm not that hungry."

"Very well, Madam." Warford exits the room, gently closing the door behind him.

The weekend was filled with charity events, which are an important part of my life and Mother's legacy. When - Mother was alive, I gave her grief about attending those events. I saw them as a nuisance and waste of time –boorish and frivolous. She never gave up, though. She believed that because God had blessed us with so much, it was our obligation to help others that were less fortunate. I poo-pooed that notion and bullied my way through life, fully aware that my spoiled elite view of our world disappointed her immensely. I had my celebrity friends and money to do what I wished. My name meant everything. I never wasted a moment's thought or considered that she might be right. That is until she died. Her death changed my soul. And now, those morals that she tried to instill – that I ignored and gave her grief over, I embrace, nurture, and call my own. I have continued her charity work plus added many more. I regret that I disappointed her so. My hope is that she's looking down on me and now sees the daughter she wanted me to be. That she's proud of me - forgives me.

"This coffee is really good," I say out loud, savoring the coffee and the moment. My watch says seven fifteen! I gulp the last bit, slam the cup down on the tray and hurry to the dressing room to dress for work.

As I emerge from dressing, I catch the smell of absolute deliciousness. It's Mrs. Lolly's muffins. I forget that I said I wasn't hungry, and I can't get downstairs fast enough, my mouth watering in anticipation. "There they are!" I quickly eye the selection and then snatch one…no two of the heavenly pillows of blueberry and banana. I tuck them into a napkin and call out to Warford.

"I am leaving for the office, Warford. I'll need you this morning. I have that meeting with Felicity and Morgan Fellows."

"Yes, Madam." I hear his reply, but I can't see him. He's within earshot on the second-floor landing. I wave in the air and slam the front door. My office and factory are right next door. The townhouse was an abandoned building, and being it was right next door, Mother bought it and made it into a beautiful city home. She enjoyed the convenience also, but I believe that the townhouse was more of an escape from memories. After my father was killed in the War, she had a difficult time staying at the estate in Long Island. Yes, I love it. But I miss my dogs, though! Handsome and Hattie. Maybe I'll start bringing them. I sure do miss my sweeties.

****

Sam and Annabelle

What Would I Do Without Annabelle

Brandenberger's Chocolates and Confections – Manhattan, New York, NY

8:00 a.m. - Monday, May 21ˢᵗ, 1928

The doors of the elevator open to reveal the smiling face

of Annabelle. She's petite, barely five feet tall, with fiery copper-red hair and a bubbly, contagious personality. She loves to dance, and she always has a boyfriend. Indispensable, she's my personal assistant and an all-around lifesaver in business matters. She's holding her finger up, indicating that there's a phone call for me…already.

"Yes, Mr. Cooley, she's away from her desk, but I will tell her you called. I have your message marked 'Very Important'." Annabelle is a pro at making people feel assured and important. "Yes, Sir……". Her voice trails off to barely audible as I open the door to my office and close it behind me. I just sit down in my chair when Annabelle comes in. I can see by her giddy expression that she has news, probably a new boyfriend.

"Mr. Cooley was on the telephone, as I'm sure you heard. Says it's urgent that he needs to speak to you." She places the small, square message on my desk. She wasn't lying. She really did mark it as *Very Important.* I pick it up and inspect it even though I know what it says and who it's from. I don't know why.

"Yes, I'm acquainted with him. He approached me Friday night at Jonathon Foster's charity dinner. He wants me to host a dinner for a charity he supports."

"Are you going to?" Annabelle inquired.

"Mmmm - probably. It's for a children's home in Tarrytown. He says that they're desperate and that if they don't raise some money soon, they will be forced to close, leaving around 35 children without a place to live. I asked him for details and information. Jonathon Foster says the home is legitimate, and I know he wouldn't say that if it weren't true. Still, you know me, I like to check things out for myself. Put in a call to NYPD, please – see if there are any concerns. Now shoo!" I command jokingly. She pays my command no mind and continues with her teasing.

"Who should I talk to at the NYPD? Detective Madison? Who thinks you're the bee's knees!" Annabelle giggled.

"Ah! I hate that saying!" I exclaim, feigning a mixture of disgust and impatience. I pretend I'm impatient with her jovial poking, but I'm not. I look forward to her girlish fun. It's refreshing, and I wish I could be more like her sometimes.

"And I thought I asked you to do something about *that!*" I bark, dramatically pointing to the ugly, unwanted oversized nameplate loitering on my desk. It says,

Elegance Samantha Callahan

"I - don't like it," I say, stressing every word.

"But I love it," Annabelle replies in her best cutesy, whiney voice. "You have a beautiful name, and I think you should flaunt it." She shrugs her shoulders.

"But I just want it to say, *'Sam Callahan'*. That's it! That's all! That's what I like! And I'm the boss! Now please get it fixed!" Annabelle gently picks up the nameplate and tucks it under her arm.

"Okay. If that's what you want, consider it done," she declares, smiling and fiddling - straightening up a corner of my desk. I know it will never be fixed. I've accepted that while Anabelle claims that she will fix it, she won't. I widen my eyes and flash her the *'Is there anything else* look*'.*

She takes the hint of my look and replies, "Oh, no. There's nothing. But don't forget you need to leave by ten to go to the meeting at *Extraordinary Woman.*" I ask her to please start reminding me at nine-thirty. "And you have a meeting at four with Greg Garrison about the proposal on wage increases."

"Thank you," I reply quietly, distracted by the pile of work on my desk.

"And …". She continues, finger pointing straight at me until I instantly stop her in her tracks with a darting glance that is undeniable. "Okay. Sure. It can wait until later." She demurely agrees as she backs away. I assure her that she's tried my patience long enough with a single nod, yet smile as she scurries from my office, closing the door behind her.

I've just concluded reading Garrison's wage proposals when I hear a voice emerging from behind my office door. It's Annabelle. She doesn't come in, merely peeks through the opening.

"What!" I bark. All I can see is her head.

"First warning. It's nine-thirty. I've called Warford to pull the car around." She informs, like a kid who's just gotten into trouble.

Well, now, I feel guilty for getting short with her. She's only doing what I told her to do. I finish analyzing Garrison's wage proposals, make a notation on the report, *Board of Directors,* and check my watch. 9:55. Time to go.

My stomach is churning – funny feeling as the elevator comes to a halt at the lobby. I don't know if it's the bumping and bouncing of the elevator or this meeting causing my upset. I think it's more the latter. Still, better get Annabelle to call in an inspector to check the elevator. The doors finally open, giving me permission to leave.

Once in the lobby, I'm greeted by the ever-loyal Maurice, my trusted security guard. He rushes from behind his desk to open the doors for me while I pull on my light jacket and tie a scarf around my hair.

"Let me get those doors for you, Miss Sam!" He says with delight, wearing that contagious smile of his. Not only contagious to me, but I've witnessed his miraculous smile cure crankiness in some of the biggest grouches to grace our building. It's very mysterious and very wonderful.

"Thank you, Maurice." I smile graciously, pointing out his worth to this company. "What would I do without you? I am so fortunate to have you, and I mean it." He nods his head once in appreciation for my praise. I put an assuring hand on his arm as he opens the doors for me and says goodbye – smiling – of course.

"Hello, Warford," I say cheerfully as he opens the car door. As I settle into the back seat, I see Maurice still standing guard at the doors – faithfully waiting for me to depart. Maurice waives while Warford takes his place in the driver's seat. And we're off.

"I'm not looking forward to this, Warford," I confide, my stomach still churning and burning.

"Yes, Madam," he replies, as usual, keeping his eyes straight ahead.

I stare out the window and daydream of something I love. Flying. I would rather be flying. I don't fly as much as I used to. I need to change that. I need to change a lot of things.

****

Detective Malcolm (Mal) Madison

A Change of Career May Be in Order

Manhattan, 3rd Precinct

8:00 a.m. - Monday, May 21st, 1928

Eight o'clock a.m. Detective Malcolm "Mal" Madison is

at his desk, slumped in his chair, head back, mouth wide open, snoring like a freight train. He's been there since 4 a.m. - called to the murder scene at a high-dollar speakeasy owned by Guido "Machine Gun" Grimaldi. Prohibition has exacted the opposite result of its intent. More booze than ever means more murders than ever. Murders that never get solved. Just one mobster killing another. But it's not murders he's dreaming about. It's her. She dances through his mind like the eternal flame that never dies.

****

"Hey Mal! The Cap'n's gonna catch you sleepin!" That voice is grating and irritating. I don't want to wake up. I want to finish my dream of her. He's shaking me now, and there's no ignoring 'im. "Hey Mal! Gotta wake up, Mal!" I keep my eyes closed, hoping Joey Gallerno, affectionately known as *"Joey G"*, will shut up! The pain in my neck is excruciating, and I feel drool running out of the corner of my mouth and down my face. My eyes are burning and scratchy – pins and needles. I'm worn out. Too many nights without real sleep.

I force my left eye open halfway and struggle to focus on the ugliness hovering over me. Joey instantly sees my creased eyelid and strikes, using the opportunity to torment me, shoving his face directly into mine – his fingers obnoxiously spreading both of my eyelids apart! His breath stinks of stale cigars and garlic. The smell of it nauseates me, and I try to save myself from the stench by jerking my head sideways. But it doesn't work. He's still there, smell and all.

"Hey Mal! Gonna sleep all day, ya schmuck! We gawt work to do!" I feel spit flyin on my face – disgusting and wet. I wrench my head up off the back 'a the chair despite the pain. I've had enough of *'G'*.

"Get outta my face, G! Ya stink!" He jerks his face from mine.

"Well, excuse me," he replies, acting offended. It's fake. Nothing offends G. He's laughing and getting a big kick outta goading me. "Neck a little stiff there, pal?" He pokes and - laughs obnoxiously - showing off. I'd like to right uppercut - 'im in that big mouth a his!

"Cap'n wants to see you, Sleepin Beauty," he taunts, strutting around like I don't know what. I yank myself out of the chair, and he's still at it. "Boy, you look like gawbage! Maybe you need a nap or somethin!" Everyone in the squad room busts out laughing, egging him on. They're over-the-top loud, and they make my head hurt.

"Yeah, yeah. Funny ya goons!" I scoff, throwing my hands in the air, disgusted with the lot of 'em. I move my neck in a circular motion, tryin to stretch it - loosen it up. "*Ouch, ouch, ouch, ouch!*" I cry, my eyes watering from the sharp and stabbing pain. And here it comes. I've left myself wide open for more harassment. The Sleeping Beauty gag worked so well the first time he it again.

"Hey Sleepin Beauty! 'Bout time you woke up!" Again, the entire squad room busts with obnoxious laughter, all in unison. God help me. I'd like to bust 'em all in the jaw.

"Ha, ha, ha," I reply, leaving the jokesters to laugh it up while I go to the head. The Cap'n will have to wait. A week straight of some mobster killing another mobster over booze or territory. Gotta be something better. Just gotta be.

I turn on the water at the sink, fill my hands and splash my face over and over. The water feels refreshing, but inside I'm not good. I became a homicide detective to make a difference – help people. What I'm stuck with now isn't making a difference. Maybe it's time to think about leaving…again.

Back in the squad room, the guys are hustling around and talking about the night's arrests. I leave 'em to it. I'm starving. I pull out my wallet to check for cash. Empty. I scan the room and spot Joey G.

"Hey G! You got any cash on ya? I gotta get something to eat."

"Yeah, yeah 'ya moocha. Here," he says, rollin his eyes, pullin his wallet out. "Here's a dollar, moochey." He hands me the money and winks at me.

"And don't wink at me, stinky," I caution jokingly.

"I know, I know. You aint that kinda girl," he cackles.

I flash him a smile and put the money in my wallet. "Thanks, G. I'll get it back to ya." G throws his hand in the air, telling me not to worry about it as he walks away.

I hit the stairs running, but I'm not fast enough. The Cap'n catches me and hails me into his office. I follow him as directed and shut the door.

"Going somewhere, Mal?"

"Well, actually, Sir, I was goin to get something to eat and some coffee. Come back and get to work. Can I get you somethin, Sir?" He smiles in appreciation, then shakes his head *no*.

He hands me a message and says, "I want you to take care of this, Mal. Call him."

"Okay, sure Cap'n. River Dell County? What's goin on up there?" He doesn't answer. He seems preoccupied and far away.

"I'll let Captain Grayland give you the details. He's got a nasty one up there. Anyway, thanks, Mal. Now, go get somthin in your belly.' He sits down, which means I better get – goin' while I can. But I can't help but notice that he looks tired. He shouldn't be here. He should be at home."

"How's your wife doing Cap'n?" I ask. His eyes show his sadness, but he puts on a brave face.

"Good, good," he lies. "The doctor says she's making progress. Managing the pain." I know the guilt he feels - what he's going through.

"I'm glad to hear it, Sir. Well…tell 'er I said I'm glad she's feeling better." I feel awkward. I don't know what else to say, but I can sympathize with the denial. She's dyin. The cancer. And the worst part is the waiting. The long and tortuous waiting.

I slip the message into my pocket. It can – wait 'till get back. The squad room is loud and busy. But over the noise, I hear a voice yelling my name. It's comin from behind me. I turn to see Jerry Jenkins bein' booked in. I've seen Jerry in here more than a few times, and more than a few times, I brought him in myself. He's an editor - at that women's magazine down on Park Ave. Too bad. He's got a great job, but he can't put the bottle down. Felicity Farmer Fellows will fire him for sure. The thought crosses my mind that she's a friend of Sam's. *Sam...*

"Hey Madison!" He yells, waving like an idiot while the officer is wrangling him for fingerprints.

I just shake my head at him, scolding, "Jerry! I thought I told you the last time I saw you that I better not see ya in here again!" He shrugs his shoulders and smiles. "And you're staying away from the *big* trouble, right?" He knows exactly what I mean. The mob. Specifically, O'Bannion. The officer continues to roll his prints. We'll find him dead one of these days, no doubt.

As I break free to the outside, the warm sun hits my face, and it reminds me of her. Sam. I've got to stop thinkin about 'er. I miss her. I'm pathetic!

Inside the diner, a familiar voice calls my name from behind the counter. Maureen. Forty years she's worked here, and she's the reason it's been here 40 years. All the customers love her. I wave at 'er and stroll to the counter and take a seat. She doesn't waste a second bringing me coffee.

"Ya sittin here or in a booth?" She demands, her voice raspy from years of smokin'.

"Booth," I reply, – takin' my coffee to the corner for some peace and quiet. Maureen brings a menu automatically, but she knows I won't need it. I get my usual my usual and she immediately barks the order to the cook on her way back behind the counter. I'm not sure that it's good - that I'm so predictable.

I retrieve the message the Cap'n gave me outta my pocket. What could River Dell County Police want? *A nasty one,* Cap'n said. I quickly shove the message back in my pocket and grab my fork and the syrup. My pancakes have arrived.

****

Mal

Opportunity Knocks

Manhattan 3rd Precinct

9:30 a.m. - Monday, May 21st, 1928

Things haven't settled down much since I left for

breakfast. I'm sitting at my desk practicing my favorite character flaw – procrastination. I have a ton of paperwork from overnight, but I'm distracted by the message, so I cave to the flaw and decide it can wait. I leave the chaos of the squad room in search of a quieter place to make this phone call to the River Dell Police. Perfect! Cap'n isn't in his office. I pick up the receiver and dial the operator, keeping the message in front of me.

Call Captain Graff Grayland, River Dell County Police

Dearborn – 7534

"Yes, operator. Could you connect me to Dearborn – 7534, please" I wish she'd hurry. I don't think the Cap'n would mind, but I didn't ask if I could use his phone and …well, you know.

Finally, a voice breaks the silence! "Please hold. I'm connecting you." The phone rings only once when a lady with a very pleasant voice comes on the line.-.

"River Dell County Police, how may I direct your call?" I hesitate for a second. I feel anxious and fidgety, but I manage to spit the words out.

"Yes, ma'am. I'm returning a call from Cap'n Grayland? My name is Detective Malcolm Madison, 3rd Precinct in Manhattan. I was told to call……"

"Yes, Detective Madison. Please hold a moment." I waited for what seemed like an eternity, but realistically, it was about a minute.

"This is Captain Grayland. Detective Madison?" He doesn't sound like a New Yorker.

"Yes, Sir, I'm Madison. My Cap'n asked me to get in touch with you. What can I do for ya?"

"Well, you see, I have an unusual situation here. I've got a female murder victim who's been found in the Tall Shadow Woods near Tarrytown, and I'm needing a little assistance. Do you know where we are, Detective Madison? Tarrytown. About 25 miles north of you?"

"Yeah, I know where it is," I reply, disguising my apprehension with enthusiasm. My first thought is that they have a mob hit, and he's hoping I can help. I was really hoping it was different. "I've been there a couple of times for the weekend. Beautiful place! I'm happy to help, so what a 'ya need?" I come off interested. I've already decided that if this is a mob thing, I'm going to make my excuses and bow out. That is unless I'm forced.

"Well, I will tell you that this is, without a doubt, one of the most gruesome things I've ever seen. But what I need your help with, Detective, is that the Pathologist found a note shoved into this victim's throat. Now, on that note was written *'DD 5'*. Have you ever heard of that reference in any case you've worked on?"

I could hear something in his voice. Not desperation. No…fear. I detect fear in his voice, and it chills me to the bone. "No, I've never come across anything like that. I wonder if your victim is the fifth victim. I can't say for sure, but it makes sense, and it's a place to start. I'll ask around about it. I'll ask some of the older guys, you know, that have been around a while."

The thought "sequential killer" races through my mind. But who knows? It could be she was targeted for some reason. Pretty specific message. Was she a specific target? Cap'n Grayland continued.

"Not only was the note in her throat, but both of her hands were amputated, and there was another message carved into her chest, '*SC Die* ....' "

"Do you know who she is?" I ask-, hearing with supersonic clarity - the sound of a match strike, then a puff on a cigarette.

"Yes, we do, and that's the worst of it, Detective. She's a nun. Sister Mary Agnes. That's all we know. No one knows her birth name, which isn't uncommon. They change their name when they join the order. She oversaw the orphanage located about – five miles out of town. Been there for several years. A man named Cooley reported her missing two days ago. He's an administrator there. I just thought I'd check and see if there was anything you could dig up there in the city that would help us out. This damn thing is just disturbing, Detective. This woman has no obvious enemies. Who in the world are we dealing with that would do something like this? I could use any information you can give me, Detective."

"I'll certainly look into it, Cap'n…see what comes up."

"I appreciate it. I don't expect you to find anything. Things like this hide in the dark places…places where you and I don't dare to tread. Whoever did this intended for her to be found but thinks we'll have no idea how to deal with it. In fact, after you inquire around, I wouldn't mind if you could come up here. I could use an extra hand, and I hear you're a helluva detective. That is if you like.

Up to you and your Captain, of course."

"Are you kiddin, Cap'n? I- can be there in an hour, but I need approval. I'll let ya know, but in the meantime, I'll do some askin' around. See if it rings a bell with anyone. Good 'nuf?"

"I'd sure appreciate it, Detective. If it helps, I'll speak to your superior. I really need someone on this."

"An official request from you is the best route, I think."

Just as Grayland and I are finishing our conversation, Cap'n Mason returns.

"Give me a minute, Cap'n Grayland," I say, placing my hand over the receiver for privacy. I apologize to Cap'n Mason for invading his office. "Cap'n Grayland is asking me to come up to Tarrytown," I say softly, veiling my emotions in case the answer is *no*. Mason takes the phone, and after a brief conversation assuring Grayland that he would consider the request, he hangs up.

"I don't know if we can spare ya, Mal. It's one body after another around here. You know that. I'll have to think about it."

"Cap'n, please!" I beg. "Did he tell ya anything about the circumstances?"

"Yes, he did. It's God awful, and I understand why he wants ya, but…."

"Cap'n, cases like this are why I became a homicide detective. Not that mobster crap! Sorry, Cap'n." I apologize, leaning against his desk. I need to convince him to let me go. I calm myself and make my point. "I gotta a feeling that this killing is something else. Something sinister. This killing could be a sequential or a cult-type killing. We're talking about a murdered nun! I have to help. Please, Cap'n." I wait patiently for his answer, but he's stalling, so I change the tone hoping it will help to convince him. "Besides, think of it this way. I'll be outta your hair for a day, maybe two." I gave it my best, but he's heard enough, and I'm vetoed. I turn to leave his office when he surprisingly says…

"Alright, alright, here's what I'll let ya do. You head up there this aftanoon. It's early enough. Take a look-see and get back to me tonight. I want a full report though," he says, pointing his finger and sternly eyeballing me over the top of his glasses. I'm excited! But I don't say anything. I don't need to. He sees it and issues his warning. "Ah, ah, ah, don't get your hopes up. I'll wait for your report, and we'll go from there!"

I can't get out of his office fast enough! "You got it, Cap'n! Will do! But can I go home and change first? I won't make a very good impression in these clothes - goin on two days."

"Yeah, yeah! Get outta here. And you need to take a car! On official police business, so take a car." He waives me to get out, then yells, "But no promises!"

"I know, no promises," I yell back, heading into the squad room, asking Joey G and the rest of the guys if they ever heard of a murder like this. No one knew of anything, but they all began immediately searching - files and heading to the street to their - informants.

"Thanks guys, and be sure to let the Cap'n know ASAP if you find anything. This is a nasty one. I'm outta here to Tarrytown."

I drive as fast as I can to my apartment, clean up and change clothes. I'm ready to get up there and get started. No need to call Grayland. I'll just show up. He'll be there.

"DD 5…SC die." I say those words to myself over and over. *Very cryptic.* "Who are you, you sick… I'm gonna find you. Ready or not, here I come."

****

Sam

Daydreaming of Days Gone By

Extraordinary Woman Magazine – Manhattan, New York, NY

10:30 a.m. - Monday, May 21st, 1928

Warford's voice startles me! "Oh!" I had dozed off.

"Shoot!" I need to check my makeup and wipe my eyes a bit. They feel tired and scratchy.

"Give me just a minute, Warford." He acknowledges my request and patiently waits as I hurriedly rummage around in my bag, looking for my makeup compact and lipstick. But I can't find it.

"Agh! I left it at home!" Warford doesn't budge. "Well, Warford. I guess they will just have to take me as I am today. I'm ready."

Warford rounds the car to the back-right-passenger side and opens the door. He offers his hand to help me out. I glide out, straighten my jacket, and take a deep breath to calm the nervousness I feel. Warford surprises me with a compliment.

"Pardon my forwardness Madam, but you are lovely. And I dare say that anyone who says otherwise is either an idiot or blind. You are the spitting image of your beautiful Mother." His eyes are frozen forward, never making eye contact. I'm touched by his caring candor, and it makes me smile. Only Warford could compliment one so beautifully and properly.

"Thank you, Warford," I say with sincerity. "You don't need to wait. I'm sure Felicity's driver, Lewis, can take me back to work. Lord knows how long this will take."

"As you wish, Madam."

He shuts the car door as I take the first step toward the doors of *Extraordinary Woman Magazine.* I haven't been here in a very long time. When - Mother was alive, I was here on many occasions. We'd meet Felicity for lunch or an afternoon of shopping. My sweet Mother…

I remember encountering the most interesting people here. Models, reporters, fashion designers, make-up artists. This magazine was and is at the forefront of enlightening and empowering women, instrumental in the perpetuation of ideas that demand change, shattering antiquated judgments and perceptions of women, no matter the age, no matter the color.

I stand before the behemoth building, daydreaming of days gone by, when a shrill and demanding voice shocks the life out of me, popping my daydream bubble and forcing me back to the moment. It's Felicity, and she's waiving frantically for me to come in. I wish I had a moment longer with those precious feelings and memories. Just one minute more.

****

CAROLYN MCWHORTER

The Man on the Sidewalk

Back from The Dead

The Corner Near Extraordinary Woman Magazine

Mid-Morning - Monday, May 21, 1928

I lower the newspaper that covers my face, making eye

contact with Warford. He discreetly acknowledges me but doesn't stick around. He must avoid suspicion, especially from Sam. He goes about his business as she instructed him to do. I stay put, right on the corner. I'm here to protect Sam and help put an end to certain individuals' covertly wicked activities. I guess I can take comfort in the fact that Felicity never changes. I won't have to approach her. She'll come after me. The look on her face was priceless. She didn't quite finish the job. I'm still alive and kicking, so to her, I'm an absolute threat. I'm back from the dead, and she knows exactly why I'm here. It's right here in the paper, Felicity. The last one. The last Diamond Doll. I re-read the story on page 3.

WOMAN FOUND MURDERED, MUTILATED, IN UPSTATE NEW YORK

A woman was found dead near the edge of the Tall Shadow woods yesterday. Police sources say that according to the River Dell County Coroner, she has been dead approximately three days. Captain Graff Grayland had this to say. "We are not releasing her name at this time. We are trying to contact next of kin. We are classifying this as a homicide and that's all I'm at liberty to say for now."

There's more, but I don't need to re-read the gory details. I know who she is and why she was murdered. And I know, all too well, who murdered her. Sam has no idea of the darkness that has shadowed her throughout her life. An unintended fallout of Valentina's crusade.

I swore I was finished with this life, but I made a promise to Valentina, and I will never break it. Until my death, I will keep that promise just like she kept her promise to me all those years ago.

****

Felicity

But I Killed You Myself, Why Aren't You Dead?

Extraordinary Woman Magazine – Manhattan, New York, NY

Mid-Morning - Monday, May 21st, 1928

I see the beautiful Sam frozen and staring at the building

right outside the front entrance. Morgan and I are so glad to see her. She's like our own daughter. But I don't want to talk about that. I open the door and step out to greet her when someone catches my eye. There, on the corner, leaning against the building. Who is that? Can it be? It's him! Yes, yes. It's him! I'd know him anywhere! But that's not possible!

My heart begins to race. I don't want him to think I saw him. I yell for Sam to come inside, trying desperately not to show how frantic I am! My tone of voice startles her, but she says nothing. I glance in his direction one more time. I just need to be sure. I'm certain. The good looks. The dark hair. He knows, and I'm in trouble. No point in denying we don't see each other. It's done.

I grab Sam by the hand and pull her toward me and give her a huge hug to distract her - hurry her inside. I take another long look at him. I want him to see that I've noticed him. He makes eye contact. I - notice that Warford has gone. I follow Sam inside, struggling to hide - my sheer panic.

"Are you alright?" Sam asks with concern. I blame a sudden onset of a migraine headache, but I'm not sure it's working. Images of Valentina flash through my mind, like a ghost from the past haunting me.

What am I going to do? He was supposed to be in the grave for eight long years, but he's here. The truth cannot be known. I have to put an end to him. That's all there is to it. But this time, I won't botch the job.

****

Sam

Felicity's Lost Her Mind

Extraordinary Woman Magazine – Manhattan, New York, NY

Mid-Morning – Monday, May 21st, 1928

Something's wrong with Felicity. I could see it the minute - we met outside her building! - One minute she's all smiles, waiving me to hurry up, but by the instant it takes me to get inside, she says she has a migraine and is not feeling well. She's distracted, manic, and distant – completely not herself. I have never seen her like this, and I'm not sure what to do.

"Felicity, what's going on?" I ask, sternly but with sincere concern. She doesn't respond. "Felicity?" I ask her again, touching her shoulder, trying to comfort her. And in an instant, like someone flipping a switch, she wraps her arms around me and hugs me so tightly I can barely breathe then she simply walks away. I rush after her, grab her hand, and gently demand, "Are you sure you are alright?" But I'm instantly sorry that I did that. Her expression knocks me off guard and frankly makes my skin crawl.

"Yes, Darling. Forgive me. I don't know what came over me, but rest assured everything will be alright," she replies, disarming and dark, her smile forced – her words cold and meaningless.

I can't muster a reply to her bizarre behavior. I nod in agreement, but her demeanor is creepy. I try to let go of her hand, but she has mine in a death grip. She stares wickedly into my eyes. I feel the pinch in my gut, and although I'd like to just leave, I don't. I change the subject to the reason I'm here in the first place.

"Let's go get this awful meeting over with so we can get out of here," I say with silliness, smiling, hoping it will push her to get a grip! "We could have lunch afterward and spend the rest of the day together – like we used to. You and Morgan haven't been over in such a long time Warford and Mrs. Lolly can plan a lovely dinner for us tonight…."

Her face changes right before my eyes - there's a malevolence in her voice that's indescribable. "You remind me of your mother. Dear, dear Valentina." She pauses, staring me down, her eyes dark, a controlled hint of hatred apparent. "I don't think we'll be able to make dinner tonight My Dear, and the meeting will have to be rescheduled to another time. We'll be in touch." She turns and walks straight away from me! I'm mad and fed up! I don't know who I just talked to! She has lost her mind! Morgan suddenly appears out of nowhere and blocks Felicity's path.

"Everything alright?" He asks, his question dripping with suspicion. I march straight over and confront them both, flatly stating that I've had enough.

"I don't know who you think you are, Felicity, but I refuse to take your abuse. How dare you talk to me like that. I don't know what happened here today, but I'm sure it has nothing to do with me. Now, if you'll excuse me, I'm leaving. If you could be so kind as to have Lewis drive me back to my office, I'll bid you a good day. Oh, and before I go, let me just say bluntly that should you decide that a meeting is necessary in the future, don't call me. I'll take some time to decide if my offer still stands. Apologize to Miss Mitchell for me."

End of conversation.

I instantly turn and walk away with no intention of ever going back. I know Felicity is following me, but she utters not a word until we get outside. She attempts an apology, but I shut her out – denying her that satisfaction. She reluctantly accepts my rejection and instructs Lewis.

"Lewis, please take Miss Callahan wherever she needs to go."

"Yes, Madam."

Lewis opens the door, and I slide in, glaring at Felicity

through the window glass. Lewis takes the driver's seat and asks cautiously, "Where can I take you, Miss Callahan?"

"To my office, please, Lewis," I reply, controlling my anger. After all, it's not his fault. My watch says it's 11:00. Good. Plenty of time to get my work done and prepare for the Board of Directors Meeting tomorrow. I feel a stomachache coming on. Maybe something to eat will help.

"On second thought, Lewis, drop me at *Piamini's.*"

"Yes, Miss Callahan."

I keep replaying the scene with Felicity over and over in my mind. What in the world could have possibly prompted that bizarre behavior? I'm so angry! And hurt! I've always thought the world of her and considered her more than a friend! But I don't think I'll be speaking to Felicity for a while. For a good long while.

****

Lewis

Driving Miss Callahan

Arriving at Piamini's Garden Restaurant

10:45 a.m. - Monday, May 21st, 1928

Ah! A parking place – right in front! I easily maneuver the huge Rolls Royce into the one and only parking space and announce to Miss Callahan that we had arrived at *Piamini's Garden.*

"Thank you, Lewis," she replies as she gathers her things. As I open the door and help her out, she says, "You can go now. I'll walk to the office from here." Miss Callahan is obviously very upset, and rightfully so. She has no idea of the trouble that's returned to the Fellows' doorstep. And that trouble's name is Antonio De Cordova.

De Cordova – a confidant of Valentina and Warford – the assassin Felicity and Morgan thought dead, is alive and well. They very well know what this means, and her treatment of Miss Callahan shows her desperation.

Madam Felicity spotting De Cordova - watching her, tells her one thing. That Warford is fully aware of her manipulation of

Sam and why, and he has resurrected the master to clean up some messes, and one of those messes is her and her husband. Madam Fellows is panicking… scrambling for a solution, but it's too late. Living a dirty life has caught up with her. The lie will be exposed. The clock has run out. And it's about time. Yes, yes…about time indeed.

****

Sam

Table for One

Piamini's Garden Restaurant

11:15 a.m. - Monday, May 21ˢᵗ, 1928

I stroll into Piamini's, still on fire over the scene with Felicity. There's no one at the reservation desk, and I'm patiently waiting when I hear my name from behind the bar. It's Jimmy, the waiter that always jokes with Felicity.

"Miss Callahan!" He says joyfully.

"Hello!" I respond, setting my anger for Felicity aside – taking all the friendliness I can get.

"Need a table?" he asks.

"No, but I'd be most grateful if you could get me a menu of your take-out selections."

Jimmy hurries right over, escorts me to a seat at the bar and asks, "Would you like a cold drink while you wait?"

"No, no. Well…does it take long? I guess I could if it's going to be a bit."

"Not long at all. About 15 minutes. There are only a few selections right now, but soon there will be more to choose from."

"This looks delicious, Jimmy!" I say, enthusiastically pointing out the spaghetti and meatballs. "Four orders to go, please." I order four because I notice through the restaurant window that Lewis is still waiting for me by the car. I guess he decided I didn't need to walk the rest of the way to work. How gentlemanly of him. He reminds me so much of Warford.

Jimmy was right. Sure enough, in about 15 minutes, the food was ready.

"I'm impressed! Tell the boss he's going to make a killing on this. Excellent business decision, but better get that new menu ready!" I bid farewell to Jimmy, his smile and undivided attention a bright spot in an otherwise dismal and upsetting morning. Lewis is waiting for me by the car. I graciously thank him for waiting on me and give him his food from the take-out bag.

"I know you probably won't get a lunch break today, Lewis, so I took the liberty of getting you a meal."

"Thank you, Miss Callahan!" "That's just wonderful of you. And it smells so good!"

He's smiling from ear to ear, which raises my spirits. Lewis's declaration that the food smells good prompts me to poke my nose in the sack and breathe in the deliciousness. Lewis parks right in front of my office, opens the door and helps me from the car. As I walk toward my building, I turn and wave again as he toots the car horn and pulls away, the huge Rolls roaring down the street.

In the lobby of *Brandenberger's,* Maurice greets me with a smile. He thanks me a thousand times for the lunch as I get on the elevator, the delectable smell filling the car.

Annabelle is at her desk, as always. She graciously accepts the lunch I brought for her, thanking me for thinking of her and raving about the 'new thing' takeout.

My desk is piled with several organized stacks of work courtesy of Annabelle. Work that could have been done instead of wasting time with Felicity. I dismiss that bitter thought and resign to letting it go, refusing to allow the distraction to control my thoughts - any longer. I set the takeout bag on the small table adjacent to my desk, hang up my coat and reach into the bag, my mouth watering for the delicious food. The same thought occurred to me that occurs to me at almost every meal. I'm hungry - but I'm alone. Table for one. I'm always a table for one.

****

"Jazzy" Jerry Jenkins, Editor

Her Majesty Wields Her Ax

Jenkin's Office - Extraordinary Woman Magazine

12:00 p.m. - Monday, May 21ˢᵗ, 1928

Jazzy Jerry sits at his desk, his mania for a drink

consuming his every thought. He hasn't had a drink in hours. No alcohol in jail. And after that phone call this morning, his nerves are raw. He's been warned for the last time to either pay up or take O'Bannion up on his offer. "You scratch my back. I'll scratch yours." The scratches of a guy like O'Bannion run deep and will likely bury you. He checks his watch. "Where the hell are they?" he says under his breath. "I just wanna get this over with."

****

At that moment, Sharon buzzes my office and announces, *'Mr. and Mrs. Fellows are here to see you.'* My heart rate quadruples, and I take a deep breath to try and steady myself - quickly smoothing my hair and tidying my desk. Little good it does. I'm an insufferable slob.

Her Majesty flings the door open in her usual rude and obnoxious fashion, helping Morgan through. *'The Queen has arrived,'* I say, under my breath. I can't stand her! And Morgan? He's nothing but her lackey. But at least I can tolerate him. Most days.

"Hello, Jerry. How was jail this morning?" Felicity says with complete sarcastic disgust.

She helps Morgan to the chair closest to my desk. "You alright, darling?" She overly dotes. Morgan assures her he's fine. Felicity throws her jacket in the opposite chair from Morgan for effect, gets a cigarette from her fancy handbag, puts it to her lips and stares me down, waiting for me to offer her a light. I obey her veiled demand and retrieve a match from my desk drawer. The Queen has a fancy lighter, but she's punishing me. She does love her petty delights. I light her cigarette and slide the ashtray to the corner of the desk, and wait for 'her majesty' to wield her ax.

"So, Jerry," Felicity says, clinking and tapping her fancy cigarette extender on the edge of the ashtray. "What are we going to do." She draws out the words, beating me with 'em, pumping her own ego. I can't say I don't deserve her venom. I'm not a model employee. A damn good editor – horrible employee. I just wish she would cut the bull and fire me already. I get it, I get it. The Queen is all powerful.

"Jerry," Morgan interjects. *He speaks!* I think to myself. He rarely speaks. Just her. "I think what Felicity means is - there are so many problems. And you know what they are, Jerry."

I don't say a word. "We won't bail you out anymore. We just won't do it. The magazine is suffering."

I don't want to risk saying something I'll regret. And if I thought begging would do any good, I'd do it in a heartbeat. But obviously, landing in jail was the last straw. "Something has to be done," Morgan continues, "Felicity has wanted me gone for a long time, and what the Queen wants, the Queen gets."

"This magazine has been a cornerstone in Felicity's family for generations."

Cornerstone! Felicity's family! Liars! I know the truth about 'em both. But they don't know that I know. I've been saving that information for a rainy day. I debate myself as to whether the rainy day is here. I'm sure the information will fetch big bucks, and I know just the person to sell it to. I wisely decide to keep the peace for right now and apologize.

"I'm sorry," I say in my best suck-up I'm pathetic voice. I lower my eyes, assuring the Queen that she's won, and I'm whipped. "I know I owe you a lot. You gave me a job when everyone else in this business wouldn't. You've bailed me out, put up with my drinking, advanced me pay. And if you give me another chance, I swear, I swear, I will turn this thing around. I will." It's surprisingly easy to say that because I know I'll never have to do it.

My apology brings on a silence that's tense, thick and drags on for what seems an agonizing lifetime. The Queen stands up and walks around the desk, circling me like something that's about to eat me, takes a long drag from her cigarette and blows the smoke directly in my face!

"Apology not accepted, Jerry," she replies in that raspy voice of hers. She does have a way of making you feel like dirt under her feet. Not going to say I'm surprised. I knew she wouldn't, but I had to try.

"You're fired, Jerry, as of right now. I – we – we (she had to remember to include Morgan) want you out of here now," she says as she takes the final drag off her cigarette before crushing it in the ashtray.

I'm a little enraged, but I don't show it. I won't give her satisfaction! I just need to keep my cool and just do as she asks. I got the info, Queeney. Your time is coming… And soon. "Fine," I reply, respectfully agreeing with her conclusion. That throws her off, but as usual, the Queen must have the last word.

"Good boy. You're just bad, bad, bad, bad, bad, bad, bad for business Jenkins. Bad – for – business," she says, lighting another cigarette, this time with that expensive lighter of hers. I pay her final comments no mind and start gathering the minimal possessions off my desk.

Felicity makes a big show of pampering Morgan. She always does that. She's an excellent actress. I'll give her that. The truth is, neither of 'em can be trusted, and they don't even trust each other. They're grifters of the worst kind. I've had my share of trouble, but these two take the cake. I'm going to take O'Bannion up on his offer. Says something, right? Imagine that. I'd rather work for a brutal gangster like O'Bannion than these two. Figure that one.

They wait for me to vacate the office like I'm gonna steal something. What's to steal? And they act like it's all my fault that this magazine is failing! Yeah, right! They're broke! They act all hoity-toity, but they don't have two nickels to rub together. Outside the office door I stop for a second and toy with the idea of eavesdropping. I'm tempted, but – realize that getting caught isn't worth it. With what I know about the dealings of those two, it doesn't matter.

****

Warford

Truth Be Told

The Callahan Townhouse – Manhattan, New York, NY

12:30 p.m.- Monday, May 21ˢᵗ, 1928

I do not know what happened between Felicity and

Madam, but Annabelle said she was very upset about their meeting this morning. Antonio telephoned to say that Felicity spotted him as Madam was arriving, so I suspect she took her anger and fear out on her. Madam has not informed me of a quarrel, but knowing Felicity Farmer Fellows, as she likes to call herself, I am positive it got ugly. Poor Madam. I am relieved Antonio could be reached and that he made it his priority to come. The murder of Sister Mary Agnes tells me the copycat *Butcher* has surfaced again, and Madam's life and the life of Anashe are in grave danger. The darkness is rising again, but I guarantee it will be the last time.

Valentina's insistence that Madam remain unaware makes for a difficult situation. Part of me understands why she did not want her to be trapped in such a life, but I know Madam. She will feel betrayed and lied to. I hope Valentina's good intentions to hide the truth until it needs to be shared do not backfire, her daughter rejecting her legacy because it was kept from her, albeit for her own safety.

Those of us closest to Madam hoped and prayed that she would never have to face the ugliness surrounding the diamond. I must tell her tonight. Tell her of people in her life who are not who she believes them to be – including her own Mother. I stayed on all these years, a promise I made to Valentina to protect her daughter and guide her through the darkness to come. That is my promise, and I will keep it.

****

Maurice

The Bureau Man

The Lobby of Brandenberger's Chocolates and Confections

12:43 p.m. - Monday, May 21ˢᵗ, 1928

"I'm sorry for your wait, Sir," I say, extending an apology for a telephone conversation that took way too long to the tall, serious-looking man before me. "Now, how can I help you?"

"My name is Dominic Del Ray. I'm a Special Agent with the Bureau of Investigation. I'm here to see Samantha Callahan."

Del Ray pulls his wallet from the inside pocket of his suit-jacket and opens it so I can inspect his credentials. They appear to be legitimate Bureau identification, but I'm suspicious and a tad worried. I wonder why a Bureau man would need to see Miss Callahan? I inquire about his visit, but he avoids my question and offers a vague and evasive explanation.

"I just need to ask her some questions," he says, like Mr. holier – than thou, with a hint of sarcastic mind your own business security man attitude that's hard to miss. "Nothing to worry about," he says, forcing a fake smile. "Really," I think to myself. "I doubt seat," I say firmly, looking him straight in the eye, dead serious.

He can see that I'm not buying his tough-guy bull and changes tactics. Suddenly, he's making light of the reason for his visit. This change doesn't alleviate my suspicion, and I just keep looking him straight and unwavering in the eye.

"I'm just hoping she can help me with an identification, that's all." I'm not buying it. One of Hoover's boys…here…just to get an identification?

"Right," I say suspiciously. "Well, you must not be very important if the Bureau can't find anything better than that for you to do, Agent …what was it again? Del Ray? I mean, my goodness!" I ignore his dirty look and call Miss Annabelle.

"Yes, Miss Annabelle. I have a Special Agent, Del Ray, here to see Miss Callahan. Can I send him up?" Miss Annabelle, of course, has questions of her own. "Yes, Miss Annabelle, I don't know. He says he needs to see Miss Callahan. He wants to ask her some questions. His name is Special Agent Del Ray. Yes, Miss Annabelle. I'll wait for your call." I place the receiver back in the cradle and inform the very Special Agent, Del Ray, of my instructions.

"Miss Annabelle - that's Miss Callahan's assistant, is going to see if Miss Callahan has time to talk to you right now. She will call me back after she speaks to her. So, if you would like to take a seat, Sir (I emphasize Sir), I would appreciate it."

Del Ray takes the hint that his importance around here may not be the same as his own image of his importance, and he moseys to a chair and sits, waiting for who is the supremely important one in this building. Miss Sam Callahan.

****

Del Ray

A Familiar Face

Front Window of Brandenberger's Chocolates and Confections

12:45 p.m. - Monday, May 21ˢᵗ, 1928

What's taking her so long? I utter in my head. I am tired

of sitting, so I get up and start to putter around the lobby of Brandenberger's under the watchful and irritating eye of Maurice, the security guard, waiting for Her Highness to agree to see me. I stand and stare at the boring view out of the huge front windows. *A grocery delivery truck – how interesting.* It's parked out front and down the curb a short distance. An old man is unloading groceries from the truck and putting them onto a cart. He pays the delivery driver, who gets in the truck and drives away. The old man is pushing the overloaded cart inward on the sidewalk when the best thing of the day happens. I see a glimpse of his face. *I know you! Who are you, little grocery man? Now where have I seen you before?* Then I remember. Yes! I know who he is, and he's on my list. Sam Callahan's flunky. My eyes covet him until he disappears, and I smile a little smile inside. That's Sam Callahan's townhouse. Well, well, well. Things are looking up!

****

Maurice

Miss Callahan Will See You Now

The Lobby of Brandenberger's Chocolates and Confections

1:00 p.m. Monday, May 21st, 1928

I have called his name three times, but he's so engrossed

in whatever's out that window that he's not hearing me. He makes me walk over to him, and as I touch his arm to get his attention, he jumps - startled, swinging wildly and nearly punches me in the face.

"Agent Del Ray!" I call, defending myself from his swing. His face has changed. *What in the world was he looking at?* He's a little unnerving, and I have half a mind to ask him to leave. I just wait and say nothing. Wait for him to snap out of whatever mind warp he's in! He smiles at me, you know, *that* smile, apologizing for swinging on me. But something just isn't right about this man.

"It's alright," I reply, defensive and ready for anything he may do next. "I didn't mean to startle you. Miss Callahan will see you now. However, she's scheduled for a meeting in 20 minutes. She says she doesn't have much time."

"Well, I better get going then," he says, leaving abruptly.

"The kind of people that work at the Bureau…not good," I say out loud, amazed that these are the people we are supposed to trust!

He wastes no time. He boards the elevator, and I ring Miss Annabelle. "He's on his way up. Might want to keep an eye on him." He pushes a button on the pane, and the doors begin to close. How did he know what floor Miss Callahan was on? The ringing of the telephone redirects my attention from Agent Del Ray.

"Brandenberger Offices. This is Maurice. How can I help you? Oh! Hello Mr. Warford. How are you today?" "Yes…yes. I will certainly do that, Sir. Yes, Sir. Thank you, Sir. Good day."

Mr. Warford requests that I leave the side door to the connecting tunnels unlocked. I don't ask why. It's none of my business, but it does make me curious. Those doors haven't been left unlocked since Miss Valentina was alive, and that's been a long time ago. Odd he would ask now. I walk down the long hall that seems to go on forever toward a secluded area at the end. I stop at the side door and go through the keys on my key ring one by one. It's been so long since I unlocked this door that I don't remember what the key looks like.

"There you are!" I exclaimed under my breath. I key the door and open it. This tunnel is old, dark, and damp. I can't help thinking, *'What in the world would Warford want with the tunnel after all this time'.* I stand just inside the door, squinting my eyes, trying to focus in the dark, but the smell of extremely stale air is overwhelming and gets the best of me. I back out of the doorway and quickly close the door, making sure it's unlocked and return to my post. The half-eaten lunch that Miss Callahan brought for me is waiting at my desk, and I want to finish it. I can't help thinking about Del Ray – and the tunnel, which hasn't been used in years. Coincidence? Maybe. An uneasy feeling settles in my bones. I don't know what it means, but this is one of those strange days... Very strange…

****

Annabelle

I Wish I Were a Fly on the Wall

Sam Callahan's Office – Brandenberger's Chocolates

1:00 p.m. – Monday, May 21ˢᵗ, 1928

I quickly clear my desk, disposing of the lunch containers and straightening paperwork. Maurice just informed me that a Bureau man is on his way up. What could he possibly want with Sam? I'm anxious it may have something to do with me. Finished with tidying, I knock on Sam's door.

"Come in," she replies. I open the door to peer in and see her at her desk working.

"He's on his way up." She nods, stows business papers, hands me important files to return to the filing cabinet, and locks other paperwork in her desk drawer. I arrange the visitor chair directly placed front and center of Sam's desk. The visitor's chair isn't always front and center, but the Bureau Man is different.

I hear the outer office door opening, and I instantly leave and greet him. I don't want him to just wander into Sam's office. He presents himself confidently. His tallness and gorgeous features are breathtaking, and I find myself struggling to make an extra effort to conceal my admiration for his stunning good looks when I greet him.

"Agent Del Ray, welcome," I say, greeting him with an outstretched hand.

"Miss Annabelle, I presume." He says, taking my hand. I instantly take note that he's *one of those*. His charm and good looks are disarming, and he prides himself in the ability to use those attributes as a most effective weapon, especially with women.

"Yes, I am," I reply, a feeling of déjà vu overtaking me. I've seen him somewhere - can't put my finger on the where. "How nice to meet you. Miss Callahan is ready to see you," I add, reminding him of just who is in charge. We shake hands, and exchange smiles as I promptly direct him towards Sam's office. My thoughts were racing as I led him to Sam. *"Special Agent, huh... I wish I was a fly on the wall. Information like that would go a long way to getting me off the hook, and my debt would be paid in full, and I'd be rid of them for good!"*

"Right this way, please." I direct, guiding him through Sam's office doors.

Sam doesn't stand to greet him. Something she learned from her mother, Valentina. *When you are meeting someone, and the meeting is likely to be uncomfortable, always remain seated at the desk.* At the desk, you have leverage. At the desk, you have power.

Don't shake hands and direct them to sit in the chair directly in your line of sight. Valentina was a businesswoman in a man's world long before women were accepted or respected as businesswomen. Her ways were learned the hard way, and they worked. Now, they are Sam's ways, and they still work.

As planned, Agent Del Ray notices that Sam remains seated at her desk, not bothering to stand and greet him. He appears surprised and somewhat irritated by this. I commence the introductions.

"Miss Callahan, this is Special Agent Del Ray." Sam doesn't inquire about his name or his title. Instead, she keeps eye contact with me. He appears to bristle a bit, and I can see that he's not used to such treatment. He's uncomfortable, and that's the way she likes it. Del Ray obviously doesn't. I take my cue and ask, "Is there anything I can get for you, Miss Callahan?" She darts her eyes straight to Del Ray.

"Would you like something to drink, Special Agent Del Ray?" She asks, in a tone that only slightly hints at condescension, patiently waiting for his answer – a stony smile radiating for effect. "A soda water - Ginger Ale perhaps?"

I discreetly watch him from the corner of my eye. I struggle to place where I know him from. I just can't put my finger on it, and I'm even more nervous that the reason for his visit centers around me. Maybe my wish to hear their conversation is a wish I shouldn't have made.

"No, thank you. Nothing for me." He replies curtly.

"Very well," Sam replies. "Thank you, Annabelle. That will be all for now, and no interruptions, please."

"Yes, Miss Callahan." I take my leave, close her doors behind me and sit down at my desk. I'm anxious and feeling very guilty. Sam's always been very good to me. I should confide in her, but I can't. The warning was loud and clear. If I've seen Del Ray, then he's seen me - somewhere.

****

Sam and Agent Del Ray

Don't Let the Door Hit You

Sam Callahan's Office – Brandenberger's Chocolates

1:05 p.m., Monday, May 21, 1928

Outwardly, Sam acts calm and cool, but inside, her guts are churning. "What could he possibly want with me?" "Maybe it has something to do with Mother's death. No one was ever caught or arrested for the bombing, and it's been eight years. It must be that. Nothing else it could be…right?"

Special Agent Del Ray is also thinking to himself. *If she only knew what I'd really like to do to her, it would wipe that fake smile right off her face!* He's itching to crawl across that desk of hers and snap her neck. *Patience, patience,* he thinks. *Besides, if I do that now, I won't get the pleasure of killing her after she spills about the diamond. I look forward to that – immensely.*

****

I guard from behind my desk, eyes directly on him. Is he uncomfortable or thinking about something else? He's not engaging me - a rather odd, far-away look in his eyes. I don't speak. He asked for this meeting, so if he wants answers, he'll start talking. And he does just that, but nothing important. Not to me, anyway. No, he starts with the one thing I hate more than anything else. Small talk.

"So, Miss Callahan, how long have you been at the candy factory?" "I raise my eyebrows at him, signaling that I find his question a little, well, stupid. His demeanor instantly changes. He gets the meaning of my facial expression."

"A long time," I respond, a slight hint of sarcasm. "Surely you didn't come here to ask me that, Agent Del Ray." I've sized him up. He's always the confident-rock solid one - sure of himself. He doesn't require validation from anyone. He's arrogant about his extremely handsome features, and he wields it as a weapon. He's tan, so he's not from New York. I don't trust him. Not because he's a Bureau man - no – something else. Something chilling about him I just don't like.

"Elegance Samantha Callahan?" he says, repeating my nameplate. "Your name is Elegance?" He says, sincerely desperate to break the ice. He leans closer, face level, to the nameplate. He looks at me from the top of his eyes, his gaze smoldering. Good try, but that won't work on me.

"I suppose you find that name amusing?" I reply. My voice is heavy with accusation, but in truth, I really don't care what he thinks.

He stands up straight with all his tallness, relying on his heavenly handsomeness to soften me up.

"If you must know, I think it's quite amazing. I don't think I've ever heard such a beautiful name."

I don't respond, but I must admit, I struggle not to succumb to his charms. After all, I'm not dead. But I suppress those feelings and instead confront him. I despise being manipulated.

"Why exactly are you here, Agent Del Ray?" I'm curt and a little rude – I demand an answer. I'm putting an end to his little game, and I'm gonna hit him right where it hurts – in his ego. "Why don't you stop trying to charm and woo me and just get to the point of your visit." Funny how a statement like that can put out a fire. His smoldering gaze quickly turns to ash which pleases me. "I'm sure you didn't come here to ask me how long I've been at my family's factory or to talk about my amazing name. Truth be known, if you were worth your salt as an Agent, you would already know those details, so I'll ask you again. What do you want? Are you here with news about my mother's death?"

"No. That is not why I'm here." He says flatly as he pulls a photo out of his jacket pocket along with a small notebook.

"Oh…" I reply, hiding my disappointment. He hands me the photograph of a woman in a nun's habit. An odd feeling comes over me. I don't know her, but there's a feeling of familiarity I can't deny.

"I'm here to ask you some questions about this woman. Do you know her? Have you ever seen her or met her?" Now he's all business, impatient as he waits for my response, notebook in hand.

"I'm sorry, Agent Del Ray. I don't know her. I've never seen nor met her." I reply coolly. The feeling of familiarity pounds in my head, but I'm certainly not going to tell him that. I'll Keep it to myself.

"Do you know if your mother or anyone else in your family knew her? Maybe you met her through your charity work." I inspect the photo again, silent about my feelings, and answer his question.

"No. I'm sorry I haven't. May I ask why you think I would know her?" He ignores my question and instead asks another one.

"And what about your mother – or father? Would they have known her?"

"I'm quite sure I don't know, Agent Del Ray. I didn't know all my mother's and father's friends and acquaintances. My father died when I was eight, as I'm sure you're aware, and as for my mother, she never introduced me to or indicated to me that she had friends in The Order." My patience is wearing thin with Del Ray. He's fishing, and I've had enough! "I don't know her, Agent," I say forcefully. His eyes change, controlled fury replacing his usual come-hither stare. I decided the meeting's over. "Now, if that's all – *Agent* - I have another meeting soon and a lot of work to do."

I don't give him a chance to rebuke my demand for him to leave immediately. I rise from behind my desk and offer to walk him to the door. He remains seated and incredibly ignores me and continues to fish for answers.

"What about anyone who works for you?" I bite my tongue and answer him calmly but with tension.

"Agent, I have house staff, but I can't speak for them as to whether they know her. There are a few of my and father's friends that I have remained close to, but I can't tell you whether *they* know her." He writes something in his little notebook.

"I'm going to need a list of names from you," he demands. "Your house staff and the friends you mentioned." I refuse to dignify his demand with an answer. He knows he's stepped over a line.

"Look," he says in a manipulative tone, his weapon of charm returning front and center.

"No! You look!" I interrupt him, and I've had it with him! "I've been hospitable to you and cooperative despite the fact that you insisted on interrupting my workday – unannounced! You shove a photo in my face and insist that I or someone I'm connected to must know this woman even though I have assured you I do not know. Now, I understand you have a job to do, but I'm about to make that job of yours somewhat of a nightmare." I buzz Annabelle. "Annabelle, can you get me Mr. Hoover on the line, please? You've got about 15 seconds to get out of my office Del Ray." I begin counting. "15, 14, 13." To my astonishment, he continues to defy my request for him to leave, blatantly daring me to follow through with my threat. "12, 11, 10, 9, 8, 7, 6."

"Sam, I've got Mr. Hoover's office on the line," Annabelle reports.

"Thank you, Annabelle. 5, 4, 3, 2, 1. Edgar! How are you? Yes, it's been a while. Edgar, I wonder if you could tell me about one of your agents. Yes, Agent Dominic Del Ray...." Ah, the slamming of the door. Good riddance and goodbye, Bureau man.

****

Annabelle

The Lie

Annabelle's Desk – Brandenberger's Chocolates

3:30 p.m. – Monday, May 21ˢᵗ, 1928

Sam is at her desk, trying to work but is understandably

distracted. Today hasn't been the best of days. First, the scenes with Felicity and then Del Ray. She's on edge, and I'm treading lightly.

"I'll send Garrison right in when he gets here," I say on my way out, a muffled *'thank you'* in my ear as I leave her office and return to my desk. I'm dying to ask her about her meeting with the handsome Special Agent Del Ray, but I don't dare. Best leave that alone.

I don't know how much longer I can continue to lie. I love Sam. She's supported me through many tough times, but I don't think she can cure this. My stupidity has cost me a lot, and if I could, I'd turn back the clock and do things differently. I'm trying to figure out a way to make it right. The clock on the wall says 3:30. Garrison will be arriving soon for his meeting with Sam. I have time, so I - take a chance a call. I'm terrified. If Sam catches me - maybe that wouldn't be such a bad thing. Maybe I should just tell her the truth! *Aah!* I scream under my breath, slamming my fists on my desk. Deceiving her like this is tearing me up! I'm such a coward!

Ring...Ring......Ring...Ring. My mouth goes dry – like I'm chewing cotton. I have a sudden onset of panic and start to hang up, but it's too late.

"Hello," he answers. My guts are tied in a million knots, my voice is shaky, and I can barely speak. I'm paranoid that Sam will appear and expect to know who I'm talking to.

"It's me," I reply in a hushed tone. "I have news." His disgusting heavy breathing churns my stomach. Second thoughts race through my mind, but I don't dare hang up. That will just make things worse.

"Are you calling me from her office!" He knows I should be at work. "I told you never to call me from there! How stupid are you!"

He hangs up on me, slamming the receiver so hard, it's like a hammer to my eardrum. I gently replaced the receiver back on the telephone, nervous that my little stunt just escalated an already deadly situation. I need to get myself together. My hands are shaking uncontrollably. I press them down in my lap, but it's no use! The terror I feel is only topped by my shame. Tears well up in my eyes, but I can't cry! *If she catches me crying, she'll make me explain!* I take a handkerchief from my bag, dab the tears from my eyes and fan my face with my hands. *Calm down. You must calm down,* races through my mind as I breathe in and breathe out, desperately trying to get control of myself. Unfortunately for me, Greg Garrison arrives for his meeting with Sam and catches me with tears in my eyes. Relieved he declines to comment, I buzz her office and announce him.

Bzzzzz…Bzzzzz

"Hi, Annabelle."

"Greg Garrison is here for your meeting," I inform her, not a hint of emotion in my voice.

"Send him in. And you can go ahead and go home. I'll see you tomorrow."

Her generous offer is not a welcome one. I've increasingly become frightened of being alone at home. I know that there's someone watching me. I can't arouse her suspicion or risk her asking any questions by refusing, so I thank her graciously and prepare to leave for the day. But inside, I'm a mess. I don't know what I'm going to do, but I know that time is running out, and I must do something soon. Very Soon.

****

Captain Graff Grayland

Things I Should Have Said

River Dell County Coroner's Office, Tarrytown, NY

Early Afternoon - Monday, May 21ˢᵗ, 1928

"C'mon, c'mon!" My patience is thin, and I obnoxiously yell to the air as I stamp out the last of the ten cigarettes I've chain-smoked, waiting – for Dr. Alexander to return to the morgue. I just want to punch something! I'm so mad, and manic thoughts invade my mind. *I wish I had known who you were! I could've protected you! Why didn't you tell me? I could have stopped it. I could've.*, I say out loud, tears streaming down my face. I feel sick. I – scurry to the back of the building to find a discrete place to puke my guts up. I don't want to lose my mind over this, but I'm on the edge, and I'm not sure I'll win this battle.

Sister Mary Agnes - who never did anything but help people – loved abandoned children - selfless and caring like the others. My thoughts begin a reign of terror, torturing me further into collapse. *It's just wrong! Can I handle this again? Can I handle it? I don't know. This is my fault. I should've stopped it before! Why her? Why not me! I'm a pathetic mess! But she – she was a gift from God.*

"I'm a humble servant of God," she always said, "and my only purpose is to do as he commands me with joy." She saw past my drunkenness and instability and never judged me – helped me heal from the pain of the past more than she'll ever know, and regrettably, I don't remember ever thanking her. Not even once. If not for her – the bullet I set aside special for just that moment…if not for Sister Mary Agnes. I can't handle this alone. I need someone else to take this one.

I stumble back around to the front of the building, still cursing Dr. Alexander under my breath. As I round the corner, I see a police car pulling up. Oh no. It's that detective from Manhattan. I wasn't expecting him until later today. And now he's going to see me…like this. "What time is it anyway? 1:00. *Where is Dr. Alexander, for crying out loud?"*

He gets out of the car and looks around. He's looking for me. How did he know I was here? Nina! Now that he's here, I find myself wishing he wasn't. Too late. He's seen me, and he's waving. He's walking toward me, hand extended. He looks young, but he impressed me on the telephone. I nervously wipe my hands on my pants, realizing what I must look like. Don't want to shake hands with sweaty palms. Wouldn't blame him if he got right back in his car and high-tailed it out of here. I really hope he doesn't. I need him. And I need a drink! I hope my breath doesn't stink like vomit. *Hold it together, and don't embarrass yourself any more than you already have, Grayland.*

"Detective Madison?" I acknowledge as I extend my hand to shake his. I'm surprised, considering my appearance, that he seems very receptive.

"Cap'n Grayland. Nice to meet you. Miss Nina told me I would find you here. I hope you don't mind me just showin up here unannounced, but she said you wouldn't mind."

Nina!

"Born and raised in New York, Madison?" I probably shouldn't have made it so apparent that I noticed his accent, but I am experiencing a blank and struggling for anything to say.

"Yes, Sir, Brooklyn, Sir."

I nod and grin, an awkward silence takes over. He's astute enough to assess that I'm struggling though I'm sure he doesn't know why. I need to stop this! Be a superior officer and take control. Trying to get a handle on that.

"Are you okay, Cap'n? I know this must be difficult. Miss Nina said that the victim was a friend of yours. My condolences. I'm very sorry, Cap'n."

With that one simple gesture, I know he is meant to be here.

He could have taken one look at me and fled, refusing to tolerate my condition. He's sensitive and kind – and a great detective, according to his Captain. Sister Mary Agnes would have liked him. They would have been great friends. He reminds me of me when I was younger. A me minus the torment and need for self-destruction. A me I would like to see again.

I check my watch. 1:10! "Thank you for coming, Detective."

"Well, thank you for askin' me, Cap'n. I really want to help," he replies, grateful and sincere. "Can I ask you a question? Do you not get along with the Docter or…. It just seems you're a little upset, and don't get me wrong, I get it. You want to get in there – get her taken care of, but…"

"Naw," I say, rudely interrupting. "I'm just not myself today. Doctor Alexander is a fine pathologist, one of the best. I'm just feeling impatient and helpless…"

"How about you and I head back to the office," I suggest, feeling the need to give the fool in me a rest. "I'd like to wash up, and there's nothing we can do until Dr. Alexander arrives."

What I really need is a drink, but I hope my conscience will help me fight that battle. Besides, if Chief Tuttle sees me like this, he'll probably fire me. As well, he should. I'd deserve it.

"Just follow me to the station," I instruct. "It's not far from here." Then I remembered he's already been there. Madison pays my slip of memory no mind. He just gets in his car and does exactly as I told him to do. He follows me. Sister Mary Agnes would say that God sent him to me. I don't know about that, but I'm sure glad he's here.

****

Detective Malcolm (Mal) Madison

The Evil Killings

The River Dell County Police Department, Tarrytown, NY

Early Afternoon – Monday, May 21ˢᵗ, 1928

Cap'n Grayland isn't exactly what I expected. He was in

quite a state back there. When I talked to him on the phone, he sounded like he had it all together. Didn't let on that he knew the victim. I guess we all handle grief in our own way. And I should know. What kinda person does it take to murder a nun? I think this qualifies as an evil killing. That's what the older cops call murders that go beyond any comprehension. I mean, don't get me wrong, all murders are beyond comprehension, but there are those – you know, murders that are so heinous that the only explanation that works is that they're just pure evil. *The evil killings.* I think the murder of the Sister is like that. Turns my stomach and makes me sick.

The Cap'n looks fragile. Rightfully so. He didn't seem happy to see me. Maybe I should've called first – not taken him by surprise like that. I hope he wasn't embarrassed. I think, considering the nature of things, it's a good thing I came, even if it's only for a short time. He's shaken, and now that I know she was his friend, I'm glad I'm here to help him out. I know what's going on with him, though. He tried to hide it, but I know the look. Seen it many times. He needs to get rid of the booze. Exercise the demon, as my father used to say. He never did, but I'm hopeful the Cap'n will.

Reporters! Oy, for the love 'a… Shoulda known they'd be showing up sooner or later. I'm gonna do what I can to help him through this. He will get it together. He just needs a little time and support. Gotta be hard on the guy, you know?

****

Captain Graff Grayland

Life One Minute at a Time

River Dell County Police Department, Tarrytown, NY

Early Afternoon - Monday, May 21st, 1928

We arrive at the station to a swarm of reporters, and immediately, my blood pressure skyrockets. I stick my left arm out of the window and motion for Madison to follow me around to the back entrance. They're like a pack of wild animals in the front. And poor Miss Nina will have to stall 'em off. A couple of 'em sprint toward my car, shouting questions as I drive by. I have to play nice, or the Chief will have my hide. I have my orders.

"I'm putting you on warning, Grayland. No more fighting with reporters." His accent is thick, like Madison's. "I know you don't like dealing with 'em, and well, after what happened in LA, I can't say I blame ya, but I just can't tolerate it." That was all he said. But the look – the look on his face was clear. He meant exactly what he said. I like the Chief. He's a good man. He gave me a fair shot after L.A., and I won't forget it. So, I show my respect and do what he says. But man 'o man, do I struggle not to just pop those guys one!

Madison and I arrive at the back door. He doesn't say much about the reporters, just rolls his eyes dramatically.

"I see you love 'em as much as I do," I say jokingly. He laughs and rolls his eyes again. Inside the station, Nina is trying her best to keep the noise to a minimum. Her expression begs me for help to control 'em, but I just keep right on walking toward my office. My blood pressure! It's spiking through the roof! But I do feel bad that I left her to be harassed and disrespected. I see her out of the corner of my eye, raising her hands in frustration, but if I get involved, there will be a fight because I can't stand 'em. I say I'll be fine, but I won't! And I'm not getting into that situation! I direct a Sergeant and two patrolmen to assist her in keeping some control and lowering the noise.

Me, minus the alcohol, is a little tricky right now. My legs buckle a little as I'm watching the chaos in the lobby. I'm grateful the wall was there to rescue me, or I'd be heaving myself up off the floor.

"Are you alright, Cap'n?" I hear Madison's voice echoing in my ears. My head is swirling - like I'm spinning down a drain. I don't answer him right away, so he asks me again. "Are you alright, Sir?" I'm trying to regain a little composure and insist I am fine. If only that were true. I flip a flimsy excuse for my near collapse and start walking toward the head.

"I just need to go wash my face and get some water. Would you go help Nina, please – I just need a minute. Then we'll talk." I summon a passing patrolman. "Hey, Carpenter. This is Detective Madison. He's here to help us with the Sister's case. Both a' you go and help Nina. I'll just be a minute." I feel like a jerk shoving him off on someone else, but I've got to have a minute to myself. Hopefully, I can make it through without a drink.

I make it to the head, slam the door and lock it. The dirty, stained sink bears my weight as I take stock of my miserable self in the mirror. The prominent diagonal crack splits my face in two, revealing something twisted. One half - the man I want to be. The other – the man I've become. As I study myself, it hits me that maybe the crack is really in my soul. How did I get here? How do I fix it? How do I get back to me? The whole me, not this disgusting remnant I've become. Sudden desperation for an answer overwhelms me, and I feel more lost than I've ever felt.

Again. It's happening again. I say under my breath, calling up memories of things I've tried desperately to bury. I honestly don't know if I can take it! I'm ashamed and broken by what Madison must think of me, what my men must think of me! My whole body is shaking from the inside out, and I can't think straight! I'm weak and sweating like a pig! '*Ahh – booze, booze, my jealous, destructive lover. You've helped me to hide and gotten me through many a night. But I give you permission to leave now. Please, leave me alone'.* I stare blankly at my soulless image. I'm a coward! Hiding out in here, avoiding everyone and everything – but mostly – avoiding myself.

"I'm so sorry, Sister, but I don't think I can take it," I say to the half of the reflection that I hope is still intact. I fight back tears and beg for help – reaching for some comfort – resisting that old urge to end it all. But I don't run for the bottle, and that brings a little smile.

"Okay. If I'm not to end it, how do I begin to pull myself out of this pit?" The split face in the mirror doesn't answer me. "So, I'm to battle this alone, am I?" I continue to stare down my reflection, declaring that I must make it right this time, even though I know I may not be able to. I allow the reflection to win for the moment and rinse my face. The cold water feels like heaven, and an amazing feeling comes over me. A feeling I always felt when I talked with Sister Mary Agnes.

She always inspired me to like myself, which was a miracle because I haven't for a very long time. But what could it hurt to ask? I'm not good at humbling myself, but I'm on my last dime here. What do I have to lose?

"Lord, what you must think of me," I pray. "You know I'm not a praying man, but I need your help. Sister Mary Agnes, who loved you with every fiber of her being, told me once that you never give us more than we can bear. I don't know if that's true, but I know she believed it with all her heart, and she had certainly seen more heartache than I, so I ask you to show me how to bear this. Tell me what to do. Tell me how to keep going. Sister Mary Agnes said that you never give up on us. Please tell me you haven't given up on me. Amen"

I hope that didn't sound stupid. I don't know. Can you sound stupid to God? A rush of emotion doubles me over that dirty sink, and I sob as I've never sobbed before. So much pain! It burns like a fire in my bones from years of regret and doubt. Years of life over the edge, a crushed soul riddled with guilt and self-loathing. Years of dealing with my demons and years of trying to find the light in even the smallest crack of the darkness. Then like washing over my soul, it occurs to me. Maybe the light isn't at the end of the tunnel. Maybe it's at the beginning. Yes, the beginning. I vow a new beginning for me.

Sister Mary Agnes always told me to live life one minute at a time if that's what it took to keep going. So that's what I'll do. Life - one minute at a time. What a wise woman my friend was.

A small surge of strength overcomes me. Small, yes, but strength I didn't have before. Small is better than nothing. I wipe my face, straighten my hair a bit and prepare to defeat my demons. *The light.* Now, to go find Madison - and get ahold of Dr. Alexander. Life begins. Minute one – minute two…

****

Dominic Del Ray

Mind Games

The Lobby of Brandenberger's Chocolates and Confections

1:45 p.m. –Monday, May 21st, 1928

I get off the elevator and see the ever-loyal Maurice at the

security desk. He stands to greet me and shake my hand.

"Special Agent Del Ray! Leaving us so soon?" His words are kind, but his tone has a hint of disdain. It's obvious he's glad to see me leave.

"Afraid so, Maurice. Thank you for all your help." He's loyal. *Wonder if he's loyal enough to cover up for her.* On the heels of that thought, I ask him about Sam Callahan's townhouse next door. I'm curious to hear what he says about it. I walk toward the doors and then turn around abruptly, pretending I've forgotten something.

"Oh, yeah! Maurice. Miss Callahan's townhouse. She said it was next door. So, is it? Right next door, I mean?" I ask, smiling coyly and pointing my finger.

"Yes, Sir. Right next door." Maurice replies, obviously treading cautiously.

"Miss Callahan's Mother renovated that building so that she didn't have to drive all the way from the estate in Long Island during the week."

"Did you know Miss Callahan's Mother? What was her name?" I snap my fingers like I'm trying to remember.

"Her name was Valentina." He makes it clear with his tone and expression that his patience is zero and he will not answer another question from me. There's the intentional, crushingly uncomfortable moment of silence between us until I announce my departure.

"Well, thank you, Maurice. You've been a big help." I do an about-face and exit through the front doors, heading straight to my right - towards Sam Callahan's townhouse.

I stop at the very – large double - doors and look up. It's five stories tall! Why would anyone want a five-story townhouse? Interesting. I check my watch. *Oh, Sh...*! The time has gotten away from me! I need to get to the office! I hail a cab and instruct the driver to take me to Bureau Headquarters.

During the cab ride to headquarters, I see her beautiful face in my mind. I can't stop thinking about her. Nor do I want to. She is, without a doubt, the most beautiful, strong, smart, irritating, but *elegant* woman I've ever encountered.

"Elegance Samantha Callahan. How beautiful you'll look on a morgue table. How very, very beautiful."

****

Sam

Questions

Sam's Office - Brandenberger's Chocolates

4:00 p.m. Meeting - Monday, May 21ˢᵗ, 1928

I - accompany Greg Garrison to the door, and assure him that I will do my best to convince the board that raises are in order.

"Thank you, Greg. I'll be sure to get these figures to the Board so raises can be discussed at next week's meeting."

"Do you think the Board will approve the raises for everyone, Miss Callahan?"

"You know I can't guarantee anything, but I'm going to do my best, Greg. And business has been great this year due to our fine employees, so fingers crossed. I think I can safely say there will be an increase, but how much – well we'll have to wait and see. I'll do my best."

"Thank you, Miss Callahan," he replies. "I know you will."

Greg Garrison is one of my best employees, and he is always looking out for the workers. He's been here a long time, an original hire of - Mother's. There is a sentimental attachment to him and many others that have been here for many years. I always think about what she would have done for them if she were here. This company wouldn't be what it is without them.

I'm suddenly overwhelmed with a crushing feeling of loss. Flashes of memory run through my mind. Her beautiful face. Her contagious laugh. She was such a presence in my life. I'm ashamed that it took her dying for me to figure that out. Things I should have said like, I am so grateful you are my mother, my mentor, my friend. I sit at my desk, alone in silence. I take her photograph from its place on my desk and hold it up in front of me. How beautiful she was, inside and out.

"I miss you Mommy."

Tears pool in my eyes, and as I gaze upon her beautiful face, I can't imagine why the Bureau would question me about her. I put her back in her place, and pick up the telephone. I ring the number and wait for an answer.

"Yes, Warford. Listen, I had a visit from a Special Agent Dominic Del Ray from the Bureau this afternoon. Yes. Dominic Del Ray. You wouldn't know why he would be interested in Mother, would you? He was asking whether she knew someone – a nun. Do you know anything about that?"

"No, Madam," he replies. "Not that I'm aware of."

I've known Warford my entire life. I can hear it in his voice. He's lying to me. Why would he do that? I don't push the issue. Face-to-face is better.

"Thank you, Warford. I'll be there shortly."

I abruptly hang up the phone, more anxious than ever about Del Ray's visit. Why would Warford lie? What's he hiding?

I look at her photograph one more time, wondering what it is that I don't know. Del Ray's questions – the nun in the photograph – his glaring insistence of a link. Warford is lying. Questions burning in my mind.

"What's going on, Mother? What's going on?"

****

Antonio De Cordova

Mama

The Midnight Arms Hotel, New York City

Late Afternoon - Monday, May 21, 1928

In my dreams, I return home – to London. The same images play in slow motion over- and over -and over, and I re-live the time with my Mama. I remember the love and the laughter – and the horror. I see the day I wish I could forget. The day my precious Mama was taken from me. The day *The Butcher* changed me. My sleep is the conduit to the memory. I'm a young boy terrified and hiding. Hiding to save my life! I was a boy who survived death, and now I'm a man who dispenses it.

I'm there – in the small apartment we called home in London. I call it home, but it's really a hiding place for Mama and me and the Sisters. Sometimes there are others there. Ones who were rescued from the diamond mines in South Africa. It's only because of Valentina, Mama, and the Sisters that they are alive and given a chance to be free. They risked their lives on many occasions to help them. The apartment is in a poor part of town. The ones who hunt us are less likely to look here, and it's easier to hide. Mama's light is the only thing in this place that makes it a home. Only people we know we can trust are aware of our location. On that dreadful day, there were only four others in the apartment. Four others – no children – just me. I can smell the delicious chicken and vegetables cooking in a pot over the fire, and I can't wait to taste it, but I'm more excited about the cake. I beg Mama to let me eat the cake first. Valentina brought it. It was my 12th birthday party, and she promised a special treat. Valentina always keeps her promises.

Mama's face shows her regret. "I'm so sorry that you don't have friends to invite to your birthday, Mijo."

"It's ok, Mama. I don't mind. It's important that we help them. If we don't, who will? And I have you, Mama, so that's all that matters." I show her my biggest, if not somewhat forced, smile to reassure her that I'm okay.

"Te quiero muchisimo, Mijo! I'm so proud of you, my Angel! I promise everything will be alright, and we will always be together." She gives me a crushing bear hug and kisses my cheek a dozen times, making that smooching noise that I love so much. My Mama….

She's smiling, always smiling - and I reach out to her to touch her face with my hand. Little did I know that would be the last time I would see her. Her voice echoes in my ears, saying, "I love you, My Angel," loud and clear. My heart yearns for all of it. Her love, her laughter, her hugs. I am happy. She's there, and I feel safe.

"Mama! Mama!" I recall hearing every glorious sound. Valentina, Sister Mary Anna, and Sister Mary Collette are holding hands and skipping, circling around me, singing Happy Birthday. It's a moment of pure joy, and they are singing just for me. And then, in the blink of an eye, the joy comes to a crashing end and is replaced by indescribable terror! My chest is burning, and my heart is pounding! I can hardly breathe, the pounding of my heart echoing like a sledgehammer in my ears. But that sound…that sound creeps into my ears; the sound of the thunderous crack of the front door being kicked off its hinges and sailing through the air until it crashes to the floor. I instinctively run and hide in a small cabinet, where I witness the unfolding of a massacre.

Two smaller men enter first, followed by the huge man, the man with the machete. They yell and scream, scaring Mama and the Sisters! I cover my ears to block it out but keep my eyes open. The terror captured my breath, and every inch of me was trembling. One of the men grabs Mama violently and holds her so she can't move. She discreetly glances my way, aware of where I am hiding, careful not to tip them off to my presence. Mama's voice resonates in my head, reminding me of where I'm supposed to be and what I'm supposed to do.

"No matter what you see or what you hear, you hide my Angel. You hide, and you don't come out! Someone will come for you. Someone will come for you, so you promise me, promise me you will stay quiet. Cover your eyes and ears, and don't you dare look." But I do look. I feel sick, so I cover my mouth and close my eyes - concentrate very hard on what Mama said. My head is swirling! I can't think straight! I wish I could catch my breath!

"This must be what it feels like to die." I thought.

From the corner of my eye, I see the tiny light beams streaming through the cutouts on the front of the doors. Then I realize I have a view of everything. Mama said not to look! I don't want to look, but I can't help it. I can hear Mama and the Sisters screaming in terror. It's at this moment that I realize Valentina is not in the room. I don't hear her voice. I mustered my courage and slowly turned my head to peer out where the tiny light beams stream - through. I quickly squinch my eyes shut, too terrified to open them again. I fight with myself, scold myself! Be a man not a coward! I slowly open my eyes and look. That's when I see it. The horror that will forever burn in my soul.

Sister Mary Anna and Sister Mary Collette, tied down, heads bowed, praying to God. But not to save themselves. They are confessing their love for Him, thanking Him that they are about to see Him at last. This act of love for God angers the two men who are still restraining Mama. She is crying and pleading with the men to spare them, but they laugh at her and tell her to shut up.

There's the other one. The large man with the machete. The silvery blade reflects the light revealing its razor - sharp intention. His face is branded into my mind, and I will never, for as long as I live, forget it. He is the devil! He is pompous as he stands before the Sisters, taunting them, taking pleasure in the terror he inflicts as he swings the machete through the air. He mocks their prayers and jokes with the other two men as he stabs them, taking pleasure in the cutting of their skin and the bleeding of their wounds. But he wasn't finished. He raises the machete. The Sisters scream to God as the blade comes down, severing one hand, then the other. He finishes by slashing their throats. The men drag Mama out the door, and she is gone. I can't move – every muscle is frozen. I scream over and over, but there is no sound, no sound at all.

"Ahhhhhhh! Ahhhhhhhhh! Ahhhhhhhhh! *No! No!"* I scream out, struggling to breathe, sweat pouring, tears streaming down my face. Time and time again, I have sat on the edge of the bed collecting my bearings, taking a moment to realize I'm not in that cabinet anymore. What does it matter? I may not be in the cabinet anymore, but I will always be the boy who was in it, witnessing horrors unspeakable. The seed of that day has made me the man that I am. A killer.

The aftermath of the nightmare brings on as many memories as the nightmare itself. And sitting here, alone, on the edge of this bed, I remember. I remember it like it was yesterday.

"Where is my Mama?" The boy in the cabinet cries to himself. His heart aches for her. Would he ever see her again? He knew the answer to that. He's trapped, even though the devils are gone. The thought of walking past the Sisters makes him sick. Sick in his stomach and sick in his heart.

"Antonio, Darling. Antonio, Darling, look at me.!" It's not his Mama.

"A voice!". The boy says in his head. *Am I dead?* " "Is it an Angel? Maybe – it is Mama!"

"Antonio, Darling. Antonio, look at me.!"

"Valentina?"

"Yes, Darling," she whispered. "It's me, Valentina." She puts her finger to her lips to shush him and whispers, "We must be very quiet now. We're getting you out of here." She takes my hand and tries to help me from the cabinet, but I resist. I'm terrified to come out. She tries to console me – coax me out. "I understand you're scared, Antonio, but you aren't safe here. We must go quickly!" She takes my arm to help me out. I can barely stand, but Valentina holds me upright as I hobble along beside her, her arms supporting and guiding me. She covers my eyes to block the sinister scene in that apartment. I didn't tell her I had already seen it – witnessed it. Witnessed everything. And I wonder how Valentina managed to escape the same fate as the others. The same fate as my Mama.

"Keep your eyes covered, Darling. We're going out. I have a carriage waiting outside, and we'll get some food and water and get you all cleaned up. Everything will be alright."

I don't speak. I fail to see how everything will be alright. Nothing will ever be right again.

Valentina rushes me downstairs to a carriage waiting in the alley that takes me to a secret location where I stay until boyhood ends and manhood begins.

The boy in the cabinet never sees his Mama again.

Valentina saved my life that day - she raised me –gave me everything, and loved me like her own. I would never betray her. As I battle my way back from the past, it occurs to me that, once again, I have lost time. My watch says five o'clock! I don't know why time matters; I have no place to be. I'm here until Warford summons me. Still, I need a wash. The wash basin that serves as a sink will do just fine. I remove my filthy shirt and lay out my one and only spare. The water feels good as I rinse my face and run wet fingers through my hair, the effects of the nightmare still hanging thick. I should have known better than to try to sleep. I never sleep. As I gaze upon the water swirling around and around in the basin, I'm left with the thought that haunts me. Will - my life - ever change, ever truly be worth the trouble. Then there's the knock at the door.

I know who it is, and frankly, I'm surprised it took her so long. I dry my hands, get everything in place and open the door.

"Hello, Antonio. Can I come in?"

"Felicity. Fancy seeing you here. What took you so long?"

****

Felicity Farmer Fellows

Death, A Dish Best Served Cold

Antonio's Room – The Midnight Arms Hotel, New York City

Late Afternoon – Monday, May 21, 1928

Antonio blocks the doorway, grinning, leaning against the door frame, his copper-toned muscular body glistening with sweat.

"I've always thought you were a beautiful specimen," I say seductively with a hint of sarcasm. His expression is one of disgust. I expected no less. He's not happy to see me. In fact, I'd say he wants to see me about as bad as he wants Ebola. I don't want to kill him, but I have no choice. I know Antonio. He won't stay quiet. He'll ruin everything and I won't stand for it. I made a mistake the first time. Believe me. I don't intend to make the same mistake twice. This time I'll do the job right and put him in the grave myself.

"Can I come in? I just want to talk, I promise." He scoffs and steps tighter into the doorway.

"Get out of here, Felicity, before you get hurt," he replies, threatening with cool confidence.

"I'm not here to fight with you, Antonio." He continues to block the doorway, but he doesn't tell me to leave, which I take as an opening. "I want to get some things out in the open between you and me. Can I come in?"

"No-," he says flatly, those dark, beautiful eyes seething with hatred.

He intentionally slams the door shut, obviously aware that I have inserted my foot between the door and the frame. The door strikes my foot, causing agonizing pain to shoot up my entire leg. He's got it pinned, and he's laughing, enjoying the pain he's inflicting. He opens the door slightly, just enough to release my foot, then slams the door in my face.

"Antonio! Let me in!" I demand, pounding on the door and choking down a scream from my throbbing foot. "Antonio! Antonio! Open this door!" I pound, suddenly realizing that I'm drawing attention. Good thing this place doesn't cater to a clientele worth worrying about. "I'm not going away! I want to talk to you!" He doesn't answer. "Antonio!"

Ah!!! I'm not getting anywhere! I try a different approach. A more tactful approach. I tap lightly on the door and beg him to open it and let me talk to him. "Please, please open the door." I wait in silence. Maybe he will change his mind. Nothing… I tap - again. "Antonio. Please open the door. I promise I will behave myself. I just want to talk to you."

I put my ear to the door, trying to detect any sound coming from the other side. Nothing. I keep my ear pressed to the door when out of nowhere, he jerks it open, knocking me off balance, and I fall forward. A shrieky squeak escapes from my throat, and I barely catch myself before heading face-first onto the floor. I regain my composure with no help from Antonio, whose wicked smile says it all.

"Getting a good laugh, are you?" He's covered in sweat and needs a change of clothes. He's as impolite as usual and doesn't offer for me to sit, not that I would anyway, in this filthy pit. God knows what bugs you might catch. I scan the dirty room, remembering a time when Antonio and I were allies. I was a different person then. And that was a long time ago.

"I'm offended at the complete filthy grossness of his room." He doesn't appreciate my snotty assessment of his living quarters and is quick to put me in my place.

"We can't all kill just to be rich, can we, Felicity Farmer Fellows," he replies with an edgy sarcasm emphasizing every word of my name. "That's some name."

I ignore his poking, but his British brogue and his gorgeous features I can't ignore. I always had a thing for him. I like the younger ones. I hobble to the only chair in the room, throw his dirty shirt out of it to the floor, and sit cautiously. It doesn't work. A puff of dust accompanied by a nose-curdling odor broils up out of the cushion and hits me in the face.

"This is disgusting," I say, clapping my hands together, knocking off what dust I can. Antonio shrugs his shoulders and puts his hands on his hips.

"I'd offer you something to drink, but I'm saving my best stock for company that I actually like…and invite."

"Funny," I reply, curling my lip and rolling my eyes. He pushes his hair away from his face, showing off his gorgeous features. He is beautiful. What a pity.

"Where have you been all these years, Antonio?" I inquire, knowing full well he won't tell me.

"Well… that's just stupid, Felicity. Because I'm positive you didn't come over here to ask me where I've been," he replies as he flops on the bed, stretching out and propping his head up with his hand, his black hair hanging ever so slightly on his forehead. I really hate being so attracted to him. Makes what's inevitable so much harder.

"Mmmm, yes. Well, I only ask because I thought you were *dead*…so you can imagine my surprise when I saw you skulking around my office building today." Outwardly, I'm smiling.

Inwardly, my guts are churning. Because the fact of the matter is, I'm good, but Antonio is better. I hired a hitman to kill him, and obviously, the idiot I hired didn't quite get the job done. Now I'm in the dangerous position of cleaning up the mess.

"No need to sugar coat things, Felicity," Antonio replies in a wicked playfulness that triggers the hair on my neck to stiffen. I'm no fool. He could tear me apart with his bare hands. I must play it cool if I have even a glimmer of hope to get the drop on him. That's the only way I'll come out of this alive.

"Yes, let's not sugar coat, " I reply, adding a little sting laced with contempt. "Let's get to the reason you're really here." The look of surprise on his face is fake. He knows exactly what I'm asking. "You obviously wanted me to know that you're here. It's also obvious that Warford brought you here. That can only mean one thing, and I can't let that happen, as I'm sure you well know."

"Oh, I know it alright." He sits bolt upright on the edge of the bed and inches toward me, leaning in, his voice growling and deep, a blast of breath from his nostrils landing on my face for maximum intimidation effect. "Truth is, I find you rather revolting, so I won't dance around the bloody bush, yeah? You know why I'm here. But do you want me to spell it out? Ok, I'll play the game. You found out where Sister Mary Agnes was, and you called in your copycat to make it look like the Butcher. I'm here to kill him and anyone else who stands in my way. That clear enough for you?"

"And Sam?" I ask breathlessly, my heart beginning to race.

"Well, let's not start lying to each other now, 'eh Felicity? It's so – tawdry and petty." He moves closer, so close that our lips are almost touching. I'm terrified and aroused at the same time. I sit, perfectly still. I don't dare make a move. If he wanted to, he could snap my neck in a second without batting an eye or making a sound. "You have a keeper, and I know who it is, so let me set you straight. I know what you've been up to all these years, right? Sam would never suspect you - thinks you care about her…would never think you would hurt her…not a clue of your depravity. But we know better, don't we? And Valentina certainly knew."

I'm completely shocked at this news, but I try my best to hide it. Slippery Valentina. She knew all along. She always was the best. Hard to fool. Clever, clever girl.

"My, my, my… A little surprised at that revelation, are you? I guess you're not as good as you think you are." He leans in closer. "Certainly not as good as Valentina." I can feel his hot breath on my face as he issues his warning. "I won't let you hurt her, got it? However, you caught me in a generous mood today. I'd say that's good for you, right? So, here's my offer. You and Morgan have 24 hours to leave town and disappear, or I'll kill the both of you. He slowly backs away from my face. He's cool as a cucumber, and deadly serious. The hairs on my neck are still standing, and my heart is beating wildly from fear."

"You can't tell her, Antonio. She can't know...." He abruptly puts his hand over my mouth to shut me up! I'm shaking my head, my muffled protests escape through his fingers, but he just keeps applying pressure.

"It's too late for that, Felicity. You see, I have been informed that there is an Agent with the Bureau of Investigation who, shall we say, is far from the right side of the law, and he's already approached Sam! Now why, pray tell, would a Bureau man need to talk to Sam? Now don't lie, love. You know who he is. He's killed before, right? Does Los Angeles ring a bell? And now Tarrytown."

He removes his hand but continues to lean over me, warning me that he means business.

"Now, if you'll excuse me, I'd like to finish washing up. I've got things to do. Get out," he orders, grabbing my hand and yanking me from the chair, forcing me toward the door. At the door, he violently whirls me around and points his finger in my face and reminds me, "Leave town or die. Twenty-four hours."

He opens the door to let me out, then turns his back on me as he heads toward the bathroom. I shut the door to make him think I left. I can't believe he just turned his back on me like that. I'm all giddy inside at his apparent carelessness, and I pull the revolver I have tucked in my handbag and move toward the bed. I hear the water splashing as I take a pillow and cover the barrel of the revolver to muffle the sound of the shot. I remove my heels and sneak over to the bathroom door, positioning myself outside and lying in wait for Antonio to emerge. The sound of splashing water stops, and I ready myself, finger on the trigger. Any time now. Any time… My heart is racing, and I'm struggling to breathe. He crosses the threshold - his eyes lock with mine. I point, ready to fire when I hear the sound,

Pew-Pew!

My legs give out from under me as a razor-sharp pain takes my breath away. I hit the floor, aware that instead of me killing him, he's killed me. I can't speak. I feel hot tears well up in my eyes, then gently roll from the corner down my face. Time slows to a crawl, and I'm fighting to breathe, gasping painful short bursts of air. My heart is slowing…slowing…slowing down. He leans over me, his face fading in the blackness, but not before I hear him say,

"Sorry, Love. You're just not that good," as I take my final breath on this earth and fade away.

****

Antonio

Felicity Farmer Fellows is Dead

Antonio's Room – The Midnight Arms Hotel, New York City

Late Afternoon - Monday, May 21ˢᵗ, 1928

Standing over Felicity, an eerie calm embraces me as it sinks in that a chapter in this horror story is now closed. I knew it would come to this because she had no choice. I was surprised it took her so long. I expected an ambush before I even got back to the hotel. But…she shouldn't have overestimated herself. She should have known better.

Felicity's treachery had ruined lives for years. Everything she had was bought with blood money from the backs of those who at one time trusted her. I promised that Sam would not end up like them. All dead – murdered and she didn't bat an eye to sacrifice them. Of course, she never did the dirty deeds herself. She had help with that.

Warford said it would come to this. He knew Felicity all too well. He won't be happy about the attention it will draw, but she's one – less danger for Sam to face. I need to get out of here and warn him, and there's clean up to do. The sooner I tell him, the better.

I check myself for blood, then look at my face in the mirror. Clean. I quickly rifle through Felicity's handbag for anything that will give a name. And there it is. Her little black book. I hope it confirms what I suspect. The name of her paid assassin. I shove it into my back pocket and put a shirt on. I don't touch her. I'll leave her right where she is. I signed into the hotel under a false name, so no one would connect me with her, and since her plan was to assassinate me, I'm positive she made sure she wasn't followed or seen.

I gather up what few belongings I have and go to the only window in the room. I open the window and scale down the fire escape to the alley below, and start walking toward the truck. I need to get to Warford. Warford will take things from here.

****

Sam

The Lair

Her Office and Townhouse

Late Afternoon – Monday, May 21ˢᵗ, 1928

I continue to stare at - Mother's picture, trying to shake the nagging feeling that's haunted me since my encounter with Del Ray. Warford's lying and Felicity's bizarre behavior at the magazine today have me feeling anxious and unsettled. I need to work, but I can't concentrate. The strange events of the day keep replaying over and over in my mind. I keep telling myself that everything is alright, that it's just one of those days, and I'm making a lot of something out of nothing. But I'm obviously having trouble listening because I can't get my mind out of overdrive and focus.

This photograph was taken when I was about 5. I remember that day so clearly. It was taken for a newspaper article. She was being honored by one of her charities, but I can't remember which one. Of course, my father isn't in it. And at that exact moment, it hit me! I had never seen any pictures of - Mother *before* she married my father. That has never occurred to me until just now! Every single picture I have is of her and my father is *after* their marriage and after I was born. My mind explodes with questions! *"Is it important, and does it mean anything? Am I overreacting to something that is likely nothing? Why would the Bureau be interested in you, Mother?* Why do I feel like I'm on the outside of something that involves me, but I'm in the dark about it?"

"That's it!" I shout at no one, placing the photo back in its place and buzzing for Annabelle. She doesn't answer, and it dawns on me that I let her go home early. I grab my coat and lock the office. I'm going to see the one person who always seems to have all the answers!

Warford! If anyone has an idea of what's going on, he will. As I pass Annabelle's desk, I notice she's left it in a mess again. I see a piece of paper randomly laying on the floor. I pick it up - and intend to put it in the trash, but the message written on it catches my attention. There's no letter head, but the names stand out to me.

You need to contact Mr. Foster about your agreement. Soon!

Harold Cooley

Cooley? Foster? I wonder if that's the same Mr. Cooley who has been badgering me for donations for the children's home in Tarrytown. And *Foster?* Not *Jonathon Foster* Jonathon Foster is my lawyer. Why are they contacting Annabelle? Maybe it's meant for me, and it just doesn't have my name on it. Weird...I shove the note in my bag. The thought crosses my mind that maybe she needs a lawyer for something, but I can think of no apparent reason why Cooley would be communicating with Annabelle.

The elevator doors open in the lobby, and Maurice is at his usual place at the security desk. He stands to greet me as always.

"Miss Callahan! Is there something I can do for you?"

"No, Maurice, thank you. I'm calling it a day. It's been a Monday for the books." He has a look of concern, but he doesn't' say anything. "Good day, Maurice, and you have a pleasant evening."

He responds with a smile and a wave, "Yes, Ma'am, Miss Callahan. You, too*!*" But, before I get to the doors, I hear him calling me.

"Miss Callahan! Miss Callahan!" I turn to see him quickly walking after me. "Miss Callahan, could you please tell Warford that I opened the door to the tunnel in the hallway as he asked me to? I tried to call him, but he didn't answer."

Maurice's comment stops me dead in my tracks.

"Maurice, what are you talking about? What door – what tunnel?" I ask. But his expression says it all. He's told me something that maybe he shouldn't have.

"Well, you know, Miss Callahan, that door back in the long

hallway that goes to the tunnel," he says hesitantly…like he just inadvertently ratted information that I obviously wasn't supposed to know.

"I know nothing of a tunnel or a door!" I yell. He hangs his head. I have never yelled at him like that before. "Show me!"

"Now, Miss Callahan, I really think you should…"

"Show me, Maurice!"

"Yes, Ma'am. This way." Maurice replies timidly.

He leads me to the end of the long hallway and points to his left. And sure enough, there's a door, perfectly concealed, blending in with the wall. I'm shocked! In all these years, I never knew, and no one ever told me about a hidden door and tunnel! What could they possibly be used for?

"Open it," I command. He sputters and stammers, trying to explain. "It's not your fault, Maurice. Don't worry about it."

"Thank you, Ma'am," he replies, relieved that he's off the hook and that his job is intact. Maurice does as I tell him. He opens the door to a tunnel dark and dank, and I can't see a foot in front of my face!

"Where does it go!" I demand. He hesitates to say. "My patience is spent, Maurice!"

"To the townhouse," he says sheepishly.

"Really! Where's the light?" Maurice reaches toward the wall, pushes a button, and lights begin to come on, chink, chink, chink one by one for as far as I can see.

Warford! I am so angry! How dare he keep something like this from me!

I follow the lighted tunnel, battling mixed feelings along the way. It is amazingly futuristic, and I am admittedly impressed, but I'm angry that no one trusted me to know about it. What else don't I know? What other surprises or lies have I yet to face?

It seems that I have walked for a long time when I finally see the end and a door. I hesitate, not wanting to turn the knob, afraid that I might encounter something evil or supernatural on the other side. It's a crazy notion, but this is a crazy circumstance, and I find myself debating what to do. I need to do something. I can't just stand here and do nothing. I gently put my hand on the knob and turn it slowly. The sound of a loud click resonates from the other side of the door as if a large latch has been released. I instinctively look behind me even though I know there is no one there. I suddenly feel very nervous and take my hand away from the knob. But how will I know what's on the other side if I chicken out and don't walk through? What would Mother do? I cautiously open the door and truly can't believe my eyes. The room on the other side of the door is the study of the townhouse. My study! I enter the study and quickly turn to examine what's on the other side. The wall of books! The wall of books I had spent my entire life looking at hides a tunnel between the factory and the townhouse! I am dumbfounded and angry! Why, why, why was I never told? Why was I not trusted? Why all the lies and secrecy?

Warford's voice captures my attention. He's barking orders outside the study door. He's coming in! How perfect that I am standing in this room waiting for him. The sight of me standing in front of the open, hidden door to the tunnel stops him in his tracks, and he doesn't know what to say.

"Hello, Warford. Surprised to see me?" My tone is sarcastic, and I am on fire! My anger is blatant. His demeanor changes, and I can't tell if he's relieved that I finally know or if he's just surrendering because he's caught.

"What's this Warford? And don't you dare lie to me!" His eyes drop to the floor, his silence only angering me more. "If you want to continue to work for me, you'd better start talking. I know you lied to me earlier when I asked you about Agent Del Ray, and now I find that, apparently, I have been lied to about quite a few things! What else is there, Warford? What the hell is going on!" I despise swearing. It's a gross display of lack of control, but it flew out of my mouth before I thought.

He puts his index finger to his lips to politely shush me, which completely astounds me, considering that he's in a heap of trouble and I'm on the verge of firing him! He locks the door to the hallway and respectfully motions for me to sit. I do as he asks, but every step I take toward the chair conveys my hostility.

He walks toward me, finger still on his lips, reiterating the need for quiet. He kneels at my feet, looks me straight in the eye and says in a hushed voice, "It's time. And I will tell you everything, Madam – but not here. You have every right to be angry. You *have* been lied to, but I can explain. All I ask is your word that you will listen and try to understand."

I whisper back frantically, "Understand! Understand what!" He quickly gestures for me to remain silent again.

"Follow me," he says, walking back through the open wall of books and then closing it behind him. He guides me sharply left, then pushes on the wall.

"Secret walls, too!" I exclaim.

Again, he puts his finger to his lips to shush me. I'd like to break that finger right off his hand. I'm so angry, but when the doors automatically open on cue with the parting of the wall, I am beyond shocked and amazed that there's an elevator right before me. He leads me inside and pushes a button labeled "5". The doors close with a creepy silence that mimics otherworldly. My nerves are screaming, and I find myself wondering if this is a dream beyond my imagination. The elevator engages and jerks slightly as it begins its ascent. I know where we're going. We are going to the sealed floors of the townhouse. The floors that I was always told were "under construction". My heart starts racing wildly, and my breathing increases with every second!

"It's alright, Madam," Warford assures. "All will be revealed. I promise."

I squeeze my eyes closed tightly in an anxious attempt to shut out the unknown. And just as I begin to calm down a bit, the elevator jerks again and then crawl to a stop. The doors glide open ever so silently. Warford takes my arm, leading me through the doors into the pitch-black. I can't see anything, and in a pang of panic, I cry out,

"Warford!" He puts his arm around my shoulder and squeezes me tightly, and then, a burst of light!

I can't believe my eyes! A room, a very large room filled with tables and radios and filing cabinets that line one entire long wall! Hundreds of huge maps cover the walls, cobweb-covered sheets shroud whatever lies beneath them. Warford stands in the light, hands on his hips, admiring the room as if it were a shrine.

A million questions are swirling around in my mind, but I can't speak. I'm completely overwhelmed and don't know what to think about any of it. He looks at me and smiles.

"Here," he says. A gentlemanly gesture of his hand directs my attention to two large Victorian chairs. "Let's sit down. And if you allow me, I will explain. And then, I have something special to show you."

"What is all this?" I ask, reeling from feelings of confusion and excitement, battling each other for the most attention. We sit, but my eyes continue to wander. "Mother always said that the fourth and fifth floors were blocked off because they weren't finished. I thought that wasn't quite true. Was this always here? What is all this for, Warford?" There are pictures and maps and radars! But, why?

He leaves his chair and kneels at my feet, his face soft and understanding like he used to do when I was a child and needed comfort. His voice has a tone that is undeniably unique to Warford. I had forgotten that until this moment, and those memories come flooding back. He offers me a handkerchief to wipe away the tears - welling in my eyes. As I wipe my eyes and my running nose, he says sincerely,

"Madam. I'm bloody sorry about this. This was not the intention of me or your mother."

"You or Mother? What do you mean?" I want to be angry with him, but I just can't muster the strength. "I feel so betrayed, Warford. I mean, obviously, everything I ever thought or knew or felt or saw - all lies! And I don't even know what the lies are about! Did my father know? And what does all of this have to do with Mother? I mean, really! All this stuff. What was she a spy or something!" I laugh, knowing that notion to be ridiculous.

But Warford's not laughing– and his expression confirms that very thing.

"What! She was a spy!"

"Yes, A British spy, to be exact. In Her Majesty's Intelligence Service. And she was very good at her job."

I feel like someone just punched me in the gut! I break down again, bawling like a baby, shaking my head, completely in denial. The flood gates have opened, and I'm not sure I can stop.

"Elegance Samantha Callahan!" He shouts. He knows that will get my attention. Mother was the only one to ever call me *Elegance,* and she was the only one who used my full name to scold me. "I'm sorry, Darling. I know how this must seem very surreal and unfair, and you have no reason to trust me, but I'm asking you to trust that none of this would have been kept from you without good reason. I'm asking you to trust that I kept it from you because that's what your parents wanted. I'm asking you to trust that I have always had your welfare and safekeeping at heart. That I promise."

I want to scream! Rebuke everything Warford is saying. Call

him a liar! And in my mind, I am. But my heart sees the sincerity in his eyes and the longing for me to believe him.

"Okay," I reply, sniffling and wiping my nose. "So why are you telling me now? What's the importance of dragging all of this out now? Does this have to do with Mother's death?" He takes a deep, long, drawn-out breath.

"We'll get into all of that later," he assured. "There are things you need to be told, things that were kept from you for your protection, and now it's time for you to know. But I'm not going to tell you the full story. Not yet. Your Mother left some things for you."

Warford goes to one of the many filing cabinets that I first noticed when we walked into the room. He takes out a box and brings it to me.

"In this box are things that Valentina and your father left for you. Look at them. It will help to begin to shed some light on the life she led before she married your father. It's photographs and things she wanted to show you but couldn't for your protection. She hoped this day would never come. But now that it has…"

I sheepishly peak inside the box, but I don't touch it. I'm curious but not completely resigned to digging into it. I'm anxious, confused, and resistant. I've never felt this way in my entire life. I've always been secure about who I am and what I'm supposed to be doing. I thought I knew everything about my mother, my father, and the life they led. But contained in this box is a deep, dark unknown, and I'm not sure I want to know.

"I don't know if I want to look." My voice cracked from crying and fear, and I felt the need to negotiate with Warford. "What if I just walked away now? Didn't look. I could go on as if none of this happened. Or I could leave New York! I have a house in Los Angeles. I could go there and start fresh."

Warford shakes his head, and I realize there will be no negotiating – no running. He stands to leave, abandoning me to wrestle with it by myself.

"Here's what she wanted you to have." He says I am in danger. He says that in this box…; He says that I have decisions… "The unsavory truth is, Madam, you only have one of two choices. You are in danger, and you can either face this head on or you can try to hide and hope you survive. The chances of that are slim. It's that simple. Now, I know you are strong – just like her. She was what she was and was never ashamed. And I should know. I worked with her until her death, and I stayed with you because I because I - well, I'm very fond of you. I promised Valentina and Collin, and I kept my promises. That is why I ask you to trust me. So! I'm going to leave you to it, and while it's your decision, I'm hopeful that you will appreciate and take to heart what she left for you. I think you'll find it quite enlightening."

Warford smiles, nods in respect, then walks away. My eyes follow him as he enters the elevator.

"I'll be back," he assures as the doors begin to close. Then, he is gone.

I hesitantly turn my attention to the box of Mother's things at my feet. He said I was in danger. He said that in this box are pieces of Mother's secret life. He said I have decisions to make and that those decisions will change my life forever, one way or another. Part of me wants to see it, but part of me doesn't. I'll leave the box for now. I'm undecided as to what I'll do.

This room has a life of its own. My eyes scan the walls, taking in the countless maps, the huge tables, and the numerous radios, all obviously important to her work. The irony of this is I can completely imagine her as a spy. She was strong and wise and clever. This is all just so surreal.

A memory suddenly comes to mind. A moment I had forgotten. I was around nine, and I was up on the step ladder, pulling books off the shelf in the study. I had no intention of reading them. I was simply bored and filling time. Mother scolded me in a tone that I had never heard from her before.

"What are you doing, Darling?" She called me Darling, but her tone was harsh. She orders me to get down, but she doesn't give me time. She immediately grabs me and sets me down gruffly on the floor. I looked up at her, and my feelings shattered. I don't understand what I've done, and I immediately start to cry. Her attitude changes at the sight of my anguish, and she takes my face in her soft hands and wipes away the tears as they fall down my cheek.

"I'm so sorry, my Angel," she apologizes, her eyes filling with tears. She fumbles for the right words to say – the right explanation for her behavior. "I'm so sorry, Angel, but it frightened me seeing you up on that ladder. What if you fell? What would Mommy do without her Tiny Angel?" She kneels in front of me and takes me in her arms. She hugs me so tight that I can barely breathe, but I don't care. My shattered feelings healed – her hug was all I needed to make everything right again. "Let's go see what fabulous treats we can find in the kitchen, shall we? And a tall glass of cold milk?" Everything is bliss between us again.

"I'll race you, Mommy! The last one in the kitchen is a rotten egg!" I take off like a shot!

"You little cheat! You didn't say *go!*" she exclaims playfully. I'm giggling with excitement as she chases me through the house.

When I reach the kitchen first, I tease her, singing, *"I won, I won,"* chanting it over and over. We laugh and dance in a circle until she lifts me up onto the counter. She takes two of Mrs. Lilly's delicious cookies from the cookie jar and pours us each a glass of milk. We drink milk and eat too many cookies. All is water under the bridge. But I am never allowed to be alone in the study again. It never occurred to me until this very moment that her scolding was rooted in fear – that she was directing my attention away from something she didn't want me to discover.

The memory of that beautiful moment with my mother – the laughter – the closeness fades - tears are streaming down my face as the reality of why she scolded me that day becomes clear. She scolded me – not for being on the ladder, but because I was too close to the book that would open the hidden door. She didn't want me to find it – didn't want me accidentally opening the door, forcing her to answer questions that she didn't want to answer.

Agent Del Ray's visit today was a fishing expedition for information surrounding the secrets of my mother. The box is sitting there, waiting for me. There may be something in there he's looking for. I don't care about Del Ray, but I need to know what that something is and how I fit into it. I want to delve into the secrets of her life, her death and everything since. It's something I must do for her and for myself. Everything I thought I knew about her is now shrouded in mystery, except for this.

My Mother loved me and – she was a spy.

****

Warford

She's Needed Killing for a Long Time

The Callahan Townhouse

Early Evening - Monday, May 21st, 1928

I return to the main floor only to be confronted by Mrs.

Lilly, who is desperate to talk to me. She has the audacity to reprimand me for my sudden disappearance.

"Where have you been? I've been looking all over for you!" She scolds me, and before I can get a word in, she immediately barrages me with an explanation. "Antonio has arrived, and he's demanding to see you. He refused to leave even though I told him you were unavailable. I let him in but told him that he must hide in the broom closet out of sight of the other staff and Madam. What is he doing here, Warford? What's going on? Are we in trouble? Is Madam in trouble…"

I am short on patience with her persistent chatter. I have the highest respect for her, but she does tend to babble when overexcited.

"I did not summon him, so there must be a problem. Now go

– go about your duties. I will take care of our *broom closet guest.*"
I shooo her out of the kitchen, and even though I have reassured her that I will take care of everything, Mrs. Lilly storms away in a huff, extremely put out that I did not offer further information. I need to handle this on my own. Antonio's unsummoned arrival means trouble, serious trouble.

In the kitchen, I position myself in front of the broom closet door. I cannot help but find this a little humorous, and I catch myself uncharacteristically chuckling quietly. It is funny, though. One of the most dangerous assassins employed by the British Intelligence Service is locked in a broom closet by Mrs. Lilly, who notably is a keen operative in her own right, but still – it is comical. I compose myself and yank the door open to find Antonio seated on a bucket. I almost laugh out loud, but he's a haggard mess and clearly has disastrous news.

"What's happened!" I ask forcefully, commanding an immediate answer. Antonio stands from the bucket. He does not answer immediately. "Well? What is this all about?" I insist, impatient with his silence.

"Yes, well - I killed Felicity," he stammers before coming to the point.

"What!" I exclaim in utter disbelief.

"Warford, I didn't have a choice! I couldn't stay at the hotel, so I came here. Before the police showed up."

"Oh! Well! For a moment there, I thought you were going to tell me something disastrous." I'm sarcastic, stunned, and outraged! Not because he killed Felicity. She has been begging for a bullet for a long time. For as long as I've known her, as a matter of fact. But the repercussions of such an act! And the timing! "Antonio! Do you know what this means? And her husband! What do we do about him? It won't be long until all hell breaks loose! I'll figure out something to clean this up. Everything that's happened today is completely unbelievable!"

Antonio simply stands there, taking my wrath calmly, not saying a word as usual. I stop – take a breath – and collect my thoughts. I suddenly feel like I owe him an apology.

"You know, Madam discovered the tunnel today. An accidental slip by Maurice-. -What a mess!- She's up on five right now, and hopefully, she's looking through the things Valentina left for her. We - are in a corner my friend. There will be no easing her into it. What did you do with the body!"

"I cleaned and left her there. Nothing else I could do. I knew you would know what to do, so I got out of there." I can see that Antonio is somewhat regretful.

"I'll take care of it. I have an idea. You can stay here tonight because you need to stay out of sight!"

"Right, you're going to kill me in my sleep then?" Antonio jokes.

"No, Antonio, I'm not," I reply, slightly offended. "Such a smart mouth!" Antonio smiles his ornery smile; the smile I remember from when he was a boy. "Once she is discovered, the police will be all hands-on deck looking for her killer, and I am going to give 'em one. I just need a little time to think." I reply, already planning and plotting in my head.

I open the closet door, and Antonio and I step out. I summon Mrs. Lilly, but she doesn't respond, so I start to go find her when Antonio stops me.

"I want to clarify something," he says. "You know Warford, I know my reputation. I earned it. It's my job – killing people. But not this time. Felicity came after me. She saw me today – outside her building, and when she came to my hotel room, I knew what the outcome would be. She came to kill me, plain and simple. I gave her an option – a way out. Leave within 24 hours, but if I ever saw 'em again, I'd kill both her and Morgan. But I knew she wasn't going to leave my room until she'd done what she came to do. I just wanted you to know that I tried to avoid it. I had no intention of killing her. At least not today."

I'm humbled by his account of the events with Felicity. I should have expected it, knowing the kind of operative she was. She had a black heart, corrupt and particularly vicious, even when the job didn't call for it. Valentina knew it. Everyone did. I should have listened to his explanation instead of instantly flying off the handle. I am confident that Antonio did what he had to do – what I would have done were I in his shoes.

"Alright, Antonio. Forgive my ignorance and rush to judgment? Everything will work out. It always does. Son, I'm going to let you in on a secret. I have been thinking about this for a long time, and I have decided that after this is settled, I am retiring. To a beach somewhere. I am tired."

"I know, Warford. Oh! By the way," Antonio adds. "I took this from her bag. Some interesting names in there. Can I go to the beach with you?" Antonio smiles and hands me the black book. "I'm tired, too."

Mrs. Lilly arrives. "Antonio will be staying," I explain. She rolls her eyes and leads him away. I did not answer Antonio about the beach. He has suffered so much tragedy in his life, and I guess it's not a stretch to think that he is tired, too. That he is also ready to enjoy life. This will be my final battle, my promise fulfilled.

Madam crosses my mind. She has had a lot to deal with today. I hope I can convince her to carry on – not run. I hope I can convince her of the truth about Felicity and others she has grown to trust unknowingly. I do not relish having that conversation with her, but it is one that must be had, and it would have come regardless of Antonio's actions.

I open Felicity's black book and scan the pages. Two names in the book confirm everything. Now, to take care of them once and for all.

****

Special Agent Dominic Del Ray

The Good Little Agent

New York Bureau of Investigation HQ

Late Afternoon - Monday, May 21ˢᵗ, 1928

I enter the corridor leading to the office that houses my

desk, feeling more than confident. I love it when a plan comes together. Sam Callahan knows everything. Can't tell me her -mother kept her in the dark all these years. Sam's the key. The keeper of what I want. The keeper of my future as a wealthy man. She'll give it to me. No doubt. Making one fear for their life does have its advantages. And I'm very good at that. The best in fact.

I'm itching to get this wrapped up – get back to Los Angeles…find a buyer, then I'm home free. Being on loan from the LAPD to the Bureau has been beneficial, no doubt – in more ways than one. But I *hate* New York. Hated it the minute I stepped off the plane!

No, beautiful Los Angeles is more my style. Escorting movie stars and playing on the beach. Yeah, that's the life. There are too many tall buildings and too much concrete here for my taste. I miss the sound and smell of the ocean. And the people! The people in LA are relaxed – like to have a good time! Not here in *The Big Apple*. These jerks are so uptight! And half the time, I can't understand what the hell they are saying because of that accent they have. God! It's irritating as hell!

No. My beloved LA is much more fun for a man of massive wealth. I *will* have massive wealth. Foster can shove it straight up his…I smile at the other agents as I stroll by. Gotta keep up the charade for just a little while longer, and then I'm home free. It is starting to grind on me a little, though. Tolerating these hacks! I don't think I've been this fake friendly to anyone for this long ever! I'd be just as happy to put a bullet in their head. But there I go again, wanting to solve everything with killing. I admit I have lost patience, but it won't be much longer. After what I saw today, I'm so close I can almost taste it.

I drape my jacket over the back of my chair. Time to play Special Agent. Just need to keep my cool for a little while longer. My desk is a mess, and I shuffle through the strewn papers laying on top. Never was one to be organized. I don't give a shit anyway. Not like I'm doin' this for real. Sean McDonald is the Special Agent in Charge, and he's always on my back to clean it up. I'd like to shut his mouth permanently, but I won't. I have bigger fish to fry.

I move some papers around to make it look like I've done some work, but mostly, this charade is a pain in my ass. I wish McDonald would hurry up and get here. Ah! and there he is, returning from God knows where. He's having an affair. Always late, extended lunches, the weekly hotel room. I know because I've followed him. That kind of information always comes in handy.

He's a short man, so his steps are short and choppy, and when he walks, it looks like he's running. *Ha!* It's hilarious to watch. Irritating little shit, though! But I do what I can to get along. I cross the room so I can meet the twit half-way as he heads to his office.

"Sir, I've got news about Sam Callahan. Got a minute?" I follow along beside him like a lap dog, trying to get his attention and make him feel important.

"Forget about her!" McDonald barks. "I need you to go to Tarrytown and check in on that murder! Since that's the reason you're here. The *only* reason." I dismiss his little juvenile dig even though I'd like to shove my fist down his throat.

"Yeah, yeah, the murder. I'll get up there tomorrow," I reply, playing innocent. It's fun, and it keeps my skills sharp. Besides, I need to stay away from there for a few days. And I don't want to go to Tarryt…Tar…Oh, whatever in the hell the name of that town is! Besides, The Daughter is there. And even though she does get the job done, I don't like her. She's twisted…worse than me if you can believe that! *The Daughter,* I joke in my head. Her parents must really hate her.

McDonald flies into his office at about 100 miles an hour, pulls his jacket off, smooths his balding head with his hands, pushes up his glasses, adjusts his pants, pours himself a glass of water, sits down at his desk, buzzes his secretary for a file, puts a peppermint in his mouth and straightens his tie in the time frame of 20 seconds flat. He's a neurotic boob of epic proportions. I've never seen anything like it!

"I want you to head up to Tarrytown tonight, Del Ray," McDonald orders from behind his desk.

"What? Tonight?" *No, no, no, no, no!* I thought. *This isn't part of my plan!* I continue to press McDonald to see things my way. "I can go up there tomorrow because, listen, I talked to Sam Callahan today, and I know that she knows the victim. She's involved up to her eyeballs, and I think she can shed some light on some of the players that I'm certain are involved. *And* I saw a man outside her townhouse today taking groceries inside. He's in the file! I'm on to something. I know it!"

"Sooooo?" McDonald replies in an over - exaggerated tone. "You can follow up on that later. I need you to go look at this. Now! Besides, you cannot just start accusing Sam Callahan."

I'll give him that. She has a direct line to Hoover. Saw it with my own eyes. Almost got my ass in trouble. But I have another plan in the works. Standing in front of McDonald, I find my mind indulging in a lovely daydream A daydream about putting one right between his eyes, his bloody dead body slumped on his desk. I smile as I end that lovely thought. Can't always have everything the way you want it. However, my dream has caused an adrenalin rush, and I lose my cool just a bit trying to get his attention.

"Sir!" By the look on his face, he doesn't appreciate my enthusiasm, so I apologize. "Sorry – Sir. But listen! I don't plan on accusing her yet, but the man that was going into her townhouse – I've seen him before…"

"So, who is he?" He rudely interjects.

"I don't know yet. I wanted to check the file over the next couple of days. I'm telling you, Sir, he's in the file." He's interested, but he's not convinced and shoots down my request.

"No," he says flatly. "He's probably just household staff and, therefore, completely irrelevant. You can follow up on that later. Tonight, you go to *Tarr-y-town*. Contact the local cops first thing and report. We'll go from there."

"But Sir, I really think that this…"

I pushed it too far, and he held nothing back, letting me know that he was drawing the line in the sand. I push down my anger and disgust and act like a good little agent.

"This comes from the top, Del Ray! Theeee Top!" he shouts, rising slowly from his chair, jamming his hands on his hips. "Now, do you know who theeee *Top* is in this organization? Well! I can tell you it's not me, and the last time I checked, it's not you! Now, I'm happy to patch you through to Director Hoover so you can tell him how you think your plan is better than his if you like."

"No, no Sir. That won't be necessary." McDonald shakes his head in victory. His obstinance has determined my next move. I'm going to shake the tree and see what falls out. I need to make a phone call and get things in motion.

Wandering amid my own thoughts, I realize that McDonald is glaring at me over his glasses, wondering why I continue to litter his office with my presence. One of my favorite fantasies returns. It's the one where I climb across his desk, grab him by his scrawny little throat and choke the life out of the smug little turd. Wouldn't that be great? But instead of offing him right now, I politely say,

"Thank you, Sir - from the bottom of my heart." He fails to appreciate that snide remark and barks orders at me as I turn to leave.

"A car has been assigned to you, Del Ray. You can pick it up on your way home. See Angela for your travel orders, hotel expenses and meals, and so on and so on."

That was it. The boob had spoken. And being that I'm such a good Special Agent and respect my superiors so much, I take the liberty of slamming his office door as I leave. I knew right then that I wouldn't be back. My time had come, and I had played Foster's game long enough.

****

Detective Malcolm Madison

Waiting and Wondering

River Dell County Police Department, Tarrytown, NY

Mid Afternoon - Monday, May 21ˢᵗ, 1928

Sargent Mullins' voice is deep and ominous, like a drill instructor. "This chaos is – not – going – to – happen! All of you will file out of here, and – if – and – only if you choose to stay, you will be allowed to assemble starting at the sidewalk and moving toward the street! Be assured that if you feel the urge to start inching your way past the sidewalk, you will be dealt with swiftly. I will not allow this type of chaos in this station, so consider yourselves warned! This is the only warning you will get. Follow the instructions I have given you, and we won't have a problem! Now! You at the back, turn around and face the doors, and walk in an orderly fashion out of them. The rest of you do the same. When there is something to tell, you will be told! Thank you."

I push past the grumbling and griping minions and post myself out on the front lawn, where I start barking orders of my own.

"Head to the sidewalk, please and stay behind the inside line. Thank you. Head to the sidewalk, please and stay behind the inside line. Thank you."

I must have said that same thing a hundred times. Surprisingly, there weren't any problems. I did notice some of 'em get in their cars and leave. But not enough of 'em to really make a dent. There is still a huge crowd waiting. Waiting for the big story. I guess I can't blame 'em. They have a job to do, too, but man, they can sure make ours hard sometimes. Not much of a fan of reporters. I don't know a cop, who is.

Sergeant Mullins - appears from the rear of the crowd and stands on the stoop for a minute, making sure that they are standing where he told 'em to. He motions for me to come inside, but he doesn't wait for me. My time here so far has been sort of a waste. I have nothing to report except the herding of reporters. But I'm still waiting for Cap'n Grayland to emerge.

"I can't believe you're not married, Detective Madison. Why, if I were 20 years younger...." Miss Nina says flirtatiously, giggling and slapping her hand on her desk. "It's not often we get detectives here from the city. And such handsome ones too," she adds, scrunching her nose.

"What about you, Miss Nina?" I ask. "Husband? Kids?" She suddenly becomes very melancholy and quiet. "Oh, I'm sorry. Did

I say something wrong?" My eyes dart to the Sergeant, who remains silent. It's obvious I've hit a nerve. She pulls a photograph out of her handbag and hands it to me. It's a photo of a young woman. I compliment Miss Nina, telling her how beautiful the young lady is.

"Thank you, detective Madison. That beautiful creature is my daughter, Polly." Her voice cracks with anguish as she looks at the photo, tears welling in her eyes. "I'm sorry. Will you excuse please?"

She abruptly leaves her desk and disappears to what I'm assuming is the ladies' room. I start to apologize for upsetting her, but Mullins says not to worry about it. "She cries like that every time she talks about her. It's not you," he says. "Polly was killed two years ago in a head on car accident coming home from the city. She was a model and did a little acting. Had dreams of moving to Los Angeles to be in the movies. Polly was a good girl."

Miss Nina returned, seeming more composed and recovered. I don't say anything else. I know what I had to endure, but I can't imagine living with losing a child.

"I'm going out to monitor the herd," I announce jokingly. She cackles, and I'm relieved that my joke lightened things up a bit. Sergeant Mullins asks me if I need 'im to go with me. "No," I reply graciously and stroll out the doors to the anxious crowd imprisoned on the sidewalk.

They immediately start yelling questions, talking over each other, each wanting to be the first to break the big story. They can't stand the thought of the reporter next to 'em gettin the big scoop. Three o'clock. I wonder if the Cap'n is alright.

Just as that thought crosses my mind, I hear Sergeant Mullins calling my name. "Madison! Cap'n wants ya!" *Finally!* I think. Wonder if there's any word from the coroner?

As I walk through the door, I notice that Cap'n Grayland looks a lot better than when we arrived.

"Hey, Cap'n Grayland! Feeling better?" He nods in the affirmative and thanks me for asking.

"I'd like for you to stay a few days – if you agree, of Course. I've already spoken to Captain Mason, and he's approved it."

"Yes, Sir! Thank you, Sir!" I exclaim, excited to dig in.

"Do you have a room for the night?" Grayland inquires.

"No, Sir, I don't. I came straight to find you and figured I'd get something later. Or sleep in the car." Miss Nina scoffs, picks up the phone and dials a number immediately.

"You are not sleeping in your car, Detective! I'll take care of it! I'm calling over to the Mayfield Hotel to reserve a room right now. I play bridge with Mona, who works at the reservation desk. Or maybe it's Mini today. Whichever doesn't matter. Don't worry, it's all taken care of."

"Nina! Call Dr. Alexander and tell her we're on our way, would you?"

Miss Nina grumbles at Grayland's interruptive request. "I will in just a second. I'm trying to get a room for Detective Madison if you don't mind!" He grins at her curt retort. The ornery look on his face shows that he likes poking at her and getting under her skin. She's not amused, and she shoots him a dirty look as he returns to his office and shuts the door. The thought crosses my mind that he's searching for a bottle, and that requires privacy. But he's only in there a couple of minutes when he emerges with a clean shirt and combed hair. I guess I need to quit comparing him to past experiences and cut him some slack.

"Miss Nina! You get her!" he shouts.

"Yes! She's there, and she's expecting you."

"Finally! Let's go, Detective. Daylight's burnin'."

"I reserved you a room, detective." Miss Nina announces, full of pride, that she could help. I take her hand and kiss it, thanking her for taking care of that for me. She blushes and giggles and shoos me away to the coroner. After I made her cry earlier, I made sure to make an extra effort to make her smile. She's a real nice lady.

We exit the back door and get in Cap'n Grayland's car. He starts it and slams it in reverse – squeals the tires and tears out of the parking lot, gravel flying. He smacks a pothole at the end of the drive going so fast, I'm surprised the car still has a bottom!

"Sh....," he says under his breath. I just smile and keep quiet. "So, how long have you been a detective?" Grayland asks as he drives like a maniac.

"I've been a detective for five years. But I was on patrol before that for two," I reply, holding onto the door for dear life. - He raises his eyebrows in surprise like he didn't expect that. "What about you? How long have you been doin' this?"

He expels a huge sigh as if the burden of that question equaled the weight of the world. "Well, let's just say a long time. I've been here for two years. Before that, LA."

"Mmmm, my curiosity is peaked! Do tell! I bet LA's exciting – all those beautiful women and the movie stars…" I'm waiting for an answer, but I sense that LA isn't something he wants to talk about, so I don't push. I want to ask him how he ended up in River Dell County, but I didn't get the chance. He roars up to the front and comes to a screeching halt at the River Dell County Coroner's office. He slams the car - into park and opens his door. *I guess we're here,* I think to myself, reaching for the door handle. Time to meet Dr. Alexander and get a first look at our victim. He throws a list of instructions at me as we approach the front door.

"Now, Dr. Alexander is a little prickly, but she's excellent at her job. Be very careful not to talk down to her."

"A woman doctor!" I exclaim. I'm surprised and more than a little intrigued. The Cap'n raises his hand to make a point.

"Yes," he stresses, "a woman doctor, and she's a genius – the best in her field. And she's – well – never mind."

He didn't say any more; he just turned and headed for the door. I don't' get a chance to tell 'im that I'm fine with a woman doctor. I've just never seen one.

"And no swearing," he whispers as he battles to open the door, swearing and yelling that someone needs to fix it! Once defeated, the door is opened, and we enter the morgue. I'm looking forward to meeting the brilliant and mysterious Dr. Alexander.

****

Dr. Olive Alexander

Confessions May or May Not Be Good for the Soul

River Dell County Coroner's Office, Tarrytown, NY

Mid Afternoon - Monday, May 21ˢᵗ, 1928

As I make the final stitch in Sister Mary Agnes, I feel an emptiness inside. It's the final stitch, and yet it symbolizes the beginning. The beginning of something I had put in that secret place in my mind – in my heart. The place that had remained padlocked away from my daily life and only appeared – though less and less – in my dreams.

I first became familiar with the children's home when I was an Assistant Coroner to the previous River Dell County Coroner, Dr. John Monroe, now deceased. God rest his soul. One of the children had been hit on the head by a rock while fighting with another child. Dr. Monroe had always offered medical services to the home because the so-called reputable physicians in Tarrytown considered the children beneath them because they were too poor to pay. After all, these were not children who fit the criteria of upstanding pillars of the community. They were seen as urchins that weren't worthy of their valuable time.

The Head Mistress of the home came straight to the morgue to request that Dr. Monroe come take care of the boy. He was in the middle of an autopsy and couldn't leave, so he suggested I go. My expectation was that the Head Mistress would refuse the offer of help, considering my gender and my color. But she didn't bat an eye. She grabbed my hand, and I grabbed my medical bag, and away we went. I was quite taken aback by her willingness to accept my help. It's not many that would trust a woman doctor, but even fewer that would trust a black woman doctor. I didn't know her name or anything about her, but I felt a familiarity toward her that was instantly seated in my soul. I instantly felt like I knew her from somewhere.

I pushed the feeling to the back of my mind, redirecting all my energy to the emergency I'd been called to treat. I had never treated a living patient, and I was exhilarated by it – hopeful that I could continue seeing the children on a regular basis but resolved to the fact that I would not be asked. Imagine my surprise and joy when, on the next occasion one of the children needed treatment, the Head Mistress requested that *I* come. Of course, I jumped at the opportunity. Another emergency gave me a chance to practice medicine, but it also gave me time to interact with her and the children.

Eventually, I began to voluntarily visit the home regularly to check on the children's health and, admittedly, to enjoy some play time. I admired the children. Their resilience to the harsh circumstances of their residency at the home inspired me. I felt at home there among my kindred spirits.

For quite some time, I only knew the Head Mistress as the Head Mistress. But that dramatically changed when, late one night, she called me to the orphanage for emergency. One of the children, Sally - a sweet little girl, five years old, suffered a horrific seizure. It was touch and go for several hours, but finally, Sally rested, and I stayed by her side. The Head Mistress asked me if I would like to join her in the kitchen for a cup of tea. Sally was asleep and stabilized, so I graciously accepted.

"A cup of tea would be lovely," I replied. I pulled Sally's blanket over her and then followed the Head Mistress to the kitchen, where she had prepared tea and some sandwiches.

"The sandwiches are peanut butter," she said unapologetically. "The Lord provides for us, and we must be grateful. But if you don't care for peanut butter, I could make you some toast and jam if you like?" I could tell that she was grateful for what they had but wished she could offer more. "I know it's not fancy, but it's all we have."

Not fancy, I thought. The sandwiches were beautiful. She had taken the time to cut them into elegant little triangles. It touched my heart that she had taken such care to treat me like royalty and to offer me food that I'm sure was in short supply. When I was a child, it was not uncommon to be denied food for extended periods of time as punishment, so peanut butter was a real treat to me.

"Peanut butter! I love peanut butter." I exclaimed softly. I wasn't about to make her think that I didn't appreciate her hospitality. She was one of the few that had ever trusted me - treated me with respect. So, I took not only one sandwich but two. "Delicious!" I declared as I wiped the corners of my mouth with a ragged napkin, which she took the time to fold.

I noticed her watching me as I enjoyed my sandwiches and sipped my tea. She was trying to be discreet, but I'm afraid it wasn't working. I wanted so badly to tell her that I had a nagging feeling that I knew her from somewhere…that she was so familiar to me. But I wasn't yet comfortable enough to inquire. Finally, she broke the ice. And judging by her question, I guessed that she felt the same familiarity with me, too.

"I feel like we've met before," she said, directly to the point. She took a sip of her tea and paused to gauge my reaction. I hesitated a second, trying to think of what to say. A wave of panic suddenly swept over me. The very conversation I'd wanted to have with her now terrified me, and I sat frozen. Scared to death! I didn't respond. *Does she see how uncomfortable I am?* I thought. Obviously, she did because she immediately apologized. I felt guilty that I had made her feel silly. She fumbled at continuing the conversation.

"Oh, how feeble-minded of me," she said, making it as if she was experiencing a failure of mind. "It's just that – well, I don't suppose this has ever happened to you, but – I just feel like we've met before. But I know that's not possible. Is it?" I got the odd sensation that she wasn't just asking the question. She was making a statement.

She lifted her teacup to her lips and sipped delicately, still watching me for a reaction. I stayed the course of silence even though I had the urge to ask her why she felt we had met before. I should have told her I felt the same way, but fear stopped me. I think I was so afraid because deep down, I knew she was part of my past, a past I had hidden for my entire life. I fiercely dreaded dragging it up. I felt like such a coward, but her words caused a stirring in my soul that was relentless, insistent that I follow her lead and simply ask. She continued to sip her tea while, in my mind, a battle raged. Do I follow the path of possible discovery, or do I shut her out? The indecision was paralyzing, and I was rendered powerless to do either. Suddenly, her voice shatters my self-torturing silence.

"Oh, how silly of me," she said, poking fun at herself again, her tone hinting that, once again, senility was to blame for her outlandish thoughts. "There's just something so familiar about you that gnaws at me. But I've lived a long life and met many people, so it's probably nothing."

I nodded and smiled at her, but I wasn't smiling inside. The war was still raging, and I was determined not to remember. She put her tea in the saucer and fiddled with her apron, brushing sandwich crumbs from the table into her hand. And just when I thought her prying was over…

"You have a unique accent. It's a mixture if I'm not mistaken. A little South African is mixed with your British accent. Am I correct?" She raises her eyebrows, waiting for me to answer.

She had backed me into a corner, and I began to panic. I was harnessed to my inability to respond to her on one side and my yearning to tell her everything on the other. I realized I was holding my breath, a tactic I learned as a child to keep from crying – screaming out. That's it! I couldn't take any more of her innuendo, so I confronted her!

"Do you know me?" I shouted. "Do you know who I am?" I lashed out at her, but she remained calm. "Yes, I am from South Africa! Yes, I was raised and went to medical school in London! And yes! I moved here and was given this job! What of it!" I broke down, sobbing and gripped with fear, my chest so constricted I felt as if I could not take another breath. She took my hands and consoled me – gave me a handkerchief.

"There, there, it's alright, Anashe." I darted my eyes quickly to her face, but they were so filled with tears that blur was all I could see. I wiped my eyes with a vengeance and abruptly stopped crying – in shock. How did she know that name? I hadn't heard that name in a very long time.

"Now," she said, rising to get more tea. "I believe we have a mutual friend. *Valentina?*" At the very mention of her name, I began sobbing again. She poured more tea, pulled her chair closer to mine and put her finger underneath my chin. "Look at me, Anashe," she said gently. "I know who you are because I was there, and I know you remember me. I recognized you immediately." The tears rushed forth again, and I felt they would never stop.

"Oh, Sister Mary Agnes. I'm so sorry. I had a feeling in my spirit it was you. I don't know why I was so afraid," I sobbed.

She spoke not a word, just comforted me while I released the pain that had followed me my entire life, and when there were no more tears to cry, she reassured me that I was no longer alone in the world.

"I had always wondered what had happened to you, especially after Valentina's death. She was a master at keeping a secret. I prayed that God would bring me to you. And it appears that he has." She lifted her Rosary to her lips, kissed it gently and thanked The Lord for answering her prayer.

Watching her embrace her faith and trust in God reminded

me - rejuvenated me – and gave me a new sense of purpose. God brought me to Tarrytown, and now one of the amazing women I owed my life to was here with me.

Valentina was a part of my rebirth. A rebirth I had forgotten. She rescued me – gave me a new name – and provided me with a chance to live rather than leaving me to die at the hands of the rebels in the diamond mines of South Africa. Valentina, Sister Mary Agnes and the other Diamond Dolls risked their own lives so that I might live.

I felt a crushing pain of regret and guilt on the heels of the memories that began to flood my mind. Had I wasted what they had given me by hiding and living in constant fear – not living to the full potential of the blessing God had given me?

"Thank you, Sister. Thank you again for showing me that the path before me is the path I'm anointed and called to be on."

"It's not me, dear. Thank The Father."

"Yes, you're right. And I promise I won't forget again." She nodded, a brilliant smile radiating from her face. *Thank you, Lord, for returning my guardian angel,* I thought.

I checked on Sally, said my goodbyes to Sister Mary Agnes and made my way home. It was late, and I was exhausted, but my spirits had been lifted to a new level for the first time in a long time.

She was my guardian angel. My whole being changed forever when God placed her in my path for a second time. And now, as I look down on her, I know that the monster who murdered her could be after me also. *The Butcher* is here, but I won't run. I won't hide. I will tell my story to Captain Grayland, the consequences determined by God. The frightened little girl of South Africa is gone for good.

I hear Captain Grayland's voice outside the window of the morgue. My stomach tightens, but I'm determined to reveal all to him. I've kept that secret for far too long, and I owe it to Sister Mary Agnes – to all the Sisters - to myself – to Valentina. *I won't forget, Sister,* I say under my breath.

"Doctor! Dr. Alexander!" I can't ignore the scraping of the morgue door and Grayland yelling, swearing under his breath at the heavy steel door that never seems to open smoothly. Grayland stumbles around the corner into the morgue. I chastise him with my eyes for cursing. He realizes that I heard him and immediately apologizes.

"Sorry, Doc. I'm going to bring some oil over here and oil that door. That thing gets me every time."

The man following him is straining to keep his composure. I don't show it, but beneath my cool exterior, I'm giggling at him too. Quite frankly, if he does oil it, I'll miss the enjoyment I get out of watching him battle it.

"Who's he?" I demand, pointing to the man hanging back behind Grayland.

"Well, Doc. This is Detective Malcolm Madison," Grayland says.

"But my friends call me Mal Ma'am," he replies, tipping his hat. It's notable he's not turning and walking straight out the door. I'm impressed.

"Where are you from, detective, and what are you doing here?" I point blank ask him. I notice that his eyebrows raise at my directness. "Don't take offense. I'm this blunt with everyone. You'll find that I'm generally direct and to the point. I like to have everything out in the open, so if you have a problem with my color, say now. If you have a problem with me being a woman, say now. If you have a problem with my directness, say now. You won't offend me. I like honesty, and quite frankly, we don't have enough of it, so..."

I put my hands on my hips and wait for him to respond. He looks to Grayland for support, but Grayland directs him to answer the questions. Madison is uncomfortable, but his response impresses me.

"Well, Doctor Alexander, I have to say that I *am* surprised by your color and your gender. Not that I don't believe that a colored woman doctor is perfectly capable, it's just that I've never seen one – worked with one. So, in answer to your question, *no,* I don't have a problem with your color or your gender. The only problem that I can think of is if you don't know how to do your job. But according to Cap'n, you're a genius, that you're the best in your field, so I can't think of one single problem I'd have with you, Doctor."

He takes me by complete surprise with that statement. Grayland seems impressed as well. His demeanor commands attention. From his perfect posture to his commanding voice with a heavy accent, Detective Madison's honesty is refreshing, and I am instantly at ease with him.

I motion them closer to the light. I gently roll the sheet back to reveal the carving in her chest. It's shaped differently, but I had seen carvings similar as a child. In fact, I bear a carving myself. I know exactly what this means. The severed hands, another gruesome and nauseating act so familiar to me. I had seen this level of viciousness on occasions too numerous to count. And as I stand here and look upon her mutilated body, I can only take comfort that she is with God now. She is with the love of her life.

I roll the sheet from her feet to her private area. Grayland is struggling. They were good friends. The Sister had touched his life as she had mine, and I share in his heartbreak. Detective Madison stood silently, with his hand over his mouth, his expression one of shock. I do my best to overcome my own pain and offer some words of comfort.

"Are you alright? Do you need a minute?" Grayland shakes his head *no*. He wipes the tears from his eyes and nods that he is ready to hear my findings. I take a deep breath and swallow hard, fighting back the urge to burst into tears. Detective Madison moves in closer, preparing to take in every detail of my report. "Yes, well. The autopsy of Sister Mary Agnes reveals that she has been dead for approximately three days. I note nothing remarkable internally that would contribute to a natural death. She appears to be in reasonable health for a woman her age. She bears premortem markings of being gagged and bound at the mid-forearm on both arms and around her ankles, suggesting that she was tied up while she was still alive. I also found a note shoved in her mouth. I don't know what this note means, but I'm sure it's significant to her killer."

I retrieve the note from the tray and wait for Grayland to glove his hands so he can inspect it. He opens the note gently. Reads it silently, but an odd expression overtakes his face, as if he recognizes something.

"Have you seen something like this before?" I ask. He doesn't respond, and I don't press the issue. I move on.

I point to each area, my hands shaking – my heart pounding.

I'm never like this, but it's Sister Mary Agnes. I steady myself with a deep breath and continue my report.

"Gentlemen, there's no doubt that Sister Mary Agnes was tortured before her death. Directing your attention to the mark on her chest. This mark was made with a knife that is razor sharp. I believe it is a machete." Mal's expression changes. I know he's wondering how I know that a machete was used. I ignore his curiosity and move on. "As you can see, it plainly says *SC die*. Now, I don't know what that means, but it appears to be a warning."

Grayland is very quiet. I get an uneasy feeling that he knows something he's not telling.

"The carving on the Sister's torso is quite clean, smooth, and concise, and I believe that the message itself is personal toward someone else. The cuts were administered premortem. As you can see, there was bleeding and notable trauma around the cuts. Her hands have been severed, premortem, at the wrist. They were removed cleanly, indicating one strike. This also supports that the blade used was razor-sharp. And last, but certainly not least, the fatal wound. Her throat was cut. That's my preliminary report. I haven't taken measurements yet or examined her organs, but as soon as I do, I'll let you know."

I feel nauseous. I know what she went through. I'd seen it first-hand many times. Hideous evil visions of what she endured cloud my mind, and I struggle to ignore them and focus.

"Do you need a break – a minute before we move on?" I ask. Grayland declines, robbing me of my own excuse to step away and compose myself for a minute.

"Okay, gentlemen, if you could help me turn her over, we'll look at her back. As you can see, Sister Mary Agnes' back is a canvas of old beating scars. It is truly horrific. I counted approximately 100 lash marks. The age of the scarring varies, but all of them are old. The instrument used to inflict these beatings was a whip made from dried hippopotamus hide. It delivers brutal punishment because when the hide dries, the edges become razor sharp." It takes every ounce of strength I can muster to talk about this horror. I managed to hold myself together by the Grace of God, but Detective Madison couldn't stay silent any longer.

"Excuse me, I don't mean to question you, Doctor, but how do you know this? You talk like you know exactly what happened to 'er. I mean, machetes and whips made from hippopotamus hide. What are we talking about here? You're describing these things like you've seen 'em firsthand. So, have you – seen 'em firsthand? Have you seen anything like this before Cap'n? Maybe LA? Because if you have insight into who may have done this to 'er, you owe it to 'er to speak up. No matter how painful. Not to mention, it's your duty."

Grayland turns his back and rubs his face with his hands, his composure crumbling. Madison is smart and deductive. And he's right. I owe it to her. I can't be silent any longer.

"I've seen this before," Grayland confesses, surprising both Madison and I. Madison confronts Grayland.

"You've seen this! You've seen this before?" Madison asks in a mildly confrontational tone. "Why didn't you tell me from the beginning? You've wasted so much time! We could've been using other departments and resources! Could've been lookin for this guy! You didn't trust me, that it? You didn't trust me."

"No!" Grayland insists. "No! I didn't want to face it, and that's the truth! It was all me! It had nothing to do with you! Yeah...I've seen this – this - grotesque...!" Grayland hangs his head, knowing he's made a grave error in judgment.

"You knew – seen it before and couldn't take it. The Sister faced it, Cap'n! But you can't face it? And you, Doctor! What's your story? Both of you obviously share something in common here – I'm guessing that you didn't realize – but neither of you came forward – didn't think that this connection was relevant – for three whole days! Shame on you! Shame on you! And I may not be the sharpest person, but I have been doing this long enough to know when people are lying! So, excuse me if I remove myself from this – this sham and get back to Manhattan. I don't think I'm needed here. Now, if you don't mind, Cap'n, I need a ride to the station to get my car."

I have never felt so low and ashamed in my entire life. Madison is right. Both Grayland and I were so wrapped up and wallowing in our own fears, to be honest and help out a -friend.

Madison abruptly leaves the autopsy suite, with Grayland on his heels. I can barely hear their argument, but I can hear enough to know that Grayland is desperately trying to persuade Madison to stay. At first, he says *no*. But after a few minutes time, the arguing stops, and they come back inside, but with one stipulation. That we both tell the truth. Mal is the neutral eye. No emotional baggage – no emotional ties – no emotional connection to the demons that affect me and Grayland. We need him. The ghosts of our past haunt us and torture us with impunity, and if we are ever to lay those ghosts to rest, we must relinquish our fear of unmasking our pain and let him in.

"Doctor – Cap'n Grayland. I'm sorry. I know she was your friend. But you should've told me. You want my help, then you've gotta quit avoiding, and, like you said, Doctor, be honest. You owe it to the Sister and obviously to yourselves! It's torturing the both of you!"

Madison's words burn like fire in my bones. I'm overcome with a feeling of extreme guilt that I hadn't gone to Captain

Grayland with my information because the fact is Madison is right. I knew what the elements and details of her death said immediately. The injuries inflicted on her were undeniable, and while I suspect that Grayland knows there were others, I know the *reason* there were others. I know the what and the who about these atrocities. If Captain Grayland says he's seen this before, then that means there have been others who sacrificed for me. We will never be free unless I tell the truth. It's time to share the story of Anashe. A little girl from South Africa.

"Gentlemen, I would like to make a formal statement. I can no longer hide in fear and stay silent, hoping that I can outrun the devil. That is not what God put me on earth to do. So, I want to confess. I know what happened to Sister Mary Agnes, and not just from a Pathology point of view. I know exactly what happened to her and the significance of it. I don't have a specific name, but I know him as *The Butcher*. And if you've seen this before, Captain, chances are he is the one who did this. Were they nuns?" Grayland doesn't answer. I repeat my question. "Were they nuns, Captain," I demand.

"Yes. They were nuns," he says flatly. "Would you like to quit stalling here and tell me how in the world you know that information? Were you in LA?" Grayland's question hit me in my soul. I knew there would be no more hiding – no more denying.

"Doctor?" Madison inquires on the heels of Grayland's question, a hint of impatience apparent.

"No, I was not in Los Angeles, but trust me, I know what happened. But I think it better to show you first, then explain."

The silence is deafening. They patiently wait as I remove my apron and begin to unbutton, one by one, the many buttons on my work blouse. I pay no mind to their reactions. I expect such. But I know that finally telling my story and showing the atrocities I endured…coming out of hiding is the only thing that will set me free.

As I pull my blouse down to my waist, I am at peace, revealing scars that have crippled my soul, both inside and out exposing the deep and controlling anguish that I have hidden since I was a child. Bearing the torture, the fear and self-contempt, strangling any attempt to really live and embrace my existence. Secrets that have kept me bound for far too long. I refuse to be crippled by fear any longer. I am empowered, and this is what God has prepared me for. This is my moment, and I'm not going to waste my opportunity to fulfill a purpose. I raise my eyes to meet theirs as I bear my secrets for them to see. I am strong, and I do not cower. The tension in the room is heavy, and they're speechless at what they are witnessing.

My body and soul stand as evidence of the evil that I have

witnessed and that I have endured, like so many others. I feel free - for the first time in my life. *Thank you, Father.* Now I know what Sister Mary Agnes meant. How blessed I am to have known her. Grayland and Madison witness in stunned silence, but what does one say to such a thing?

I allow my blouse to fall, revealing the scars of Anashe. I feel the weight lift, showing me a new way to live. I don't speak. I simply trace the outline of the carving on my chest with my finger – the mark that eternally binds me to the rebels – a branding that runs deep. A branding that scars my skin as well as my spirit. A slave to the diamond mines that I escaped from with the help of Angels. A new beginning. I am prepared to tell all without hesitation – without shame.

"Thank you, Dr. Alexander," Grayland says, his tone quiet and surprisingly comforting. Detective Madison turns his back and allows me privacy to raise my blouse and button it. My emotions are a jumble. I am relieved yet terrified – strong yet weak – happy yet sad. But I did it. My past is now out in the open, and I've never felt such peace.

Mal brings me a chair. I collapse like a rag doll and begin to cry. They allow me a moment to reconcile with the huge step I have taken in relieving the pressure of a life of fear. They allow me to cry until all the hate, bitterness, and guilt has left me, affording me the opportunity to rebuild myself from the ground up, waiting patiently for a que to continue.

"I want to tell you everything. Both of you," I say, confident and assured that I'm on the path to healing and justice.

"Me too," Grayland says. "It's time."

I take comfort that my visual confession helped him to confront demons of his own. I feel a sense of solidarity with him. Evil has wickedly scarred both of our lives in ways that are unique to each of us.

"Got a notebook, Madison," Grayland asks. Madison's hand jumps from pocket to pocket, searching for a notebook he hopes is there.

"Found it!" He opens it to a clean page. "Why don't you just start at the beginning, Doctor? It's your story, and I wouldn't have the first idea what to ask you."

Mal looks upon me with admiration and respect, ready to hear everything. Captain Grayland squeezes my hand. I'm ready. Deep breath, deep breath. Into the light, I go….

****

Anashe, Captain Graff Grayland & Mal

Soul Cleansing

River Dell County Coroner's Office, Tarrytown, NY

Late Afternoon – Monday, May 21st, 1928

Captain Grayland holds my hand tightly as I close my eyes and begin the journey back to a time in my life that's buried deep in the recesses of my mind. I beg them for a moment. A moment to fixate on the memory of where it all started. The diamond mines of South Africa.

It all began very innocently…

"My birth name is Anashe. I remember being about five." I notice the silence around me. I keep my eyes closed tightly, refusing to be distracted – focusing on that day.

"It's just me and my mother. My father had died, so I never knew him. I'm – playing – running up and down on a mound of rocks along with three or four other children older than me. I see my mother in the distance. She's hanging clean laundry on the line to dry. We are playing a game – tag, I think. It is a time in my life I remember being truly happy."

"I become bored with the game, and I decide I want to play on my own. I wander a short distance away from the others, taking notice of a tiny area of loose dirt. I pick up a flat, thin rock laying to the side of the soft dirt and begin to dig, pretending I'm on a treasure hunt. I find rocks mixed in with the dirt. The rocks are my treasure, and I collect as many as I can, laying them to the side. I am enjoying playing on my own. I'm digging and digging, moving the dirt around, when suddenly, there it is! A rock of such beauty. Big, bright, beautiful. I've never seen anything like it."

The sun's rays magnify its beauty, and it sparkles like nothing I have ever seen. I don't put it with my other rocks. I want to keep it with me. It seems – magical, and I am mesmerized. It is the most beautiful thing ever. And it's mine. The rock has me spellbound. I don't want to stop looking at it - holding it up to the sun and watching it sparkle. I hear the chatter of my playmates coming from behind me, yelling, asking me what I have in my hand. I don't want them to take it from me, so I hide the magical rock in my shirt and take off running for home. They follow, yelling for me to let them see it, but I don't want to. My mother sees me running quickly toward her. The others are still yelling that they want to see it! They keep pointing to my shirt, grabbing at me! I fight them, protecting my treasure. My mother breaks in between me and the others!

She scolds them and sends them on their way. She gently

takes my face in her hands and looks into my eyes. Her face is worn – weathered from the sun, but her eyes… She asks me to show her what I have. I resist! I don't want anyone to see what I have found. Her eyes become stern, and the tone of her voice commanding! She orders me to show her! I - have no choice but to obey, so I reveal the rock. I thought she would be happy that I had found something so beautiful. But she wasn't. She panics and instantly grabs the rock from my hand, harshly warning me not to say a word to anyone about what I have found. I don't understand! I don't understand what I have done wrong. I just – I just want to keep it! She sternly whispers that I should have left it where I found it, that I shouldn't have picked it up! I begin to cry, and she realizes what she has done. She hugs me tightly and then looks me in the eyes again with such fear and panic that I will never forget. She warns me that I cannot tell anyone about the rock. But the children already know. Her eyes dart off in the distance. We can hear the chatter of our neighbors growing closer and closer.

"Don't speak! Don't say anything!" she warns. Her voice frightens me. She hides the rock underneath the scarf at the back of her head and composes herself. She hides her fear and greets the neighbors with politeness and joy. Of course, they are curious about the rock and insist that my mother show it to them. They say they were told how beautiful it is. She's desperate to hide the truth. She tells them it was nothing and that she got rid of it. They become

silent, and it's obvious they are suspicious, but they appear to accept her answer and leave. She doesn't make a move to go inside until they are out of sight. She grabs my arm and pulls me inside the house, frantically warning me. *"Anashe! You must never mention this. It will bring trouble."*

"I was horrified! I didn't understand how a simple rock could bring trouble. I assure her I won't say a word. But it was too late. Our neighbors didn't believe my mother. So, to gain favor with the rebels, they betray us. And before we knew it, they had us surrounded, and they were questioning my mother about the rock. They are who she feared the most. Evil men whose only goal in life is to perpetuate their evil purpose by controlling and terrifying people into mining diamonds. They demand to see the rock. But my mother denies having it. They punish us by taking everything we own enslaving us in – those mines."

Eventually, she tells me of the rock's value - that the rock was not just a rock but a diamond. You know, one would think that the diamond would have been our salvation out of poverty, but it delivered us to the devil! They wanted the diamond plain and simple. No one was going to have something that they thought was theirs, but my mother continued to deny she had it.

"Every hour in that mine seemed like a lifetime. Continual beatings with hippopotamus hide whips, starvation, and continual threats with the machete. Those were their preferred methods of control. Our lives changed in an instant! And it was my fault! It was my fault that my mother and I were subjected to such cruelty. If only I hadn't picked it up. If only I ….."

Captain Grayland immediately jumps to my defense.

"How could you have known? You can't blame yourself."

"I know that now, but at that time, I felt a tremendous amount of guilt. I survived by living inside my head – dreaming of freedom – looking to God every minute for a way out - some way to get us out of the horrible situation I had put us in. I waited, and I prayed. I knew the odds of escape were zero. That's how I came to have the mark. We didn't try to escape, but others had tried and failed. At first, they killed anyone who managed to escape and were caught. But the rebels soon figured out that killing them simply meant one less slave. That's when they decided we needed to be marked. That way, if anyone did get away, they could identify us by the marks on our chests. And the rebels knew that no one would help you if you were marked."

"I still remember the pain and agony as they carved into me. But I was fortunate in a way. I overheard my mother and other adults talking. Anyone caught helping an escapee - was punished by having their hands amputated, just like Sister Mary Agnes. An example of the consequences for helping an escapee."

The tears flow down my cheeks, dripping into my lap as I recall the terror and horror of life in those mines.

"My mother's health deteriorated. She endured beatings and sexual assault. She was continually harassed by the rebels - trying to get her to give up that diamond. But she denied to her dying day that she had it. She knew that the diamond was our leverage. That if she gave it to them, they would kill us – instantly. She eventually died from abuse, overwork, and starvation, and without my mother, I was completely alone. I resigned myself to that life, a life devoid of anything human, and I completely tucked myself away. But I would discover later why the rebels never found the diamond. Her cleverness gave me a chance to live."

I'm exhausted.

"I need a moment," I say, wiping the tears from my eyes, taking a deep breath, and exhaling the pain. Grayland and Madison both agree that a break is in order.

I lead them to my office, where I have an ice box. They seem surprised that I have such a luxury in what they perceive as a dismal place. I get three glasses out of my desk drawer and set them up for filling.

"Water or lemonade," I ask as I open the door to the ice box. "I'm prepared, gentlemen," I joke lightheartedly. "I spend more time here than I do at home. I also have peanuts or soda crackers if you would like something to eat."

They decline the snacks but are more than gracious for a cool drink. They both want water, so I take the pitcher of water out of the ice box and fill their glasses. They drink the water down quickly, enjoying every gulp. I refill them promptly, sit down at my desk, and leisurely sip the lemonade I poured for myself.

"Do either of you mind if we continue in here? I need to get out of the morgue." Grayland and Madison agree in unison. I'm much more relaxed now, but I feel utterly drained and anxious to get this over with. I need to finish caring for Sister Mary Agnes. "So where was I?" I ask, searching my mind for the place where I left off. Detective Madison reminds me.

"You were saying that your mother had passed, and you were alone…."

"Right," I reply, arming myself to combat the extreme emotions I know will rise as I continue. "I was alone. My mother is dead. I think I was about seven at the time. Again – guessing. Time didn't exist in that horrible place except to drag on."

"Two years gone by," Mal says, seemingly astounded that so much time had passed.

"Yes, and I was one of the lucky ones. *Lucky* - Sounds strange, I know, but I was saved. Most died there, young, and old.

The rebels took *us* because they got a tip-off about the diamond I had found. From the neighbors, you know. Trying to save their own skin. Can't blame 'em, though. It's all about survival. The rebels were selling the diamonds to a British chap I can't remember his name - to buy weapons. Anyway, I was lucky. One day, The Lord answered my prayers."

"A British chap, you say?" Madison interjects. I don't get the chance to address Mal's question before Grayland interrupts.

"How so," he asks. "How were your prayers answered?"

"Well, for some time, missionaries had been coming to the mine – forced to stay on the edge. The Rebels tolerated their presence, but they were kept away from the slaves who were being forced to work – not allowed to speak to anyone. But they faithfully came every day and watched. Sister Mary Agnes was one of those missionaries."

"Sister Mary Agnes. Weren't they afraid?" Mal asks. "Weren't they afraid of being killed?"

"Surprisingly, no. And here's why. I overheard two of the rebels talking one day, and while I got the impression that they would very much like to kill them – stop them from coming there every day - they were too frightened to, because they were people of God. I know how unbelievable that sounds, considering their viciousness, but I got the impression it was a true fear. It was a true concern. They believed that if they killed them, God would come for them. Sister Mary Agnes and the others were aware of that fear and used it against them. She used their fear of God's Wrath to talk her way into the mine. She made a deal with them – something that sounded like a benefit. She offered to take care of the orphaned. Children whose parents had died - any child that was alone. Of course, the rebels certainly didn't jump on that opportunity immediately, but Sister Mary Agnes was persistent. She kept at them, and they finally agreed. She convinced them that by allowing her to take care of the orphaned, we would be better able to do more work and that God had sent her there for just that purpose. I don't know what we would have done without her. She truly was a God send."

Tears well up in my eyes, remembering the pain and the sacrifices she endured - how she cared for us and loved us.

"I'm sorry," I say, regaining control of my emotions. "That memory of her burns in me. Because the fact is, gentlemen, I wouldn't have survived without her. She was my first initial contact with anyone from the outside. And she sacrificed for us. She sacrificed everything! Those marks on her back - those are there because she sacrificed herself to take beatings that were meant for us! The children! She bore the pain and anguish."

I can hardly speak; my throat starts to close as tears flood my eyes, and I recount the times I heard her scream in anguish and pain. She wouldn't have done that had she not loved us with all her heart. Grayland and Madison listen intently in disgusted disbelief.

"There are no words, Doctor," Mal says, a clear tone of sadness in his voice. "I don't know what to say. I'm so sorry for you, for her, for your mother. I've never heard anything like this."

"Well hang on. I'm not done. There's much more to tell," I warn as I take a drink of lemonade and catch my breath. "I'm nine, I'm guessing, and Sister Mary Agnes is still with us. By that time, there's only a handful of children left. The Rebels would drag in new workers, but they were mostly adults. Then, one day, I noticed three strangers at the edge of the mine. I could see they were rich – dressed in fancy clothes. They had daily conversations with the leader of the rebels. Sister Mary Agnes also spent a lot of time talking to the lady in the group. When I asked her about the lady, she said they were just investors in the mine, and the lady was quizzing her about the workers. Especially the children. I was very curious about this lady. She was so elegant and refined. I wanted information, but the Sister sternly cautioned me about stepping out of line and asking too many questions."

"Anashe, it's best you keep your curiosity to yourself," she said. "They were always accompanied by two men who stood behind her. I was amazed that they weren't run off or killed, but I

guess the Sister informed the rebel leader that they were also people of God, and they came with lots of money. Those two things combined assured their safety. After every meeting with the lady, the Sister would wait until she thought we were asleep and silently – not making a sound – she would hide something in her Bible. I never let on that I saw her, but I knew that there was something going on between her and the lady. Sister Mary Agnes kept her Bible with her, never letting it out of her sight. She had two Bibles. The one she read and the other one she just kept. That always puzzled me."

"That mystery was solved when, one night, she stirred us all out of our sleep. She ordered us to quickly get our few belongings and swiftly walk to the perimeter where the lady and the two men were waiting with a coach. She instructed the adults to run away, giving them provisions and warning them not to ask for help. I grabbed the only thing I owned. My mother's Bible. The rebels were all lying on the ground, and they looked dead, but I couldn't be sure. We wove in and out of their bodies on the way out, and I remember the terror I felt as we stepped around them. I kept thinking that one of them would reach up and grab me – kill me. But the Sister kept pushing us along until we reached the fence. We climbed over and ran to the large coach waiting for us. They put us - into the coach and hid us with blankets. When the coach started to move, I remember feeling anxious, frightened, and guilty. I know it sounds ridiculous, but part of me didn't want to leave. I had no family – no place to really go. What was to become of me? And I felt such guilt."

"Guilt? Why guilt," Madison asked, leaning forward with his elbows on his knees, taking in every word.

"I felt guilty because my mother was buried at that mine, and I didn't want to leave her there alone. It pained me a great deal – leaving her there. All the way to the fence, I kept looking back, hoping I would see her behind me."

I pause for a moment to remember her. I remember her mannerisms, her laugh, her fun-loving spirit, her undying -devotion, and love for me.

"Anyway, we traveled to Kimberley, South Africa, without incident. During that time, the lady took particular interest in me. Sister Mary Agnes had told her that I had no family. I remember when we got to Kimberley, the other children were met by two nuns who ran an orphanage in Kimberley. I suspect they were your nuns from LA, Captain. So, while the others were going with the Sisters to the orphanage, I sat off to the side, scared and alone, having no idea what to do. I had a secret. I just didn't know what to do with it. I was terrified to bring it up for fear that I would end up in the same situation that the secret got me into in the first place. I had the diamond."

"You had the diamond!" They exclaimed in unison.

"Yes, like I said before, my mother was clever. She also knew of the rebels' superstitions, so she hid the diamond in her Bible. They wouldn't touch it. She always told me to never let that Bible out of my sight.…keep it hidden, but don't be obvious about it. You can imagine my surprise, opening that Bible and seeing it there. I hadn't laid eyes on it since the day we were taken. She never mentioned it, not one time- - never let on she had it. And neither did I. I didn't even tell Sister Mary Agnes. Mother had chosen the perfect hiding place. So, I have this extremely valuable diamond, but I'm terrified to try to sell it. Didn't want to tip anyone off that I had it. I didn't want the trouble it would surely bring. But as it turns out, I didn't have to worry."

"Riding in the coach, the lady introduces herself and reveals to me that Sister Mary Ages had informed her that I had no family." She asked if I would like to come to London with her. She offers to take care of me and assures me that I will want for nothing. Naturally, I was very hesitant. I trusted Sister Mary Agnes, but I didn't know this lady. Don't know if I can trust her. But the more I talk to her, the more comfortable I become with her proposition. I - decide that if Sister Mary Agnes trusts her, I can trust her, too. I had to trust that God would make the way.

"I keep my secret and mention nothing about the diamond to

anyone. I just cling to my Bible – *never* letting it out of my sight. The lady makes good on her word, taking me to London to live with her. And although she was gone quite a bit, I was always taken care of. She used her influence to get me a good education and get me into medical school. She relocated me here, and I've been here ever since. But she has since passed away."

"What you went through, and then to find people willing to help you. That's amazing, Doctor," Mal says, his tone sincere and comforting. "And you say your benefactor has passed away now?"

"Yes. She died eight years ago. I didn't see her much after I got to the United States. But I still see the man – the one who rescued us. Often, I have caught a glimpse of him watching me. I've known him practically my entire life."

"You said there were two nuns in Kimberley?" Grayland asks. "Do you know their names? And how did you hear that your benefactor died? Was it natural causes or something else?"

"No – I don't remember the names of the nuns in Kimberley," I reply. "As for my benefactor, I learned of her death from an article in the local newspaper. The article said that she died in the bombing on Wall Street in 1920, I believe. Why? I was very upset to hear about her death. I loved her very much, and I owe her my life. I know what would have become of me had she and Sister Mary Agnes not come into my life. I owe them everything."

"The bombing on Wall Street! You're saying she died in the bombing on Wall Street? And the man's name – the one who checks on you. What's his name?" Madison's questions put me on alert, his demeanor signaling he may know the identity of my benefactor and the man.

"Yes! The article said she died in that blast! She was at her bank, I believe." "What is going on, Detective Madison?" He doesn't answer but asks a question. And this question is one thing I was told never to talk about. It was the one thing Valentina absolutely forbade. The one secret that kept everyone safe.

"C'mon, Doctor! I know that you know – or at least you suspected."

The hair on the back of my neck is standing on end. I know what Mal is driving at. As I have gotten older, looking back at the circumstances surrounding my escape from the mines, I have come to certain realizations that I have *never* spoken about until the night Sister Mary Agnes, and I had our discussion at the children's home. I teetered back and forth – denying the thought – embracing the thought. But none of it seemed to matter – until now. Anxiousness wells up inside me. Mal has figured it out. Do I really want him to concur with my suspicions? And what about Grayland? I know he has something to say. He said as much.

"Okay – fine." Mal states with a hint of indignance. "I'll be the one to say it. This story of yours indicates only one thing to me. We're not dealing with ordinary people here. Thirty or so rebels were incapacitated all at one time. The mysterious lady giving the Sister something she's hiding in her Bible. Everyone in that camp manages to escape. A wealthy lady, a group of nuns. She manages to get you out of South Africa virtually unscathed?"

Mal's eyes dart from me to Grayland, impatient with my unwillingness to confirm his theory. He sighs with a hint of disgust, judging my failure to respond as obstinance and obstruction. But that's not true at all. I don't say because of a little fear and a lot of respect for Valentina's instructions and wishes.

"Okay, don't say - whatever." Mal continues, "but I know what this means, and we are way in over our heads here. We may not even be able to touch this for the simple fact of who we're dealing with! We're talking about people who can lie their way into extremely dangerous situations like that and come out unscathed while either killing the people they are dealing with or incapacitating 'em...no matter. Who's more dangerous, I ask? I'm tellin' ya, Doctor, your mystery benefactor is."

"A spy!" I exclaim, the words flying out of my mouth untethered. "There! I said it, Mal. I know you think that I had a sinister motive for not saying, but you must understand that I was trusted never to tell. She told me almost immediately that my silence ensured my safety and the safety of everyone involved. I knew what she was. British Intelligence. And Sister Mary Agnes said to me once that there were other nuns involved. The *Diamond Dolls*. Five to be exact. But she also said that it was a rogue mission. That British Intelligence never officially sanctioned that mission."

"That explains a lot, I'd say," Captain Grayland says quietly.

"Captain? Care to share your connection now?" I ask gently. He hesitates at first but seems to make peace with himself, and he begins his story.

"Sister Mary Agnes and I were great friends. I met her right after I moved here and started this job. She was very supportive, wise, and caring. Other than that, I knew very little about her. I never bothered to ask. So, unfortunately, I can't provide much about Sister Mary Agnes personally. However, when I was a detective in LA, I was assigned to a similar case. Two nuns were murdered in a similar fashion. There were similar signature wounds and notes left. Those notes read *DD #3* and *DD #4*. They didn't have those horrible marks on their backs, though. I believe they were the two nuns you saw in Kimberley, Doctor. Sister Mary Clarice and Sister Mary Francis were their names. But listen, you two. Like Mal, I have a very bad feeling about this. I think something sinister and far-reaching – something that has festered for years has resurfaced, and someone is looking to finish what they started a long time ago. And Mal may be right about something else. We may not be able to do anything about this. It will take someone who can operate without boundaries to take care of this one. We need to be careful. Very careful."

"What happened, Cap'n?" Madison asks. "What happened in L.A.?"

"It was just like Sister Mary Agnes. Unimaginable these killings. I'd never seen anything like it. Dominic Del Ray and I were assigned to investigate. From the very beginning, his behavior raised red flags for me. The longer the investigation went on, the more certain I was that he knew more about the killings than he was saying. I strongly suspected that he knew who did it and why or worse – that he had committed the murders himself. LA is corrupt. Sometimes, your enemies are the ones closest to you. I had two choices. I could report my suspicions to my superiors, or stay quiet. But I refused to stay quiet. There was something off about that guy. But he had connections, important ones, and everyone knew it. Del Ray had been reported so many times. Not even a reprimand. In fact, he's highly decorated - hailed a hero, if you can believe that! It wasn't long after I said something about it to my Captain that I was fired and dragged before a review board – my career and personal life destroyed. Del Ray told the brass that the reason the Sister's murders weren't solved was because I mishandled the evidence, and even if we caught the guy, it would never hold up in court. And they believed him. He was the one tampering with the evidence. I believed he was covering his tracks then, and I believe it to this day. I know he murdered them. I know it in my bones."

"What happened to Del Ray after you left? Anything?" Madison inquires.

"Ha!" Grayland laughs sarcastically, shaking his head. "Well, believe it or not, he was offered the opportunity of a lifetime. Yep! Can't get promoted much higher than to become a Special Agent with the Bureau of Investigation now, can you." He sighs a bitter sigh, his eyes haunted by the evil.

As I listen to Captain Grayland explain the events surrounding his tragic firing from the LAPD, I realize that I may have misjudged him. I have heard the gossip, and while I like him very much, I have often wondered if his position here might constitute a mercy hiring Chief Tuttle giving a washed-up cop a second chance. Everyone deserves a second chance, and I know that better than most. But the drinking – well, now I know and who's to say that I wouldn't react to something that sinister any differently?

"I'm sorry Cap'n. I misjudged you and what you've been through," Madison says, extending his hand.

I'm impressed by Madison's ability to see flaws within himself. Some cops find it impossible to point the high-powered finger at themselves.

"Doctor. I have a confession to make," Mal announces. "I believe I may know who your benefactor is. And because I know - this, I also know that there's a lot at stake." Madison locks eyes with me. I know that it's ridiculous to continue to withhold her name with everything that's happened. I make the decision not to conceal anymore, but before I can reveal it, Mal reveals it first.

"Valentina Brandenberger Callahan," he states. "And the man who checks on you – his name is Warford." He knows he's right, and there's no point denying it. "Valentina Brandenberger was *the* wealthiest and most influential lady in New York City period. She owned *Brandenberger's Chocolates and Confections.* She came from old money, which came from her parents, who were also in the candy business in Sweden. She was married to Collin Callahan. He was killed in WWI. She has a daughter named Sam. Sam Callahan. *Sam Callahan. Sam – Callahan. SC-SC.*" Mal is deep in thought, repeating his words over and over. "*Sam Callahan. SC Die! SC Die!* That's it!" he exclaims, looking worried and a little panicked.

"The carving, Sam Callahan – *SC Die.* SC is Sam Callahan." Madison is up on his feet, pacing around like a caged cat, thinking out loud and bordering on frantic.

"Madison, would you like to let us in on what you are thinking, or are you just going to keep pacing?" Grayland asks. Madison stops and directs his attention toward the captain.

"The carving! The carving! *SC* Die refers to Sam Callahan. It would make sense. This all connects to her mother, Valentina. Someone's after Sam," he declares. "Sam Callahan is in danger. The carving is a message, and it's a warning. But why? She wasn't even born during that time. Something's missing. Something we're not seeing."

The more Madison talks, the more his panic escalates. He's in love with her. There's no doubt about that.

"I gotta get ahold of Sam! I gotta call her! Warn her! Cap'n, I think we need to ask her to come up here and talk to us. Right? She needs to know!"

"Madison, did you have a relationship with Sam Callahan?" Grayland presses, completely ignoring his manners. "Because if you did, and you can talk to her, that could be very helpful." Mal doesn't admit anything about his relationship with her, but he does say that he can contact her.

Something is riding the edge of my brain. My mind is reeling around a certain something that I can't put my finger on. Something I heard - something I saw – *DD*. I know that from somewhere. I'm so frustrated! *Help me think of it, Lord. It's important.* I repeat it over and over in my head, blocking out Mal's continued panic about Sam Callahan. I close my eyes and try to pinpoint in my mind exactly where I know that from. *…think, think, think!* I repeat the letters, hoping they will trigger a memory. I leave my office and walk into the autopsy suite, grab a pair of tweezers and pick up the note. I stare at it! I repeat it! *C'mon, c'mon!* Visions of London. My life in London…Valentina…I keep coming back to something in London, London! Then it hits me. *Yes!*

"Gentlemen!" I yell. "I know what the *DD* stands for." *This is for you, Sister,* I say, blowing her a kiss before I run back to my office to relay the news. "I remember once when we were in London. I was standing outside Valentina's office door, and I overheard her talking to someone. I wasn't supposed to be there. Anyway, I remember Valentina was concerned because she said, and I quote, '*The Diamond Dolls are in danger, and we need to do everything we can to protect them.* The Sisters were the *dolls.* They were numbered. There were five. Sister Mary Agnes was *DD#5.* It says it right here on the note. All the *dolls* are dead. All of them.'"

"That's good work, Doc," Mal says with a reassuring smile. "Now, to get in touch with Sam Callahan. And you need to be careful too, Doc."

We are making headway, and I feel in my bones that, finally, many questions from the past will be answered, except for one. Mal said it. They are looking for something. He hasn't made the connection that they are looking for the diamond, and I chose not to disclose its location. Only I know that information, and I intend to keep it that way.

I'm anxious about Valentina's daughter. How will she react to me? Does she even know about me or who I am? Valentina told me once that Elegance and I would be sisters one day. I hope she was right, but if not, I know this. I survived my soul cleansing today – a milestone long overdue. If I survived that, then I can survive anything.

****

Annabelle

Bullseye

Sam Callahan's Townhouse

Early Evening - Monday, May 21ˢᵗ, 1928

I'm scared to death! When I got home from work, I found

my apartment door kicked in and splintered into a million pieces. It's obvious they think I have it. That means it's only a matter of time until I'm dead, and I can't call the police. Foster has cops and mobsters in his pocket. I spent the entire afternoon in a café down the street, afraid to go home – paranoid – that every face I saw could be the one sent to kill me. I'm cornered, and Sam's in terrible danger. I should have gone to her in the first place, but I couldn't face her. Now, we're both out of options. I hope she'll understand. Maybe even forgive me once she hears the whole story. Regardless of her response to my betrayal, I need to warn her. I just can't believe the mess I've made.

"Are you alright, Miss?" The cab driver asks. I can see his eyes in the rear-view mirror, darting back and forth from me to the road. He must have heard me crying. I take the handkerchief from my bag and wipe my eyes. "Yes, I'm alright." There's an awkward silence between us, like he's expecting an in-depth explanation for my sobbing. I lie. "My grandmother just passed away," I reply, blowing my nose. "I'm really gonna miss her."

He's sympathetic and says how sorry he is, which is an opening for him to tell of his grandmother's death and how it was a blow to his whole family. I'm glad he's talking because if he's talking, it relieves me of the burden of doing it. All I can think about is how to even begin to explain to Sam that I have been spying on her.

The cabby pulls over and stops. "Here you are, Miss." As I open the door, he offers further consolation for my loss. "Just remember. Tomorrow is another day. Things'll get better."

I thank him for his gracious words of sympathy and shut the door. He speeds off, leaving me on the walk outside Sam's townhouse – alone – scared – knowing what I have to do and not wanting to do it. But they trashed my apartment looking for that diamond. Telling her the truth is certainly more favorable than lying dead on the slab for both of us.

I briskly walk to the door- -start to knock but hesitate. My heart is racing, but there's no backing out now. No one answers, so I knock again. Warford answers but acts like I've interrupted something.

"Miss Annabelle. What can I do for you?" He says with impatience.

"Hello, Warford. I need to see Miss Callahan, please."

"I'm sorry, Miss Annabelle, but Madam is indisposed. I have orders not to disturb her. You'll have to wait until morning." He slams the door in my face, but I refuse to back down. I - pound with fury until he finally answered again.

"I apologize, Warford, but I must insist. I need to see her. NOW!" I don't wait for him to invite me in. I seize the moment and push past him into the front entryway. Mrs. Lilly is standing quietly behind Warford, waiting for instructions to take me somewhere to wait.

"I'll tell Madam you are here," he concedes, "but like I said, I have instructions not to disturb her. All I can do is try. So please, go with Mrs. Lilly and wait. Thank you." He orders Mrs. Lilly to take me to the sitting room.

Mrs. Lilly is gracious, and after leading me to the sitting room, she asks if she can serve me any food or drink. "No, thank you, Mrs. Lilly. I'm not very hungry. Just a drink, please." I belt the drink down in one gulp and ask for another. "Actually, just bring the bottle if you would be so kind." Mrs. Lilly's face wreaks of disapproval, but she brings the bottle and sets it down on the table next to me. Her judgment doesn't bother me in the least. I need all the courage I can get. And Prohibition be damned! Sam *always* has the best courage.

Warford and Mrs. Lilly are whispering outside the door. Mrs. Lilly is tattling to Warford about my drinking, no doubt. *Where is Sam?* My manic thoughts are interrupted by Warford, who clears his throat very loudly in advance of his announcement.

"Madame will be with you shortly, Miss Annabelle. I rang her room, and she asked that you give her just a moment. In the meantime, is there anything else I or Mrs. Lilly can do for you?"

He waits patiently for my reply. "No, thank you Warford. And I apologize for just showing up unannounced like this, but it's important. It's very important." Warford bows and makes his exit. I sit back down and take another drink. Something strange is hanging in the air here. Very strange.

The phone rings, and I hear Warford answer. From his tone, I suspect he's giving orders again. I do manage to make out the name *Antonio*, and *yes, it's being handled*. Who's *Antonio*? I down another belt of liquor and wander the room to pass the time. There are pictures of Valentina on the fireplace mantle. One picture particularly catches my attention. It's Valentina with Big Ben in the background. I take it down from the mantle and take a closer look. She looked so young, and she certainly was beautiful. Sam favors her. But who's the little colored girl standing beside her? Curious…

"Annabelle?"

"Sam!" Her voice startles me, and I drop the picture on the floor. "Oh! How clumsy of me!" I exclaim as I bend over to pick it up, embarrassed to the bone. "I'm so sorry, Sam. I was just admiring the pictures of your mother. Thank goodness it didn't break." I instantly feel intensely uncomfortable. Her obligatory smile with her eyes full of impatience rattles me. She takes the picture from my hands and gently returns it to its rightful place on the mantle.

"What's going on, Annabelle? Warford said that there was an emergency and that you insisted on seeing me." Her voice is controlled, not completely void of emotion, but colder than usual.

"Sam. Thank you for seeing me. It is an emergency – for both of us. I need to tell you something - something serious, and the truth is, I'm not sure how to start." My heart is racing, and I'm shaking. Tears fill my eyes as I try to find a way to tell her that I have been blackmailed into spying on her.

"Annabelle? What is it? What's going on?" I don't respond because I don't know how to say it. All I can do is cry. Then, Sam surprises me by asking - an unexpected question. "Does this have something to do with the note I found on the floor by your desk today? Why is Jonathon Foster contacting you, Annabelle? I can't help you if you don't tell me what's going on. Here – come sit down and let's talk."

Sam summons Warford. "Warford, could you please bring a handkerchief and some water for Annabelle please." Warford bows and leaves the room, only to return a minute later with a handkerchief and water as requested.

Sitting by Sam on the sofa, my heart aches. What if she doesn't believe me? I need her to believe me. "Okay." I begin, sniffling and wiping my tears. "I need for you to believe me when I tell you that I didn't mean to get caught up in it – and I'm so ashamed."

The tears spill from my eyes to my cheeks, muting my voice until I regain my composure. Sam takes my hand and pats it gently, patiently waiting for me to say what needs to be said.

"You've always been so good to me, Sam. That's why this is so hard. I need you to understand that at the time, I thought I had no choice." I sniffle. "And then the man, you know that Mr. Cooley – well – he said that he would help me, but I had to do something in return – not something for him but something for his boss. So, I agreed to it! But I haven't given them what they want! And these people will kill you if they think they've been crossed. That's why I'm scared! I'm so scared! When I got home today, my apartment had been broken into. They think I'm lying to them. I owe you the truth, Sam! I have to tell you!"

"Annabelle, you're babbling. I don't understand a single

thing you just said. Now, calm down and start from the beginning."
I stop crying and pause a moment to organize my thoughts. "I'd like
Warford to hear this too. Is that alright?" Sam asks.

"Sure – fine," I reply hesitantly, realizing that she's not
asking my permission but, instead, is making a veiled demand as if
he's a witness to my statement. Warford stands a short distance
away, listening but not intervening.

"Alright. Go ahead from the beginning," Sam says with a
hint of a sigh. I draw in a deep breath and begin.

"Well, one night a few weeks ago, I was at a club. I went
there with a friend, but she needed to leave early. I wasn't ready to
leave, so I stayed. That's when I saw Mr. Cooley at the club with
Jonathon Foster. I didn't think they saw me, and I didn't speak to
either one of them."

"How do you know what Cooley looks like?" Sam asks.

"Well, he came to the office one afternoon when you were
out. He wanted to talk to you about your pledge to contribute to the
children's home in Tarrytown. Remember, I said he called you
several times about it."

Sam nods that she remembers his persistent calls.

"Anyway, I was at the club and went to the ladies' room." I
start to cry again, remembering the event that triggered my bad

decision. "I'm sorry. This is so hard. Anyway, just as I came out of the ladies' room, a man came around the corner and point-blank shot another man dead! He wasn't more than a foot from me. I'm in shock! I don't know what to do! His blood is all over me!"

"Did you recognize either of the men?" Sam asks, shocked that I had witnessed a murder right before my eyes.

"Well, no. I didn't know either one of 'em." I blow my nose and take a sip of water. "But Cooley shows up and says that the dead guy is one of O'Bannion's goons."

"Cooley!" Sam exclaims. "What was he doing there?"

"Cooley was standing right behind the shooter!" I stress, pointing my finger in the air with one hand and wiping my nose with the other., "I didn't think much of it at the time, but now I know. Cooley and Foster set up that murder. That's how I got rooked into spying on you, Sam. They set me up to get to you."

Sam's eyes widen at the revelation, and even Warford, who hadn't said a word, darts his eyes in my direction. I'm so relieved it's finally out in the open.

"The shooter," I explain, "throws the gun right at my feet. And I don't know why, but I stupidly bent over and picked it up! I'm standing there with the murder weapon in my hand. Cooley immediately comes over to me and says that the police have arrived, and they are going to instantly accuse me because I'm covered in his blood, and I'm holding the murder weapon – a weapon my fingerprints are on. That's when he tells me who the dead guy is and says that if the cops don't get me, O'Bannion will! I set the gun back on the floor, but it was too late. Whether it's the cops or O'Bannion, either way, I'm caught. And stupid as it may sound, I believed him. I believed that the cops would think I shot that man, and Cooley and Foster would not say otherwise. That was made very clear. Then Cooley makes an offer. He says his boss has a lot of clout, and he can make it disappear – completely with the cops and O'Bannion. I told him I would tell the cops and O'Bannion what happened and that I refused to be extorted."

"Extorted!" Cooley laughs, cigarette smoke spewing from his mouth and nostrils. "Being extorted is the least of your worries, girlie. Go along, or you're gonna wind up dead! No two ways about it. Now make up your mind. Do you want to live? Or do you want to die? Pretty simple if you ask me."

"I decided that I wanted to live, and I would do whatever foul thing they asked me to do."

"So, what did they ask you to do, Annabelle?" Sam asks, stopping short of passing judgment.

"He says that if I can find something they think you have, his boss can get me off the hook with the cops and O'Bannion." My tears are uncontrollable, and I am sobbing so hard I can barely speak. "I didn't see any other way. And since I just wanted the cops and O'Bannion to leave me alone, I agreed. But I want you to know, with all my heart, that I'm not here just for me, Sam. I'm here to warn you. They set me up, yes, but the person they are really after is you."

"Well, that's quite a story, Annabelle. And I wish I could say that I believe you, without a doubt. But I'm questioning whether you are really concerned for me or if you are trying to do some pre-emptive strike just to cover yourself. You must understand that after what you just told me…"

"I know, Sam and I completely understand and deserve that. I'm not arguing or denying it. I know how this all sounds, and you've been nothing but gracious to even listen. All I can say is I'm sorry, and I don't blame you for questioning my motives. Yes. I need your help. But more than that, you're my friend, and I would never forgive myself if I didn't warn you."

Sam sighs and intentionally avoids eye contact with me, completely understandable after the bombshell I just dropped. But, for her safety, I must convince her that what I say is true.

"Sam, listen to me. Cooley's boss. It's Jonathon Foster, your lawyer. That's who Cooley was sitting with at the club. They knew I was there and that I was alone. I don't know how they set it up.

But they did. I have nothing to lose by coming to you. Because they're going to kill me, I know it. And they will kill you if you don't give them what they want."

The expression on Sam's face is one of utter confusion. I truly believe that she has no idea what I'm talking about.

"And what do they think I have, Annabelle?" she asks, her tone accusing and sharp.

"A diamond! A big one. Worth millions." I reply, exaggerating' *'millions.*

"A diamond! I don't have a diamond – not one like that, anyway. Why would they think I have something like that?"

I glance over at Warford with a look that begs his input. The mere mention of the diamond has given rise to a strong reaction in him. Sam notices it, too, and her demeanor mysteriously changes.

"I don't know," I insist. "But I was instructed to look for evidence that you have this diamond, or better yet, find the diamond and let 'em know. Cooley said that he had a source that told him that you have it. We are all in danger, Sam! We -need do something! Maybe call Madison. He'll know what to do, and I know he'll help. You can't just sit here waiting for them to come. You must do something!"

"Foster is obsessed. O'Bannion – dirty cops on his payroll.

No witnesses, right? He's coming after you. Foster is convinced you have this diamond! And that's the truth. And I'm sorry I ever agreed to do that, Sam, but on the other hand, if I hadn't agreed, I would have never known that they were after you. So, that's it. I just had to tell you the truth. Thanks for seeing me, and I'll see myself out now. Thank you for everything you've done for me. Watch your back."

"Annabelle, wait!" Sam yells, following me until she reaches out and grabs my arm gently. "Where will you go? You can't go out there! Like you said, it's not safe."

I don't know what to say, and I'm humbled by her generosity, but I can't in good conscience accept her help.

"I'll find someplace. Take care, Miss Callahan." Just as I'm about to open the sitting room door, Sam says to Warford.

"Warford. Would you please put Annabelle in a guest room and have Mrs. Lilly tend to anything she requires?"

"Yes, Madame." He replies in his usual manner.

I'm so relieved! I can't believe it! Sam is going to help me. My chances of survival were slim out there on my own, a bullseye on my back. "Thank you, Sam, thank you," I say, my voice cracking, overwhelmed with emotion. I can't believe that she is offering to protect me after what I have done. That's what I respect about her.

That's Sam.

"This way, Miss Annabelle," Mrs. Lilly directs me by putting her arm around my shoulders. "I'll show you to your room."

"Thank you, all – for everything," I say, but it doesn't really sound like enough. But I am relieved that I took the step to come here tonight and talk to Sam.

The room is lavish and fit for a queen. But I don't feel like a queen. I feel like a betrayer. But I have made my peace with Sam, and I'm relieved. If I were to die tonight, all would be right with the world. I plop down on the huge, soft bed. I feel safe for the first time in a long time. No more running – no more hiding. It's early, but lying on the bed relaxes me, and I feel myself dozing off. I haven't had a good night's sleep in so long. I see a blanket at the end of the bed and pull it over me, relishing the feeling of comfort and of being safe and sound. I'm going to be alright. Nothing can happen to me here. Nothing can hurt me.

****

Sam and Warford

You Remind Me of Valentina

The Callahan Townhouse

Early Evening – Monday, May 21ˢᵗ, 1928

My head is pounding, and I have a splitting headache. I rub my temples, hoping to relieve the pain that's throbbing and pulsating through my brain. Warford pours me a drink and sets it on the table beside me. He clears his throat, an indication that he has something to say, but waiting for my permission.

"What is it, Warford?" I ask, secretly praying that there's nothing more to talk about today, realistically knowing that escape is not forthcoming.

"Well, Madame, I know today has been full of difficult revelations, but I feel I must warn you that what you learned today isn't even the tip of the iceberg. There are developments that I must tell you about, and they are of such a nature that I must tell you now."

"I saw the pictures, and they mean nothing to me. What am I supposed to know about them, Warford? I mean, diamonds,

Jonathon Foster – Mother. None of this makes any sense, and I'm about at my breaking point. Do you have the answers, Warford? Better yet, do I want to hear the answers? I feel like this is a dream, and I'll wake up tomorrow and go to work and have lunch, and everything will be normal. But that's not going to happen, is it Warford."

I swirl the scotch whiskey around and around in my glass, waiting impatiently for his reply.

"I know the answers to all the questions, Madam. All of this is a shock and hard to understand. I think the biggest struggle inside you is reconciling your feelings about your mother being an operative. You see her now as a bad person when that could not be further from the truth. Your mother was everything you thought her to be and more. There are many people in this world who owe their very lives to her and others. And for that, she was never apologetic. Spying is a nasty business, and it naturally brings fierce enemies. And those enemies often masquerade as friends. Greed – murder – sedition. You name it. The ugliness of spying knows no boundaries. She kept you away from the ugliness because you were one of the things in her life that was pure and beautiful. Do not ruin that by misjudging her before you know what you need to know. She loved you more than anything. Hang on to that. You are going to need that strength for what is to come."

"I'm sorry, Warford. And you're right. I have had those thoughts. Thoughts that because her profession was what it was, her memory is now tainted. I haven't felt this helpless since the day she died. I'm floundering. I don't have a trick or a lesson or a saying of hers to help me even begin to know how to deal with all of this. I'm alone, and I'm scared that I never knew her at all."

"Well, you're not alone. You have me, and there are others you can rely on. You know, your mother and I - were friends and colleagues - for many years. I worked with her – supported her – and believed in her. And I'm here to tell you that – while there was immense darkness in our work, there was also light. She had her dark moments early on, but she chose to change that – used her connections in the covert world to help people. And that person is the Valentina you call *Mother*. So, whatever you learn in the days to come, remember that about her. Cling to it with every fiber of your being and never let it go."

"I trust you, Warford. You know that. But put yourself in my shoes. How would you react if you were in the same position? Everyone has lied to me. And I know you say it's for my protection, but that doesn't help. I could've been trusted with all of this, but I wasn't given the chance. I just wish I'd been given the chance."

"I know, Madam. And you're right. You have not been treated exactly fairly. But it was not for lack of trust. Your mother sincerely hoped that none of this would touch you. I see now that keeping these things from you, for whatever reason, was a mistake. We should have handled it differently. I promised her that I would tell you everything and arm you with whatever and whoever you would need to battle it, and that promise still stands. Now, the question is, are you willing to let go of the hurt feelings and face this head-on? Eradicate it once and for all. Or are you going to bury your head in the sand and hope you survive? It is entirely up to you. And I will be with you whatever you decide."

"Tell me everything, Warford. I don't know about carrying on any legacy, but for right now, I want to fight. I'm not a runner, and I won't be threatened. So, tell me everything."

"Excellent, Madam. I must say that in this very moment, you remind me more of Valentina than you ever have before." He pats my shoulder and stands. "Now, I will tell you everything about the past, but first, I must tell you of the more pressing present – day's events that will all make sense when you know everything. I'm so proud of you, Sam." He smiles and walks away, barking over his shoulder that he will be right back. He's never called me *Sam* before. I rather like it.

As I wait patiently for Warford to return, I study the pictures of my mother situated on the mantle of the fireplace. The picture that had captured Annabelle's attention earlier also captures mine. The picture of Mother with a young colored girl at her side. It has been in the exact same place for as long as I can remember, yet I never really looked at it. *Who's the girl?* I wonder. Mother never talked about her. I take the picture down from the mantle. It's London, that's obvious. This girl is important to Mother. I can see it in their faces. But why?

I look at all the pictures on the mantle. The pictures of my mother and father together make me smile. I miss them both terribly and wish they were here. I need them more than ever now. I hold tightly - the photograph of Mother and the girl. I want to look through Mother's box again. Maybe there's another photograph of her – some clue to tell me who she is. Warford has not returned yet, so I summon Mrs. Lilly.

"Yes, Madam. What can I do for you? Can I get you something to eat? I baked one of your favorites. Peach Pie." Mrs. Lilly's smile is always a glorious sight to behold, and it makes me feel warm inside.

"I can smell it!" I exclaim, "And it smells divine. Mrs. Lilly, can I ask you a question?"

"Of course, Madam. Anything." I fight the urge to ask her if she's an operative also. I'll leave that for later.

"Would you tell Warford that I'm going up to the ...." I stammer.

"Going up to the sealed room, dear." She says with a sly look, finishing my sentence.

"So, you do know!"

"Of course, dear. All the household staff are operatives," she says.

"Right. How silly of me," I reply sarcastically. "Then please tell Warford where I am and send up some sandwiches and slices of your delicious pie. It's going to be a late night."

"I'll get on it right away! And by the way, Madam, I loved your mother, and I will stand by you no matter what."

"Thank you, Mrs. Lilly. That means a lot to me," I say as she walks away in the direction of the kitchen.

I shouldn't have been sarcastic with Mrs. Lilly. None of this is her fault, and I'm grateful I have so many experienced and loyal people around me. As I ride the elevator to the sealed room that takes up the 4th and 5th floors, I think about what Warford said about Mother. She was an honorable woman, a woman of valor, and I need to remember that. I loved her, and she loved me. I need to remember that and trust that what she did, she did because she knew in her heart it was the right thing to do. *Follow your true heart, Angel. It will be your most trusted guide.* And she did just that.

My mother – the spy with a heart of gold and a velvet-covered iron fist. How could I be anything but proud of a woman like that?

****

Sam, Warford and Antonio

The Mysterious Man

The Covert Room, Callahan Townhouse

Early Evening - Monday, May 21ˢᵗ, 1928

My patience is wearing thin. Warford is taking his sweet

time getting up here. It's six o'clock. What could he be up to? I guess

it's only been 20 minutes since I left him downstairs, but time has

slowed to a crawl. I told Warford that I went through the box, but I

barely looked at anything. – I'm - resistant and don't want to see. I

don't understand what importance these things carry. Still, if Mother

left them for me, it means something.

I take two photographs from inside the box and lay them out

side-by-side. The first is Mother and a woman. It's the same woman

in the photograph Del Ray showed me! I look again to be sure, but

yes – yes, that's her! *So, you did know her!* And by the looks of it,

they were close. The second Mother is with a group of five nuns,

dressed in traditional habits. There are no names – no dates – no

location noted. And there she is again! At least, I think that's her.

She wasn't wearing a habit in the photograph Del Ray showed me.

I don't know. It's hard to tell. The photograph is old, and the habit obscures her hair, but I'm reasonably certain that's her. Mother and a group of nuns. What does that mean?

I reach in and pull out another photograph. This one is obviously Mother with a young and very handsome Warford. I smile at the image. Hard to imagine a young Warford. But who's the boy? Again, no names or dates.

At the very bottom of the box lies a packet. It reads, *Confidential – Eyes Only - Elegance*. I use my finger to pry it open and extract the contents. It's folded. Obviously, a map. I unfold it until it's opened to the full. South Africa. I inspect it closely, straining to read what is written outside a red circle, signifying an area intending to draw attention. It says **Target Diamond Mine 1** in very small, bold black letters.

"Target diamond mine!" I exclaim. - There are more photographs in the envelope that accompany the map. My mind cannot begin to accept what they depict. Sickening images. Men, women, and children with horrendous scars obviously created by brutal beatings – emaciated, nothing but a rack of bones - holding shovels and picks – sheer despair distorting their features into something too painful to comprehend. Men with machetes, wearing uniforms suggesting some sort of militia. It's an overwhelmingly ghastly scene, and it turns my stomach. I can't look anymore. I quickly begin to gather them up, intending to put them back in the envelope, when one face catches my eye. My heart skips, and I can't take my eyes off it. It's the face of a young black girl holding a large pick. Her expression penetrates my soul, for it is not one of terror but of resigned submission.

I know her!

I immediately compare the photograph of my mother and the young black girl I brought from the fireplace mantle. There is no doubt. This is the same girl, and I now understand what the box is all about. It's a visual account of things never spoken. I'm torn – excited that I made a connection - evidence of her with Mother in two locations – London and South Africa. Heartbroken – wondering if this girl is still alive – realizing her importance, something I've failed to take an interest in. Until now…

A painful pang of regret and disappointment burns inside me. How blind I was. This girl has been on our fireplace mantle ever since I can remember. She was a part of my mother's life, yet I never once asked about her, and I'm ashamed of my self-centeredness. Mother took special care to keep her in a place of honor, like family, where she could see her often. She's connected to my life, and I don't know how or why, but I know who can tell me. He knows exactly who she is.

The elevator doors open, and Warford walks into the room carrying a tray of food and drinks, a mysterious man in tow. They're chatting like old friends, and I'm instantly anxious – and curious. I fixate on his face, hoping to kindle a spark of recognition, but nothing. Someone I've never met. I cautiously step out from behind the table and ask the obvious question.

"Who's this, Warford?" I confront in a controlled but slightly curt tone. I'm suspicious, and I waste no time sizing him up. He's handsome – I'd guess middle to late 30's - dark-skinned. The mysterious man remains quiet as I impatiently wait for Warford's reply. He strolls past me, ignoring my commanding impatience and places a tray of sandwiches, peach pie and a pot of tea on the table in the sitting area.

"Please, Madame. Come sit – eat. I'll explain everything."

Warford and the mysterious man make themselves comfortable in the huge Victorian chairs, and he motions for me to join them. But I prefer to stand, reluctant to engage with the mysterious man. Warford hands me a plate of food, but I refuse, waiting impatiently for an explanation. Warford can see my impatience, yet he continues to fail to introduce me to the mysterious man. He's testing me, and with every bite of food they take, I become more aggravated.

"Doesn't Mrs. Lilly make the most delicious sandwiches," the mysterious man says, chewing slowly, taking delight in every bite.

"Warford!" I shouted, demanding he pay attention to me.

They both instantly stop eating. Warford's irritation is evident, but I don't care. I demand an answer now!

"Madam," he says in a forceful yet respectful tone. "This may be a good time to talk about *trust*. Do you really think this man would be here if I hadn't asked him?"

I immediately realized that my outburst appears childish and foolish. I retreat, demands in hand, and apologize to smooth things over.

"I – apologize, Warford," I say, my words stiff and begrudging. I'm aware that my apology is notably transparent and lacking some sincerity, which Warford notes immediately. The eyes of the mysterious man dart between me and Warford, observing the tension – waiting.

"You failed the test, Madam. Without trust, we have nothing. You could have sat and eaten; trusted that if this man is here, he is someone you can rely on – extended a hand in friendship and comradery. Instead, you immediately suspicion. He would not be here except at my request. You are rude, demanding, and untrusting, and if you cannot trust me, then who will you trust? So, since you insist, allow me to introduce you to Antonio De Cordova. Antonio is family. Valentina raised him in London after his mother, Maria, was murdered. Maria was a very important part of Valentina's operation in the South African diamond mines."

Warford's dressing down makes me feel like a complete fool, and I deserve it. I shouldn't have reacted that way. They both punish me with silence, apparently determining amongst themselves that if I don't trust Warford, they unite in refusal to share anything else. I had no idea Antonio was such an integral part of Mother's life and work. And how would I? I went on the attack, not allowing Warford to explain. Childish and unwarranted. I apologize sincerely this time and attempt to reverse their blatant shunning.

"The diamond mines?" I inquire, awaiting their reactions, hoping I'm forgiven. There's a second of silence, and I'm worried I'm still in the doghouse, when Warford breaks the silence with a reply, apparently deciding that my apology was sufficient to earn my way back into their good graces.

"Exactly," He states. "And I'm delighted to see that you have been doing some sleuthing." He glances toward the table, observing that I've laid out photographs from Mother's box. "Many years ago, Antonio and his mother Maria fled from Spain seeking political asylum in England. They ended up in London. Seems as though a particularly violent group of anarchists didn't appreciate Maria's resistance to their political agenda and targeted her and Antonio for assassination. It was just the two of them. Antonio's father was assassinated a few months earlier. They had nothing when they arrived in London, only the clothes on their backs. Through a series of events, they met Valentina, who took them in. Maria volunteered to help in any way she could with the Diamond Doll operation. It was her way of repaying Valentina for her kindness and support. Maria was instrumental and extremely valuable in aiding Valentina to hide people freed from the diamond mines in South Africa, after their arrival in London."

Antonio sits quietly, his eyes fixed straight ahead. "Sadly, Maria was taken and presumed murdered, and two others were murdered in their apartment right before Antonio's eyes by rebels exacting revenge for Valentina's work." Warford breathes a heavy sigh, visibly shaken by the tragic memory, while Antonio's demeanor stiffens, but I can see that he's struggling to block it out.

"Antonio," I implore with remorse. "Please forgive me."

"There's no need for an apology, Miss," Antonio replies, sincere but devoid of eye contact. "I understand your skepticism. You are not to blame. We shouldn't have tested you like that, right Warford."

Warford offers no reply, and the subject is dropped, but Antonio's gesture of chivalry has captured my attention. He didn't have to stand up for me. I didn't deserve his support. He could have refrained from making the point to Warford, but he didn't, and I find myself drawn to him. His exotically handsome features disguise an unknown I can't put my finger on. His British accent bears an aristocratic tone, much like Warford's, much like Mother's, but unlike them, he radiates a dangerous charm and quietness that is positively fascinating, and I wait with hidden anticipation for anything he has to say.

"May I say it's so nice to finally meet you, Miss Callahan," Antonio continues politely. "I feel I've known you your whole life even though we've never met. Valentina was a kind and caring woman, and I owe my very life to her. I wish we could've met under different circumstances. As for me and the purpose of my presence here? I am a specialist, requested to do what I do best. Take care of things that require tending. I apologize for barging in on you like this, but I'm afraid I needed Warford's help with a bit of a problem…"

Warford clears his throat, an obvious signal to Antonio not to divulge further details. It's clear his interruption is intended to silence Antonio.

"Thank you, Antonio," Warford says, rudely taking control

of the conversation. "And yes, Madam, I summoned him."

I don't understand any of this, and I search for the right words to say without sounding condescending or juvenile.

"Well – thank you for your loyalty, Antonio. It's reassuring to have you on my side. That said, I'm going to be honest. I know you are still avoiding telling me the full truth. We've established why you're here, Antonio, and that you were requested to come. However, nothing has been offered as to who you are. You were important to Mother, and that eases my mind, but both of you are still concealing and avoiding. I declare enough is enough. I've been kept in the dark for far too long, and I demand to know everything. Stop protecting me from things that I need to know, and just get on with it. You ask for my trust; well, I'm asking the same of you. Agreed?"

"Yes, Madam," Warford replies, "you are absolutely correct, and we owe you the truth."

"Then what are we waiting for? No time like the present," I say, conveying that I'm tired of the secrets and surprises, and the time has come to discard excuses to hide details and spill it.

"Yes, Madam," Warford replies, a slight gleam in his eyes. "Antonio is a British operative, as you probably guessed, but he's a specialist – an assassin," he says comfortably as both men munch on sandwiches as if it's just another day at the office.

I'm shocked and unnerved, but I don't show it. *What in the world have you gotten me into, Mother?*

"The best," Warford continues, "trained by none other than your mother. Surprised?" he asks. *Of course, I'm surprised!* I think to myself, but to him, I smile slightly and reply.

"After what I've learned today, Warford, nothing surprises me about Mother." I can see the wheels turning in his head. He doesn't know how to take my comment, but he declines to reply and continues with Antonio's curriculum vitae, taking another sandwich from the tray.

"He knows the specifics of everything - *Valentina* inside and out. He knows her enemies, and now yours, and what they are after. Valentina left instructions to call Antonio should the need arise. And here he is. I know you are anxious and hurried to know everything, but I say join us – let us eat and enjoy a moment of peace before we detail the horror. All will be revealed shortly. I promise."

I don't argue. I honor his request and enjoy the food prepared for us, relieving the hunger pangs in my stomach that I have stubbornly ignored.

"There is one last thing I'd like to discuss with you, Warford." Warford's expression turns to dread, his moment of peace gone. He should learn not to jump to conclusions. "Please, continue to call me Sam. The truth is, I never really liked being called

Madam. Mother was *Madame.* I'm Sam, and I think our relationship has developed beyond old boundaries, don't you?" Warford's expression is one of exquisite surprise. I've said something right today. "I think considering everything that's happened today, it's fitting. I don't view you as my employee. I never have. More like a father and a friend. You were always there for me during the darkest moments."

He offers a simple nod in appreciation for the respect, clears his throat of the emotional knot and says with an endearing smile, "I'll try to remember." It's apparent that my gesture touches him deeply.

"Valentina's daughter," Antonio says lovingly, with admiration and respect. He is pointing to me and looking at Warford, referring to my resemblance to Mother. My heart leaps at his comparison. Antonio's comment relieves all hesitation about him, and I vow to move forward in trust and solidarity. Mother trusted Antonio very much, and he trusted her, and that's good enough for me.

"Yes. Most assuredly, Valentina's daughter," Warford replies, his voice slightly cracking and shaky, a rare display of emotion apparent. "Excuse me for a moment."

He quickly stands and, in a quick step, walks toward the men's room, returning only after I imagine he has wiped the tears from his eyes. Antonio and I try to conceal our smiles, but they don't escape Warford's attention. "What!" he barks, turning and marching toward the table where Mother's photographs layout on display. Antonio and I share a discreet smile, then join him. Maybe – just maybe – the answers are within reach.

****

Sam, Warford & Antonio

The Reveal

Covert Room, Callahan Townhouse

Early Evening - Monday, May 21ˢᵗ, 1928

Warford takes the photos one by one in hand – looks at them endearingly, and says, "Look, Antonio, here's one of you and your mother with Valentina."

"That's you, Antonio!" I exclaim, pointing to several other photographs that Warford is laying on the table.

Antonio takes the photo from Warford's hand, his painful expression impossible to ignore. "The two most important women in my life right here in this picture," he says lovingly. "At least, until now." He engages my eyes, and I feel a flutter. I don't reply, but my heart skips a beat - from his comment. His attention returns to the image of his cherished mother, the love in his eyes quickly replaced by anger and bitterness. I can't possibly know the horror he went through, but my heart is aching to reach out - say something to him – something comforting.

"She was very beautiful, Antonio. And this photograph shows that." I wasn't just complimenting him to help him through his feelings. She really was very beautiful, and it's obvious where his looks come from. He traces his mother's face with his finger – seemingly drawing power from her. Warford gently pats his shoulder and says,

"I know my friend. I know."

Antonio places his mother back with the others and abruptly returns to his chair while Warford changes the subject to the matter at hand. He passes me a photo and says,

"You see these five women, Sam?" The photograph is delicately pinched between his fingers. I saw it earlier and recognized the woman that Del Ray was inquiring about. "These are the Diamond Dolls. That was their code name. Valentina gave them that name. She said she knew it probably sounded silly, but she did not care. They were not operatives, of course, but they were essential in freeing and hiding the slaves rescued from the diamond mines."

"As well as you," I point out, tapping the photograph of young Warford. He declines to accept my small gesture of praise, continuing as if I had said nothing.

"These women were part of a very limited circle that Valentina trusted," he said, his tender tone an homage to their bravery and sacrifice.

I examine their faces more closely this time. I love that they are all smiling and waving to the camera. I feel their souls leap straight out of the picture and speak to me. True happiness, even though their very lives were at stake. Their commitment was much bigger than themselves and certainly much bigger than anything I have ever done. I suddenly feel very small and insignificant. I envy their bravery and courage in the face of such evil. It occurs to me that I have never been so important to anyone – so pivotal in anyone's life.

"Where are they now, Warford? Do you know? I would really like to find them if possible." Antonio clears his throat, and his expression grows dark and wrought with emotion. My question upset him! I look to Warford for any clue as to what I said that would cause this kind of reaction.

"They are all dead, Sam. Murdered," Warford replies, his voice deep with regret and anger.

"Murdered! All of them!" I'm shocked and strangely heartbroken. Mother's Dolls. How in the world could this happen?

"Yes – all of them." Warford's tone was flat and to the point. It was apparent that he cared deeply for all of them, and their murders affected him to his core.

Only when my mother died did I see Warford react in such a way. I sympathize with him and Antonio, and my heart is filled with a flood of emotion. "They knew the risks, and they did it anyway. *We are doing as God instructs.* That was their conviction. The risk to their own lives was very real, and they accepted that."

"Doing as God instructs is always good, no matter the personal consequences." Warford reads the note with Valentina's handwriting and smiles a smile of familiarity.

"Mother used to say that. Of course, I dismissed it - let it go in one ear and out the other. Didn't understand it. Little did I know or care, unfortunately. I failed to see that faith in her, only seeing what was convenient for me to see. I wish I had respected that part of her – really listened to her. I wish I had allowed her to pass on to me every grain of her wisdom. I heard and embraced plenty from her about business, but - if only…"

"Yes, Sam, but she was so proud of you," Warford reassures. "You've served her memory well, and that is all she asked." Warford is sincere, but that empty guilty feeling is bearing down on me, strangling me as I come to terms with my own shallowness toward her, a part of me I fiercely regret; her death - opened my eyes to things about myself I didn't want to see. I casually glance toward Antonio, who is quiet, eyes fixed on one of the many lights hanging from the ceiling. "Don't worry about him," Warford says softly. "It still upsets him to talk about this part of it. But he'll be alright."

"Why *is* he here, Warford," I whisper. Warford eases a glance toward Antonio.

"As I said before, Antonio is a specialist – a master," Warford replies, his voice soft and hushed.

"A master of what?" I ask.

"Problem-solving," he replies. I'm exasperated with his persistent cryptic responses, but I don't bother to pry any further.

Warford's voice trails off in the distance as I focus my attention on Antonio. I have never encountered anyone like him. That feeling returns - a burning in the pit of my stomach. I have always thought myself an excellent judge of people, knowing immediately their strengths and their weaknesses. But not Antonio. He's escaped my talents. Maybe that's why I find him so intriguing.

"Sam! Sam?" I feel Warford squeezing my arm. His barking, sharp tone penetrates my thoughts of Antonio and jerks me from my trance.

"Oh, yes, Warford. I'm listening," I say, a little white lie rolling off my tongue. "Please, go on."

"Yes – Now, from left to right - this is Sister Mary Anna, and this is Sister Mary Collette. They were murdered along with Antonio's mother in London – on Antonio's 12th birthday," he whispers with an intense sadness, shadowed by regret and sympathy.

"His birthday!" I exclaim. Warford raises his hand, a signal to lower my voice. I'm horrified!

"Yes. His birthday," Warford says quietly. "And he was hiding in the room when it all happened."

"Oh, My God in Heaven," I say quietly. "I can't imagine going through something like that," I add, suddenly ashamed - for the times that I complained about the most trivial of things. Warford pauses, then clears his throat as he often does when he's struggling to push down emotions difficult to deal with.

"Yes. Well, getting back to it. This is Sister Mary Clarice, and next to her is Sister Mary Francis. They were murdered in Los Angeles four years ago. Now, all the Sisters were murdered and tortured, *appearing* on the surface to have the same MO. But it's a rouse. The murder of Sister Mary Anna and Sister Mary Collette – and Maria, Antonio's mother in London - was confirmed to be committed by an assassin called *The Butcher*. To most, it would be reasonable to conclude that since Sister Mary Clarice and Sister Mary Francis were murdered in a similar way, therefore concluding *The Butcher* had returned. But what is unreasonable is the amount of time in between the murders in London and Los Angeles. A 20-year gap and the inconsistencies in the signature are undeniable to those of us who know *The Butcher*."

"Mmmm, I see what you're saying. That's a lot of time to

hunt someone down. And from London to Los Angeles?"

"We know definitively that there were three men who were involved in the murders of Antonio's mother, Sister Mary Anna, and Sister Mary Collette in London. *The Butcher* was hired and carried out the murders personally. This was not a by-the-book assassination. Most assassinations are covert – discrete. This was not discreet – not in the least. This was a message – a vicious example of what happens when you cross the rebels and their British investors. Money – that was why they were murdered. *The Butcher's* MO includes ritual-type torture - machetes, amputating hands, etc."

I can't believe what I'm hearing. What kind of monster does such things? Antonio sits quietly, saying nothing. *How does he do that?* I wonder. I don't think I could sit by quietly and listen to a discussion about the murder of my mother. I know I couldn't.

"So," Warford continues, "We knew without a doubt who murdered Maria and the Sisters in London. However, determining who committed the murders of Sister Mary Clarice and Sister Mary Francis in Los Angeles took some scrutiny. As you pointed out, an immense amount of time had passed, and you are crossing an ocean. Also, there were notes left with numbers like the killer was keeping count - the carvings on the bodies. It just doesn't fit *The Butcher* in London. Nothing like that was left at their murder scene. And there were bigger problems in Los Angeles. The police investigation was undoubtedly manipulated from the inside, and for no other reason than to create an intentional false narrative linking *The Butcher* to the murders of Sister Mary Clarice and Sister Mary Francis. Of that, I am sure."

"Why would someone want to do that?" I ask. "Manipulating police reports? That's no easy task, and whoever is doing the manipulation runs the risk of being caught. Why go to such great lengths to point the finger at an assassin from 20 years prior? Unless…"

"Unless someone is mimicking what happened in London," Warford stated with confidence. "Someone who has knowledge of *The Butcher* and his signatures. Undoubtedly, the Sisters in LA were murdered by a copycat. But not a very thorough one, I'm afraid. Let me rephrase. This person is good enough to fool local authorities, but he didn't fool us. Glaring falsehoods riddled those reports, but it didn't matter. The murderer knew that the chance of those mistakes compromising his ability to sell *The Butcher* as the murderer was not a problem. And he was right. The LAPD covered their eyes and accepted the findings hook, line and sinker. But we know better."

"Meaning?" I prod Warford along to make his point.

"Meaning, an experienced assassin has been pushing *The Butcher* as the culprit in the murder of the Sisters, which I can tell you with certainty is not possible. Because the murderer known as

The Butcher is dead. Assassinated in his bed 3 days - after he murdered the Sisters and Maria in London. Not surprising. Someone is eliminating the witness, no doubt. Dirty business assassinations."

A chilling thought crosses my mind. Did Antonio settle a grudge? He would have been very young, but still… Warford called him a problem solver. A problem solver indeed trained by my own mother. Warford continues to delve into the details, the horror of the murders of mother's friends and confidants.

"Antonio and I have pinned who this copycat is. He's well-financed, and that financier manages to keep him in legitimate law enforcement positions, creating the perfect cover. He's been quiet since Los Angeles, and we hoped he would never resurface. And he didn't – that is – until three days ago when the River Dell County Police found the body of a woman dumped in the Tall Shadow Woods. And even though her name is being withheld, Antonio discovered who she is.

" Warford taps the face of one of the Sisters remaining in the photograph. "Sister Mary Agnes, Diamond Doll 5. Antonio confirmed that the Sister was headmistress at a children's home in Tarrytown. The MO of her murder aligns with the murder of Sister Mary Clarice, Diamond Doll #3, and Sister Mary Francis, Diamond Doll #4, in Los Angeles."

"She was one of Mother's!" I exclaim as Warford points to

the article in the newspaper. "That close!"

The connection bursts forth in my mind and my blood runs cold. Tarrytown is about 25 miles north of New York City. Cooley is there! And Foster!

"Yes, Sam," Warford replies with sadness. "Sister Mary Agnes is her name. She is the last of the Dolls. The murders of the two Sisters in Los Angeles and the murder of Sister Mary Agnes in Tarrytown are identical. The assassin is here. Which leads me to the Bureau man who paid you a visit this afternoon."

"I already know you lied to me when I asked you about him, Warford. As for what he wanted, I don't know exactly. He was fishing for information, I know that. He showed me a photograph of Sister Mary Agnes and asked if I knew if she was an acquaintance of Mother's. Did I know her, or did any of my friends know her? Of course, I said no because I wasn't aware anyone did until now. He already knew Mother's connection. Why ask loaded questions?"

"Sam," Warford says softly. "I know you were upset that you were not told about your mother, but the Agent Del Rays of this world are exactly why she hid things from you. To protect you. You could not tell him anything because you did not know. And, yes, I lied to you. A phone call was not the right set of circumstances to tell you about him. So, on that note, let me tell you about our Special Agent Dominic Del Ray," he says with a tone that conveys disgust.

"Before he became Special Agent Dominic Del Ray, Detective Del Ray was one of the LAPD detectives investigating the murders of Sister Mary Clarice and Sister Mary Frances in Los Angeles."

He retrieves a thick paper file from inside one of the cabinets, bringing it to me for inspection.

"When we learned of their murders, Antonio was dispatched to Los Angeles to gather details, and he found some rather disturbing facts. There was significant suspicion that Del Ray knew more than he was telling. In fact, his partner, a detective named Grayland, was so certain that Del Ray had committed the murders that he went to his superiors and accused him outright. Of course, that information was never made public, and Grayland was subsequently forced out. - Del Ray's law enforcement career is inundated with reports of corruption and an accusation of murder, yet he secures the position of Special Agent with the Bureau. There is someone with some very powerful strings helping him. He could have never been hired by the Bureau otherwise. And – Grayland? He has landed right back in the lion's den. Grayland is now a Captain with River Dell County Police in Tarrytown and is investigating Sister Mary Agnes' case. God does have His ways, 'ey Antonio?"

Antonio simply raises his hand, avoiding a verbal response.

"Rather a twisted turn of events, wouldn't you say? Del Ray, or someone working with him, is the assassin we seek, of that I have no doubt. He was tipped off that Sister Mary Agnes was working at the children's home in Tarrytown. Your feelings about his fishing expedition with you today are right on the money. Del Ray is on the prowl, looking for something that has eluded him for a very, very long time. He was also watching me while I was unloading the grocery delivery from the truck today. Del Ray uses his law enforcement positions to get what he wants. His money source pulls the strings and makes sure that he is always positioned to further their hunt. And that money source is Jonathon Foster."

Annabelle's accusation of Foster now makes more sense! She was right! And how could I have let his deviance slip by me? I have always been confident in my judgment of people, but I never suspected him for one minute.

"Annabelle said she saw him at the club with Cooley. She said Foster is Cooley's boss. Why Del Ray, Warford? Why would Jonathon Foster need someone like him? Annabelle said he was looking for a diamond! Del Ray is hired to find the diamond?"

"Exactly, and he is not the only one Foster hired," Antonio interjects, taking Warford and me by surprise with his sudden insertion into the conversation. "The murder of the Sisters in Los Angeles is just the tip of the iceberg. Del Ray has worked for Foster for a long time, and Foster knew exactly what he was getting from Del Ray. That's why he hired him. Foster arranged for his assassin, Del Ray, to be planted inside the LAPD. He was never an officer on the street – he went in as a detective from the beginning. His purpose? To find the Sisters of course because it was believed that they would lead to the diamond. Plain and simple. But while he was looking for them, Del Ray made dirty money on the side. He just can't help himself. It's how he ticks. Complaints ranging from extortion to blackmail - running prostitutes – mob activities, you name it. But Foster cleans up Del Ray's messes, and it was well known in the LAPD that if you complained against Del Ray, you were risking everything, even death. Every officer that made a complaint against him was fired or just mysteriously disappeared. Foster's money and influence and Del Ray's ease with destroying and killing make things like that happen. Foster will do whatever is necessary to make sure that Del Ray has access and the opportunity to hunt whoever he needs to hunt to find that diamond. Even the Bureau is not out of reach. Del Ray *is* selling *The Butcher* as the murderer to direct suspicion away from himself or his cohort. He's keenly aware that there are those of us left who worked with Valentina, but I don't believe he's aware we're on to him. His ego won't allow it. Foster will never give up looking for the diamond, and Del Ray will not give up his double-cross. There's the twist. That's why he came to you. He didn't really want to know about the

Sisters. He already knows everything about them. He wants what he thinks you have. He came there to court you, not question you. It just didn't work out, it seems."

"Court me! What...But I don't have it!" I exclaim, completely in the dark as to why Foster or Del Ray believe that myth. "And the murder of the Sisters in L.A. and now Sister Mary Agnes in Tarrytown? What do they have to do with the diamond other than their connection to Mother?"

"The murder of the Sisters in L.A. and Sister Mary Agnes," Warford replies, "has nothing to do with revenge like Antonio's mother and the Sisters in London. That motive centers strictly around finding the diamond. The sad thing is, they – knew – nothing. They died for nothing."

"They died for nothing," I repeat, overwhelmed at the monstrosity of Foster and Del Ray. "Did Mother *ever* have the diamond they're looking for," I demand, thinking that if it is hidden, and I can get my hands on it, then it needs to just be handed over – put a stop to this once and for all!

"No!" Warford exclaims forcefully. "She *never* had it. She never saw it. But she knew who did, and she protected her with everything she had, and I still do! That is why the Sisters were murdered. There were past connections with Valentina and with the rightful owner. Therefore, Foster and the others believed they must have known something."

"So, there is a diamond – and still protecting *her*? Protecting who?" I demand. "Who are you still protecting, Warford!" Warford hesitates to reveal her name as if it is a name that was never to be spoken.

"Warford," I say gently, "You cannot keep this to yourself any longer. Innocent people have given their lives; tortured and killed in ways that make God Himself cringe. I know you feel an allegiance to her – you want to continue to protect her, but there's no honor in withholding her name any longer. If they find her, they'll kill her, that I know – and so do you! So, for the sake of everyone, living and dead, who are you protecting?" Warford breathes deeply, an expression of surrender on his face. He knows he can no longer keep this secret.

"Anashe. Her name is Anashe, and her story began long ago."

****

Sam, Warford & Antonio

Anashe

Covert Room – 5th Floor, Callahan Townhouse

Evening – Monday, May 21st, 1928

Back in the sitting area, I pour us all a cup of tea. I've never been fond of tea, but Mother was an aficionado. Our cupboard was filled with exotic blends from all over the world. The pungent earthy aroma and rich flavor remind me of her, calming my nerves and soothing my emotions. A moment of exquisite quiet from the smothering chaos. But it all ends too soon as Warford begins the tale of a girl named Anashe and her diamond…her very, very large diamond.

"It wasn't long after Valentina arrived in London with Anashe," Warford explains, "that I received word that a story was spreading. The rumor mill was abuzz people talking about a legendary diamond that had made its way to London from the mines in South Africa. I don't know who knew about the diamond nor who began the tale. How does any rumor start? The mere mention of it caused Valentina and I grave concern, and even though neither one of us had ever seen it, she was aware that Anashe possessed it. She told Valentina as much. Valentina hid the diamond in a safe place while Anashe was young but gave it back to her when she came to America. I'm not aware of the reasoning behind that. Valentina never said, and I didn't ask. All I know is that I promised Valentina I would continue to watch over her, limiting contact unless necessary, and that I would do everything in my power to protect her, and I kept that promise. Foster does not know who she is; that is why he is still hanging on to the falsehood that Valentina had and then passed it on to you. And it's also the reason Anashe is still alive, and unfortunately, you are the one under fire. That unintended blowback would have distressed your mother terribly. She never ever planned on this happening to you. She wouldn't have done it had she known it would put you at this level of danger. Warford rushes to the table and returns with the photograph I had brought from the mantel of the young black girl and my mother."

"This is her," he says, admiring the image lovingly. "Valentina and I, along with all five Diamond Dolls, were instrumental in Anashe's rescue from that wicked place. Valentina took responsibility for her. Her mother was killed in the mines, and she had no one. The legend of the diamond with beauty beyond description begins and ends with this young girl."

I lightly stroke the photograph of Mother and Anashe, taking in the expression on their faces…expressions of love and admiration…and trust. A pang of jealousy rattles around in my spirit. I have no right to be jealous. I never tried very hard with Mother. I was more interested in getting under her skin than having a loving, trusting relationship with her. And it's a painfully bad decision that I've had to come to terms with. But now I see why having a close relationship with me was so important to Mommy. I wish I had tried harder and not taken so much for granted. Looking at them together, it's clear why the photograph of Anashe and Mother had a special place on the mantle. Their relationship was special, something that stood the test of time. Warford gently takes the photograph from my hands and continues to stare at it as if mourning something he failed to do. He finally relinquishes it to me, and I gently place it back with the other memories that now mean more to me than ever. I take his hands in mine, a loving gesture of understanding. We each have our own regrets regarding Mother, and we each, including Antonio, battle them in our own way.

"We all have scars on our heart, Warford. But I say, we use those scars and warrior up. Let's make Mother proud."

"Yes, Warford," Antonio agrees. "If not for you, those people…" Antonio truncates the compliment, seemingly aware that Warford knows the meaning behind his words.

"Yes, Warford. If not for you, Mother, and the Dolls…so

many lives you saved. And you saved me when Mommy died. Tell us everything, please," I coax. "Tell us this exciting legend of the diamond!" We make ourselves comfortable, and as he begins the tale, his aristocratic tone, dramatic and alluring, draws me into the midst of the sordid past, surreal and exciting as if it was spun from the corners of his imagination and not anchored in truth.

"The rumor spread like wildfire and quickly evolved into legend. Walk into any pub or place where people gathered, and that's what they would be talking about – arguing about. A diamond of enormous size and unimaginable beauty, told to be in the possession of a child who escaped the diamond mines in South Africa."

"The legend portrays the story of a child who found a mystical diamond of untold beauty while playing one day. It told of the enslavement of the child and her mother, forced to work the diamond mines for refusing to relinquish it to the rebels. The child's mother hid the diamond from the rebels from the time of their internment until the child's mother was killed in that mine. Upon her mother's death, she discovers the hidden diamond and, like her mother, continues to keep it hidden, defying the rebels, risking her very life to honor her mother's sacrifice and ensure the diamond's safekeeping. She succeeds, killing the rebels with her bare hands and escaping with the diamond, making her way to London."

"This legend worried me a great deal because legends begin with a shred of truth, and it is the truth of the story that attracts those who seek to benefit the most at any cost. Especially when the legend revolves around something so valuable, which brings me to a sight holder named Alonzo Foster. He was keenly interested in the legend and began the search for information. He was adamant that the legend was not a legend at all. He became obsessed with finding the diamond. He hit a lot of dead ends until he met a British operative who made him an offer too good to refuse."

"You called him a sight holder. What is that?" I ask, laying aside for the moment that the name *Foster* has caught my attention. "And who was this other British operative?"

"Sight holders are a middleman in the diamond industry, Sam," Warford explains. "The sight holder employs highly skilled people called cutters. They cut and shape the diamonds and prepare them for sale. Alonzo Foster knew that if he could find this diamond, it would make him an extremely wealthy and influential man in the diamond business. Oh, he had money, but his business was dependent on the truly wealthy - company owners. He knew everything would change if he could find this legendary diamond, cut it – and sell it on the black market, making him millions. The hunt for the diamond consumed him. He spent a small fortune on private detectives who were hired to follow reported sightings of the diamond. Even the slightest tidbit of information was investigated.

He searched and hunted for the diamond until the day he died, financially ruined and bitter never finding it. On his deathbed, Alonzo made his successor promise he would continue the search. So, Sam, as I'm sure you noticed, the last name of the sight holder was Foster. You've no doubt made the connection. That successor is Jonathon Foster, Alonzo Foster's son."

"I knew it!" I exclaim in excitement, but also somewhat confused. "But I don't understand why Mother would allow Jonathon Foster to handle all her legal affairs if she was completely aware of this treachery and what he was up to. A rather dangerous game to play, isn't it?"

"That was Valentina's way," Warford replied, offering a defense and explanation regarding Mommy's judgment.

"Valentina was a master at manipulating her enemies. She and the way she manipulated her enemies, and she was a master at keeping them close. She could mislead them, con them, coddle them, lie to them, and misinform them, all while leading them to believe that they were manipulating her. She knew every move they made and why they made it. They thought they were getting away with taking her for a ride. But they couldn't have been more wrong. She pulled the strings that they thought they were pulling. She always harbored hope that Foster would abandon his search for the diamond, but that was not to be. So, by allowing Foster to believe that she had the diamond…hidden…where only she knew of its location, she kept the advantage, which ensured the safety of the rightful owner of the diamond. Whenever discussions of the diamond arose between them, Valentina always asserted her opinion of the silliness of Foster continuing to bleed money chasing something that was nothing but a legend. He had carte blanche access to all her financial records, which, of course, showed no indication that the diamond was included in her assets. And trust me, he inspected her finances with a fine-toothed comb. He found nothing because there was nothing to find. Her finances were in impeccable order, as you well know. Every penny accounted for."

"If Foster had access to Mother's finances and couldn't find anything, why continue searching? Why continue to insist that I, or anyone else for that matter, have it?" I ask, aggravated and a little scared. "What kind of person continues to pursue at any cost, including murder, something they can't even prove exists?" I cast a glance at Antonio, who continues to be quiet and nonassertive. He seems content to just listen and wait for Warford to bring him into the conversation.

"Well," Warford continues, "Jonathon Foster made a promise, didn't he? To his father, who is on his deathbed. He swore that he would never give up looking for it. And Alonzo is the one who first indicated that Valentina had the diamond in the first place. Greed…pure greed. That's the catalyst that drives the madness. But

I also think there's another factor driving his obsession. He's failed! He's failed to do the one thing his father begged him to do before he died. It's his failure that fuels his insanity more so than his greed. It's made him a twisted and wicked man, committing atrocities beyond comprehension to find it. Foster's psychopathic pursuit led him to this point, and unfortunately, he won't give up. Because he can't imagine Valentina leaving something so valuable in the care and responsibility of someone else, especially a young girl who has never admitted to its very existence. Alonzo Foster never murdered anyone to find the whereabouts of the diamond, but his son Jonathon has no issue in doing just that. And with pleasure! We know through intelligence that Jonathon Foster ordered the execution of the Sisters in Los Angeles, and he ordered Sister Mary Agnes' murder in Tarrytown because he thought they had information that would lead to the diamond. They gave not one shred of information as to its hiding place. So, he's refocused again, and his target is logically you."

My resolve to beat this animal transcends my initial inclination to run, and the more I hear, the more resolved I am that running is not the option I'll be taking.

"And Cooley? What's his role in all of this? What's his stake? I know there's got to be something in it for him." "Cooley really fires me up. He a liar and schemer, and even if I didn't have it in for Foster, I'd be sure to get my hand on him."

"Cooley is Foster's right-hand man," Warford replies in scoffing disgust. "He's the cleaner...the one who keeps Foster's hands out of the dirt. He's insulation, directly handling Del Ray and any others who do the dirty work. And Cooley, for the most part, does not get his hands dirty either. That's why I was shocked to learn that he had wormed his way into a position at the children's home in Tarrytown. Foster believed Sister Mary Agnes to be the key. She was the closest to Valentina. Not much they didn't share. Foster and Cooley underestimated their prey. They didn't count on the Sister refusing to tell them a thing. Now they have another murder on their hands, and they're back to square one...which is you, Sam."

"Okay, square one...but I still don't understand, Warford. Foster could have gotten to me at any time. I've been to charity functions and dinners with him, and his family had them to the house in Long Island...had them here! Why am I still alive!" I declare, raising my hands to the sky as if reaching for heaven, asking God Himself for an answer. "There must be a reason he hasn't killed me. He's been given so many opportunities over all these years, even when I was a child! What's stopped him? What's stopped him?" I reassert, hoping for an earthly answer but realizing the answer may lie in the divine.

"Foster was being fed information by someone close to you," Antonio interjects out of the blue, catching Warford and me off guard.

He's sat there all this time, not saying a word. Warford was right about him. He'll speak when he has something to say. He's a man of action, not words. He has our undivided attention.

"What do you mean someone was feeding him information? Someone close? You mean someone other than Foster?" My heart is flip-flopping in my chest, and I'm doing my best to grasp what Antonio just said. "Is everyone around me some sort of threat?" I insist, my voice a mix of disbelief and panic! I sit there, speechless. What else can I learn today that will shatter everything I thought I knew about my life and the people in it?

"That someone is someone you've trusted your whole life," Antonio continues in a mysterious, macabre manner that sets me on edge. "Someone Valentina knew was an enemy but kept them close. Someone hired originally by Alonzo Foster. Someone who intentionally kept the focus on Valentina and then you after Valentina's murder. I'm sorry, Sam. You should have been told that the bomb blast that killed Valentina was carried out to kill Valentina, and you should have been told that a long time ago."

"What!" I exclaim, shock and rage welling up inside me. I've been punched in the gut, and I can hardly breathe! "That's not possible. No. No! She was killed an innocent victim of that blast! Isn't that right, Warford? Isn't that what you told me, Warford? That's what the Bureau of Investigation determined!   That

Anarchists set off that bomb, that's what they said!" I'm so angry, I can hardly stand to be in the same room as these two. My breathing is heavy, and my heart is broken. I glare at Warford, and I pointblank ask him, "Did you know about this?"

"Sam…" he stammers, struggling for the words to smooth over this hideous lie.

"Did you know!" I scream! "I want the truth! How dare you…how dare…!" I collapse in the chair, sobbing, hating, despising the sight of them both!

Their silence says everything! That's all the confirmation I need. Another lie! But this one cuts me to the bone. I'm shattered. I can't comprehend a justification for keeping that from me. How can I ever trust either of them again? And Especially Warford!

"Why! Why!" I cried, devastated and furious! "Why didn't you tell me, Warford? I deserved to know!" Warford doesn't back down. He stands his ground and dares to attempt to justify a reason for this cruel and utter betrayal.

"Sam, I know it is a shock, and I know you are angry, but we did what we had to do. And understand it or not deserve the truth or not my job was to keep you safe, and if someone was so bold as to blow up a bank just to kill your mother, with no consideration for her or the countless others they surely knew would die, what makes you think they wouldn't come after you if you knew the truth! We knew the truth, but we left it alone. I won't apologize. I did what needed to be done, and if Valentina were here, she would agree with me!"

"Oh, stop it! Just stop it!" I scream. "I'm sick of hearing that! Just sick! Do you hear me?" I bolt straight out of my chair. I couldn't even be near them! I can't look at them! How dare they lie to me about something like this. I can't stand it! Why! I pace around, not knowing what to think or what to do. I want to just leave! Get out of here and never come back! I feel eyes on me, and I turn to see Warford standing behind me. He tries to talk to me, but I refuse to listen. He follows me, begging me over and over. I'm so angry, I'm shaking!

"I'm so sorry, Madam," Warford apologizes. "I know this is a shock, and I understand you are upset. You see it as another lie. But to Antonio and me, it was not a lie! It was a necessity! If you knew the truth You would not be standing here now, and it would have only taken hours for them to snuff you out! Now!" he rages, the anger in his voice escalating, "I know you have had a lot thrown at you today, but you simply could not know! End of story! And throwing a tantrum about it now does not help you or me or Antonio! There is no time for it, no time! So, refuse to understand it if that will make you feel better, but know this, Madam! Nothing we've done was ever intended for anything but your safety. It was never intended to be malicious or to hurt you in any way! This is not about what you should or should not have known! It was about keeping you out of this as much as possible and keeping you alive! And quite frankly, I'm weary of reminding you of that. For all these years, Antonio and I have had one single purpose. To protect you! So, I demand you make up your mind. Either go or stay, but if you stay, you must accept that there will be things brought up that were kept from you and that it was never the intention for you to know such things until such time that you needed to know! And that is all I have to say. I leave it up to you to decide."

Warford abruptly turns and walks away, returning to his chair across from Antonio. I despised the harshness of his words that stung like shrapnel, leaving me unable to respond and wondering if I was kidding myself in thinking that I'm even remotely capable of handling this! Maybe I need to rethink fighting. Maybe running is truly the better option.

Antonio says nothing, of course, but his expression explicitly implies that he's in complete alliance with Warford. What to do? I don't know. I'm angry, but I know I can't leave things like this with Warford and Antonio. Warford demanded that I make up my mind. So, my mind is made up. They would die for me, and that I know. And I'm mad as hell that I wasn't told about Mother, but I know he's right. I wouldn't last long on the run. It occurs to me that these men and all these people that Mother put in place have sacrificed their lives for me for years and on many occasions. So, I'm angry, but I'm also grateful. What would I do without them if they left. I slowly walk toward Warford, his angry eyes avoiding me.

"I've made a decision," I tell him, hoping they don't decide I'm not worth the trouble anymore and are the ones who do the leaving. That notion terrifies me. What would I do without them? What would I do if they left me?

****

Sam, Warford and Antonio

The Last Glass House

Covert Room 5th Floor, Callahan Townhouse

Late Evening - Monday, May 21st, 1928

It seems we have been in this room a lifetime, but it's only

been a few hours. A very long and tortuous few hours.

After a brief pause to compose our emotions, Antonio Jonathon Foster's direct connection to me. The one who continued to bait him with direct knowledge that I had the diamond.

"Felicity Farmer Fellows." He annunciates, adding disdain to every part of her name. "Felicity is dead. I'm sorry, but I had to kill her," he says, cool and unemotional, as if it was akin to driving down the street…eating cereal for breakfast…getting dressed. His callousness stuns me to my core, and I'm shocked at his ability to make such a declaration with glaringly obvious ease. I'm trying to digest the ugly truth that my longtime friend, Felicity, was playing for the dark side and that her professed affection for me was simply an evil thrill for which she was supplied with a paycheck. And the hits just keep coming!

"Listen to Antonio, Sam," Warford urges, obviously noting my distress about the shocking news regarding Felicity and interceding on behalf of Antonio. "I promise you will understand. Listen to him." I nod my head in agreement. There's no denying that if Antonio says she was corrupt, then she was corrupt.

Antonio delicately pours me a cup of tea, which strikes me as somewhat weird. The coldblooded killer making tea. Interesting…

"The life I have led demands that I confront situations in a straightforward and very harsh fashion, Sam." Antonio's voice is nothing like what one would think a killer would sound like. It's deep and seductive…and along with his looks, it's hypnotizing, and I find myself glued to every word. "Please forgive me. I'm afraid I am not a gentleman at times. I have forgotten my manners, and I should have put that news to you differently. I know she was your friend, and you trusted her. Especially after Valentina…well…. I shouldn't have told you like that," he says apologetically, presenting delicately the tea he's made for me. He then offers Warford a cup, who graciously accepts and begins to delicately sip in true English fashion. And finally, Antonio takes his own tea and returns to his chair for more of what I can only imagine are more assassin stories. But to my surprise, he utters not a word.

Antonio breathes the aroma in, sips the tea delicately, and

places the cup back on the saucer. I watch him intently, wondering why he's become so quiet, and then I realize. He's patiently waiting on me - to signal that I am ready to hear the rest of the truth. He's not one to rush. I know it's time to face what is hopefully the last glass house of my life to be shattered.

With a heavy heart and tear-filled eyes, I say, "Okay, Antonio. I'm ready. You can tell me…tell me about Felicity. Tell me everything." Antonio takes the cue and begins.

"First, I want to share with you that I sympathize with you. I know what it's like to have your world torn apart. It's happened to me to both Warford and me many times throughout the years. But we adapt. This life chose us, and we do what needs to be done despite our heartbreak. Adapt or die. Neither of us started out that way, but just like you, circumstances, good and bad, put us in a position of no choice. Everyone in your life did what they did to keep this away from you. But there are people who will not let it go. It has nothing to do with you, but that doesn't matter. What matters is what drives them. Greed, failure, or just pure evilness. I've seen a lot of all of it. And I often wonder what my life would have been like had that day not happened if my Mama would have lived. I have moments times when the memories invade my mind, but I refuse to wallow in them. I can't. My survival and the survival of those who depend on me won't allow for it. I've done some bad things, but killing Felicity Farmer Fellows was not one of them. The truth is, I didn't set out to kill her. I defended myself. She came after me. She had to stop me from revealing the truth to you. And I assure you, it was a situation that I could not avoid. If I had wanted her dead, she'd have been dead a long time ago. She gave all of us plenty of reason to do it. So, as harsh as it sounds, I don't regret it. She was not the person you thought her to be, and she is a player in the death of *all* the Sisters and my Mama. She is also the reason that you have stayed on Foster's radar."

"What do you mean?" I ask, looking for clarification. "I don't understand. Felicity always said that Mother asked her to look after me. Even when I was young, Mother and Felicity were friends. I remember it! We were just talking about it the other day when she asked me to do an interview for her magazine!"

"I know, I know!" Antonio asserts, assuring me that he knows I'm finding his information difficult to swallow. "And you believed in that friendship, and you trusted her. She counted on that trust. After Valentina was killed, she did exactly what Valentina encouraged her to do. You believed it was friendship, but what she was really doing was keeping an eye on you."

"But Mother and Felicity were friends!" I exclaim, unable to discount what I have believed for so many years.

"Well, that's how it appeared, but remember what Warford said. *Valentina was a master at keeping her enemies close.* She knew Felicity's motives, and she encouraged her to watch out for you, not to encourage friendship between you and Felicity. The friendship was incidental, but to keep her close so that Warford could keep an eye on her and you."

"That's exactly right, Sam," Warford declares. "Valentina knew what Felicity was up to."

"And what was she exactly?" I asked. "A spy, no doubt like Mother like both of you."

"An operative? Yes. Like us? No!" Antonio insists, with an underscoring tone of offense to my comparison. "An operative's life is dependent on the ability to carry out a lie, but Felicity always gravitated toward the dark side, not above sacrificing other operatives to accomplish her own self-serving goals and ambitions. It all began when she had an affair with Alonzo Foster. It didn't last long, but he did tell her of his search for the diamond."

"And Morgan? How does he fit into all of this?" I can't believe that Morgan would be involved, but I also know with certainty that he does what Felicity tells him to do, there's no question about that.

"Morgan was also an operative," Antonio explains. "That's how they met. They were married and operated as a team for British Intelligence. But they botched a mission in Germany. They were assigned to infiltrate the German government and obtain information about the military movements of the German army in World War I. The Germans uncovered their spying, and they barely escaped with their lives. *That's* how Morgan was injured. Trying to escape Germany, not as a war hero."

"They're certainly good!" I exclaim with bitterness. "I'll give them that! I never suspected any of this for a minute!" I'm consumed with the feeling of complete and utter disgust for their lying and treachery.

Antonio takes a sip of tea.

"It's good you didn't know," he replies. "That's what saved you all these years. They would have killed you without hesitation to hide it. Formidable and ruthless, especially Felicity. She was the real planner and schemer, and Morgan followed her every step. After their narrow escape from Germany, they decided they wanted out. Germany was too close a call. They wanted to relocate to New York. But it seems they have a huge problem. The problem is that they are flat broke. They beg the British Government to set them up, claiming that they deserve it after all the work they've done for Queen and country. But British Intelligence has had enough of them, and not only will they not fund their move to the United States, but they also outright release them. Disavowed! Now, Morgan and Felicity are really in a bind. They have no money, and the British government has cut them loose. What do they do? They devise a scheme. They know that if they can legitimize themselves as wealthy socialites with just one aristocrat or one person of means and influence, they'll have it made. They choose a target. Felicity's former lover, Alonzo Foster. She arranges to meet him at a party, and they introduce themselves not as Felicity and Morgan Banes, their real names but as Morgan Fellows and his wife, Felicity Farmer Fellows. Catchy! Wouldn't you agree. Sounds regal, don't you think?"

"Wait a minute," I interrupt. "Did you just say that Fellows isn't their real name?" I repeat, astounded by what I'm hearing.

"You heard correctly," Antonio replies, assuring me that I have not misunderstood. "They bait Alonzo assure him that they can help him with his problem of locating the elusive and legendary diamond. They offer him information, saying that Valentina or one of her Diamond Dolls has the stone and assure him that they can easily find out where every one of the Dolls is located. It was a lie, but Alonzo Foster is desperate, so he makes a deal with them. He gives them an obscene amount of money, which Felicity counts on, especially given her and Alonzo's history. She and Morgan immigrate to New York City and, with their newfound wealth, courtesy of Alonzo Foster, weave their way into society circles. No one suspects a thing."

"They started *Extraordinary Woman* magazine, easily

maneuvered about in New York society circles, and were not only accepted but adored! Just as you've seen, Felicity has a way about her. She can charm her way into anything and generally charm her way out. They were flying high, but problems began to pop up. Starting the magazine and weaving their web has depleted the funds Alonzo gave them. So, they posted a letter to him requesting more money. They receive a response, but it's not money. Instead, they are told that Alonzo has died. Now, that's a turn up. They are really in a bind. That bit of news was a huge blow, and they are desperate. That's when they decide to contact Jonathon Foster, the heir to Alonzo."

"They feed Jonathon the same story they fed Alonzo, but to their disliking, Jonathon isn't as forthcoming with the money as Alonzo was. He's certainly interested in the information, and he pays them some money, but as per usual with those two, it's not enough and he refuses to pay them anymore. So, Felicity and Morgan begin searching for the diamond for themselves. They figure if Foster can find it with their help, they will just find it and keep it. This goes on for some years, Jonathon continuing to rely on them, unaware of their double cross. It's at about this same time that Valentina arranges a 'chance' meeting with Felicity, and they become friends, each having their own motives. Valentina knows of Felicity from London. She's heard enough about her. She is, again, keeping her enemy close, and Felicity is befriending

Valentina, believing she has the diamond. I hate to tell you this Sam, but Felicity is the one who hired the culprits and set up the bombing that killed Valentina. She was making way for Foster to check every inch of her finances to discern whether there was an anomaly apparent that indicated a massive money transaction. And Felicity also knew the location of the Sisters in Los Angeles, and we know what happened to them. "

"Fast forward to Sister Mary Agnes. Felicity is the one who pinpointed her location. She was in Tarrytown on a magazine shoot doing a story on the children's home, no less. Not a story that Felicity would usually see as interesting or newsworthy, right?"

I had to agree there – most definitely not Felicity material.

"I believe Felicity recognized Sister Mary Agnes right away, and Cooley was sent there with Jonathon Foster's help to keep an eye on the Sister's movements who she associated with. What better way to accomplish that than to get him a job there as an administrator? Valentina was always one step ahead. She changed Anashe's name, and that's what saved her. Otherwise, Cooley would have certainly made the connection to Valentina and the diamond. When Cooley is unsuccessful, Foster brings in Del Ray to extract information. Well, that brings us up to the present and the murder of Sister Mary Agnes." Antonio stops, resting his head in his hands.

I don't know what to say. I'm overwhelmed with a crushing

emptiness as I imagine the horror that the Sisters and Antonio's mother endured and how a woman who was like a second mother to me could commit such heinous acts.

"I do have a bit of good news," Warford says, cutting our agony with a semi cheerful tone. "You'll be happy to know that Morgan is also no longer a problem. He's out of commission completely. He won't be stirring things up for quite some time."

"Out of commission?" I reply. "Is he dead?" I ask, half hoping that Morgan met the same fate as Felicity.

"No, he's very much alive, but I've taken care to ensure that he's out of our way for good. Morgan has been arrested for the murder of his wife."

"Good!" I declare defiantly, torn as to whether I should ask how that feat was managed. "Do I dare even ask? Explanation?" I inquire, not sure I really want or need to know. Antonio is stoic, but I've come to realize that that doesn't necessarily mean anything. He wouldn't show it if he did know.

"I'm glad to explain it to you if you insist," Warford says, not wanting to rock the boat but offering an alternative. "But I think it's a better use of our time to prepare you for what is coming rather than dissect the sordid details of what's already happened. However, it is possible he will call you Sam. He still thinks he can trust you. Just be prepared."

"And I doubt Foster will take his call," Antonio adds, seemingly confident that Foster has washed his hand of the Fellows. "It's in Foster's best interest to distance himself. If anything, Foster's already put out a hit on him. His reach is far and wide, and that includes jail staff. Morgan is in a dangerous position. My guess is that he's staying quiet and will gladly take the blame just to stay alive."

"Let him call." I declare firmly. "I won't help him."

"We'll confront that situation if it presents itself," Warford replies.

They both nod, prepared to move on to the next item on this unbelievable agenda. I stand up and stretch. Every muscle in my body is screaming, and I can't sit any longer. I'm looking forward to the moment when they tell me that this is the end of the sordid tale and t that everything that needed to be said has been said. But this isn't that moment.

"Alright," Warford says with a sigh. "We must discuss Annabelle. At this point, I think it best for her to just lay low, but I don't discount the possibility of recruiting her to help with Foster and Cooley. If she agrees, it will be risky but helpful because she already has a connection with them. I believe it's something we must consider."

"I agree she could be an asset," I reply. "But I want to see what transpires. These people are dangerous, and I don't want her getting hurt - or worse. They already ransacked her apartment. Scared her to death! Was that little maneuver a threat or tactic intended to warn and scare her? Was it intended for my benefit? Either way, I'd rather keep her out of it if possible."

"I don't believe they think she has the diamond. It was a calculated scare tactic to put pressure on her," Antonio says. "They knew she would waste no time coming to you, Sam. Tell you everything. It could be they thought you'd use it to bargain for her life. It's a weak tactic simply poking and prodding, hoping to hit something, which shows me that they are more desperate than ever and they're running out of leads. Strong arming Annabelle appears that they are grasping at anything, which could work to our favor should we choose to use it."

"We all agree, then? Annabelle will stay out of it unless her involvement becomes an absolute necessity." Warford and Antonio nod in agreement, and I'm relieved. The charity dinner planned for the children's home suddenly comes to mind.

"Warford, remember I told Foster and Cooley that I would sponsor a charity dinner for the children's home. That's coming up next week, right?"

"Yes, it is," Warford replies. "But I don't think that is a viable opportunity. Too many people and we are not going to have the luxury of waiting. This is on top of us now, and time is of the essence. Foster has upped the ante. We must prepare to meet this head-on this very minute." Warford pauses and lowers his eyes to the floor as if he's searching for the right words to say.

"I know that look," Antonio says. "What's going on?"

"Warford?" I ask, bracing for whatever bombshell he's about to drop. He looks up at me and smiles. Not a smile of friendliness and comfort. More like a smile of *I have something to say that you may not like.*

"Alright, here it bloody goes then. I received a telephone call from an old friend of yours today, Sam. It was unexpected, to say the least."

"What friend was that?" I ask, perplexed as to who he could possibly be referring to.

"Detective Malcolm Madison," Warford replies carefully.

"Mal?" That name gets my attention. I feel like someone just reached into my guts, grabbed a handful, and began to twist. I haven't thought of him in a long time, and any time his name is mentioned, I promptly dismiss it and pay no mind. Our love affair is a thing of the past, and I have made peace with it. Still, I find myself with butterflies in my stomach at the news that he called. "What in the world could he want? Is it about Felicity? He's assigned to her case, isn't he?" I knew that it had to be something to do with Felicity, and it made sense he would contact me.

"No, Darling, it is not about Felicity. He did not even mention it. Apparently, he is not even in the city. He is in River Dell County helping with the investigation into the murder of none other than Sister Mary Agnes."

"You're joking!" I exclaim. "Why would he be involved in that up there?"

"I don't know," Warford replies, bewildered. "He didn't explain, and I did not ask. He offered no explanation or particular reason for his call, but he did say that he is concerned for you because of a piece of evidence that was found on the Sister. Something threatening. He believes it pertains to you, and he is asking that you come up to Tarrytown and talk to them about it. So, you see now what Antonio and I have been saying about you being in extreme danger. This is serious, Sam and we have got to tread carefully."

"Evidence? And who's 'them'?" I insist.

"*Them,*" Warford replies with emphasis, "meaning himself and Captain Grayland, the homicide detective from LA and, of course, the coroner."

"The detective who investigated the murders of the Sisters

in LA with Del Ray," Antonio adds to Warford's explanation.

"I remember.   But evidence *on* Sister Mary Agnes?" I inquire, feeling spooked about what they found, and curious about what kind of evidence relating to me was on Sister Mary Agnes? I'm thinking out loud, struggling to reconcile that direct evidence pertaining to me was found on a murder victim. "Mal wouldn't have called unless it was serious, so, of course, I'll go," I say confidently, hiding the overwhelming fear inside me. "When does he want me there?"

"It will put you out in the open," Warford warns. "And I am not sure if this is the proper way to handle it."

Antonio agrees.

"And what am I accomplishing just sitting in this room?" I demand. "Both of you are starting to wear on my nerves." My voice is calm but stern. It's the voice my mother taught me to use in business dealings. The voice of control. The voice of power. "First, you tell me that I need to step up, take charge and clean up a I don't know a covert mess, and then you tell me that because I'm in danger, I shouldn't do what you said I should do. And according to what you said to me earlier, Warford, they're out to get me! The danger is everywhere, you said! Whether I run or whether I stay! Mother would want me to fight, you said! Which is it! I need a decision now."

I say to him exactly what he said to me, and I wait for a reply. But neither of them breathed a word. They know I'm right, and I'm quick to throw it in their face.

"Good! I thought you'd see it my way. I refuse to hide out like a scared rabbit when others sacrificed their lives. I don't believe that to be very honorable. Besides, we need to pay our respects to the Sister. She was important to Mother. And Mal wouldn't have called, believe me, if it wasn't something significant."

Warford and Antonio exchange glances, reconciling with the fact that I've made up my mind and I speak sense, but Warford, being Warford, refuses to let it go without a final word.

"It is not that I don't trust Mal, Sam, but there is more that needs to be considered before you talk to him. There are elements he is not aware of, and I believe it best to keep it that way until we get a grasp of the situation up there."

"Ok alright, what situation?" I ask. Warford responds with stern conviction.

"The situation is this. If he is assisting in the investigation, that means he has encountered the River Dell County Coroner, who just happens to be Anashe, a/k/a, Dr. Olive Alexander. She's the owner of the diamond. She is the child who found the diamond and carried it out of South Africa. She is the girl in the picture. Now, do you see the need for caution?"

"Mother's Anashe?   She's the Coroner in River Dell County." I don't say anymore. I don't have the words. I hold my head in my hands and press on my temples the complexity of it all is beating my brain to death.

"She's in grave danger," Warford warns. "Anyone involved in this investigation is! Del Ray is here and killing, and he won't hesitate to do what he needs to do or what he's ordered to do. So, you see the need for extreme caution here. Until we know what Anashe has told the police, we must approach this very carefully. I guarantee that Del Ray is planning on entrenching himself in this investigation. That's his purpose for being here. He was feeling you out to see what you know, and I guarantee he will be showing up in Tarrytown soon. If he sees you there, you're in trouble. In fact, we're all in trouble! If we are going, we need to beat him to it. We need to be up there very early tomorrow morning! And when Del Ray realizes, if he hasn't already, who is heading up this investigation, he won't hesitate. He will kill them all except for Dr. Alexander. He will want information from her, and we all know what that means. We cannot fail Valentina, and we cannot fail Anashe. We will not get a second chance."

It's amazing to me that after all these years, Warford's devotion to Mother and Anashe hasn't wavered. Not one iota. Just like his devotion to me. I smile at him, reach out for his hands, and squeeze them to reassure him that I'm with him all the way, just as he has reassured me throughout my entire life.

"We'll all be alright, Warford. Your promise to Mother and Anashe won't be broken. You have my word. We leave for Tarrytown tonight, but first, I want to take Annabelle and Mrs. Lilly to Long Island. Warford, you handle the other staff. I don't want anyone to stay here. Long Island is safer." Warford and Antonio look at me as if they've seen a ghost. "Well! Are you going to just sit there, or are we going to get moving?" I order.

As Antonio, Warford and I depart, walking briskly toward the elevator, an immense feeling of power floods my spirit. For the first time in my life, I feel like I am part of something bigger - and more important than myself. This is Mother's legacy to me - the good and bad and I am embracing it with the full force of my being. As for Anashe, she is also part of Mother's legacy, and Mother loved her very much. She is the sister I never had, and I am determined to do everything in my power to protect her. *I promise Mother. I promise with all my heart.*

****

Sam

The Murder of Annabelle

Callahan Townhouse

Late Night– Monday, May 21ˢᵗ, 1928

Mrs. Lilly is waiting in the study as we return from the upper floors. She seems impatient, announcing that Annabelle is still resting and inquiring as to whether she can begin to prepare a late supper.

"Thank you, Mrs. Lilly," I reply, "but there won't be time for that. Please get things together. We're leaving for Long Island in one hour. I'll raise Annabelle." My watch reads 8:00. "Everyone is ready to leave by nine. I want to be in Tarrytown as early as possible, but I'm going to Long Island first. Mrs. Lilly, please call Mrs. Dwyer and let her know we are coming."

"As you wish, Madame." I hear her faintly say as I ascend the stairs to Annabelle's room.

I knock on Annabelle's door - and wait for her to respond. No response. I open the door and enter, noticing that she's lying on the bed in her clothes, curled up and covered with a blanket. My abrupt entrance startles her from her peaceful sleep.

"Sam? What is it? What's going on?" Her voice is groggy and sleepy. "Annabelle, you need to get up. We are leaving in an hour to go to the house on Long Island."

"Sam? What's going on?" she asks again, her voice quiet but with soft tones of sleepy confusion.

"I'm sorry, but I don't have time to explain it right now. I'll explain it in the car. I need you to go downstairs and help Mrs. Lilly get what she needs to get done, please. I'll be down shortly." Annabelle continues to sit quietly on the bed, stretching and yawning, trying to wake up. I lost my patience with her and raised my voice. "Annabelle! You need to c'mon. We are leaving!" Her eyes widen at the harsh, commanding tone of my voice, and she quickly throws the blanket back and slides from the bed, her feet hitting the floor. She fluffs her hair with her fingers, runs her hands down her dress to straighten it, and darts toward the bedroom door. As she opens it, she glances back at me over her shoulder before closing the door behind her.

I quickly change – out of my dress and into a pair of - leather pants, a blouse, and tall, black leather lace-up boots. I retrieve from the darkest corner of the closet a wide, heavy-duty belt equipped for carrying two handguns and ammunition. I swing it around my waist and buckle it, surprised at its weight. It's been a very long time since

I wore it last. In fact, I can't remember when that would have been. I pull my custom made, long leather coat from its hangar and sling it over my right arm and then my left. I'm a mixed bag of emotions as I hurriedly dress in clothes that haven't seen the light of day for I don't know how long. I'm exhilarated yet scared, and I haven't felt scared for a very long time. I shake off the fear like the dust on my boots. I don't have time to get mired down by such things now.

A fleeting thought of Morgan Fellows sitting in a jail cell tickles me as I dig through the pockets of my jacket. I'm rather shocked he hasn't called me, but also relieved. I wouldn't go anyway. The thought of Morgan Fellows quickly dissipates as I pull a small piece of paper from my right-hand jacket pocket, its jagged edges preserved as if time in the pocket stood still. I unfold it gently, opening it to reveal the writing inside.

I love you,

Mal

My heart becomes heavy – a constricting lump forms in my throat, and I'm overwrought with emotion. I have never seen this! He had to have put it in my pocket the day I took him flying – the day he flew for the first time – our last day together – the day I told him goodbye. I remember now. That day was the last time I wore this jacket.

I loved him so much, but our love was plagued with a toxic

situation that was too much for me to bear. Mal needed to be with his dying wife, not spending her last moments on this earth with me. We didn't plan to fall in love. It just happened. Maybe because he needed relief from his loneliness and the grueling horror of his wife slowly dying – and maybe - my need to be loved by a man. But Mal wasn't just any man. I loved him more than anything, but the day I accidentally ran into Mal and his wife at the hospital changed that forever. The sight of her frailty, obviously on death's door, made me feel dirty and ashamed. Before that day, she was merely a name, not a person. Before then, I could lie and convince myself that what we were doing was okay. But seeing her so frail and desperate to hang on to every minute - I couldn't handle it. The guilt was simply too much to bear, and I resigned myself to the reality that my relationship with Mal – while beautiful in its way - was something I had to end.

As I hold the small note in my hand, tears fill my eyes as I recall the last words that we spoke to each other. We accepted that our love was for a purpose whose time had run out. I gave him the courage to face his wife's impending death, and he gave me the courage to face life without my mother. Bittersweet - tragic that, once again, we are drawn together by circumstances that are against us. How tragic, indeed.

I long to leave the strangle-hold of the day behind and just stay in the moment of the beautiful note, but I can't. My life has changed, and Mal is a part of my past. I crush the note in the palm of my hand, symbolizing once and for all those days are gone. I'm tempted to throw it away, but something stops me. Instead, I gently and with loving care, press the crumple out with my fingers and put it back in my pocket where I found it - where Mal left it. Deep breath. Another deep breath. I wipe the tears from my eyes and put him out of my mind - close off my heart. I walk to the side of the bed and sit down. I've been running on high adrenaline all day, and my legs feel like lead. I open my bedside bureau drawer- no real purpose in mind, just one of those things you do because. There's a pack of cigarettes hiding in the corner.

I rarely smoke anymore, even though it's all the rage these days. Felicity smoked. Her long, elegant, black cigarette holder comes to mind and brings a smile to my face. The way she held it between her fingers was so flagrantly fashionable and dramatic. She always looked as if she just stepped right out of her own magazine. Felicity. Things didn't quite work out for you, did they?

I smoked a lot in college – thought it made me look like part of the cool crowd, you know – independent woman and all. All it did was give me bad breath, make my chest hurt - cause my clothes and hair stink. Mother frowned on it vehemently, so I smoked more around her just to irritate her. So childish. *Forgive me, Mother,* I say out loud, taking the cigarettes from the bedside bureau. I strike a match, the familiar smell of sulfur filling my nostrils. I light one up, taking delight in the crackling sound of the tobacco as it is kissed by the fire of the match. I take a long, slow drag and enjoy every bit of it. There's about one swig of scotch in the carafe, so I pour it into a glass and take a sip. Prohibition! It's really been rather a stupid attempt to control a vice that people refuse to let go of. Oh well. I'm not a politician and have no desire to be one. Apparently, I am a spy by proxy. A spy! *Ha!* I laugh to myself. Who would have thought? Not in a million years would I ever. One swig and it's gone – one final lovelorn drag off my cigarette before stubbing it out in the ashtray. I can faintly hear Warford barking orders downstairs. Just one more minute alone is all I need. Just one more minute. I rise from the bed and look out my second-story window.

The city lights and the night sounds coming from the street below comfort me. A welcomed distraction shattered only by the voice in my head scolding me to stop wasting time and get downstairs. I start to surrender my window vigil, fully intending to go downstairs, but something stops me. Something catches my eye down on the street. A large black sedan is moving past the townhouse very slowly. People on the sidewalk begin to scream and scatter! My gut tightens, squeezed with dread. My mouth goes dry as I see what looks like the glimmer of a gun barrel. And in a split-second, a hail of bullets, *Tat – tat-tat-tat-tat-tat-tat-tat-tat-tat-tat-tat-tat-tat-tat-tat-tat-tat-tat-tat-tat-tat-tat-tat-tat-tat-tat-* earsplitting pings, shattering glass – screams!

"Oh God! Oh My God!" I scream as I fall to the floor, ducking - covering my head with my hands – avoiding the window – paralyzed by shock and fear as the shooter sprays bullets back and forth - the sound of shattering glass piercing the night air! And as fast as it started, it stopped – the squeal of tires on the pavement – the sound of the sedan racing away! I'm scared to death to look! I'm frozen. I can't move! People are screaming in panic! But is it from the street or inside? *Downstairs! I need to get downstairs! No, no, no! Oh, please! Please! Please let everyone be alright!* I scream in my head as I crawl on my belly across the floor toward the bedroom door. I reach the door, extend my arm to the door handle, and pull it down! The door cracks open, and I peek out, frightened of what I might see. I roll on my left side, grab the door, and kick it open, pulling myself into the hallway. I listen! Someone's crying!

"Warford! Warford!" I scream. No answer. "Warford!" I scream again. "Antonio!" I hear the crying again! It's Annabelle or Mrs. Lilly! I crawl to the stairs and instantly stand up on my feet, running as fast as my legs will carry me down the long staircase. Shattered glass is everywhere, scattered about the floor and outside on the sidewalk. The heavy burgundy drapes bow as they are sucked by the wind through the glassless window frames. The front of the townhouse is obliterated. "Warford! Antonio!" That's when I saw Mrs. Lilly lying in the foyer. She's bleeding profusely from her face, shards of glass protruding like tiny spears. She's on her side in a fetal position, her hands covering her ears.

"Mrs. Lilly! Mrs. Lilly! Are you hit? Are you shot!" I shake her a little to make her realize that I'm trying to talk to her. She removes her hands from her ears to hear my voice, and it's then I realize blood has pooled in her eyes, and she can't see me.

"Madame! Oh Madame! I can't see!" She shouts in anguish. She reaches for her eyes to wipe them, but I grab her hands, keeping them away from the wounds.

"No! Mrs. Lilly don't touch your eyes! Just wait. Just leave it. Just be still!" She nods erratically and lowers her hands from her face. "Are you shot!" I ask again forcefully, hoping she will hear my voice - despite her terror!

"No, no, I don't think so," she replies, her voice cracking and wavering from fear.

"Do you know where Annabelle is?" I ask desperate for an answer but trying not to panic her more.

"I heard her scream. It came from over by the kitchen." Mrs. Lilly replies, her eyes squeezed tightly shut, the blood mixing with the tears that stream down her cheeks.

"Warford!" I scream again. Mrs. Lilly instinctively tries to rub her eyes again and again, I warn her. "Don't touch your eyes until we know if they have glass in them, Mrs. Lilly. Can you sit up?" I help her sit up and prop her back against the foyer wall. "Mrs. Lilly. I need you to listen to me. I need to leave you for a minute and find everyone else. Now, don't move - stay here, and I'll be right back! And don't rub your eyes!" I command. She nods her head, eyes squeezed tightly, and I start calling for Annabelle.

"Annabelle! Annabelle!" I scream, running frantically through the house, checking the sitting room and the study. Nothing. Wait. Something on the floor. Blood! Large drops of blood lead toward the kitchen. I follow where the trail leads, and that's where I find her. Annabelle - on the floor - motionless. I fall to my knees beside her. Her beautiful face is sliced and stabbed by glass, her hands covered in blood, grasping her abdomen, her eyes open, a dead stare that is unmistakable. "Annabelle! Annabelle!" I scream her name and shake her, refusing to let her go, refusing to believe that she is dead. "Annabelle!" I cry, my shoulders shaking violently, suppressing the agony inside me that's trying to escape. I can't hold it back any longer. "No! No!" I cry, pushing strands of her blood-soaked copper hair away from her eyes. I hear Warford calling my name, but I don't answer. I'm paralyzed with grief. "I'm so sorry, Sweet girl," I say, cradling her head in my arms, thinking that if I just give her a minute, she will open her eyes.

"Madam! Are you alright!" I glance at him over my shoulder, tears streaming down my face. "Oh, Dear Lord." Warford squeezes my shoulder and softly says, "I'm so sorry, Madam. She's gone. She's gone." He pulls at my shoulder, trying to convince me to leave her, but I refuse, pulling away from him, crying… crying.

"Annabelle," I say again, repeating her name as if that gesture will make everything alright. Warford squeezes my shoulder again. "She was a rare and beautiful woman with a contagious personality. Funny and daring and always happy. I loved that about her." I wipe the tears from my eyes. Warford helps me to my feet. And it strikes me! "Mrs. Lilly. Oh, God! Mrs. Lilly! I left her in the foyer!"

"Antonio is with her, Madam," Warford assures me. "He's taking care of her, and she is going to be fine. She has some glass in her face. It looks worse than it is." He smiles a sympathetic smile, puts his arm around me, and leads me to the study where Antonio is taking care of Mrs. Lilly.

"Alright, everyone!" Warford barks. "We need to get out! Antonio, would you please get that case, and I'll get this one."

"What about Annabelle?" I ask, heartbroken at the thought of leaving her behind. "I don't want to leave her here alone." The tears begin to flow again.

"Madam, the assassins have come to your front door. Death has come calling for you. I am sorry about Annabelle, but we must leave immediately. She will not be alone. Mrs. Lilly will stay with her and handle the police. They will be arriving soon, and we cannot be here when they do. Foster has police on the payroll. This is an example of how far he will go to get what he wants. I'll take this."

I know he is right, and as hard as it is for me to abandon her here, I am fully aware that we can't stay. Warford grabs the handle of a long silver case, and Antonio brings a black utility bag filled with ammunition and other weapons. I quickly open my father's safe and retrieve two revolvers, holster them on my belt, along with the ammunition and two knives. Mrs. Lilly is still bleeding badly from the shards of glass in her face, and the towel I gave her is soaked, so I immediately take all the towels from the downstairs bathroom and set them beside her.

"I hope this is enough," I say as I set the towels down, making sure she can reach them without much effort.

"It's fine, Madam. Don't worry about me." I smile my bravest smile to reassure her, but I'm not comfortable with Mrs. Lilly being a decoy left to face this all on her own.

"Sam, Mrs. Lilly knows what she is doing, don't you?" Warford announces with notable confidence.

I don't feel very reassured. Warford and Mrs. Lilly are smiling at each other as if they share a sordid secret. "She is a master of diversion," he praises. "Never known her to fail. Mrs. Lilly has saved all our lives at one point in time or another. She will take care of this, and that is for certain." He and Antonio approach Mrs. Lilly, lift her right hand, and lightly kiss it. "We will be seeing you soon," Warford assures, confident in her ability to distract. "You get to a doctor and then take a nice long vacation with Mrs. Dwyer. We will be in touch."

Mrs. Lilly nods, seemingly comfortable with her assigned task and appreciative of Warford's praise and obvious admiration. As I stand before her, I realize that I've known this woman my entire life, and never did I ever imagine her to be the woman sitting before me now.

"Mrs. Lilly… "

"Go, dear," she orders, shooing me away, her eyes coaxing and demanding. "Everything will be alright. You will be alright. You have your mother's spirit, a spirit of fire." I wrap my arms around her and squeeze her tight, worried that I might never see her again, then leave her to catch up with Warford and Antonio.

Warford opens the false door to the tunnel, and we file through. I stop and turn to wave to Mrs. Lilly one more time before he secures the door, pushing the button and resetting the bookcase. She returns a wave a smile, and blows me a kiss. I'm troubled and uncomfortable – leaving behind my life, my home – Annabelle. I take a deep breath as Warford flips the switch that will light our way through the tunnel that ends at the back of the lobby of

Brandenberger's Chocolates and Confections. I squeeze my eyes tight, my heart racing, and like jumping off a cliff, I take the first step toward the unknown.

****

Sam, Warford & Antonio

The Get Away

The Underground

9:00 p.m. – Monday, May 21 *st*, ***1928***

W e sprint toward our escape. I'm scared to death of what lies ahead but determined to face it head-on. A flame of anger begins to burn in the pit of my stomach at the thought of all those who have betrayed me. Those thoughts serve me well, fueling a new and surprising strength within me. Felicity and Morgan already paid, but Foster, Cooley, and Del Ray – your bill is due.

Antonio slowly opens the tunnel door that leads into the lobby – cautiously - just a crack - instinctively poking his head through, ensuring the coast is clear. He swings the door open and holds it for Warford and me. Once through, Antonio sprints, leading the way down the lobby hall and around the corner to a door marked 'utility closet'. *Utility closet?* I say to myself, but things are moving so fast I don't have time to question. He opens the door and motions us in. On the other side of the door is pitch-black darkness – until he turns on the light, revealing a winding, narrow staircase, descending downward as if going to the pit of hell - refusing any light the landing has to offer. Warford begins the descent, and Antonio takes my arm, urging me to do the same. But I resist, hesitant to attempt to navigate the stairs in the dark. Then, a light, a single light, illuminates Warford's way. Warford waits, and Antonio again urges me to set aside my fear and forge ahead. I take the first step down and then another until I reach Warford, with Antonio close behind me.

"Stay close, Darling," Warford says, picking up the pace. Five more steps down, a ray of light blazes forth as the light behind us goes out. On – off, on – off, the lights alternate with precision as we make our way down, down, down. I'm blown away - my mind wracked with questions, but there's no time. Warford and Antonio keep me at a racer's pace, taking each step as quickly as my feet will allow. Finally, the end. Antonio comes from behind me, keying a door. A door that leads to another surprise. A garage. And a car.

"Warford?" I say, my eyes wandering the space and pointing toward a car that I never knew existed. "I don't remember…"

"It was your mother's," he replies with a tone of pride. "And now, it's yours. She commissioned it specially modified and fortified with steel doors and special glass. Armored - bulletproof. She never had to use it, but she suspected that you would. She was a master at thinking ahead."

He and Antonio open the rear door, and I peer inside. It compares to the back of a limousine. Dual seats – leather. It's stunning!

"Do not be fooled," Warford says with a gleam in his eye. "Let me show you."

My eyes glaze over in amazement as he raises the entire back seat to reveal a showcase of the latest weaponry, set up and ready to fire. I marvel at the genius of it all, of everything I've witnessed so far. *You were a master, weren't you, Mother,* I quietly say under my breath.

"All it takes is the push of a button – located on the dashboard. Should the need arise to engage these beauties, you simply move to a little jump seat there," he points, "which automatically opens when the guns are ready. Maximum protection as necessary, right Antonio?" he says, rubbing his hands together – giddy. Antonio responds with a nod and a smile but says nothing, as usual. "This is the best part of the job!" Warford exclaims like a kid with a toy, a side of him rarely seen, the proper Brit always front and center. "Isn't she a beauty! HaHa! I do miss driving British cars! American-made cars just aren't my cup of tea," he says, caressing the steering wheel as if he and the car are old lovers. "Valentina had this car sent from London."

Yeah…, I think w*ith the help of British Intelligence.*

He inspects the dash from top to bottom. It's a maze of mysterious buttons, monitors, and gauges, and he knows every button and its designed function. I watch him intently, fascinated by the otherworldly bells and whistles that are liken to a work of science fiction rather than a car. Warford and Antonio ready the car for travel, testing every switch, button, and monitor.

"A pre-flight check isn't this in-depth," I say jokingly. "Mother certainly kept…."

"Shhh!" Warford insists, exiting the car, raising his hand for instant quiet. He listens intently. Antonio and I freeze on his command, awaiting confirmation of the sound that has caused him alarm. "I hear sirens. The police are here."

I strain to hear the sound – and then - faintly – ever so faintly – sirens.

"Warford?" I whisper.

"No need to worry, now," Warford reassures, his expression diminished from level 10 to level 3. "Mrs. Lilly will focus their attention. She will make sure that they focus on the shooting. Trust me, we are fine, but we must make haste."

Antonio hurriedly finishes stowing the cases in the trunk while Warford starts the car. I immediately get into the spacious back seat and close the door. Antonio takes his seat to Warford's left in the front and nods his head that all is ready. I glance out the back window. The garage lights suddenly go out as if instructed to do so, and once again, the darkness takes over. Warford is engrossed in the dashboard – our only source of light - patiently waiting for the multitude of indicators that signal the car is armed and ready for anything. I lean forward, straining to catch a glimpse of what lies ahead through the front windshield. I feel like a child, trapped - waiting for the monster who hides, then rushes from his ill-laden corner to destroy me. But with the push of a button, all is well, and we begin to move ever so slowly - and light – light bursts forth in symphony with the car showing us the path of escape. I lean forward again, excited and scared. *More tunnels. More living lights. You prepared for everything, didn't you mother?* I say to myself, breathless, my palms sweaty with anticipation as Antonio depresses the button, declaring itself '*T. Lights*'.

Warford accelerates, the engine whining like a finely tuned ship. He rolls up the window and grasps the wheel, his delight uncontained. He and the car are one – the master and his machine – moving like a speeding bullet toward our lighted escape. Again, I'm stunned with disbelief and amazement as the highly perched lights strategically illuminate in synchronization with the car.

"Unbelievable!" I yell from the backseat, frightened but loving the uncertainty of every second, embracing the unknown. I peer through the back window, watching the lights go out as we pass. It is all so surreal – amazing. My own living science fiction novel.

"Valentina had many loyal people willing to support her - genius people – people behind the scenes – scientists, bankers – good people. Now you know why she was so successful – and why Felicity and a lot of other operatives were so jealous. She always had the advantage. She always had her secrets. Her arsenal was comprised of brilliant scientists, courageous loyalists, and fierce enforcers. '*The Essential Three*', she called them. Brains, loyalty, and tactical specialists. That's the three."

He acknowledges Antonio with a pat on the arm and a look of unwavering respect when speaking of *tactical specialists. The Essential Three: brains, loyalty, and tactical specialists.* I repeat her manifesto, burning it into my mind. Her success is my success, as always.

The car begins to slow, gears downshifting rapidly to adjust to the command of its master until movement is barely noticeable. I'm curious, and I strain to focus on what's happening in front of us, but visibility is zero. Darkness befalls us again. We come to a stop, and instantly – dim lights reveal that we are parked in an elevator box. Antonio engages a square button on the dash, and my ears are filled with the sound of mechanical gears creaking and grinding.

"Metal blocking mechanisms!" Warford yells. "Behind each

tire to keep the car from rolling during ascension! Antonio, take us up!"

With another push of a button and the gate closes behind us, mechanisms engage, and the elevator slowly carries us upward. It's a one-minute ride to the topside. Every mechanism disengages, and Warford allows the car to roll gently and cautiously forward. We exit with stealth into a large, secluded lot, surrounded by heavy fencing, concealing us from view.

Crawling through the darkness, we creep toward an iron gate that opens on queue, detecting our approach. Once through the gate, Warford turns on the headlamps. Finally, we are on the road and steaming toward Tarrytown, taking less traveled roads to avoid the heavy traffic of the city.

The car rides so smoothly, seemingly weightless, floating above the road. My eyes become heavy, and I struggle to keep them open. I rest my head against the seat and close my eyes – an attempt at a little rest, but I'm unable to shut down, and the scenario of the day plays over and over in my mind - anxious racing thoughts, my heartbreak about Annabelle, Mommy's murder, on and on images flash like a movie reel out of control! But then, a wash of calm comes over me. I see Mommy. Her hands are extended. She's encouraging me as she always did - reassuring me that everything will be alright, that she trusts me, but most importantly- she loves me. *I love you too, Mommy,* I say softly as I picture her in my mind, clutching tightly to sweet thoughts of her. How beautiful she was – how much I love her – how much I miss her – how much I need her. Although today has been full of unimaginable discoveries about her, she is and forever will be the one person I love most in this life, and nothing will ever change that.

****

Special Agent Dominic Del Ray

Shaking the Tree

Del Ray's Room – The Empire Hotel, New York City

Late Evening – Monday, May 21ˢᵗ, 1928

Del Ray paces in his crummy, dismal hotel room, smoking a cigar and downing a bottle of scotch he bought from a black-market seller in an alley four blocks away. He wishes he had bought two bottles instead of one. He's antsy. His adrenalin is off the charts. He's waiting for word confirming that the order to warn Sam Callahan has been carried out. It was a necessary move to convince her to turn over the diamond. Foster will be furious, but what the hell? Let him be mad. She needed to be shaken up. And shaken up good! Felicity and Morgan were supposed to take care of her a long time ago. But no matter now. He chuckles to himself, giddy that they are out of his way – one less obstacle between him and the diamond. Once he has that, The Daughter can have it. She's proven herself, and there's no doubt she has a hatred for Sam Callahan that burns like the devil.

He's getting impatient. Word from O'Bannion is long overdue. He fights the urge to call the NYPD for information about the attempted murder of the ever-important Sam Callahan. They'd give it to him, no doubt, but he doesn't think it smart to risk it. Someone might question why the Bureau of Investigation would show an interest so early on. No. He thinks it best to keep his distance for now. And the shooters he hired -well - they don't exactly fly under police radar.

The more he drinks, the more frenzied he becomes. His plans have not worked out. Finding the diamond, offing Foster, Cooley, and anyone else involved has dragged on far too long. He should have heard something by now! He takes a swig and downs half a glass of scotch. He refills his glass, the bottle nearing empty. He thought the Sisters in Los Angeles would lead him straight to the diamond. After all, who wouldn't choose to live over the alternative he offered? He underestimated their commitment and their faith. He underestimated Valentina's reach from the grave. He underestimated Sister Mary Agnes, who also refused to reveal the secret in lieu of a slow and torturous death. How long could he resurrect *The Butcher*? How long before someone discovers that *The Butcher* has long been dead? Valentina's people are out there. He knows his days are numbered. He needs to disappear, and quickly. But not without the diamond! No – not without the diamond. He's invested too much time and effort to abandon that fortune now. He must see it to completion, and losing is not an option.

His drunken, paranoid, erratic thoughts are abruptly interrupted by a tapping at his hotel room door. He waits. He's not sure if he really heard it or if the alcohol is playing tricks on him. *Tap, Tap, Tap, Tap.* There it is again. His revolver is laying on the bed. He tiptoes to avoid detection, picks up the revolver, pulls the hammer back very slowly, quietly, and steps ever so lightly toward the door, his heart racing. He reaches the door and calmly says, "Who is it?"

"I gawtta message for Ray," replies the hushed voice on the other side of the door.

I nervously tighten my grip on my revolver, hiding it behind my back as I crack the door open ever so slowly. I see a middle-aged, fat man through the crack, an overly gnawed toothpick between his teeth. I don't recognize him and attempt to slam the door shut, but he plants his hand on the door, preventing me from slamming it in his face.

"You need 'a let me in. I don't want anyone ta see me out here in the hallway in front a' your door."

He's calm but hints at intimidation, which amuses me. He doesn't know who I am. He thinks he's dealing with Special Agent "Ray". The tiny flame begins to burn inside me as I lock my eyes directly on him, my face wrought with wrath at his gross misjudgment of me. It's a look he knows well. A clear signal that he better rethink - reign in his attitude - and get himself in check. His expression is priceless. It's a look I enjoy – that I've seen a million times. I think I'll kill him just to make a point. I don't like being kept waiting, and I don't like his attitude.

"Who are you?" I growl, deliberate and threatening. He looks around, making sure there's no one in the hallway to hear. He's changed his tune, and he knows he better answer.

"I'm with O'Bannion, ya know?" His voice is low and tense.

"Yeah?" I reply sarcastically. "Name?"

He doesn't speak. He avoids my gaze by dropping his eyes to the floor. I don't really need to know his name; I just like toying with him – controlling him. Old habit I happen to like.

"Name!" I demand, opening the door just enough to grab his arm and pull it through, then *SLAM!* He is trapped between the door and the frame, and every shove of his arm causes him immense and excruciating pain. Puts a delightful spin on things. Makes me smile a little.

"Okay, okay, okay!" he says, anything to make it stop. "I'm Jerry, but they cawl me Jazzy." His voice is shaky and broken from trying to control the scream that is dying to get out. I nod my head and grin.

"You mobsters do love your nicknames, don't you.?" I tease wickedly. He doesn't answer. "Well, *Jazzy* – what's the message?" I demand. He answers immediately with no hesitation, his voice a mere whimper.

"The job you ask for is done. But – there was some collateral damage."

"Collateral damage?" I reply angrily, spit flying as I increase the pressure on the door, enjoying his squeal. "It better not be who I'm thinking, or Mr. O'Bannion will have a rather large problem," I threaten, pushing the door tighter and tighter on his arm, his face writhing with pain.

"No-no!" he says, choking back a scream. "Mr. O'Bannion told me to assure you that it's not her." Jazzy knows. He knows exactly who I'm referring to, and I appreciate his gracious clarification. "It was her assistant - Annabelle."

Oh! I think to myself. I'm kind of sorry to hear that. I liked Annabelle. Foster was an idiot to use her anyway. I release Jazzy's arm from the door. He shakes it and rubs it to relieve the pain - get the blood flowing again. He's just lucky I decided not to break it. "Okay, now beat it," I growl, slamming the door in his face. I sprint the few steps across the room, open the window, and crawl through to the fire escape. I scan the entire alley, and then I spot it. Jazzy's car. Perfect.

I quickly and quietly scale the rickety steps to the last rung and stop. My head is spinning from the alcohol, and I feel sick. I only have a second to compose myself. *Stupid!* I know better! But I can't let him go. No. Never. O'Bannion needs a warning, and Jazzy – well, he just needs to die. The spinning in my head subsides, but my stomach is still in an uproar. I peer down to the ground. It's a long way down, and there's no extension ladder. I'll hang from the bottom rung to close the gap. I hang for a few seconds, prepare for the pain, and drop. I hit the ground with both feet and roll - onto my side. The pain in my ankles and knees knocks the wind out of me, but - nothing I haven't felt before. These are the times when Pain Suppression training comes in very handy.

I hear the *tick, tick, tick* of shoe heels striking the pavement, heading in my direction right on time. I hoist myself off the ground and hobble ever so quietly and hide in a dark corner close to Jazzy's car and lie in wait. I hear him coming closer – closer – closer. As he rounds the rear of the car, the light of the moon catches his face. As he reaches for the door handle, I tap on the wall. Startled, he spins wildly toward the sound, fear in his eyes. He's facing me as I creep from my hiding place, standing face-to-face with him. He doesn't speak. His voice was captured by fear. He knows what's coming. There's nothing like witnessing the end, and I waste no time. With lightning speed, I strike the underside of his nose and with perfect precision, drive the bone straight into his brain, dropping him like a rock – his eyes rolled back in his head – dead. Works every time! I yank him from the ground by his coat, wrangle him into the driver's seat of his car, and shut the door. O'Bannion is the perfect cover. The cops will naturally think it's a mob hit. I wipe down the door handle, quickly check the ground for anything that could be incriminating, swat my hands together at a job well done, and walk away. Easy, peasy…doesn't get any better than that.

I stand below the fire escape, wondering how the hell I'm going to get back up there. If I hadn't been drunk, I would have thought of that earlier. A rare slip-up that could cost me. But I'm in luck! There are several wooden pallets stacked against the back of the hotel. I hustle to stack them one on top of the other until I can reach enough to pull myself up. My ankles and knees are screaming, but I scale the fire escape with moderate ease back to the open window – crawl through it into the room, and close it behind me. I limp to the bathroom, splash my face with cold water, and admire myself in the mirror. Remarkable. I do possess extraordinary abilities.

Ring, ring! Ring, ring! The telephone startled me to the point of anger. I dry my hands and collect myself. It could be the Bureau. Time to change skins. The ever steady and reliable Special Agent Dominic Del Ray might have to reappear. I hobble to the telephone and answer.

"Del Ray," I say with conviction, taking care to substitute the drunken slur with a professional and even tone. No one speaks, but they don't have to. I know who it is. I can hear that disgusting, heavy breathing. It's Cooley, the idiot! "What do you want, Cooley?" I ask impatiently. He has no business calling me. I deal with Foster and Foster alone. But I guess I'll entertain his ego – for the moment.

"You've rather mucked things up, Del Ray. That was a stupid stunt! He's not happy," Cooley replies. "Now she's *gone*, and we don't know where she is. The cops are involved. Bad move. Your job is to keep an eye on her, not take matters into your own hands unless told to do so. Not when it comes to her. Stay put until you hear from me, and I mean it. Understand?"

"Yes," I say with coolness, daydreaming of him taking a flying leap off a short pier – with my help. "What about Tarrytown? I'm supposed to head up there for the Bureau tomorrow." I have no intention of going to Tarrytown just yet, but I need to humor this moron.

"Stay put!" Cooley screams. "I'm sure you'll figure something out." There's a loud click in my ear, and the line disconnects. I laugh to myself and sigh at Cooley's inflated perception of the power they think they have over me. I pour the last of the whiskey into my drink glass and take a swig, then another, finishing it off. It burns like fire as it hits my empty stomach, heightening the alcohol-induced nausea already plaguing me. And it's not helping the pain in my knees and ankles one bit. I strain, pull myself from the chair, and hobble to the bathroom sink. I barely make it before the first heave brings up the putrid-smelling liquid that sets my throat and nostrils on ablaze. Again and again, the punishing heave forces the extraction of the whiskey until there's nothing. I rinse my mouth and my face. It's going to be a long night, but I choose to look at the bright side. My drunkenness creates the perfect excuse. As I stumble over to lay down on the bed, I peek out the window in the direction of Jazzy's car. It's still there. No cops yet. Didn't really expect any.

I fight to get my wallet out of my back pocket, then collapse on the bed. I rifle through my it, looking for the small piece of paper with McDonald's home number. I dial. No answer. I'll *stay put,* as Cooley said. Grimy little leach. It's a stretch, but someone shooting up Sam Callahan's townhouse could help with a delay. Anything to stay away from Tarrytown for a couple of days. Locate Sam. I'll notify McDonald at the Bureau in the morning and stall for time. Don't want to show my hand too quickly just yet. Besides, The Daughter is there keeping an eye on things. She'll report if need be. She's completely insane, and I dislike her immensely. But she is good, I'll give her that.

I lay back on the bed, closed my eyes, and focused my

thoughts on the diamond. Foster isn't going to know what hit him. And shooting up Sam Callahan's house, well – I'm just simply shaking the tree. It won't be long until she breaks. And then - I'll have the pleasure of killing them all and have all that money all to myself. A sinfully sweet dream as I fall into the blackness of alcohol-induced sleep.

****

Warford, Antonio, and Sam

Walls

Driving in the Rolls

Into the Night – Monday, May 21ˢᵗ, 1928

Warford quickly glances toward the back seat. Sam is

asleep. He conceals the ever-grinding feeling of guilt over the way she was told about Valentina and her past. He's not sure he would have been so strong. But he consoles himself in the keen awareness that not only is Sam's likeness to Valentina apparent on the outside, but it rages on the inside of her as well. And that is comforting. Because the reality is, as much as he'd like to protect her, there may come a point when that's not possible, and Sam will be required to entrap those who seek to entrap her. She's like a daughter to him, and this life is extremely dangerous. What if the worst happens? What if she's killed? He's disturbed by these thoughts banging around in his mind, but he knows he must set them aside for Sam's sake. Be strong for her.

Antonio is wide awake. He senses Warford's worry, and he's worried, too. He struggles, unsure of Sam's ability to handle the fallout, but he's sure of one thing. Foster and Del Ray will cave to demands. Hopefully, she can handle them from the outside – stay clean and untainted. That's his hope for her. Warford eyes the roadside for a public phone box. There was no time to call Mal before they left, and he wanted to call ahead to warn him that they were coming - and discuss where to meet. Discretion is paramount. Someone is likely watching – waiting. He spots a closed service station off to the right, a call box barely visible in the darkness. He pulls in, lights the call box with the headlamps, and informs Antonio, "I'm going to call ahead to Detective Madison. Let him know we are coming and arrange a place to meet. I'll be right back."

Antonio watches as Warford gets out of the car and enters the phone box. He keeps his eyes on Warford and surveils the surrounding area for any sign of suspicious activity. Warford picks up the telephone receiver, deposits change, dials, and waits. The minute he starts talking into the telephone phone receiver, Antonio hears Sam's voice from the back seat.

"What's going on?" I ask, stretching –and squinting my eyes to see out the front window. "Why have we stopped?"

"Warford thought it best to call ahead to Detective Madison. Arrange a place to meet," Antonio replies, eyes fixed on Warford in the call box.

I lean forward, noting that Antonio keeps his eyes straight ahead. I catch a glimpse of his features in the light of the moon shining through the window, outlining a perfect silhouette of his face. *How beautiful.* That thought made me a little uncomfortable. Everything about him makes me a little uncomfortable. Like the way the light illuminates certain lines around his eyes, enhancing his attractiveness. I'm a little embarrassed at these thoughts and instantly suppress any hint of my interest, hiding that I find him most attractive and intriguing. I felt it from the very moment I first saw him. He pulls at me in a way that no man has in a very long time, and I struggle to contain it. Shouldn't I be wary of a man who obviously has two distinct parts to his personality? My mind screams yes! Leave him alone! You don't need a man who's lived his life as an assassin, skilled in the art of murder, which he can commit without batting an eye. But my heart mysteriously and without judgment sees the other side of him. The quiet, spiritual, kind, and gentle man whose life hasn't been completely of his own choosing. Give him a chance, my heart says. And while you're at it, give yourself one too. I want to know him more. Much more.

"Antonio?" I ask cautiously. "Can I ask you something?" A tinge of panic hits me in the stomach, and I second–guess myself as to whether I should ask him anything. He turns his head but avoids eye contact.

"Sure," he replies, an uncertain tone shadowing his response

- allowing my question yet seemingly uncomfortable at the prospect of answering.

"Have you ever been married?" He squirms, his eyes dart to the left to look out the window. I can tell he's completely shutting me down - refusing my question. His combative gestures don't deter me. "Have you? I really want to know." He continues his vigil of blocking me out. His silence confirms the building of the wall. I take a step back – stop pushing. I'm disappointed.

"Alright," I respond, respecting his need to protect himself. "You don't have to tell me right now. But I'm hopeful that sometime soon, you will realize that you can trust me with the answer. I would really like to know more about *you*. Not the assassin. *You.*" He continues to stare out the window, unresponsive and stoic.

The moment is interrupted by Warford's return. I'm hopeful I made an impact on Antonio - punched a hole in that wall. That's a funny notion. That's good coming from me. I'm an expert in wall building. I'm even more of an expert at hiding behind them. I will soon have to show my face to one of those walls, and his name is Mal. Butterflies are churning in my stomach, and I'm scared. I never expected to ever be confronted by that ghost again in my lifetime. Antonio must feel the same way about his walls. Walls are a double-edged sword. They ensure stability and protection, but they also ensure bitterness and isolation. The sword will make you suffer the consequences of both. I want to change all of that.

"I mean it, Antonio. I want to know," I whisper sincerely as I retreat into the darkness of the back seat.

Warford opens the car door and slides in behind the wheel. "Mal is very anxious to talk to us, Sam. I told him we would be arriving in about 30 minutes." There's an uncomfortable silence between me and Antonio, which doesn't escape his keen sense of perception. "What's going on? Everything alright with you two?"

We both assure him there is no problem, but I detect a hint of disbelief in Warford's expression. All is quiet between the three of us as we drive to Tarrytown - toward Mal and the murder of Sister Mary Agnes – Anashe.

I'm hypnotized by the passing road, and as hard as I try to dismiss it, nervous thoughts about seeing Mal again after all this time hound me. I don't want our relationship dredged up. It's better left where it belongs – in the past - behind the wall. I reach into my jacket pocket and feel the precious note. The note was left to me by Mal at a time when our love was what kept us going. Why did I keep it? I should have thrown it away when I found it in the pocket. Something good to hold on to, I guess, but I know our love can never be rekindled.

Antonio is at the forefront of my mind, and I'm far from the same person who awoke this morning expecting nothing but normal.

I ended my relationship with Mal, and while I have fond memories, I ended it for a reason, and every fiber of my being resonates. *You can't go back.* One of the most important things that Mother taught me is to listen to that inner voice. She would say it's the voice of God telling me what to do and never to ignore it and never doubt it. Never…

****

Detective Malcom Madison

Anxiously Awaiting Sam

A Dark Road Next to the Tall Shadow Woods

Around 10:00 p.m. – Monday, May 21ˢᵗ, 1928

This road – this eerie, dark road - the same road that led

to the dumped body of Sista Mary Agnes. An inconspicuous road, known only by a few that leads from the morgue to the middle of nowhere. Warford requested seclusion. This is about as secluded as it gets. The headlamps burn through the darkness but do little to ease my nerves. I'm looking for the sign. The sign where I told Warford to meet me. *Tawll Shadow Woods*. That's it. That's it right there.

As I slowly roll up to the sign and park, I'm anxious, my guts in somewhat of a twist. I all but begged to be part of this investigation - to come to Tarrytown. Never dreamed it would be like this! That I would be faced with such wickedness. Evil killings. The murder of Sister Mary Agnes is an evil killing. Seclu*ded*. That word burns inside my brain. *Secluded. Secluded!* The murderer knew this road! No one would see, no one would hear. He could take his time. Do his business. *The Butcher!* I scream inside my head. It could be anybody! I'm at a loss, and I don't like it. Solving mob murders isn't usually too big a stretch. Most never get solved, even though ya know who did it. But this – this is different. Is this out of my league? I don't know, but I'm up to my eyeballs in it now, so there's no backing out.

It shouldn't be too much longer until they arrive. How will I handle Sam? I don't know that either. I hope… No! I can't let that interfere. This is very important. But I am worried about her. What's the connection? The diamond? The mines? Old and vicious - something that someone refuses to let rest - won't let go of. Something vengeful and deep. Doctor Alexander, Sam, Sister Mary Agnes, Cap'n Grayland, the Sisters in L.A. – all entangled together, tethered to this thing, living with the expectation that payment would come due. Pretty steep price, for sure. It is, without a doubt, the most sinister murder I've ever encountered.

Del Ray – the LA cop Cap'n spoke of. Is he this *Butcher?* Did he murder the Sisters in LA? Is he here in Tarrytown? Did he murder Sista Mary Agnes? Does he work alone, or is someone pulling his strings? So many questions – so many - but only one truth. One thing is for certain. Everyone involved is in great danger, and I'm relieved that Sam and Warford are on their way.

My mind is a mess, bantering scenarios back and forth without end. Does me no good without some answers. I'm hoping

Warford and Sam will have some. There's an evil element here, and it's gonna take tactics that are outside the law to catch this one. Where does that leave me? Do I wanna go down the path of being on the outside or…. Better get my mind straight about it. Time is runnin' out.

Sitting and waiting on Sam and Warford, I don't even hear so much as a cricket. I wish they'd hurry up already. 10:10. *C'mon, c'mon*, I say out loud, tapping my foot on the floor to break the unbearable, bone-chilling silence. I feel like a kid in bed – hiding under the covers, certain there's a monster in my closet. I don't like it out here. I need a distraction from my childish thoughts –stop scaring myself.

I haven't smoked for years, but I still carry a cigarette lighter. Never know when you might need one – I guess. Sam used to smoke – sometimes. I take my lighter from my shirt pocket and hold it in my hand, thinking of her like I've done every day for the last 2 years, robotically flicking the lid, back and forth, back, and forth – listening - c*lick-click-click-click,* open-close, open-close. It's the only sound to be heard, and it shatters the stillness and the dark of night. I realize that instead of helping to suppress my anxiousness, it's aggravating it and making it worse, escalating my already lacking confidence that I can solve or help to solve this case. I abruptly cease flicking the lid and put the lighter back in my pocket. Dead silence. Dead.

My eyes are heavy, and I'm so tired, but I don't dare close my eyes. I'd be out like a light in a minute. It's been a long and stressful day. I don't know how long I'll be able to continue the battle against my eyelids, and then – relief! A flash of light came toward me in the dark. It disappeared! No! Wait! There it is again! Please let that be them.

I'm cautious of the two headlamps heading my way. I sit up, peer down the dark road, and stay put in the car. Need to be sure it's them first. I sit and watch, mesmerized by the large, supernatural–looking Rolls Royce that glides slowly toward me and then stops. I recognize Warford but not the other man seated in the front. He's focused straight ahead with no sign of acknowledgement toward me. I wonder if Sam is with them. No sign of her yet.

I flash my lights and get outta the car, protecting myself behind the car door. The headlamps of the behemoth Rolls flash in response. Warford appears on the right side, waives, and gets back in the car. I guess that's my cue to lead them to where I want them to go. I get back in, put the car in drive, and head back to the morgue, fighting flashing seconds of blindness from the headlamps glaring through the back window. My thoughts focus on Sam. She's the one I really need – want to talk to. Warford was intentionally very cryptic on the telephone. And then there's Doctor Alexander and her tale of South Africa and Valentina. I'm excited yet apprehensive. Never dealt with spies before. But I'm gonna see it through, for better or worse.

The morgue is silhouetted in the moonlight, and I leave the roadway and pull up to the gated fence that protects the back-parking area and get out. I open the gate and motion Warford to go on into the enclosed area. I thought this would help to hide their presence, but that car! I don't know if it can be hidden! I've seen Rolls before, but obviously. This isn't your ordinary Rolls.

I surveyed the area, making sure we weren't followed. I get back in the car and drive through the gate, get out, scan once more, and close the gate. Warford meets me at the rear of the car, his hand extended, greeting me with his usual upper-crusty politeness. I shake his hand, and we exchange a few pleasantries, but my mind is on one thing and one thing alone. I'm anxiously waiting for Sam to make her appearance.

"She's in there," Warford says, intentionally holding my gaze, squeezing my hand a bit too hard, sending the message loud and clear. I get it, and I'm embarrassed that I'm so obvious.

"I didn't know if she would be able to come or not," I reply in a fumbling and juvenile manner.

"She did," Warford states in an edgy, almost confrontational tone. "And we are ready to answer any questions you have. But there are some issues we need to be clear on here, Mal. There is more to this than you know. Another side, another dimension, so to speak."

I'm intrigued by Warford's veiled admission that there are secrets to be uncovered. I won't admit what I know entirely, but I can't resist scraping him with the hint that I know quite a bit.

"I know," I reply confidently, stopping short of a know-it-all tone. "I had a rather long conversation with Doctor Alexander today, as well as Cap'n Graff Grayland. They both had very interesting accounts to share. And in fact, the name Valentina Brandenberger came up..."

"I know, I know, Mal," Warford interrupts forcefully. "All will be revealed." He releases the squeeze on my hand and walks with deliberate strides to the Rolls. The stranger in the left passenger seat opens the door and gets out. It strikes me odd that he exits the left, meaning the steering wheel is on the right. The car came from England. Maybe nothing – but it's worth noting.

I've never seen him before, but I've met the type. He's dangerous and no one to be trifled with. I can hear Warford talking – pointing at me. I'm the elephant in the room. I can't make out exactly what's being said. The stranger says nothing, simply nods his head, acknowledging me, but remains still. I have no doubt now. This man solidifies my suspicion that I'm in the presence of operatives. British operatives, to be exact. But this man is not just an operative. He's something else. Something else entirely.

Warford pulls the door handle and opens the back door of

the Rolls. I watch my heart racing as a leg emerges from inside the car to the ground. I know those boots. Know them anywhere. A lump consumes my throat, and I lose my breath as her hair – beautiful - soft black with waves ever so perfect, comes into view. Just as I remember. Stunning beauty beyond compare. My chest constricts as she engages me with a smile, those raven waves gently moving with the breeze. She mesmerized me from the first moment I met her, and she owns my heart, still.

She walks toward me as if floating on air and offers her hand. I'm disappointed, hoping for an embrace – to see that look in her eyes. The look that was meant for me and only me. But that's crazy - a lot to expect, I guess. So much time has passed between us. So, I take what I can get, accept the offer of her hand, and gaze upon her face, my heart stinging from the cool greeting and awkwardness. As I hold her hand in mine, a toxic thought worms its way into the back of my mind. After what I discovered today, did I ever really know her at all? Was she aware of her mother's life?

"Hello, Mal," she says delicately, her voice melting every suspicious thought, leaving a tinge of shame in their place. Her smile – her hand. My emotions teeter back and forth as I drink in her beautiful face, the waves of her hair outlining her perfect features. "How have you been? Good I hope." My determination to see her as a villain, crumbles into pieces, and I want more than anything to tell her that I've been miserable - that I think about 'er all the time, but I don't. Of course, I don't. I tell her what she wants to hear.

"I'm great. Everything's great. Couldn't be better." Lie! Lie! Lie! My heart sinks, but I don't let 'er see. I'm obviously the only one who has spent the last two years of their life dreaming of this moment. Her feelings for me are gone, replaced by a silent tension that's heavy and unbearable. Sam jerks her hand from mine, intentionally averting her eyes, avoiding a moment I had hoped would be beautiful.

"Well, shall we go inside," she says curtly. "There's much to discuss and not much time. And I hope Dr. Alexander is here. I'm anxious to meet her."

And there she is. The one I saw at our last meeting. The one who coldly broke my heart and my spirit and walked away. I know I shouldn't blame her, but I do. God help me I do.

I glance toward Warford, who's waiting, his eyes fixed on the ground, his face full of pity. I'm embarrassed that I allowed myself to be taken by the hope that when she saw me, she would remember what we meant to each other. At that very moment, I knew it was over. I gather what little pride I have left, straighten my spine, and point toward the back door. "This way," I say firmly but with politeness.

"Thank you, Mal," Sam replies with hollow sincerity. She walks toward the back door, Warford and the stranger following in behind her, me behind them. We are almost to the back door when Warford - decides that he needs to make the introductions.

"Oh!" he exclaims. "Where are my manners? Mal! This is Antonio De Cordova. Antonio, Detective Malcom Madison." We shake hands and exchange the expected professionally polite greetings, but it's obvious Warford isn't fooled. He leans in and threatens the both of us and in no uncertain terms.

"Let's not be inappropriate, gentlemen. I think you know what I mean, right?" Warford eyes are like nothing I've ever seen in him. A warning to be heeded. Sam is at the back door, staring back at us, waiting impatiently, which doesn't escape Warford's attention.

"Toot suite, gentlemen," he demands, his eyes reasserting his previous warning. De Cordova and I stare each other down, but only for a second, then relinquish the territorial battle, a battle I never had a chance of winning.

We converge on the door, and I start pounding - unnecessarily hard – releasing my anger spurned by rejection. De Cordova avoids eye contact with me but nods to Sam and says quietly that everything is fine. Sam flashes an inquisitive look my way, but I ignore it, continuing to beat on the door. A high-pitched, scraping sound pierces the tension between us as the large sliding bolt begins to move and then stops. The heavy metal door swings open, Cap'n Grayland standing in the doorway. His haggard appearance depicts a tired man, but to my relief, I don't smell any alcohol when we pass by him. Once inside, he bolts the door, turns, and smiles. -.

"Cap'n Grayland, this is Miss Samantha Callahan." Grayland takes her hand gently and politely says, "I understand from Dr. Alexander that Sister Mary Agnes and your mother were very good friends."

"Yes, well, thank you," Sam replies politely. "I never met her or even knew of her until today, but yes, she and my mother shared a special bond, from what I've been told. I wish I could have gotten to know her."

Cap'n Grayland's expression was one of surprise as if he didn't expect Sam Callahan to be so gracious and kind. Sam continues by introductions. "And allow me to introduce Warford Worthington and Antonio De Cordova. They both knew my mother and Sister Mary Agnes personally."

Warford steps boldly forward and shakes the Cap'n's hand. "Sister Mary Agnes was one of the bravest people I have ever known," he tells Grayland, his voice cracking ever so slightly. A surprising display of emotion from a man I always saw as rather stony. "And I am struggling with why she did not contact me – let me know she was here so I could have protected her."

De Cordova breaks his vigil of silence and mimics the condolences of Warford. I'm not impressed with this guy. He's nothing but Warford's puppet.

"Yes," the Cap'n replies, sadness in his voice. "I'm grateful you all could come, and I'm hopeful you can help shed some light on this. I've made some coffee, so please, come on through. Dr. Alexander is in her office, anxiously waiting to see you all."

He leads the way to Doctor Alexander's office. She's asleep, her head resting on her desk. Cap'n knocks on her door. Her head pops up, looking as if she's been caught doing something she shouldn't be doing.

"Sorry, Doctor," Grayland apologizes, "but they're here." Doctor Alexander's eyes search the faces - looking anxiously for someone in particular. Sam steps forward, and her eyes light up.

"Elegance?" Doctor Alexander's eyes fill with tears. Sam nods and smiles the biggest smile, reaching inside her jacket and pulling out a photograph. Doctor Alexander is so overwhelmed at the sight of it she begins to cry, holding the photograph to her chest – embracing it.

"Anashe," Sam says, crying and wiping the tears rolling down her cheeks. She throws her arms around Dr. Alexander and hugs her for what seems an eternity. There is an instant connection that cannot be denied. Doctor Alexander then saw Warford and

Antonio over Sam's shoulder.

"Warford," she says, hugging his neck and kissing his cheek.

"Hello, Love," Warford responds, kissing her hand ever so gently.

"Thank you for watching out for me all these years." Doctor Alexander's face is wet with tears, her expression one of love and admiration. Warford kisses her hand again. "Antonio," Doctor Alexander says as she throws her arms around De Cordova and kisses his cheek. He squeezes her tightly, then kisses her hand. The Doctor obviously knows him and has feelings for him. But it doesn't change my opinion, and I'll hold my tongue – for now. There's a lot at stake here, and I can't let my feelings influence what needs to be done to solve this case.

"Appears you were right, Mal," Cap'n Grayson says, patting me on the back. "Excellent deduction. But what have we gotten ourselves into?"

His words hit home, and I'm asking myself the same question, hoping and praying that the answer isn't the death of us all.

****

Sam

Breaking the Ice

River Dell County Morgue – Anashe's Office

Around 11:30 p.m. - Monday, May 21ˢᵗ, 1928

Anashe's office is crowded and loud. Everyone is talking

and even laughing, a welcome sound, a smidge of relief from the heavy sadness and fear that has engulfed our lives, except Antonio, of course. He is his usual quiet self, uncomfortable being thrown into a group conversation. I feel for him. He has no idea what to say to anyone. The life he's led – alone and isolated – has left him to struggle in social situations, happy or sad. He's miserable, that's apparent – desperate to retreat. He catches me looking at him, but he doesn't avoid. He holds my gaze, stoic and unemotional- that is until I smile at him. His eyes immediately dart to the floor, and I wonder – is he embarrassed at my attention, or is he avoiding my flirting gesture? I whisper to Anashe,

"I'm going to step outside for some fresh air and clear my mind for a minute. When I come back, I'm going to clear this room so you and I can talk. Alright?"

"Yes, that's fine," Anashe replies, reassuring. "And while you are doing that, I need to finish the paperwork on Sister Mary Agnes. There is still evidence to log and my report to finish." Her words are broken from emotion. Tears fill her eyes and stream down her cheek, as I'm sure they have many times today, and in her lifetime. I take her hands and squeeze them, an unspoken rally of support and sympathy for the loss of her friend.

"I am so very grateful that you are here, Elegance," Anashe says in a soft and endearing voice. I am instantly comfortable with her and can see why Mother loved her so. "And even though the circumstances could be better, I'm glad for the chance to finally meet you. I rarely saw Valentina, but when I did, she always spoke of her beautiful, angelic Elegance. She adored you to the moon."

My heart skips a beat. I knew my mother loved me, but I was so blind to the depth of her love and devotion. She called me *her beautiful, angelic Elegance.* "Well, now I am ashamed," I say, holding back the tears, trying to swallow the very large lump in my throat.

"Why? Why are you ashamed?" Anashe asked, genuinely concerned.

"It's silly," I say, wiping my nose and dabbing the tears that are flowing down my face. -

"No, no, it's not," Anashe replies softly. "Tell me."

I sniffle and take a deep breath, raising my courage for a full confession.

"Because I never liked my name. I never allowed her to call me that. Always insisted that she call me Sam. Samantha is my middle name, so I insisted that she call me Sam. Only Mother ever called me Elegance, not even my father. I forbid it, and I don't even know why. I loved my mother very much, but I'm not convinced she knew that. I wasn't the best daughter I could have been, which makes this extremely difficult to bear."

Anashe's expression changes, and she gives me a look of solid conviction.

"Don't be too hard on yourself. We've all had times in our lives we regret. Your soul is tormented by things you wish you had done differently, especially with Valentina. We all do. I still struggle with certain actions in my past that caused my mother and I so much pain. Unintentional actions – actions that I didn't even realize would bring such despair. I'm sure it's the same for you. We're not perfect. Nobody is – no relationship is. You must forgive yourself. Only then will you see your relationship with your mother as it really was? A gift from God. Imperfectly perfect."

Her words – so kind – so eloquent, penetrate my soul and bring me a peace that I fail to understand. Everything she says is exactly what Mother would have said had I been willing to listen.

Anashe reminds me of her. But I don't feel angry about that. It's strange. I don't know her, but I feel a kinship with her. She's empowering, something I have missed since Mother died, and her words of trust and encouragement have impacted me deeply. I hope she feels the same about me.

"Thank you, Anashe. Thank you for that." She - releases my hands, a bright smile radiating from her beautiful face.

"Now, go," Anashe commands softly, her face full of joy. "I'll see you in a while, and we will talk about everything." Her eyes glance in the direction of Antonio. "I think Antonio would appreciate you rescuing him for a moment."

Sure enough, he's still sitting quietly, suffering the situation of people. I discreetly wave at him, trying to capture his attention. He finally notices me, and I dart my eyes toward the door, an indication for him to join me for a quiet moment. He eagerly rises from his chair and follows me as I lead him to the back door. Warford is on our heels, demanding to know where we are going.

"I'm just stepping out for a minute, Warford. Everything's fine. I need some fresh air and some time away from everyone for just a minute. Some quiet. Just for a minute. Antonio is going with me because I figured you would throw a fit about me going alone, so I asked him to come and watch me." I play off Antonio's presence as protection, instantly putting the kibosh on any idea Warford may have about putting a stop to us going outside together.

"Alright, then," Warford concedes. But he just can't leave it at that. He demands the last word, no matter how unnecessary. "But stay close to the building – in the shadows. Antonio on your guard!"

Antonio nods but says nothing, a slight look of irritation on his face. It's apparent Warford's condescending tone rubbed him the wrong way. I don't blame him. It rubs me the wrong way, too, and I roll my eyes in defiance at his tone of condescension.

"I promise we'll be careful. I promise. *Please* take a break from worrying. We'll be fine," I insist, irritated, and exasperated by his constant over-protectiveness. Warford simply nods and quietly walks away, leaving Antonio and I to find a little peace and quiet – alone.

****

Sam and Antonio

Memories and Moonlight

Behind the Coroner's Office

Going on Midnight – Monday, May 21st, 1928

Antonio and I embrace the quiet beauty of the moonlight reflecting off the trees in the distance, the lonesome hooting of an owl the only sound that breaks the still quiet of the night.

"It's beautiful, isn't it?" I say softly, glancing at Antonio out of the corner of my eye. He's looking up to the sky but fails to respond to my simple question. I wish he'd come out of his shell – talk to me. But if he won't talk to me, I'll continue to talk to him.

"I've decided that I need to spend more time at the house on Long Island. Being in the city so much, I rarely get to see wonders like this. Noise, constant stress, busy with work, too many people. This is glorious, and I do believe I have been missing this in my life. Along with several other things."

I breathe the clean air, look up to the sky, and marvel at the view. "How amazing, Antonio." I point toward the sky, admiring the countless stars. "I've seen stars, but not like this. The entire sky is glowing with wonder. The majesty of it reminds me of a painting," I say, completely mesmerized.

"I remember stars like this," Antonio says, a hint of painful reminiscence apparent. "In Spain, when I was very young, my mother would make a game out of trying to count them."

Antonio continues admiring the sky. I imagine the memory of his mother weighing on his heart. A thought occurs to me. Maybe – just maybe- I can make a connection with him and penetrate the suit of armor he wears. I pray it doesn't backfire. I'll just have to take that chance.

"Let's try to count them," I say, gently – coaxing him to partake once again in a beautiful ritual created by the most important woman in his life. He resists at first, unsure whether dredging up such a memory so particular to her is something he can bear. I don't blame him. Memories can open wounds, but they can also heal them, and I refuse to lose this opportunity to make an emotional connection with him. I hesitate, uncertain if I'm making a mistake, but decide to take the leap and begin.

"1...2...3...4...5...6...". I count the stars slowly, my eyes pointed to the sky, my finger extended, placing the tip on each and every one. I turn my head slightly and glimpse him looking up, not seeming to make a move to join me, when suddenly I see a smile. A true smile that radiates from his soul. My heart skips a beat, and we continue to count the stars together. Nothing can disturb this wonderful moment.

"200!" he exclaims, lowering his head and grabbing his neck- - squeezing and rubbing it, trying to curb the pain caused by - looking up at the sky for so long. "I don't think my neck can take anymore," he laughs.

"Yes! Mine is hurting too," I agree, giggling and vigorously rubbing - my neck. I sit down on the -step -, and pat the concrete next to me. "Sit by me." Antonio hesitates, but only for a second, then decides to take me up on my offer. I sit quietly, my hands cradled in my knees, looking out into the dark of night. If he wants to talk, he will. We just shared an exquisite moment, and I won't risk him becoming uncomfortable. I just enjoy being around him, and I hope he feels the same way.

It wasn't long before his voice broke the silence, and he said, "Sam?"

"Yes," I reply softly, avoiding eye contact, my heart pounding with anticipation.

"You know, earlier, when you asked me if I had ever been married?" That's the last thing I expected him to bring up, but I'm glad he did. It shows me he's thinking about what I said.

"Yes," I answer softly, turning my body toward him. I want

him to know that everything he has to say is something I want to hear. He's still protecting himself – won't look me in the eye - but at least he's talking – not the shut out, so I'll take what I can get.

"I was taken aback by your question," he says. "That's why I didn't answer you. The truth is, no one has ever asked me that before. Something personal like that. About me."

"So, what's the answer? To my question," I reply, squelching my urge to push him too hard. I don't want him to retreat and shut down. I want to get to know this man very much.

"The answer is *no*. I have never been married." His answer is blunt and to the point, and there's that awkward waiting for more information that doesn't come. I'm frustrated with his inability to confide in me, but I'm determined to hold it together and wait – wait for him to decide that he can trust me - completely.

"Oh," I reply, withholding any other insight or conversation.

"My work," he continues, "has never been - I mean…well, my work would not be conducive to a successful marriage. Too many secrets – and lies. Doesn't make for an ideal husband. And honestly, I must say that I've just never met anyone I really wanted to marry. I've met women, plenty of them. Just not anyone I'd want to call my wife. Again, probably a byproduct of my line of work. I've accepted that I am what I am and that - marriage may not be something I can offer anyone. And I wouldn't want to bring someone into a life, expecting one thing and getting something that is completely unfair and unacceptable."

"You are what you are? And what are you?" I ask gently, still on guard to avoid the shutout.

"I'm an assassin," Antonio replies, with a tone and expression that reiterates that this is not a career but a way of life. "Have been for most of my life. Not exactly a '-*How was your day, Honey?*' type of occupation. It requires isolation, sacrifice, and a stony heart – and it's dangerous. I couldn't in good conscience begin a relationship based on a lie, nor would I put someone I love in danger. I can't leave this job at the office. I've been alright with that, I suppose. It's worked for me so far, but now… Well, I'm thinking that maybe there's something better. That I want more out of life."

My heart is pounding out of my chest, and it's all I can do to keep from throwing my arms around him, drawing his lips to mine, and kissing him passionately. "Steady now, steady," I think to myself, wanting so badly to take that leap! But I can't jump the gun! Because maybe he's just talking…and maybe his need for change has nothing to do with me. I could be making a fool of myself! That's what my head tells me. And I'm glad I thought better of it because his next question is a question that I'm unprepared for.

"Now that I have been more open with you, it's your turn," Antonio asserts, squirming a little but seemingly confident in his inquiry.

"Okay," I reply with fake total confidence. The truth is, I'm not confident at all! He takes a deep breath, lets it out, and then asks,

"Do you still love Detective Madison?"

His eyes meet mine. My heart sinks to a level of the immeasurable bottomless pit, and my hopes that we will connect are dashed. He's completely taken me by surprise! I'm at a loss for words. I never thought he would ask me about that! How did he know? He put me on the spot, and I hesitate to answer – trying to think of the right thing to say.

"Your silence is your answer," Antonio says softly, his tone edgy but understanding.

I'm somewhat put out that he instantly jumps to a conclusion based on my failure to answer within seconds of his question. But I'm desperate for him to stay. He stands to leave, and I quickly reach up, take his hand, and ask him to please sit back down and allow me to speak. As he sits - down, I make sure that his hand remains in mine.

"Look at me, Antonio," I demand, placing my fingers under his chin, raising his eyes to meet mine. He resists only slightly, then gives in, allowing himself to be completely absorbed in the moment. "I'm going to be honest with you. When Warford said that we were coming up here at Mal's request, I was worried. I was worried about the situation, and I was worried about what I would feel- - what I would say when I saw him again. Yes, we loved each other once, but that was over a long time ago, and *I* made that decision. And honestly, I didn't know if those feelings would rekindle. That is until I saw him- - talked to him. It was at - that point, I knew. I knew it was over because the entire time I spent talking to him, I was worried about what you would think. That's the truth! So, to answer your question, *no,* I don't love him anymore. But I do care about him, and I consider him a friend. I hope that's acceptable to you. Is it?"

"Yes, it is. Thank you, Sam," Antonio replies, squeezing my hand, seemingly relieved and hopeful.

"You're Welcome. Can I ask you another question?"

"Yes," Antonio replies.

"Why did you ask me that? Why – why was it important for you to know about my feelings for Mal?"

Antonio takes a deep breath, exhales, and gently kisses my hand. I'm touched by his chivalry, but it only increases my curiosity.

"Like I said, I've been thinking – thinking that maybe I want a better life. I'm serious about this being my last job – of the assassin kind, anyway. I'm tired, and while I would love to work with you and Warford, if it involves me being called on to kill, I don't want it. I've had enough. I haven't said anything to Warford yet, so I'd appreciate it if you didn't say anything either. I want to be the one to tell him that I want out."

"Of course! Your secret is safe with me."

I'm stunned. His confession is far from what I expected, but welcome news – yes, very welcome news. I am certain about my feelings for him, and now, I know he feels the same way about me. Under these new circumstances, retirement is a good idea. We need time to get to know each other without interference from things best left behind. It's love at first sight, but that doesn't mean we don't have work to do.

"I'll see this through, of course," he adds. "You think you know these people, Sam, but you don't. They don't care about you, and they will kill you to get what they want. I care about you …love you very much. It's grown beyond the promise that I made to Valentina, and I won't stop until they are no longer a threat. Then, I'll be finished."

"I love you too," I say as I move in and lightly kiss his lips, holding his face in my hands. He responds by putting his arms around me and kissing me passionately. But our kiss is abruptly interrupted by Warford's announcement that Anashe is done with her work and is back in her office. Antonio and I manage to make it look like we are simply sitting there, side by side, enjoying the evening air, but Warford isn't fooled.

"Time to go," I say as I stand, our eyes locked on one another. I walk toward Warford, my head and heart spinning. I feel Antonio's eyes on my back, watching me leave – watching every step. I turn and look at him before I go inside and smile before disappearing - beyond the door.

"Is Antonio coming?" Warford asks.

"I don't think so. Not right now. You know how he is with crowds."

"Yes, yes. Alright then." Warford looks at his watch.

"Warford, I think it would help if Anashe and I were alone."

"I understand. I'll get Mal and the Captain out of your hair. Anything else?"

"No, nothing. Thank you Warford. And Warford, I'm sorry about what I said before. Please forgive me. I'll always need you to worry about me."

"No need, Madam," he replies, a hint of happiness that I still need him radiating from his face. He pats my shoulder lovingly and walks with me to my meeting with Anashe.

Anashe stands to greet me and has already gotten us a cup of tea. Warford suggests to Mal and Captain Grayland that we be allowed some time alone. As we make ourselves comfortable, my hope is that for everyone's sake and the sake of those who have died protecting her, Anashe will trust me. Trust me like she trusted Mother. And that means surrendering the diamond. If this nightmare is to ever end, she must give up the one thing that has caused such heartbreak for so many. The one thing that has the power to repel the demons and bring us all back to a place of peace.

****

Jonathon Foster

Find Sam Callahan!

Foster's New York City Mansion

Nearing Midnight – Monday, May 21st, 1928

Jonathon Foster paces nervously inside his New York City

mansion. Paid sources inside the NYPD have told him that Sam Callahan is nowhere to be found. He impatiently awaits news from Cooley as to a lead on her whereabouts.

Del Ray has really screwed things up, stupidly escalating the Sam Callahan situation with that drive-by shooting stunt! Foster's suspicions have turned to a certainty that Del Ray's motives have extended past their original arrangement made so many years ago - keenly aware that Del Ray is manipulating the position given to him and that Del Ray is plotting to acquire the diamond for himself. Foster has lost his patience! He won't be double-crossed! Del Ray will meet a bullet, but not until Sam Callahan is found.

The phone rings. He picks up the receiver, anticipating that it's Cooley with news that the illusive Sam Callahan has been found.

"Jonathon Foster."

"Sir," Cooley replies.

"Any news?" I ask, anticipating a *no* but hoping for a *yes.*

"I'm sorry, Sir, but no."

My blood pressure rises, causing my heart to pound to the point that I can hear it in my ears. *Do I have anyone on my payroll anymore that can do their damn job!* I scream in my head.

"We – need – to find her," I growl. Cooley is dead silent, not daring another peep. Anger burns in the pit of my stomach. I have spent a lifetime hunting for this damnable diamond, and I'm not about to allow these two imbeciles to blow it now!

"Find her!" are my last words before slamming the receiver so hard that it's a wonder the telephone is still intact. I turn the dial, exact on every number, opening the wall safe to retrieve the bottle of Scotch. I don't bother getting a glass. I just open it and gulp straight from the bottle. "Sam Callahan…. I know she has it! She's hiding it just like her infernal mother! She could be anywhere!" I scream in the air to no one. *What do I do now? What…*

"Damn you, Del Ray," I curse under my breath. "Damn you."

****

Cooley

My Demise

Cooley's House, Tarrytown NY

Midnight – Tuesday, May 22nd, 1928

Foster. What to do about Foster? I'm up against the wall!

My life depends on making this right in Foster's eyes. If I want to live, I must fix this! What to do? Where to look? I'm frantic, and my hands are shaking as I drum my fingers on the table. Sweat -pouring down my face. This is deadly serious. I already talked to Del Ray- - the idiot!

"Stupid! Stupid!" I snap as I pound my fist on the table! Foster has many in his pocket, and I'm terrified. Desperate situations require desperate actions. I've gone to great lengths to keep The Daughter out of sight, but she may be my last chance. She's here – in Tarrytown - keeping an eye on the Sister Mary Agnes murder. Haven't heard from her, haven't seen her, but I know she's here. I don't like her. She's a sick twist, and I hate dealing with her. She's evil and extremely dangerous, but thanks to Del Ray, I'm out of options. I dial the Mayfield Hotel and ask for room 5.

"I'll connect you. One moment," the hotel operator says. There's a click and then a few seconds of silence. Then, *ring, ring – ring, ring*. With every *ring*, my heart rate increases. I hear a *tick*. She picks up the receiver. I wait for the sound of her voice. There's a pause, then finally…

"Yes." She answers. Her voice is quiet but seductive. It makes my skin crawl.

"We have a problem. Can we meet?" I ask, barely disguising my fear. She'll sense my fear. She'll know.

"I already know about the problem. Why do we need to meet?" She asks in a cool manner.

"You've heard then?" I continue to pry.

"Of course," she replies.

"Do you have any information?"

"Maybe," she replies in an innocent toying manner.

It's obvious that this conversation is going nowhere, but I'm not about to push her. I'm about to hang up when she abruptly states,

"One hour. The alley off Seventh Street – South edge of town. Know it?"

"I'll find it," I assure her. I'm terrified to meet her alone, but I agree. Del Ray must be dealt with immediately.

"One hour – that's 1 a.m. Don't be late."

The sharp slamming click of the receiver causes me to jump. I hang up abruptly, asking myself the question, *"What have I done?"* An overwhelming feeling of dread hangs on me. I'm bound now. I must show up. If I don't, she'll get me. Maybe not now, but sometime. She'll get me. I need to be prepared for her. She can't be trusted for a second. I'm dancing with the devil, but it's imperative that I show Foster an attempt to fix things. Del Ray is my responsibility, and I should have been watching him more closely. I let him get away from me. If I can't fix this, my fate is sealed, and I know what's coming.

My watch now says 12:02. -. One hour she said. 1 a.m. sharp. I can't be late. I throw my jacket on and pluck the car keys from the pocket. I lock the front door behind me and walk quickly to the car. The night is so still, and there's no one on the street. Meeting her in a darkened alley is extremely stupid, but I'm far from the position of power here, not with her.

I open the car door and get in, reaching underneath the passenger seat for my revolver. I feel the need for a little backup. I pop the chamber open and count the number of bullets. There are only two. I reach underneath the passenger seat again, searching for ammunition, but I can't feel anything. I know it's under there somewhere!

I get out of the car and go around so that I can search. I open the door and poke my hand underneath the seat. Still nothing. Damn! I look at my watch. 12:15. I need to leave, but I try one more time, feeling further toward the back. Maybe the ammunition box slid. I'm reaching…reaching!

I feel a hand on my forehead, yanking my head back! A sharp pain across my throat - something warm is gushing down my shirt! I put my hands to my throat! I try to scream, but there's no sound! There's blood – my blood – I feel it in my hands! I can't breathe! I can't breathe! I collapse to the ground and turn on my back, leaning half in and half out of the car - gasping for air. I can barely see the outline of a shadow. It's her I see in the moonlight. It takes the last ounce of life to instinctively reach out to her – a silent cry for help. But she won't help. No, not her.

"What's the matter, Cooley? Your throat hurt?" she taunts with evil giggling and echoing chatter that penetrates my ears as I take my last dying breath. Blackness veils my eyes, and my murderer gloats over my demise. I should have known better. I should have known… better.

****

The Daughter

A Job Well Done

The Scene of Cooley's Murder – Cooley's House, Tarrytown, NY

12:07 a.m. – Tuesday, May 22nd, 1928

I crouch - and admire my work. I should run get out of

here, but I can't resist the urge to bask in the glory. He's not quite dead yet, and I know he can hear me. He'll die soon, but I want the last sound he hears in this world to be my voice. The one who took control of his life and death. Oh, the power! It sends chills up and down my spine! Who knew that this line of work could be so – well-rewarding?

"Poor, poor Cooley," I say, mocking his struggle to die. "Such a good little soldier. But you should've known better now, shouldn't you? Now, Cooley, don't take it personally. And just so you know, no one asked me to kill you. I made that decision all on my own. I couldn't resist because, you see, I haven't had my fix for a few days, and frankly, I'm just darn good at it! Oh!"

He takes me by surprise with his final spewing and his last gurgling breath. And…. and he's dead! Job well done.

"I'd really love to stay longer, but I need to get going." I stand and straighten my nice dress – blow Cooley a kiss, and walk away. I stroll leisurely to my car parked on the next block. After all, who's going to see me? It's like a stinking ghost town in this neighborhood at this time of night.

I get in my car and sit, reliving the moment. Wow, what a rush! I'm amazed at how easy that was. It's *all* been so easy! Sister Mary Agnes – now Cooley! Well, that hack Del Ray helped. He taught me some *very* useful things. Los Angeles was a little before my time, but what worked once worked again. Honing my *Butcher* skills. It's exciting! I get all tingly just thinking about it. And Sam Callahan is a naughty girl, running off and hiding like that. Now, where could she be? Idiot Del Ray! Oh well, I'm not worried. She'll turn up. She won't stay hidden long. I can't wait for her! She's my trophy. I could care less about that stupid diamond, but I guess if she wants to give it to me before she dies, all the better for me.

I start my car and make the short drive back to the Mayfield Hotel. Tarrytown really is a beautiful town. I like it here. I think I'll stay…. till I've done all the killing I need to do here anyway. I take the parking spot near the front door, sneak into the hotel, and hide around a corner, peeking toward the front desk. The nosey desk clerk is gone. Excellent! I briskly, but with a calm manner, walk toward the hallway that leads to my room. Once in the hallway, I'm in the clear. My room is immediately to my right. I key the door and go in.

I kick off my shoes and remove my earrings. I sit down at the mirrored bureau and admire myself in the mirror. Oh, my! There's a spatter of blood on my cheek. I move in closer to the mirror so that I can see it up close. I grab a tissue and wipe it away. I return to my reflection in the mirror. There, that's better. I open the bureau drawer, take out a photograph of Sam Callahan, and admire it.

"I'll see you soon, Miss Callahan," I say with a wink and a click of my tongue. "Very soon."

I return the photograph to the bureau drawer and close it. I'm exhausted. Killing makes me tired. Too bad the day's not over yet. Del Ray, Del Ray, Del Ray. What to do about you. I think you must die. Might as well get rid of them all, then I won't have to share. Del- Ray, Foster, and Sam Callahan - the hits - just keep comin'!

****

Sam and Anashe

The Holy Hiding Place

Anashe's Office – River Dell County Morgue

15 Past Midnight - Tuesday, May 22nd, 1928

My head is pounding! Anashe and I are exhausted, but there's no time for rest now. We settle for a little quiet, and take a final sip of tea. "Would you like more?" Anashe asks.

"No!" I laugh, shaking my head. "You know, I have had more tea in the past eight hours than I've had in my entire life. I've never been fond of tea. Mother loved it though," I say, closing my eyes - enjoying the beautiful memory that began to dance in my mind so vividly.

"I remember," Anashe replies softly, fondness in her voice. "And she always had the most delicious exotic blends. It was an obsession - collecting tea."

"Yes, it was." I reply with a loving chuckle, remembering very well.

We share a laugh at Mother's propensity for collecting tea

and then drift back into quiet. I'm feeling the pressure to bring up the diamond. I keep putting it off. I'm nervous, and I don't know how she'll take it. I hope she'll take it as it's meant. Protection for her and a means to an end.

Thoughts of Annabelle suddenly flood my mind, and a rush of sadness washes over me. I haven't had time to even grieve for her. I feel terrible about that.

"Are you thinking about your assistant, Annabelle?" Anashe asks.

"How did you know about her?" I reply, surprised and bewildered. *Does she have a crystal ball?* I wonder in my head.

"Warford told me. Well, I should say he was telling everyone about what happened earlier at your house, and he mentioned that Annabelle was unfortunately killed. I'm so sorry. He said you were close."

"Yes, we were," I reply, fighting back tears that are welling up in my eyes. "She worked for me for three years. They used her. She was lied to and tricked into this mess by the same people who have kept it going all these years. The people that need to be stopped once and for all."

I pause for a second. I'm working up the courage to mention the diamond - approach Anashe respectfully. She suddenly gets up abruptly from her chair and goes to a heavy filing cabinet on the other side of her office. She pulls and tugs at it - moving it, shoving it, pushing it to expose something.

"Can I help you?" I ask. "That looks heavy!" I'm perplexed by what she's up to.

"No. I got it," she replies with determination, stooping down to the floor and removing a piece that disguises a hiding place. She reaches in, retrieves a box, and brings it back to her chair. She sits with it in her lap, takes a deep breath, and hands it to me, seemingly anxious for me to open it.

"Anashe? What is…." My heart is beating out of control! I think I know what it is, but I don't want to seem too eager.

"Open it," she says, her mouth hidden by her teacup. This is it. She's giving me the diamond, and I didn't even have to ask. I gently open the box that hides an old Bible inside. I feel odd like I'm not supposed to be touching it. Anashe is anxious and nervous. She's crying. "Take it out," she instructs, her voice broken and emotional. "What you need to stop all of this is in there," she says, her eyes filling with tears and her pinky finger pointing to the Bible.

I'm excited! I can't ignore the butterflies in my stomach. Then, I see the pain on Anashe's face, and I suddenly feel ashamed of my excitement. The pain in her eyes breaks my heart, and I remind myself – that the diamond has many facets – most of them not very beautiful.

I gently take the Bible from the box and blow the many years of dust away. Anashe is rocking back and forth, wrought with emotion. It hurts me to see her like this, so I gently suggest an alternative.

"Anashe, why don't you go wait with Warford? This is obviously very painful for you and…"

She stops rocking, takes the Bible from me - and gazes upon its cover. She holds it tightly to her chest and grips the crucifix that adorns her neck – closes her eyes, and begins to pray. Tears stream down her face, and as she prays under her breath, spiritually connected to something I can't see, I'm moved by her devotion, and I fight back the tears pooling in my eyes, waiting to fall down my cheek.

"Amen," she says, concluding her talk with God.

She opens the Bible toward the middle, hesitates briefly, then extracts it. She cradles it in her hand, wraps her fingers around it, and squeezes it tightly. The diamond fills the palm of her hand, and I am stunned by its size and beauty. Even in its raw state, it is the most beautiful thing I've ever seen, and I am mesmerized. I gasp at the sight of it, my hand covering my mouth, astounded by its perfect magnificence. It seems to have a life of its own. A divine life. It's easy to see why Anashe picked it up as a child. A beautiful treasure that drew her into its majesty.

"Here," Anashe says, handing me the diamond. I take it from

her and hold it in my hands. "I'm sure you already know that this is what they're looking for. I want you to take it – make things right. And when this is all over, I want you to keep it."

"Anashe no. I don't want to keep it. It belongs to you,"- I insist, puzzled by her reasoning behind granting the diamond to me.

"No," she replies softly. "It does not belong with me. Ever since I found it, it has brought misery, pain, death. I want you to have it and do with it what you need to. All I ask is that when you are done making things right, you find a way to use it for good. It belongs to God. It always did. I believe that human eyes were never meant to see it. But I did. I didn't know any better then, but I do now. Valentina tried to convince me of this a long time ago. I don't know if I refused to give it up because I thought it was my cross to bear or because I thought keeping it was what my mother would want me to do. But no more. God wants me to do something different, something good. So, I turn it over to you and trust that you will carry out His Will."

"Beautifully spoken, Anashe. We will stop them, and I promise *we* will find a divine purpose for it."

"That is God speaking to you through it. You will stop them. I know - you will," she replies with confidence.

"I admire your faith. It inspires me, and I'm truly honored that you are trusting me to take *temporary* take care of it. You say it belongs to God. I don't know much about Him, unfortunately, but if He allowed you to find it and keep it, then He must be okay with you having it. Right? Tell you what. How about when all of this is over, you and I figure out the divine purpose for it together."

Anashe's eyes dance with hope – her smile radiant and in agreement, and I feel a happiness that I haven't felt in I can't remember how long. "After all, we are sisters. From now on, we do everything together."

"Oh, Sam, do you mean it? I mean, are you sure? I mean, people will talk, you know, my color." I realize what she's saying, but I don't couldn't give a flying hoot.

"Anashe, let me ask you something. Do you believe that Mother hid you all these years because of your color or because she was worried about your safety?" She answers without hesitation.

"Valentina cared for me and was an honorable woman, and I wouldn't be alive if not for her."

"I don't care what color you are. You are my family, and I am yours. We belong together. And once we take care of Foster and his crew and we get the diamond into a secure place, you will be able to live a normal life. No more fear. We're family, and I mean it. Mother wanted that, and I want that. She kept your photograph on our fireplace mantle. She saw you - every day of her life, and so did I. I just didn't understand it all. You are family, so yes. I'm sure, and I don't care what people think. Whatever comes, we'll face it - together."

Anashe nods her head, and tears stream down her face. "Oh, Sam. You remind me of Valentina so much. I have missed her so these past years."

I take her hands in mine and pull her from her chair - wrap my arms around her, and hug her tightly. I respect her immensely.

"I see everything must be going well," Warford says with a chipper tone, interrupting our girl talk.

"Oh, Warford!" Anashe exclaims, wrapping her arms around him and kissing his cheek. He notices the diamond on the table.

"Good Lord in Heaven!" he exclaims. "I never dreamed!"

I place the diamond back in Anashe's mother's Bible and hide it in my jacket pocket. "It's not leaving my sight," I declare, and Warford nods in agreement. I take Anashe's hands. "I'm going to get Antonio now. I'll be right back." Anashe smiles, and I leave to retrieve Antonio from the back stoop. As I open the back door, Antonio turns to look. He's still sitting in the same place where I left him. The time has come to initiate the collection of debts long overdue. Debts that will be paid.

Detective Malcolm Madison and Captain Graff Grayland

Meet Fiona Mitchell

The Mayfield Hotel, Tarrytown, NY

1:00 a.m. – Tuesday, May 22nd, 1928

The parking lot is dark, but the lights shine brightly in the Mayfield Hotel lobby. "Man am I starving. I think my stomach is beginning to eat - itself! How 'bout you Cap'n? You hungry? Thanks for calling the hotel and arranging for some food. I don't know how much longer I could 'a made it on the Doctor's snacks. I'm glad she had 'em, though. They sure helped."

Cap'n called the hotel desk clerk, who was more than happy to make us some food. Cap'n told her we were working late on the case, and she said she'd get right on it. He hasn't said much on the ride over. He looks tired. But he's gone without a drink all day, so I'm grateful for that, and I'm sure that has something to do with his quietness. I'm proud of him. I hope he can stick to it. I wish my father…. He never could. He just couldn't beat that demon.

"I can taste it now, Sir," I exclaim, pounding my hands on the steering wheel, excited that I finally get to eat some real food! He looks at me and chuckles. "You ready?" I open the car door and start to get out when the Cap'n grabs my arm.

"Wait just a minute, Mal," Cap'n asks. "I want to talk to you about something." He's solemn like he's carrying the weight of the world on his shoulders. *Oh no! He's gonna tell me he doesn't need me anymore.* That is my immediate thought, and my heart kinda sinks. That's the last thing I wanna hear. I want to see this through - to the end.

"I've been doing some thinking," he says softly but with conviction. "I'm tired Mal. Real tired. I've been through a lot these past few years, well, hell, all my life, it seems like. But today, reliving what happened in LA and what's happening here now, it seems things have come full circle. I think it's a sign."

He pauses, keeping his eyes fixed on what appears to be nothing specific, seemingly gathering his courage and strength to say what he needs to say.

"Cap'n?" I reply, utterly surprised that he didn't say what I thought he was gonna say, and curious about the meaning of what he just said.

"I like you, Mal," he says sincerely. "And it's obvious that you are a good detective. So, here's the million-dollar question.

Would you be interested in taking my place? Would you want to live here and work here?"

"Whoa! I'm flattered by your confidence in me, Cap'n, I really am – but retire? Are you sure? I mean, I know this has been hard, very hard – Sister Mary Agnes - and I understand you feeling that way now, but…" He cuts me off, assuring me that his decision is final.

"I've made my decision, Mal. No question about it. Like I said, I'm tired. I want to live a little before I die. The notion of mortality has been weighing heavily on my mind lately. I'm on the mend and thinking clearly for the first time in a while. I have not had one drop of alcohol since yesterday morning. You know, I used to think I would never be one of those cops who turned to the bottle…well – you know – it's surprising how clear your mind is without it. And I've never been clearer and more certain about anything. So, what do you say? Think about it at least. I think you'd be an excellent fit for this department."

"I don't know what to say, Sir. I will. I will most definitely consider it, and thank you for your confidence in me."

"Good!" Grayland replies, extending his hand to seal the deal with a shake. "Can't ask for any more than that. Now, how about that food? I'm starving."

Inside the hotel, Mini, the night clerk, is dusting the front desk. She greets us as we come in and exclaims,

"I've got your food ready, Captain!" She scurries outta sight and reappears with a huge box of, from what I hear, pure deliciousness. "I hope you're hungry. I made you a feast, and look. We just got in these new takeaway containers. Isn't that marvelous! But I'm sure you see this kinda thing all the time in New York City, don't you, detective." I don't get a chance to answer before Mini starts listing all the food she made. "I made some ham sandwiches. There's left-over meatloaf with mashed potatoes, some corn, and green beans...."

I'm delighted to take every bit of this food off her hands. The Cap'n takes his wallet out of his pocket to pay the bill and praises her cooking. "Thank you, Mini. It looks and smells fantastic, and I don't know what we would have done without you. And thank the manager for us also." Cap'n hands her the cash for payment. She takes the money, smiling and beaming with pride. He grabs the box of food from the counter, and we turn to leave.

"Say hello to Nina for me!" Mini exclaims. "And Detective Madison, your room is still waiting for you. Do I need to extend your stay another day or two?"

Before I can answer, a woman's voice interrupts from behind me.

"Yes, Detective Madison. Are you going to extend your

stay?" It's that reporter – the one outside the station earlier today. I'm surprised to see her wandering around the lobby so late. In fact, I find it odd that she's even still here. All the other reporters have left. The Cap'n notices her seductive manner but refrains from commenting. I greet her cordially, but I'm wondering what her game is.

"Hey! Miss…?" - I hate it when women pull out the sex card to get something. I see it in mob dealings all the time, and it really gets under my skin. I don't play her game. I remember her name, but I won't give 'er the satisfaction. Reporters…always looking for an angle.

"It's Fiona Mitchell," she reminds me, "but my *friends* call me Mitchy. Remember?" Her movements are intentionally seductive, an obvious attempt at manipulation. "And you must be Captain Grayland."

She extends her hand for a delicate handshake, probably hoping he'll kiss it. But his face is blatantly stoic and unresponsive, and even though she can see his hands are full, she instantly bristles, reacting to what she perceives as Cap'n Grayland's rude refusal of her hand. Inexplicably, her eyes fill with obvious anger and perceived insult. Her overreaction strikes me as very odd, and a pang of caution rises in my gut. *Somethin's not right with her,* the caution warns. And then -just like that- like flipping a switch- her personality changes, laughing the situation off when she realizes the Cap'n and I are judging her behavior. Her eyes dart back and forth from me to the Cap'n, and there's an awkward silence. She distracts from the uncomfortable silence by turning her attention back to me.

"Well," she says. "You didn't answer my question, Detective." Her voice is again dripping with sexual overtones. *What's she after?*

"And your question was?" I reply, again refusing to give her the satisfaction that her presence means anything to me – the warning still beating my gut. I didn't get this feeling from her when I first encountered her outside the station yesterday. No. She's different. There's a wickedness about her now that I didn't notice before. She's giving me the creeps. She must have realized her female wiles were being wasted on me. The seductive smile disappears, and she begins to back away as if to retreat. But Cap'n Grayland - he doesn't let her off the hook so easily. He fires questions at 'er – putting her on the spot – requiring an answer.

"What are you doing up so late, Miss Mitchell? And why are you so interested in Detective Madison here?" Her expression immediately turns angry! "I haven't seen any other reporters around, so why are you still hanging around? What is it you're waiting for?" His tone is condescending, and he intends it to be. He waits for her answer.

"Well, Captain, since you must know," she replies with a hateful, sarcastic tone, "I'm up so late because I couldn't sleep, and I thought I'd inquire as to whether I could get a cup of warm milk. And as for your question about my presence here, I have been instructed by my editor to follow up on the Sister Mary Agnes murder. Is that a crime?" Cap'n could have let it drop right there, but he doesn't. He pours more fuel on the fire.

"But you're fully dressed," Cap'n observes.

"Fully dressed. So? What does that have to do with anything?" Her sarcasm has escalated to angry indignance, which is changing levels second by second.

"Well, you just said that you couldn't sleep," he replies matter-of-factly. "That's why you are wandering around the lobby so late. But you are fully dressed. Usually, when one is trying to sleep, they are in night clothes. You're not in night clothes, Miss Mitchell. Maybe that's why you can't sleep."

The Cap'n hit her below the belt. The cat is now the rat caught in her own trap. I fight to hold in the laugh that's trying desperately to bust its way out, but I can't help it. The laugh escapes. However, I do manage to control it with one laugh and a smug smile. The Cap'n brought her down in short order. Her face says it all. Her breathing is fast and hard, and it's all she can do to suppress the obvious anger raging inside. This is the second time since she approached us just minutes ago that I've seen that expression. She's a time bomb with a short fuse when she doesn't get her way. That much is apparent. She shuts her mouth - and doesn't say another word. As she turns her back and stomps off, Cap'n gives her a stern warning.

"Stay away from my Detective, Miss Mitchell. I mean it," he yells as she quickly retreats and disappears down the hallway, never looking back.

"Warm milk, huh?" The Cap'n jokes.

"Yeah," I reply in disbelief, my gut churning about the obviously unstable Fiona Mitchell. As we walk toward the door to leave, Cap'n Grayland hollers to Mini over his shoulder,

"Thanks again, Mini." We hear a - faint, *you're welcome*- as we pass through the front doors heading to the car.

The drive back to the Coroner's Office is quiet. Grayland hypnotically stares out the window, and I replay the encounter with Fiona Mitchell in my head, dogged only by my empty stomach and the divine smell of Mini's food filling the car. The office is straight ahead. I dismiss Fiona Mitchell and redirect my thoughts to a hot meal and maybe a nap. But my gut is nagging me about - Fiona Mitchell. My gut doesn't let go so easily.

****

Fiona Mitchell

Poking the Beast

Room 5 – The Mayfield Hotel

1:15 a.m. – Tuesday, May 22nd, 1928

The angry scream inside is tearing me apart as it tries to claw and rip its way out into the open. I'm so enraged! – shaking – fumbling to key the door. Once inside, I slam the door, the force of the slam shaking the walls. The bureau mirror is my witness as I pound my hands against the wood and examine my reflection – twisted but honest. I laugh – a disguise for the scream I've managed to subdue.

"How dare him!" I growl at the face in the mirror. "Nobody treats me that way! Nobody!" A delightful resolution to his gesture comes to mind and is cemented in the stony confines of my very being. It's decided. "Well, well, well. Congratulations, Captain Grayland. I'm pleased to inform you that you've won a coveted spot on my list. Yeah…you sure did. Your prize will be delivered soon. Very soon…"

****

Sam, Antonio, and Warford

Take the War to the Enemy

River Dell County Coroner's Office, Tarrytown, NY

2:30 a.m. – Tuesday, May 22nd, 1928

As Warford, Antonio, and I gather around a small table

in Anashe's office, our otherwise civil discussion turns to argument as we plan the details of *Operation Diamond Doll.* It's unofficial – a strictly symbolic gesture to honor Antonio's mother, Maria, and the Sisters, affectionately named by mother - The Diamond Dolls.

"It's 2:30 am," I report after checking my watch, my mind fogging over and ceasing to function from lack of sleep. "I vote we get a little nap and talk about this in a bit. I'm so tired I can't think straight. I just need an hour, and I'll be fine." I'm begging, and I hate that I sound so weak, but I can't help it. And I am certain that I'm not the only one who needs a little shut eye. It's just neither of them will admit it.

Warford defers to Antonio with a wave of his hand. I'm in hopes he'll agree to a little rest, but he ignores my plea and begins laying out the scenario step by step.

"Here's what I'm going to do," Antonio states, exhibiting no signs of lack of sleep.

"Uhggggg! I growl? Antonio, please! This is not going anywhere. It's 2:30 in the morning! Please, I just want to shut my eyes for a little while!"

"I know, I know," He answers with irritation. "This won't take long, and then I promise we'll all take a rest. I just want to go over it. It's important," he stresses, begging my indulgence with his eyes. *Dear Lord, does he ever sleep?* I bluster to myself.

"Let's begin," Antonio says, checking his notes one last time, running his finger down his list, and taking everything in before his presentation. It's obvious he's done this many times before, an example portrait of notational organization and details. Who knew that an assassination required the planning mind of a corporate CEO?

"First off, Sam," Antonio points out, "your role will be to contact Foster. You inform him that you want to discuss the 'item' he's hunting you for, using it as payment to call off his goons. Of course, he will demand to see it – proof that what you say is true. I want you to arrange to meet him - tomorrow at midnight – at his residence. He will immediately call Del Ray and put out a hit on you. He will enlist Del Ray because, by now, Foster is aware that Felicity is dead. He normally would use her for such an easy job, but now, all he's got is Del Ray. Del Ray will have to make the hit at Foster's because that will be their golden opportunity. I'll set up surveillance and wait for Del Ray to show up. Once they are together, I'll enter through the kitchen. I'll do them both and make it look like they killed each other. Easy. The gun's untraceable, and so is the ammunition. Bought it with me from - London. Company issue."

"What about Foster's wife?" I ask. "Won't she be home?"

"Well, as it happens, she's not," Warford replies. "She's visiting a hot springs spa and isn't scheduled to return for another week."

"I guess it's settled then," I concede, my tone curt and impatient – all I can think about is sleep!

"See, that didn't take so long," Antonio says, a gentle jab at my whining. "We'll discuss this further in a few hours, after some rest when our minds are clearer. I just wanted to outline everything."

"Halleluiah!" I exclaim as I immediately stretch out prone on the couch, pulling a blanket over me – closing my eyes. The time for retribution is near, but for right now - sleep – glorious sleep.

****

The Daughter

Foster and Del Ray Must Die

New York City

3:30 a.m. – Tuesday, May 22nd, 1928

Ah, New York City. What a wonderful place. I've missed

it, even though I've only been away for a few days. I'm not staying long. Just long enough to take care of a couple of things – well, a couple of people actually. Foster called me. Called me to clean up his mess! That's right because I don't make mistakes. Del Ray overstepped - let his greed and impatience rule his actions. What an idiot. And Foster! Wrapped up in his daddy's obsession for years but getting nowhere. Pathetic! I've had enough! How Mother and Father ever got mixed up with them is beyond me. Well, I'm cleaning things up, and then there will be no one standing in my way-, except for one. But she won't be a problem for long. Tick, tock, tick, tock. The mouse ran up the clock.

First order of business – buy a newspaper. Not only do newspapers contain – well – news, but they also make an excellent tool for the assassin. One of the first lessons taught to me by Mother was, use it or not, one can never go wrong with having a newspaper handy. Ah! Here's what I need right there. I'll just pull right up and ask the newsie to bring me one. I would normally get out, but not this time. I don't want to be seen. Don't want anyone to be able to describe me later. I don't make messes like that. Never. I'm just in time. The papers are being set out for the day's sales.

"Hey, kid! Bring me a paper?" I yell.

The boy takes a paper from the top of the pile and runs it to me. He's very young. Cute kid! I pay him four cents. Two cents for the paper and two cents for a tip.

"Thanks, lady!" he says excitedly, waiving as I drive off. Two cents – that's a lot of money to him, and you know, I like doing what I can.

I take stock of my tools as I drive toward Del Ray's hotel. Got my paper, got my plan, got my cyanide. I'm ready. Looking forward to enjoying a drink with Mr. Del Ray. Not far now.

I want to park my car in the alley behind Del Ray's hotel, but I spot something I don't like. Someone is sleeping in their car! Damn drunk! I can't park here! What if he wakes up! I back out of the alley and drive around the block to the front of the hotel and drive by slowly, slowly, peering into the huge front lobby window. Is the night clerk at the desk? No. Sleeping? Maybe. I hope.

I park my car about half a block down from the hotel and across the street. I check my bag just to be sure. Good. I know exactly where the cyanide is, and I brought extra. As I take the newspaper in hand, -the bold headline catches my eye.

FELICITY FARMER FELLOWS FOUND MURDERED!
HUSBAND ARRESTED!

There's her picture! Wow – Felicity was murdered! And Morgan was arrested! I try to read the article, but I can't make out the words. It's too dark, and I don't dare risk shining a light. Well, I guess I'm all alone now. My heart sinks for a split second. Oh well. Not the end of the world. My split second of upset has subsided. I'm just sorry that I wasn't the one who was afforded the pleasure of doing her in. But! Can't have everything, I guess.

I fold the paper, clutch my handbag, get out of the car, and cross the street. It's quiet – no traffic, which is surprising, but I'll take it. Less chance of being seen. I peer briefly through the front window of the hotel to check once again for a desk clerk. No desk clerk to be seen. I enter through the front door, quickly stroll across the lobby like I belong there, and climb the stairs to the first floor. I scan the numbers on the doors as I make my way down the narrow hallway. There it is. Del Ray! I tap on the door lightly. Don't want to wake the neighbors.

"Who is it?" Del Ray yells from the other side of the door. He's drunk! And he sounds like he just woke up – still in a stupor, which makes me happy. He'll be easier to take care of.

"It's me," I reply in a soft and reassuring tone. "I need to see you. We need to talk."

The doorknob turns, and he opens the door just a crack. I see an eye and part of his face, the sickening odor of liquor wafting out through the narrow slit. It's overwhelming, and I cover my nose with my hand to block the offensive smell. He's suspicious of me. Imagine that. I take advantage of the headline in the newspaper. I snap the paper open, fully spread, exposing the bold headline announcing Felicity's murder. This is my way in and my leverage. Mother was right. The newspaper is truly an assassin's best friend. He cracks the door a tad more, allowing him to see clearly what I'm showing him. I don't mince words.

"You've been a bad, bad boy, haven't you? Foster's a little mad, to say the least. He thinks you did this. If you want my help, you better let me in." – It's a bold face lie. Something I do very well. He's skittish and reasonably so, but I won't be denied. I threaten him. "Del Ray, if someone sees me in this hallway, it's going to get ugly, and I know you don't want to see me get ugly."

I don't have any intention of getting ugly. I wish to remain anonymous because I have another fish to fry. But he doesn't know that. However, he is fully aware of what I'm capable of. Sister Mary Agnes and all that nasty business is all the ammunition I need. He quickly opens the door, a compliant and silent invitation to come in. "Thank you," I say politely as I pass him in the doorway. Mother always said to be polite. "You've outdone yourself, Del Ray. The smell in this room is nauseating, and you are the perfect picture of disgust."

"What do you want?" he demands nervously. He's sweaty and obviously not well. Too much alcohol. Like I said. Idiot.

"Tisk, tisk – so touchy," I say, intentionally condescending. His face tightens with anger, but he knows there's nothing he can do about me. "Why don't you pour me a drink and go - splash some water on your face. Then we'll talk."

"Get it yourself! All I have is what's left in that bottle," he replies indignantly, his speech slurred, almost unrecognizable. He's wobbly on his feet. The happy thought that he'll just pass out crosses my mind. Sure would make killing him so, so easy.

"Oh, never mind then!" I snap, faking irritation - retracting my suggestion for a drink. "Are you sure you're alright? Can I get you a glass of water?" Del Ray doesn't respond. He's on his feet, but barely. He'd be on the floor if not for the wall. "Here," I coax, walking to him, placing my arm around his waist to assist him to the bed - escorting him to his final resting place. "Come over here and sit down before you fall down! Careful, careful. There. Now stay there," I command. "I'll get you some water."

I reach into my bag unnoticed, grab the tiny vial of cyanide, and head to the bathroom. I glance over my shoulder. He's sitting on the bed but struggling to stay upright. I can't believe my luck! This is a real gift – way too easy. I don't need the water-because he's drunk enough, I can simply put the cyanide directly in his mouth. I'll bring water to him anyway since I said I would, but I leave the tablet in the vial.

I pick up the filthy glass sitting on the edge of the sink. I'm tempted to clean it, but decide why bother. Not going to matter anyway. I fill it with water, shove the tiny vial in my pants pocket, and check Del Ray once again. I have to say I'm tickled watching him continue to fight to stay upright, the assassin in him refusing to give in. He knows why I'm here, and he's in no condition to fight me. I've often wondered what it must feel like to be in the grip of certain death. To know there's nothing you can do to stop it. Curious. I'll never know what that's like. I'm too good – too skilled to be in that position. I'm the assassin's assassin, trained to be the cream of the crop, not the target. *No,* I chuckle to myself. That's an absurd notion.

I sit quietly on the bed beside him and offer him the water. He inspects it and then does exactly what I figured he'd do. Sets it on the floor beside him untouched, looks straight at me, and in his drunken slur demands,

"What do you want!"

I just smile at him – rise from the bed, get my handbag, and open it.

"What are you doing!" he shouts.

"Calm down already! I'm just getting a cigarette." Getting a cigarette is merely a distraction. I don't smoke the nasty things, but it gives me cover to retrieve the cyanide vial from my pocket and open it. But even as drunk as he is, he'll try to put up a fight, and it's not worth the risk. No. I need him out cold. I need… And there it is. A glass ashtray – sitting on the bedside table, just waiting for me. Perfect.

I target Del Ray out of the corner of my eye, and in one fell swoop, I grip the ashtray, swing it around, and hit him square between the eyes. I hear the bones in his nose crack, and blood begins to gush from his nostrils. I dropped him like a rock. He's out cold on the bed. I slowly straddle him - - tip the vial up-, and watch the tablet tumble ever-so perfectly into his mouth. Then, I gently - push his lower jaw closed. I can feel him writhing beneath me as I take in the fullness of his seizures and labored breaths, the white foam flowing from his mouth. One last seizure, one last breath. His body goes limp. His eyes never open. "It's done," I sigh, taking a couple of extra breaths just to calm myself of the adrenalin rush. I pat him on the chest and look at him. I feel a little sad that it was so easy. I lift myself off him and begin to clean up.

I retrieve the glass from the floor and wipe it down with a dirty towel that's lying in the bathroom, then place it back on the edge of the sink, remembering to wipe down the faucet handles. I remove a pillowcase from a pillow on the bed and use it to wrap up the ashtray. I'll hide it in the newspaper and take it with me. I'll dispose of it on the way to Foster's. I carefully put the tiny vial back inside my bag and take one last look around. I can't leave anything behind. Oh! The newspaper. I place the pillowcase containing the ash tray in between the folded newspaper and tuck it under my arm. One more look. I take a little time. I didn't touch anything, not the door, not the…I wiped down the sink. Yes. Job done and clean.

I get my handbag from the chair and head for the door – using the end of the towel to hide my prints, I turn the knob slowly, cracking the door just enough to allow me to peek out into the hallway. Not a person in sight. I exit the room, shut the door without making a sound, and walk quickly but calmly – silently down the hallway back to the stairs. On the second stair down, I stop - peer downward in the direction of the front desk. No clerk. I descend the stairs at a quickened pace, without panic, and dart straight out the front door - stroll down the sidewalk, cross the street, open the car door, and get in. I take a deep, long breath and laugh in relief. I start the car and drive for about 20 minutes, then toss the pillowcase from the window of the car. Now, to delete problem number two. Mr. Foster, prepare to die.

****

Dr. Alexander, Mal & Captain Graff Grayland

Dead Body

The River Dell County Morgue - Tarrytown, New York

7:00 a.m. – Tuesday, May 22nd, 1928

Dr. Olive Alexander is asleep at her desk, her head resting on her crossed arms. She's startled awake by the telephone ringing. She reaches over, groaning and stretching her stiff neck as she picks up the receiver. Barely awake, she can hear the panic in Nina's voice on the other end of the line. She's desperate to talk to Captain Grayland.

"Nina! Nina, slow down!" Dr. Alexander says in a raised voice. "I can't understand you. Start again. Captain Grayland? Tell him what? Oh, Dear Lord! A murder! Hold on, Nina. Let me get him for you. Hold on. I'm going to put the receiver down. Don't hang up. I'll be right back, okay? Don't hang up."

I've disturbed Sam, who's sleeping on the couch with my jacket. I apologize as I scurry from my office in search of Captain Grayland. I begin calling -out his name, waiting for him to answer. I open the door to an extra storage room and find him and Mal sleeping on couches and Warford and Antonio on cots.

"Captain! Captain!" I exclaim in a hushed tone, shaking his shoulders to wake him. He detects the panic in my voice and flies off the couch, rubbing his eyes. "Nina is on the phone," I inform him. "She says someone's reported a dead body." By this time, Detective Madison is awake, and he wastes no time getting up and throwing on his shirt. Antonio and Warford are awake, too, and although they offer help, there's nothing they can do. Grayland and Madison strap on their guns and head straight to my office, where Nina is waiting on the phone. Sam is up and wondering what's happened as Grayland takes the call.

"Nina! Nina, what's going on?" Grayland is trying to calm her, but I can hear her voice coming through the receiver. "Okay. It's alright, Nina. We're on our way. What's the address?" He motions for a piece of paper and something to write with. Mal pulls a small note pad and a pencil out of his shirt pocket, but as Grayland writes the address, his expression changes from concern to shock. He looks at Madison and then responds to Nina. "So, you say it's Cooley, huh? You're sure it's Cooley. Nina, get Rice over there right now and instruct him to take a sheet to cover him up."

I notice that Sam, Warford, and Antonio exchange glances, eyebrows raised as if this news is no surprise – something expected. Grayland instructs Nina not to say a word to anyone. "There's a reporter around town named *Fiona Mitchell*. I don't trust her – tell her nothing if she starts poking around. Not a word, understand? Madison will put out a press release later."

"Madison will put out the press release. – Odd," I think to myself. Grayland has always been very controlling about press releases-- has always insisted he - do them, and now he's handing it over to Mal. The click of the telephone receiver brings me back to the reality of the room as Grayland begins to report – on Nina's call.

"As I'm sure you all heard, our Mr. Cooley was found dead this morning outside in his driveway. A neighbor reported it, and from what Nina says, it's a bloody scene. Doc – get ready. We need to get over there."

First Sister Mary Agnes and now Cooley? And judging by the reactions of Sam, Warford, and Antonio, I know these murders are connected. I know it. Sam hugs me goodbye. I grab my medical bag and follow the Captain and Detective Madison out the door, dreading what we may find and extremely disturbed by the apparent evil that has invaded Tarrytown.

****

Sam, Warford & Antonio

I've Heard the Name Fiona Mitchell

River Dell County Coroner's Office, Tarrytown, NY

Early Morning – Tuesday, May 22nd, 1928

Sam, Warford, and Antonio are on edge at the news of

Cooley's murder. Their immediate thought is that Del Ray has arrived in town and has murdered Cooley to keep him quiet.

"Del Ray is here! We weren't fast enough-!" I exclaim, pacing around the room, scared that we may be next. "Thats got to be him! We're too late! Your plan is somewhat foiled, Antonio. There's no way to get him and Foster together. Now, what do we do? How do we handle this?"

"Now, Sam, we need to just think about this for a minute and not panic," Warford stresses. "We must keep our heads and wait to see how this thing unfolds. That is all we can do for the moment."

Antonio is pacing. He never paces. He's always the calm, cool, collected one. If he's pacing, that means trouble. If Antonio's worried, there's something to worry about.

"What are you thinking, Antonio," I ask. He stops pacing and rubs his face with his hands. He doesn't answer right away. "Antonio?" I'm looking for reassurance from him, but I'm not getting any. Everything is wrong, wrong, wrong! "We should have gone back to the city and taken care of them last night! And it's my fault!" I exclaim, panic setting in. "I knew it! Now, Cooley has been murdered, and we don't even know where Del Ray is!"

"And something else we need to consider," Antonio says, "is that if Del Ray is here, and he assassinated Cooley, then Captain Grayland is in direct danger. He knows Del Ray, and if Del Ray is eliminating connections and he knows Grayland is here, Grayland is in real danger."

"You're right, Antonio," Warford replies, "and I think that there's no question that we must warn him. Anashe as well. Bloody hell, we all are! We know he killed the Sisters in LA and Sister Mary Agnes to get information on the diamond. Anashe spent a lot of time at the children's home– with Sister Mary Agnes. They have history together and were friends. - It would not be a problem for Del Ray to come to the same obvious conclusion. We must find him!"

"I agree," Antonio replies. "It's priority one. If he's tracked Grayland and Anashe, then he knows where you are, Sam. In his mind, you're the ultimate target. The one he's gunning for."

"Indeed, so what's the solution?" I ask, pushing down the

fear inside. "What do we do? We can't just sit here and wait! I can't imagine if something happened to Anashe or Grayland or any of us!"

"Okay, okay, listen," Warford says with impatience. "We need to calm down. This happens in this line of work. It is part of it! But if we allow the panic to take over, nothing will come of it but failure. As Valentina said, *panic will be your downfall.* We must take a breath and look at this logically, methodically, and rationally. Flying off the handle will not help. It will only create more problems. Calm down. I am going to make us some coffee, and then we will work this all out, but until then, I do not want to hear another word!" He leaves the room, and Antonio and I just sit and look at each other, not saying anything as ordered.

Warford returns with coffee for me and tea for himself and Antonio.

"Thank you for the coffee, Warford." I sip my comfort in a cup, grateful it's not tea. I remain silent, my insides tied up in knots. We dropped the ball, and now Del Ray has changed his course and escalated the situation ten-fold.

"I'd like to suggest something," Antonio says.

"Go on," Warford replies, his eyes glancing over his cup.

"Well, first, I believe it would benefit us to step back - do a little sleuthing. Sam, you have Del Ray's number from his card. Call it. Inquire as to whether he came in for work today. If he hasn't shown up, don't push for information, but try to get a feel about whether he's been in contact with the Bureau. He probably has, but you never know. If he's murdered Cooley, he may be off the rails and gone totally underground until things cool down. I hope not. I'd rather have him out in the open."

Warford agrees.

"Give it a bit. Wait until eleven or so. That should be plenty of time for him to show up for the day if he's going to."

"Yes, Antonio. I like it. Let us see what we can find out," Warford replies. "But at some point – soon - Anashe and Grayland will have to be told."

I'm listening to Warford and Antonio when it hits me - something Grayland said. "Yes, of course. I'll call. But you know, there's something that Grayland said that is nagging at me."

"What is it?" Warford asks, setting his teacup down and paying full attention.

"Well, he was talking to Nina; isn't that her name?"

"I believe so, yes," Warford replies, returning to his tea for a sip.

"Well, Grayland told Nina that he wanted absolute silence

about Cooley's murder. He told her that there was a reporter who had been snooping around, and he didn't want her to get ahold of any information until he approved a press release. He said her name is Fiona Mitchell."

"Fiona Mitchell," Warford says, repeating her name as if she's someone he should know but fails to remember. "I don't know her, but now that you bring it up, I have heard that name somewhere. I just do not know where."

"You heard the name from me, Warford. She's the reporter that Felicity assigned to interview me for the magazine. Fiona Mitchell. What's she doing here – reporting about a murder? *Extraordinary Woman* doesn't report crime stories. It's not that kind of magazine. I guess she could be freelancing. But I just think it's odd. There's only one way to find out." I jump up and go to the telephone.

"What are you doing?" Antonio asks.

"Well, I'm doing some sleuthing. I want to talk to someone at the magazine who can tell me about Fiona Mitchell. Felicity said that she is a *new* reporter. Seems strange that a new reporter would be assigned to cover two heinous murders. And like I said, crime has never been included as part of *Extraordinary Woman*. It's about beauty and fluff. Not murder! I think a phone call is in order, and they'll never question me."

It's a little early, but I dial the number for *Extraordinary Woman Magazine* and hope someone answers. *Ring, ring – Ring, ring.* I hear the click on the other end of the line. The operator connects me to reception.

"*Extraordinary Woman Magazine,* how may I direct your call?"

"Yes, good morning. I'd like to speak to Felicity Fellows, please." Warford and Antonio look at me like I've lost my mind!

"Uhm, excuse me ma'am. Are you a friend of hers?" the receptionist asks.

"Well, yes. As a matter of fact, I am. This is Sam Callahan. Is she in?"

"Oh! Miss Callahan!" she exclaims. "Well, I'm surprised you haven't heard." Her voice cracks, and she starts to cry. I feel a bit cruel and guilty, but it can't be helped.

"I'm calling from out of town. Heard what? And why are you crying?" I ask sympathetically with a touch of panic to conceal my lie.

"Well, I hate to be the one to bring you this terrible news, but Mrs. Fellows was found murdered late last night. And they've arrested Mr. Fellows for it. Can you believe it!" I can't help but feel sorry for the poor girl. After all, she knows nothing about Felicity's extra- curricular life, and she is genuinely upset.

"No! I hadn't heard! That's awful! I can't believe it!" I shriek, whipping up a fake cry myself, making a huge scene about how much I'll miss her and how tragic her death is, and then, I take the opportunity to pry a little. "Well, what will happen to the magazine? Is Mr. Jenkins running things?" I continue to fake cry and listen while the receptionist discreetly blows her nose into the phone.

"No," she replies, sobbing. "Mr. Jenkins was fired yesterday. Gordy Mills is handling things."

I don't recognize that name, which may be a stroke of luck. Hopefully.

"Gordy Mills? Oh, okay. Well, do you think you could transfer me to him?"

"Of course - hold one moment. I'm sorry, Miss Callahan. I just don't know what we're going to do without Mr. and Mrs. Fellows."

"It's perfectly alright. I understand. I'm just in shock at this terrible news! I'll miss my dear friends." I say, still fake sobbing and rolling my eyes, hopeful I don't sound phony.

"I'll connect you." I hear a click and wait. Finally, a voice answers.

"Gordy Mills," he answers.

Antonio and Warford are sitting – waiting patiently like a couple of gossipy hens - - on pins and needles for the juicy news.

"Yes, Gordy. This is Sam Callahan. Yes, *the* Sam Callahan." I reply, crossing my eyes and sticking out my tongue – acting completely immature as Warford's expression tells me.

"What can I do for you, Miss Callahan," he asks, friendly and willing to help.

"Well, Gordy, I'm out of town, but I'm hearing some just awful, awful news! What's going on!"

Gordy goes on to explain the terrible state they are in since someone murdered Felicity, and to make matters worse, Morgan has been arrested for it. I reply with as much sympathy and understanding as I can muster.

"I am so shocked! She was such a dear friend. I just don't know what I'm going to do. I guess the question I called about originally is trivial, considering poor Felicity." I smile great big at Warford and Antonio, still hanging on every word. Gordy assures me that nothing I have to say is trivial. "Well, like I said, this is so trivial, but I had promised Felicity I would do an interview for the magazine with a reporter that she apparently hand-picked. I've never met her, so I thought I would get in touch and talk to her over the phone. Maybe break the ice a little. But I'm sure that the interview will be canceled now. In fact, I insist on it."

There's an awkward silence.

"Gordy? Is everything alright?" I flash a look and shrug my shoulders at Antonio and Warford. I don't know why he's so quiet.

"Miss Callahan," Gordy says with hesitation and a hint of embarrassment. "I hate to say this, and I don't want to upset you. But the truth is, I don't know what you are talking about. No one said anything to me about an interview with you. I am so sorry. Please accept my apology. I just took over yesterday after Jerry was let go, so I hope you'll pardon my ignorance. I'm a bit overwhelmed. Please, what is the name of the reporter? I'll have them contact you immediately."

"Gordy, I completely understand, and I don't want you to worry about a thing. You get to it when you can. But Felicity said the reporter's name is Fiona Mitchell."

"I'm sorry, who?" he replies, obviously bewildered by that name.

"Fiona Mitchell. Felicity told me her name is Fiona Mitchell." More silence. "Gordy? Are you there?"

"Well, I'm afraid I owe you another apology, Miss Callahan, but we don't have a reporter named Fiona Mitchell. I don't mean to question you, but are you sure that's the name Mrs. Fellows gave you?"

"I'm *very* sure. She even wrote it down for me," I lie.

"I see," Gordy replies. "I'll certainly do some checking, but I've been here three years, and we've never had a reporter named Fiona Mitchell. I'm a little confused as to why Mrs. Fellows would tell you that."

"Oh, well, I don't want you to worry about it, Gordy. I'm going to check my notes again. I probably made a mistake. But if you could check also, I'd appreciate it. I just can't imagine where I got that name from. No matter! I'm sure I'll figure it out. Thank you, Gordy."

I hung up the phone, stunned and angry.

"You heard it!" I exclaim. "I can't say I'm surprised. I had a feeling."

"So, who is Fiona Mitchell, and how is she connected to Felicity?" Antonio says as he paces, thinking out loud.

"So – Extraordinary Woman doesn't' employ a reporter by that name," I say, trying to reason a connection to Felicity. "That means something, there's no doubt. And she's here - in Tarrytown reporting on these specific murders? Coincidence? Mother would say there's no such thing as a coincidence. And I agree. I think it's time for me to meet the mysterious Fiona Mitchell. I'm sure Mal or the Captain knows where she is – could arrange a chance encounter with her. Wouldn't that be interesting?"

"Oh, I don't know, Sam," Warford protests. "That may not be such a good idea. Especially now that we have no idea who she really is and what she is up to. It is most likely that she is working for someone. Maybe Foster."

Antonio nods in agreement with Warford, but I'm not persuaded.

"Well, we can either sit here like sheep and wait to be slaughtered, or we can take some action. To me, doing something beats just sitting here doing nothing. And – we're in it double deep if Del Ray and Mitchell are working together, which is more than a possibility, and you both know it as sure as I'm standing here. I say we take control – head straight into the lion's den. I want to meet her, and I'm going to keep the interview. Maybe between now and then, we can figure out who she is. It's either that or ask the one other person we know who can tell us something about her."

"You are speaking of Morgan," Warford sighs, his resistance to the idea glaring.

"Yes! If Felicity knows her, then it's a sure bet that Morgan knows her, too. We could get the information from him, but we run the risk of Morgan getting word to her that we're asking, and then every bit of leverage will be gone. I really think that talking to

Morgan is not a great option. It's riskier than drawing her out."

I wait for Warford and Antonio to come to a consensus, hoping that the prospect of speaking to Morgan is a risk that he's not willing to take and he will readily agree to my original suggestion to meet Fiona Mitchell myself. He's thinking, he knows he must choose one or the other. His usual flat denial won't work this time. I won't allow it.

"So, which is it, Warford," I press for an answer. "An arranged meeting where I have Mal and Captain Grayland for backup or a visit to Morgan?" I've backed him in a corner, but before he states his decision, he does the one thing he always does when he's forced - to commit to something he doesn't like. He defers to Antonio.

"Warford, I know you don't like it," Antonio affirms, treading carefully, "but I think Sam is capable. And the interview is already set, so unless it's canceled, which hasn't happened, there's no other option but to smoke her out." Antonio pauses, thinking for a second. "I agree with Sam. I think we should talk to Captain Grayland and set something up. We need his support on this, and I will go as well. And since Felicity thought I was dead, it's doubtful this woman will recognize me. This is too dangerous a situation not to take the upper hand, and if it were anyone else but Sam, you would be ordering this type of operation. So, what do you say? I don't see any other way."

"Thank you, Antonio. I agree. So, Warford?" I ask, placing

the ball entirely in his corner.

"Alright. You got me. We will engage the assistance of Captain Grayland, and I will work on keeping my personal feelings a little more under control."

"Thank you, Warford," I say as I kiss him on the cheek. "This will work. I'll be fine."

I'm alone, deep in thought, my mind flooded with scenarios of how my meeting with Fiona Mitchell will play out. I'm nervous, I must admit, but I'm determined. This is the right thing to do. I know it. I still need to telephone the Bureau and see what information I can get, if any, on Del Ray. Then, the call to Foster, and tonight, Antonio will do what he does best, then hopefully, we will be on the road to ending this. Everything needs to run like clockwork – for everyone's sake.

The sound of slamming car doors and muffled voices resonate from outside. They're back! I anxiously peer through the front window. Anashe, Grayland, and Mal are huddled together, and although I can't hear what they are saying, I can only imagine that they are discussing what must have been a grisly scene. *What happened to you, Cooley? What happened, indeed?*

****

Sam

Living Life Hour by Hour

Anashe's Office – River Dell County Coroner

Mid Morning – Tuesday, May 22nd, 1928

I hung up the phone after a one-sided conversation with a

receptionist at the Bureau, not knowing what to think. She refused

to provide any information on Del Ray's whereabouts except to say

that he wasn't available and didn't know when he would be. It didn't

matter what I said. She was tight-lipped and intentionally secretive.

I expected that, but it was worth a try. I wouldn't leave my name,

but I doubt that made a difference. Besides, if they tell him I called

and gave him the number, he will certainly hone his radar and find

us for sure. Sobering thought, but then again, maybe that's what

needs to happen. My patience is growing thin. I'm itching to just

confront them all: Foster, Del Ray, and Mitchell. I'm being

ridiculous, and I know it. I just wish things would get moving! All

in good time, I guess. All in good time.

Warford and Antonio are outside, getting a bit of fresh air.

We've been cooped up for hours. I open the door, and there they stand, staring silently toward the woods. The woods where Sister Mary Agnes was found. The beautiful woods with ugly secrets.

"I'm off the phone," I say, disgusted and frustrated.

"No luck?" Warford asks.

"Well, it wasn't a complete bust," I reply, somewhat grateful for the information I did get. "I did manage to get the secretary to divulge that he hasn't shown up for work today, but that's it. I don't know what that means. Is he here? Is he in the city? I guess I can try again this afternoon. See what they say."

"No," Warford says. "I do not want you calling them again. I suspect he has dropped off the grid."

"He's either dropped off the grid or – he's dead," Antonio adds.

"We can only hope he's dead," I reply, knowing it's not true but harboring some wishful thinking.

"I told Anashe and Grayland – about Del Ray," Warford says.

"How'd they take it?" I ask.

"Well, Anashe is fine," Warford replies, puffing on his cigar and blowing smoke rings. "Said she would take things as they come. She's no stranger to being under threat. She's confident that we will get to him before he can get to any of us. I wish I had her faith. He has slipped through our grasp more than once. I hope this time is the charm."

"And Captain Grayland?"

"He took the news alright, or that's how it seemed. He was not the least bit happy to hear that his old partner might be prowling around, but he was not backing down. Even though I wouldn't blame him if he did. Del Ray caused him a lot of grief. A *lot* of grief. Almost ruined his life. But I think he realizes that he is lucky to be alive. Del Ray could have killed him. So yes, he is very lucky." Warford takes one more puff from his cigar and says, "Shall we go in? Get the dirt on Cooley?"

"And talk about meeting with Fiona Mitchell," I remind Warford.

"Ah, yes. Miss Mitchell. How could I ever forget?" He replies with sarcasm.

As we head back inside, my heart feels heavy. A rush of worry has hit me like a brick. Nothing is going as planned. Antonio discreetly takes my hand and gives it a gentle squeeze, his eyes soft and encouraging. I wish I could stay in this moment – just him and I. But for now, it's a life lived hour by hour.

****

Dr. Olive Alexander

Sacrifices and Separation

River Dell County Coroner's Office

Autopsy Suite, Tarrytown, NY

Just Before Noon – Tuesday, May 22nd, 1928

I peel off my gloves and set them aside for sterilization.

My report on Cooley is almost complete enough so that I can update everyone as to the cause and manner of death. Not much investigation is required on this. Slashed throat, resulting in exsanguination. As I'm updating the record, I hear a light tapping on the door.

"Can I come in?"

It's Sam, standing in the back doorway of the autopsy suite, her expression full of angst and anticipation, and although I'm not quite finished with my report, her visit is a welcomed distraction.

"Of course, just don't get too close," I reply. I take a few steps closer to the end of the counter next to the wall and invite her to stand by me.

"So, this is your work, huh?" she asks, her tone respectful but speckled with a glint of horror. She stares at Cooley's body, lying motionless, large stitches sealing the gape where his insides used to be. "Kinda looks like Frankenstein," she says calmly, her gaze fixed, her expression bitter and hateful.

Can't say that I blame her. I myself find it difficult at times to separate my duty from my feelings. But I must. No matter how hard it may be.

"I know you probably don't understand how I could take such care of a man who has caused us so much pain. I'll admit I'm struggling with this one. But I must treat him like any other person that graces my table, whether they died naturally or they are a victim. Their background or motives make no difference here," I explain, using my eyes to refer to the autopsy suite where the dead come to tell secrets.

"My calling is to give a voice to those who cannot speak for themselves, even if I don't really like what they have to say. Most doctors would never dream of becoming a pathologist because they get wrapped up in the fact that there's a dead person in front of them. We're generally taught as doctors to heal the sick, not bury them. Sometimes, it's all I can do to distance myself from what's happened to them and draw myself closer to why it happened to them. I have to remember my purpose – that last gesture of respect."

"Even the ones who don't deserve it?" Sam's question cuts straight to the heart of my internal conflict, but I can't let her see.

"Yes, Sam. It's not my place to judge," I reply. "And I must uphold the law. I expect nothing less." I feel a tinge of guilt that I withheld the complete truth. There are times I struggle immensely, but my professionalism and ethics must come first. I gather my notes and point toward the door, avoiding further conversation on that subject.

"I'm ready to report my findings if everyone is ready," I state, coercing Sam to leave the suite and meet with the others.

"Of course," Sam replies, obviously realizing that I didn't want to discuss it any longer. "Everyone is ready and waiting."

As I enter my office, I see faces that are tired and solemn. Captain Grayland is especially distracted after the news from Warford about his former partner, Dominic Del Ray. Each of us confronting our pasts - pasts that have reared up and demanded our full attention once again. Mal is on the phone, and from the expression on his face, it's not good news.

"While Mal is on the phone, I think I'll get a cup of tea. Can I get anyone anything?" I offer. Everyone says, *not thank you, Anashe,* so I nod politely and excuse myself. This office is getting to me. I would love to go home, take a bath, and change clothes. The walls are closing in. I encourage myself with the thought that it will all end soon. *Just a little while longer,* I tell myself.

"I'll go with you," Sam offers. I reply with a nod - welcoming her company.

Sam and I return to the office, the warm tea soothing my tired spirit and offering a little comfort. My watch reads 12:15! The morning has flown by. Mal has ended his telephone conversation, and he appears agitated. I wonder if his Captain in Manhattan ordered him to return. He offers nothing as to the context of his conversation, so I take a sip of my glorious tea and proceed.

"I have completed the full autopsy on Mr. Cooley, and I'm ready to report the findings. There is no doubt that Mr. Cooley was murdered. His throat was slashed from ear to ear, close to decapitation. The cause of death is exsanguination. My *opinion* based on the crime scene is this. The driver's side door was left open, but Mr. Cooley was found on the passenger side. Based on the position of his body in relation to the car and the open passenger side car door, I believe Mr. Cooley may have been searching for something underneath the passenger seat when the perpetrator came up behind him and slashed him across the throat. I estimate that the time of death to be between midnight and 2:00 a.m. The condition of the pooling blood in the driveway surrounding Mr. Cooley would support this time frame. He was discovered at 7:00 a.m. by his neighbor who was leaving for work."

"Do you have an opinion as to as to whether this was a professional hit or just a random act?" Warford asks. He holds Anashe in the highest esteem and trusts her judgment immensely.

"Officially, I can't say. That's a job for the police." I reply. "Unofficially, considering who he is and what we know about him, I'm reasonably certain that's exactly what happened. It's possible that his murderer knew he was going to leave and was lying in wait for him. Could have even lured him out for the purpose of killing him. It was late – he was in his car, obviously going somewhere. There was also a revolver lying on the seat. Who was he expecting to encounter? I have dusted it for fingerprints, but as you know, a match may be a long and arduous process, so in the immediate moment, that won't be useful."

"Thank you, Doctor," Grayland says.

"Of course," I reply, excusing myself to return to the autopsy suite to complete my work with Mr. Cooley.

As I return to Mr. Cooley, I'm filled with contradictions about this one. *Lord, help me set that turmoil aside.* I don a fresh pair of gloves and pull the sheet back, exposing his face and neck. This despicable man had a hand in the death of Sister Mary Agnes. I suddenly feel an intense wave of anger – anger like I felt in those mines. I step away! Turn my back! Close my eyes and ask The Lord for peace. That peace comes in the form of the voices of Sister Mary

Agnes and Valentina telling me that everything will be alright.

The memory of my mother creeps in behind my eyes. I remember her sacrifice, and I know that I must stay on the high road, no matter how hard, no matter how bitter I may be, because my burden pales in comparison to their sacrifices. My burden is nothing if not a blessing. That settled, scalpel in hand, I finish the autopsy of Mr. Cooley because that's the job God put me here to do. And I would never ever want to disappoint My God.

****

Mal

There's Been Some Big Developments

River Dell County Coroner's Office, Tarrytown, NY

Early Afternoon – Tuesday, May 22nd, 1928

I know they are all wondering why I'm so tight-lipped about my telephone call. I'm tight-lipped because, heck, I can hardly believe it myself! Grayland is eyeing me. He's wondering what's going on. After several minutes of not mentioning it, Grayland's patience has reached an end, and he can't wait any longer.

"What did your Captain have to say, Mal?" Grayland asks. "Are you cleared to stay?"

"No," I reply curtly. "He wants me back in Manhattan immediately. Says there have been some big developments, and he can't spare me. I told him I'd leave here in about an hour." Cap'n Grayland is disappointed, but there's nothing I can do about it. And on top 'a that, I gotta confront Sam, Warford, and Antonio.

"All hell has broken loose, and I suspect that you three can shed some light on things," I say, pointing directly at all three. I'm a little more than curious as to whether they know about the murders my Cap'n just informed me of. "All of New York City is in shock, and the department is being pressured to arrest somebody. Politics and police. Doesn't mix and never ends well."

"Mal? What's going on?" Sam inquires with uneasiness.

"I'll tell 'ya what's going on. I'm wondering. I'm wondering just how much you three know. What are you - up to? There's something going on here that none of you are saying. Don't deny it. I'm gonna tell you what my Cap'n just told me, and you three better start talking. I want -the truth. Because when I get back, I'm gonna be looking, and I'm gonna be looking straight at you three. So, what's it gonna be? And before you start thinking of the spin you're gonna put on what I'm about to tell you, let me warn you, Doctor Alexander and Cap'n Grayland told me everything. I know that Valentina was a British operative, and I suspect you are, too, Warford. And you Antonio. I don't know how you fit into this, Sam, but obviously you do or you wouldn't be here. Don't lie to me. I wanna know, and I wanna help, but I can't help if we continue to play these games and keep secrets. The time for secrets is done. The way I see it, all of you are up to your eye bawls in it. That's between you and me. There have been no names mentioned – yet – but I would suggest before that happens, you tell me what the hell is goin on here!"

****

Sam

The Secrets We Keep

River Dell County Coroner's Office, Tarrytown, NY

Early Afternoon – Tuesday, May 22nd, 1928

My voice is calm but sinister. I refused to be accused and

backed into a corner. So, I do what I always do when backed into a

corner. I confront Mal with what he knows. And I'm ugly about it.

His cloaked accusations anger me. Mother taught me how to handle

accusers. Turn the tables on them and turn 'em hard. It begins with

sarcastic pressure and ends with a demand.

"Your right, Mal," I say sarcastically. "The time for secrets

is done. So why don't you cut the *tough cop act* and spill what you

know? That way, we can better address your empty accusations.

What'd 'ya think? And, if you know what you say you know about

my mother, then you must also be keenly aware that there are some

secrets best left alone. We'll tell you what we can. We're willing to

help but don't ever threaten us again. Got it?" I'm all of two inches

from Mal's face, my breath bouncing off his skin. His eyes are

squeezed tightly, a failed attempt to retreat. Out of the corner of my

eye, I see Antonio crack a smile. Warford just clears his throat, and

Mal knows he's pushed me too far. Grayland steps in to defuse the situation.

"Now, we're all on the same side here – aren't we, Mal? Let's just calm down and talk. Nothing will get solved with us at each other's throats like this." Grayland squeezes Mal's arm, but I don't relent, that is, until Mal acquiesces.

"Okay, okay," Mal agrees defiantly as he shoves himself from the corner of the desk, pushing past me, putting distance between us. He raises his hand, points it toward me in surrender and says in an edgy tone, "You're right. I apologize. I shoulda told you before I accused you."

"That would be excellent," I say, still applying the sarcasm, not yet ready to believe him or let him off the hook. He sighs and throws his hands in the air, takes a deep breath and eases into the situation in New York City.

"What I have been told is there's been three murders in the last 12 hours. First up, Felicity Farmer Fellows – found shot to death in a hotel room – not a hotel that one would expect to find her in - by the way – and Morgan Fellows has been arrested for it and is sitting in jail. Now, what do you think about that? I take it you know something because none of you seemed shocked or upset."

Mal is doing what he does best - judging our reactions, looking for any sign of deception. He'll know a lie. I feel extreme pressure to say something, but I must be delicate about it. I won't sacrifice Antonio. I refuse. Warford and Antonio are silent – suspiciously silent and Mal has taken note of it. Every second that passes in silence leaves a mark. I have no choice but to jump in with the only thing I know to say that will alleviate the ongoing standoff.

"We know about Felicity," I admit. Mal throws his hands in the air, declaring his title as the all-knowing. "Are you going to let me talk – or should I just shut up now so you can crawl back up on your self-righteous pedestal."

It's obvious that jealousy is playing a large part in Mal's behavior because, frankly, I'm shocked that he hurled those accusations like that and is refusing to listen. I've always known him as levelheaded, never one to judge too soon. He offers no apology but begrudgingly signals me to continue.

"We knew about Felicity – and Morgan," I inform him. "The truth of it is, I believed that Felicity, Morgan, and I were friends – well – actually, more than friends. I saw them as my family, especially after my mother died. But that relationship was a blatant lie, and I was misled by Morgan and Felicity - by everyone." Mal looks at Warford and Antonio with questioning eyes. "Warford and Antonio have been keeping track of her for many years. Even Mother knew what they were and what they were doing."

"And what were they?" Mal asks in an accusing tone.

"Disavowed British operatives, Mal! Fellows isn't even their real name. It's Banes. They were running a scam. They conned money from a man in London named Alonzo Foster many years ago."

"Money! Why would they need to con money from anyone?" Mal interrupted. "They had plenty!"

"Well, that's the con right there, yeah? They needed it because the British government had disavowed them – cut them loose. That created a huge problem for them. They wanted to come to the United States, and they were desperate for money. They discovered that Foster was obsessed with finding an extremely valuable diamond. He was a sight-holder, so diamonds were his business, and he was fully aware of - this diamond's worth. Felicity and Morgan offered their services – and assured him they could deliver. They tracked the diamond by tracking the people who they thought had information. Or better yet, who had contact with the little girl to whom they thought the diamond belonged? That brings us to the murder of the Sisters in LA and now Sister Mary Agnes. Morgan and Felicity didn't kill them, but they were the pipeline of information and tracking, and we are certain they knew who murdered them. Alonzo Foster dies, and his son takes over the obsession. All reports show that Alonzo was never violent, but his son, oh yeah. These murders committed by the so-called *Butcher*. Impossible."

"Impossible? And how do you know that?" Mal asks, insinuating I'm telling a lie.

"Because!" I exclaim. "*The Butcher* is dead! Has been since he was murdered in London shortly after murdering Antonio's mother and two Sisters there. The murderer of the Sisters in LA and Sister Mary Agnes is a copycat. They've dragged up an old devil and are attempting to copy his methods to divert attention. Morgan and Felicity were so entangled in lies and murder that it's anybody's guess as to why Felicity was in that room or who she was meeting there if anyone. They were determined to have the diamond for themselves. My mother knew that. The truth is Felicity was after the diamond for herself, and she intended to leave Morgan. She told me as much when we had lunch a week ago. Morgan's your man. He knew Felicity was trying to double-cross him and leave him holding the bag. There's your killer – there's your motive." I sigh silently inside, relieved that I had found a way to lay cover for Antonio but regretting that I had to spin a lie like that.

"So, let me get this straight. The Fellows' entire life was simply one big covert operation to locate and keep the diamond for themselves," Mal says flatly, indicating that he's choosing not to believe my account. "And Valentina knew this about them, but they were friends. And not just Valentina but you as well, Sam? You'll forgive me if I question that explanation because, quite frankly, it makes no sense."

Warford comes forward to take control of the ever-cocky Detective Madison. He clears his throat and readies to cut Mal to the quick. There's no besting Warford. Grayland's discomfort grows to level red as Mal persists with his accusations and degrading attitude.

"Well, Detective," Warford says politely but firmly, "as you have boasted, you know that Valentina was a British operative. A very successful one. An operative's view of a situation doesn't always fit into the normal. Valentina had her beliefs, her convictions, and her rules of operation. She was a master of *many* covert tactics, and one of those tactics, and one she relied on heavily, was to keep her enemies close to her. Don't let them know that you know who they are and what they're up to. That way, they can be watched vigorously without raising suspicion. That is the way she dealt with Felicity and Morgan, and she dealt with Jonathon Foster the same way."

Mal's expression changes. The name Foster has struck a chord. I see it in his face!

"Jonathon Foster is Alonzo Foster's son. He is obsessed with the diamond-like his father before him. Since Alonzo's death, Jonathon has spent his life and plenty of his fortune looking for it as he promised his father he would. Jonathon Foster was convinced that Valentina had the diamond. Now, he is convinced that Sam has it. My point is that Valentina hired him as her lawyer for a reason.

To watch him. And to this day, that is what I have done. Watch him. He is violent and desperate and subject to double cross from everyone he has had on his payroll who has had anything to do with the hunt for the diamond. He has a hired assassin actively working for him at this very moment. That assassin's name is Dominic Del Ray, Captain Grayland's former partner."

Mal's expression changes again at the mention of Del Ray. "Del Ray is also in the middle of what appears to be a double-cross of Foster. He also wants the diamond. And yes, Captain, you were right. Del Ray murdered the Sisters in LA. Antonio was there and confirmed it."

"So, I was right. Del Ray did kill them." Grayland replies, relieved that his instincts were correct – troubled that he couldn't do anything to help.

"Yes, Captain," Warford replies. "And as I told you earlier, you are lucky to be alive. Others who questioned Del Ray were not so lucky. Your dismissal from the LAPD probably saved your life. His obsession has closed in on him, just like all the others who thought they could have the diamond for themselves. Still, that is why I told you about him this morning. If he has not found out your whereabouts yet, he will. And you are a threat. He will not hesitate to remove the threat."

Captain Grayland nods and thanks Warford for the

information. Mal sits on the corner of Anashe's desk, his face showing signs of disbelief and maybe just a little hint of embarrassment.

"Mal?" Grayland asks. "Thoughts?" Mal shakes his head, slaps his hands on his legs and sighs. But it's not a sigh of relief.

"I think I owe you an apology. Sam, Warford, Antonio. After hearing your explanation, it's clear to me that this is very complicated, and I was wrong to accuse you."

"What do you mean, Mal," I demand.

"What I mean, Sam is that Foster and Del Ray were also found murdered early this morning. You've got Felicity, Foster, and Del Ray, and according to you, they're all connected to Doctor Alexander's diamond."

Warford, Antonio and I are stunned! This can mean only one thing. There's another assassin! A sleeper! One we have yet to encounter.

"No! Foster and Del Ray. Murdered! I can't believe it!" I exclaim.

"Well believe it. That's what my Cap'n just told me on the phone, and that's why I have to go back to Manhattan. Now you understand the pressure. A rich lawyer, a magazine mogul, and a Special Agent with the Bureau - all murdered in one night. Now, my next question is, do any of you have – an idea who could have done this? I mean, these people were a part of your world. You seem to understand their motives and relationship to each other, so can you think of anyone who could've done this? Anything would help. Point me in a direction. Oh, and – Felicity's editor, Jerry Jenkins – was found murdered in his car in the alley behind Del Ray's hotel. Cap'n Mason thinks Del Ray did that one. I guess some material was found caught in the fire escape leading from his room, and it matches a tear in Del Ray's pants. So, there ya go."

"Jerry Jenkins was fired by Felicity yesterday," I say.

"And how do you know this?" Mal asks.

"Felicity had talked to me about doing a story for her magazine. She told me she assigned a specific reporter to do the interview. It's the same reporter you were telling Nina about this morning, Captain. Her name is Fiona Mitchell. I thought it was odd that *Extraordinary Woman* would do a murder story. So, I called. I found out two things. Jerry was fired, and they don't have a reporter named Fiona Mitchell working for them. Felicity lied, and we have no idea who Fiona Mitchell really is."

"Mmmm - Fiona Mitchell?" Mal says - under his breath.

"Like I said, the first I heard of her was at a lunch meeting with Felicity back on May 14th. Felicity asked me to do an interview for *Extraordinary Woman.* She said she had assigned a new reporter, a young woman named Fiona Mitchell. When Captain Grayland said her name this morning, it struck me as very odd. *Extraordinary Woman* doesn't report stories on crime. I talked to Gordy Mills, Jerry's replacement, and he's the one who told me that he had never heard of a reporter by that name. Which begs the question, who is she then? Gordy Mills said he has been there for three years, and there's never been a reporter by that name. Felicity is the one who first mentioned the name Fiona Mitchell. She's someone to Felicity. That means she's someone to Morgan, too. Captain, you were right not to trust her. She's up to something, and it has nothing to do with reporting."

Warford and Antonio both shake their heads in agreement. I don't mention the call to the Bureau about Del Ray. I think I'll just let that slide.

"Suggestions?" Mal asks, looking to each of us for ideas on how to deal with Fiona Mitchell. "What do we do about her? She's obviously lurking around for a reason. I'll check into her when I get back to Manhattan," Mal says.

"Well, Mal," Warford says, "I'm not going to tell you how to do your job, but I can guarantee that you won't find anything on her. She's a dark horse, and if she hasn't come up on our radar, I can assure you, she won't come up on yours."

"Hmm," I say, tapping my fingers on the desk, a thousand

thoughts colliding in my mind. "What's keeping her here," I think out loud.

"What's that, Sam?" Antonio asks, catching my attention and encouraging me to continue my line of thought. "Well - there's something keeping her here in Tarrytown. Could it be that she's a part of Foster's crew?"

"Well, I don't know if we can jump to that conclusion," Mal replies. "I mean, what do we know about her? That she lied about being a reporter, but what else? Nothing."

"Well, that's not all, Mal." Grayland points out. "Let's track this. Fiona Mitchell is connected to Felicity Fellows – the Fellows are connected to Foster – Foster hires Del Ray, so it stands to reason that Del Ray knows Fiona Mitchell. And I'm telling you, I've been in this game a long time. When we saw her in the hotel, she gave me that feeling. That skin-crawling, hair-raising feeling. Something sinister about her. She bothered me deep down. I know you noticed it, too, Mal. There's more to that girl. More than you'd want to know."

"The captain is spot on," Antonio says. "Sometimes instincts are the best weapon." Mal immaturely brushes off what Antonio has to say, so I interject my own opinion with conviction. I won't allow Mal to ignore him.

"You need to listen to him." My voice is calm as I shift my

eyes from Mal to the Captain back and forth, making plain my disdain at Mal dismissing him like that. "If anyone knows the evils these people perpetrate, it's Antonio. He's been involved from a very early age, ever since *The Butcher* killed his mother right before his eyes."

Mal's expression exhibits some shame, and rightfully so, but he clearly has no intention of apologizing. I glare at him until he takes the hint and finally offers the robotic blah, blah, blah apology, "I'm sorry, Antonio. I had no idea." An obligatory apology that I refuse to let him get away with.

"Think what you want, Detective Madison, but I've learned that when *he* tells you something, you better listen." I hadn't called him Detective Madison for a long, long time. But I mean business, and I'm sick of his condescending attitude. "And think about this!" I exclaim as I turn on him. "You need us. You need all three of us. But you know what? We don't *have* to help you. We don't need you. You are the one being put on the spot – being pressured." I lower my tone to a growl and make this last statement to Madison, the one that would haunt him should he decide to continue this holier-than-thou attitude. "I have all the money in the world, Madison. With this man's help," I stress, pointing to Antonio, "We could simply disappear, leaving you strapped with dead bodies and dead ends and *you* the one looking over your shoulder day and night wondering when you'll be next. There's another assassin." I turn to Antonio, point my finger and point-blank ask him,

"Who's the assassin, Antonio?"

"The person calling herself Fiona Mitchell," he replies with cool confidence. I return my attention to Madison.

"Did you hear that? The person calling herself Fiona Mitchell!" I stop and take a deep breath. Detective Madison says nothing. "Warford, Antonio – I'm going to say goodbye to Anashe, and we are going back to New York…"

"Sam?" Anashe comes around the corner of the door.

"Anashe," I say, acknowledging that she overheard something she wasn't supposed to overhear. "I guess you heard that?"

"Yes. I heard it, and for what it's worth, Detective, I agree with Sam."

"Mal, can I talk to you? Outside." Captain Grayland points toward the door. He comes around the desk and pats Madison on the shoulder. "C'mon, let's go outside." Madison gets up and follows him out the door.

"Anashe, I was just coming to see you," I say, apologetic and full of regret. "We need to get back to New York. I want you to come with us. It's not safe here. We can protect you there, and when this is over, if you want to come back, I'll bring you myself. But for right now, I think it's best for you to stay with me. Don't you think so, Warford? Antonio?"

"I think that's best for now, Anashe," Warford replies.

"Fiona Mitchell is here, Anashe," Antonio says, his voice drenched with concern. "I believe she murdered Del Ray and Foster, and I'm certain she killed Cooley. I don't know exactly why, but she did it. She's extremely dangerous. She fears nothing. Cooley was textbook, and I believe they will find Foster and Del Ray to be the same."

"But how do you know?" Anashe asks Antonio.

"I don't, not for certain, but if experience has taught me anything, it's taught me to follow my gut and draw the most logical conclusions. Fiona Mitchell is the logical conclusion. And if I'm right, and I know I am, she's very dangerous. It takes a special kind of evil to brutally murder three people in one night, regardless of the reason. Fiona Mitchell is a serial assassin. Sounds strange, I know, but there is a certain set of rules and codes for assassins. Serial assassins have no use for such rules and codes. This type of assassin is rare, but I have seen it. And with that in mind, there's a real possibility that she had a hand in the murder of Sister Mary Agnes."

Anashe is filled with emotion, resistant to abandoning her work, but also aware that she is in grave danger. She hears her mother's voice, like an eternal flame in the back of her mind, and she's telling her that she needs to do what Sam is telling her to do.

"Well, I am willing to come with you, but what do I do about Sister Mary Agnes? The Church has yet to pick her up. They will be here in a couple of days, and then there's Mr. Cooley. What do I do about him? Who do I notify on his behalf?"

"You go, Doctor. I'll take care of the Sister, and I'll try to locate – any family for Cooley. I'll take care of it for you." Grayland states as he enters her office with Madison in tow, Mal's demeanor noticeably different. Anashe ponders her choices while I try my best to convince her to leave.

"Okay. If you all think it best, I'll go. Captain, are you sure?"

"Absolutely. I would rather have you safe. Antonio, I overheard what you said. And I agree with you. And Detective Madison does, too, don't you, Mal?"

I don't know what Captain Grayland said to Madison, but it certainly made an impact. My guess is he told him that his jealousy was making him look like an utter fool and clouding his judgment. Madison walks toward Antonio and extends his hand. Antonio takes his hand, and they shake while Mal apologizes, sincerely this time. Then he comes to me and extends his hand for me to shake.

"Friends, Sam?" he says.

"Of course. Always." I see Captain Grayland smiling in the

background. Madison turns to Anashe.

"I hope to see you again, Doctor. It's been a pleasure to meet and work with you and an experience I'll never forget. I hope you'll heed Sam's warning and come to New York. You'll be much safer." Anashe gives him a hug. I couldn't swear it, but I thought I saw an exchange between the two of them. The eyes never lie. "I'm going to go now," Mal says. "Sam, come see me later when you get back to the city. We'll take care of Annabelle and everything else." He half-heartedly smiles and turns to Warford, shaking his hand and then reluctantly walking out the door. And He is gone.

We all awkwardly stand around, left behind - feeling a little lost. It's been a horrible day and a half that seems like a month, and there's only more of the same to look forward to until this is finished and finished for good.

"I have news about what we discussed earlier," Grayland says. "I just called over to the hotel, and the desk clerk told me that Fiona Mitchell is still there. Thought we could initiate that chance meeting if you're ready." He smiles at me and eagerly awaits an answer.

"Now you're talking!" I exclaim, excited for the opportunity to meet the mysterious Miss Mitchell. "Warford, you take care of Anashe?"

"Of course!" Warford exclaims happily, taking Anashe's

hand, kissing it gently and offering to make her some tea.

"Well, then. What are we waiting for, gentlemen?"

Captain Grayland, Antonio, and I waste no time outlining the coerced meeting with Fiona Mitchell. I'm nervous, but if she is who we think she is, she won't be hard to bait. All I need is a hook. The interview! That will work. I know it because it will be the perfect opportunity to kill me. That's why it was orchestrated in the first place. Mitchell is going to get her wish, but with a different outcome, I assure you.

****

Sam and Fiona Mitchell

Friday is a Good Day to Die

The Mayfield Hotel, Tarrytown, NY

Afternoon – Tuesday, May 22ⁿᵈ, 1928

Captain Grayland, Antonio, and I park to the side of the hotel. The captain called ahead to Mona at the front desk requesting her help in getting Fiona down to the lobby for our 'chance' meeting. She was more than willing to oblige. Seems Fiona rubs everyone the wrong way, and if Mona could help the police and help catch that witch…

I've run the plan over and over in my mind. Antonio will sit in a lobby chair and observe while I wait in the outside foyer. When Fiona arrives at the desk, I come strolling in. She'll recognize me and start a conversation because she just won't be able to help herself. She sounds like the type that likes to flaunt that she has a secret about you that you must die to find out. I say a little prayer. Please let this work. We get out of the car and head for the front entrance. Captain Grayland points toward a two-toned blue Rolls Royce Coupe.

"That's her car," he says. Little expensive for a reporter,

don't you think? Getting her money from somewhere."

We enter the hotel and take our positions. My heart is pounding out of my chest. This is the first time I've ever done something like this. Antonio assures me I'll be fine. I hope his confidence in me isn't wasted. This has to work. I peek through the glass doors into the lobby as Captain Grayland positions himself at the front desk. The desk clerk picks up the phone and dials her room. I'm anxious to get a glimpse of her. Maybe I have seen her before and just don't remember. Hopefully, it won't be long now. Antonio has a newspaper propped up in front of his face, pretending to read it. We're all set.

The time is crawling! But according to my watch, it's only been five minutes. *Where is she? C'mon, c'mon.* And then… Yes - there she is. I know it's her. She's a petite woman with dark hair, cut in the latest fashion, a dramatic bob with bangs. Expensive hairstyle to fit with the expensive dressing gown she's wearing. It's 2:30 in the afternoon, and she isn't dressed yet? There's not a hair out of place makeup is perfect. I don't know her, but she does look familiar. I have seen her somewhere. *Where have I seen her!* I think, tapping the crevices of my brain for the memory. All these things are spinning in my mind when suddenly, I remember…

She's arrived at the front desk. I take a deep breath, shake off my nerves and open the door to the lobby, strolling leisurely right up behind her. I intentionally say hello to the captain. I want her to know I'm behind her. Fiona doesn't speak to Captain Grayland. She simply darts a look his way and continues with her business. She questions the desk clerk as to why she's required to pay her bill now when she hasn't yet checked out. Mona offers an explanation that doesn't sit well, but Fiona doesn't argue much. I suspect she doesn't want a scene in front of Captain Grayland. She pays her bill and turns to walk away from the desk. I take the opportunity to intentionally bump her shoulder – make her stop and engage me.

"Oh, my goodness!" I exclaim. "Please excuse me! I'm so sorry!" She's staring at me. She knows who I am. "I'm so clumsy!" She's holding my gaze but hesitant to speak to me. "Again, I'm so sorry." I smile and turn toward the desk, worried that she may not pursue a conversation. "Do you have a room for tonight?" Mona acts like she's looking for a room. I can feel Fiona's eyes fixed on my back as I glance at the captain out of the corner of my eye. He's standing at the end of the desk, pretending to read the newspaper, popping peanuts in his mouth.

"I'm sorry, there's nothing. I could call over to the Cambridge Hotel. See if they have anything available if you'd like," Mona says, remorseful but cheerful.

"Well," I respond. "That's fine. I'll just drive back to the city tonight." I still feel her eyes on my back, but she's moved across the room toward the stairs. I know that because the clerk keeps looking that way. She's trying to help – warn me where she is.

"Well, if you change your mind, I'd be glad to call for you." I smile, say *thank you* and turn to leave. I start walking back toward the lobby door, but Fiona doesn't move. She's not going to say anything! What if she doesn't say anything? If she doesn't engage, I guess it's not a complete bust. At least I know what she looks like. Provided she doesn't change her appearance. Captain Grayland and Antonio stay put. I notice her reflection in the glass doors. My pulse jumps! She's coming after me!

"Excuse me," I hear from across the room. I turn to find her practically running toward me. I knew she wouldn't be able to help herself.

"Yes?" I reply, turning toward her.

"Please don't think me rude, but are you, Sam Callahan?"

"Why, yes, I am," I reply, fake acting a little puzzled as to why a total stranger would stop me in a lobby to talk. "I'm sorry, do we know each other?" Fiona smiles, but she's obviously uncomfortable. Antonio told me she probably would be at first. She can't help her compulsion to talk to me, but she's been put on the spot and had no time to prepare. I'll need to put her at ease.

"No. Well – we've never met. I'm Fiona Mitchell. Felicity assigned me to interview you for *Extraordinary Woman Magazine*.

Or at least I was - I don't know what's going on now. I just found out that Felicity has been murdered."

She's shockingly deceitful just as I expected. The captain was right. She's a sinister one, no doubt. I don't think I've ever seen such black eyes, void of emotion.

"Fiona Mitchell! Of course! I just recently talked to Felicity about you. What an awful tragedy," I cry, pouring on the fake tears. "Just awful! I am in complete shock, and I can't. I just truly can't believe it!" I wipe the fake tears from my eyes and heave a huge emotional sigh. "This has just been an awful week. I'm heartbroken, Fiona. I've had three dear friends murdered just this week. First, Sister Mary Agnes and Mr. Cooley from the children's home, and now - the news of Felicity. On top of that, I received word while on a business trip that my house was destroyed by a hail of bullets, killing my friend and assistant, Annabelle. I tell you; I just don't know what's going on!" I break down in a ladylike manner, dabbing my eyes and nose. "I don't understand why someone would shoot into my house!" I continue while Fiona pretends to be sympathetic. But it's clear by her expression that she's not phased at all. In fact, I swear I see a glimmer of amusement dancing in her eyes. My skin begins to crawl. Antonio and Captain Grayland were right. She's something else. Wickedness drips from her, so much so that she sucks the oxygen from the air. But I press on with the pretenses. I must.

"I'm so sorry about Annabelle. That's tough. But you knew

Sister Mary Agnes and Mr. Cooley?" she asks, her tone suggesting that her inquiry is more about information gathering rather than sympathy or grief.

"Thank you and, yes. Such wonderful people. I am a huge supporter of the children's - home. I was supposed to have a meeting with them today. I found out the terrible news when I arrived. It's shocking, just shocking! Who would do such a wicked, wicked thing? I hope the police catch whoever did this and whoever killed Felicity soon. And poor Annabelle. We don't need maniacs like that running around our streets!" And there's the trigger. Her face turns to stone - from amused to angry in a split second, her fake evil smile transparent and telling.

"Well, if you'll excuse me, I have to go," she says abruptly. "But I hope you'll still do the interview. It's been cleared with the editor, and I want to do my part to keep the magazine going."

What a bald-faced lie! How confident she is to assume that I haven't checked on her.

"I do want to do the interview," I assure her. "And I'd like to dedicate it to Felicity. I want to do that for my dear friend. And to think! Morgan could do that to her! I just can't believe any of it!" I exclaim, my river of fake tears flowing. I had to throw that in. Fiona appears to be anxious to make her escape - I offered the bait. Now, I will set the hook. "Why don't we go ahead and schedule the interview?"

"Really," she replies cheerfully, her eagerness nauseating while I'm gripped with dread.

"Yes. I want to. How about…" I take my calendar book from my bag and flip through the pages. "Let's see, today is Tuesday. How about Friday? Will that work for you?"

"Friday is great! Absolutely!" she exclaims, her fake enthusiasm dripping.

Hook, line, and sinker. It's all set. *Friday is a good day to die.* I think to myself.

"Wonderful!" I reply, noting the smug smile of self-proclaimed victory. "My house in Long Island. Do you know where it is?"

She slips up, giving away that she's done her homework.

"Yes, I do – well – I don't, but I can find it. I mean, doesn't everyone know where your house is?" She smiles a wicked smile as she twists a strand of her hair, her head cocked to the side – those black eyes dancing at the thought of my agonizing death. "I'm sorry, I don't mean to ramble, it's just that – well, thank you so much for this opportunity, Miss Callahan," she hisses, her words dripping with evil confidence, but I've got news for her. Big news…

"Oh, don't mention it. I will do anything for Felicity. You

know, she was right. You are really very nice and gracious," I say, with over-the-top sickening sweetness. But I smile and shake her hand, not like Mother said. No – a lady's handshake, soft and non-threatening.

"Please," I implore. "Call me Sam. And I loved her too. And I will miss her more than you know. Friday then," I confirm. "Come for brunch. I want to make sure you make your deadline."

"I'll see you then," Fiona replies with a smile that I wish I could slap off her face. She doesn't mention Felicity's funeral. So, I do.

"Oh, and I'll see you Thursday – for Felicity's funeral?" Her only reply is a notably arrogant nod. She has no intention of going, but then, neither do I.

As I leave the hotel and walk to the car, my emotions are a jumble of fright and excitement. I've seen her before somewhere, and her name is not Fiona Mitchell.

****

Sam and Anashe

Sisters

The Callahan Windsor Hotel, New York City

Late Evening – Tuesday, May 22nd, 1928

It seems a lifetime since I was last in the City, but it's only been 24 hours. I'm more at ease now that Foster and Del Ray are dead, but Fiona sets me on edge.

I sent Warford and Antonio ahead to the house on Long Island. I want everything prepared for Fiona on Friday. Tomorrow, I'm scheduled to see Mal at the police department for a report on the townhouse and arrange for Annabelle. Mrs. Lilly is recovering nicely and is with Warford and Antonio on Long Island. I imagine she's packing for her extended trip to parts unknown with Mrs. Dwyer. I owe her my life, and I will never forget it.

Anashe and I drove by the townhouse before arriving at the hotel. She couldn't believe the amount of damage. She just kept telling me how thankful she was that we all survived and then said a prayer for Annabelle. The police still have it cordoned off, so I couldn't go in. They did let me get my car from the main garage, though, thanks to Mal. Once the police release the house back to me,

I will start the repairs. The thought of selling it crossed my mind, but I'll never do that. Too many memories of mother there. Too many 'unique' features that I wouldn't want to be discovered.

Our hotel suite is a welcome sight. We are both exhausted and ready to sleep and a nice, long, hot bath. Finding Anashe has made me realize how empty my life has been. She was afraid that the hotel wouldn't let her in because of her color. But I told her not to worry about it. She's Dr. Olive Alexander, my sister. No one will treat her with disrespect.

"I was surprised that the desk clerk didn't make more of a fuss. You know…" Anashe says.

"Well, no one here will make a fuss. Especially since we own it."

She's sipping her champagne, a gracious 'gift' of the manager, and nearly chokes at that news. I smile and pour myself a glass.

"Own it!" she exclaims. "And you paid?"

"Well, the hotel is in business to make money. We only make money if it makes money. Know what I mean?" Anashe chuckles and agrees that this is a good, logical business analogy.

"Valentina taught you a lot about business, didn't she?" Anashe asks, using the question to lovingly bring up the relationship between me and my mother.

"Yes, she did," I reply, fondly reminiscent. "Everything." Anashe nods in understanding and then takes a sip of champagne.

"I love this! It's delicious!" she says. She takes a sip – giggles – and takes another one. "And it seems especially good since it's – well – illegal and a little naughty."

"Bubbles tickling your nose a little?" I ask, giggling at her girlish fun. She smiles and takes another sip.

"Where's the diamond?" she asks, her voice solemn, concerned.

"It is in the very capable hands of Warford and Antonio. It's in the safe at the Long Island house. It's safer with them than here in the city. No one will get past Antonio."

"You miss him, don't you?" Anashe asks, grinning and giddy. Sometimes, she reminds me more of a little girl than a doctor. I wish I was more like a little girl sometimes.

"I do, yes," I reply, a little embarrassed. "He's so different. But a good - different. I haven't felt this way in a very long time."

"Well, I've known Antonio for most of my life, and I love him. I'm conflicted about him, but I love him." Anashe's face is soft and reassuring.

"Conflicted? How so?" I ask, bewildered by her confession.

"Well – on one hand, he breaks God's commandment - he's an assassin – on the other, I'm grateful that he is. He was there for me when we were younger, and he traveled with Warford, Valentina, and me from London, and I never felt more secure. So, you see – conflicted. I don't want to discourage you, but I've lived around people like him - hidden from people like him. I know Valentina trusted him with her life, and so do I. He's good at his job. But that's just it. He's good at his job. He's lived an isolated life, so – may not be the best husband material."

"I know what you're saying. Never thought of it that way. And I know it sounds like I'm seeing what I want to see, but I don't think so. I believe that regardless of his occupation, Antonio has a good soul. I think that's what Mother saw in him most. He took on a lot of her qualities after his mother was killed. She taught him and loved him. And he loved her. That's got to count for something."

"I just don't want you to get hurt. He would never hurt you intentionally, but…," Anashe says lovingly, yet cautioning me not to move too quickly and not to expect too much. At first anyway.

"He told me that this was his last job. He's ready for a change in his life. I've been trying to think of a way to carry on my mother's legacy. Some way to help people. People who are in trouble and have no place to turn. Not necessarily monetary help. Real help. He wants to be a part of it, whatever is decided. Something to think about. I've also been thinking of selling the candy factory. I don't know if it's what I want anymore. My mind is a boggle. So many changes in such a short amount of time. Wait and see what happens, I guess. What do you think about selling?"

Anashe is shocked that I would even ask her!

"Truly, I appreciate you asking, but I don't feel like I should give an opinion on that. I was never involved in that part of Valentina's life. She gave me so much, but that part belongs to you. I'm sure you'll make the right decision."

She takes the last sip of champagne and announces that she's going to go enjoy a bath. We give each other a huge hug, and I express to her just how much I enjoyed our talk. "I'm going to do that as well. I just want to get in contact with Captain Grayland and check on the status of Fiona Mitchell."

"Don't stay up too late," she says as she heads toward the bath. I smile, pour another glass of champagne, and dial the front desk.

"Could you connect me with the operator?" I ask.

The operator connects me with the River Dell County Police Department. It's very late, but Captain Grayland answers the phone. He assures me that Fiona is still staying at the Mayfield Hotel so I can relax. She hasn't followed me – not yet, anyway. I lovingly advise him to go home and get some sleep. "I won't be able to sleep until that woman is out of town," he says gruffly. "I don't trust her, and she's just crazy enough to try something. I'm more protected here. She can't get to me here."

I assure him I understand and reiterate that by Friday, she'll be taken care of, and we call all breathe again. We say goodnight and hang up. I think I'll follow Anashe's lead - A bath and a nice long sleep. Divine.

****

Sam and Lewis

Driving Miss Callahan - Again

The Callahan Windsor Hotel, New York City

Early Morning – Wednesday, May 23rd, 1928

I open my eyes little by little, still sleepy - wishing I could ignore Anashe knocking on my door, calling my name to get up. I search the bedside table for my watch, then realize it's still on my arm. I forgot to take it off when I went to bed. 8:00! I'm going to be late for my meeting with Mal!

"I'm up!" I holler, my voice cracking with remnants of sleep. "I'll be out in a few minutes." The knocking stops abruptly.

I take no time getting ready. My wardrobe consists of the same clothes I had on when we left for Tarrytown. Thank goodness for the complimentary soap, toothbrush, and toothpaste. I wash, brush my teeth and fumble with my hair using my fingers as a hairbrush. I look forward to going home.

I open my bedroom door and am greeted by the glorious aroma of breakfast.

"Smells divine," I say, grabbing a piece of toast and a cup of coffee.

"Is that all you're eating?" Anashe asks.

"Unfortunately, it's all I have time for. I'll be lucky to be on time for my meeting with Mal at nine." A quick bite of toast, a swig of coffee, and I'm off. "By the way, I don't know about you, but I think some clean clothes are in order. When I get back, we're going shopping."

I am not at my best this morning. I'm not looking forward to this meeting with Mal. I hope his attitude is better than it was yesterday because I'm certainly not in the mood for any more of his jealous tantrums. But the meeting with Mal isn't the only thing weighing heavy on my heart. I'm also grieving for Annabelle. The shopping isn't just for Anashe and me, but also for a burial dress for Annabelle. I'm calling her parents today. Don't know how I'm going to tell them their daughter is dead. Maybe Anashe can help me with that. Yes, I'll ask Anashe.

And then there's Felicity's funeral. I don't know. I may skip it. Ha! Won't that raise some eyebrows? I'll give it more thought, and I know my appearance is expected, but after what I learned, I could really care less whether I go or not. And since I've never been one to give two hoots about what other people think, I may just stay away. So many things on my mind. I'll find a way to get through it.

The elevator doors open to the lobby, and I walk straight to the front desk. I should have reserved a car last night, but I didn't think of it.

"Good morning," I say to the desk clerk.

"Good morning, Miss Callahan. What can I do for you?" The clerk replies in a chipper voice that I'm sure the hotel guests love.

"I need a car, please." He doesn't respond, but his eyes alert me that there may be a problem. "Is there a problem?" I inquire.

"No, no, there's not a problem, it's just that – Well - there's a car already waiting for you. Didn't you request it last night?"

"No, I didn't," I reply, concerned and suspicious. Then, a - voice speaks in a low, familiar tone from behind me.

"Miss Callahan."

I turn to see Lewis, Felicity's chauffeur, standing behind me in his uniform, his hat tucked under his arm. My heart begins to pound, and my throat tightens. *What's he doing here!*

"Don't be afraid, Miss Callahan," he says in a hushed voice, putting his hand up for reassurance. "Warford sent me."

"*Warford* sent you," I reply, mistrustful and disbelieving. Lewis is fully aware that I would never question Warford. He could be using that against me, and I make no bones about my intentions. "Then you won't mind if I call him then and confirm that."

"Please do," he encourages. "He'll explain. The truth is, Madam, I drove for Miss Felicity, but I *worked* for Warford. I'm sure you're aware by now what that means. He has, as of last night at the time of his departure, assigned me to you and Miss Anashe."

"Excuse me," I say curtly, returning to the desk to dial Warford.

Warford informs me that he did indeed assign Lewis to protect me and Anashe. He is to guard and drive us where we need to go, and he's to take me to Long Island on Friday.

"I'm concerned that Fiona Mitchell will show up in New York," Warford explains. "Lewis is there to make sure that you and Anashe are safe. I trust him like I trust Antonio. I would not have sent him otherwise," he says, slightly exasperated with my continual questioning of his expertise and personnel decisions.

I scold him slightly for not letting me in on the arrangements and that I would appreciate being kept in the loop. I hang up on him - abruptly. Lewis is standing in the exact same spot where I left him, patiently waiting for me to resolve my issue.

"To the Manhattan Precinct, then Lewis," I instruct, agitated that Warford chose to keep this from me, but relieved that Lewis is here for us, and I don't have to worry.

"Yes, Madam. Right this way." He responds, placing his hat atop his head, opening the lobby door for me and directing me to the Rolls parked directly in front the hotel.

As we drive to the police station, I take advantage of the

quiet to - think about what I will say to Annabelle's parents. I forgot to mention it to Anashe – how I could really use her help. Never mind, there will be time later. Right now, I need to keep it together for this meeting with Mal. But her memory lingers in my thoughts. Flashes of her smile, her sense of humor; her bubbly and intoxicating personality which always brought me joy, tickles my heart and brings tears to my eyes. I will miss that beautiful creature - my friend - until the end of my days. Annabelle…

****

Sam and Mal

Saying Goodbye

The 3rd Precinct, Manhattan, NY

9:00 a.m. Wednesday, May 23rd, 1928

The squad room of the 3rd precinct is busy and crushingly loud. I haven't been here in a long time, not since Mal and I…well, this is how I remember it. I scan across the room, searching for Mal. A few familiar faces come into view, but most I don't recognize. I finally spot Mal in the crowd and begin to make my way through the sea of officers toward his desk. He's on the telephone, so I patiently stand and wait. He glances up at me a couple of times while he's talking, indicating he's aware of my presence – and finally, motions for me to take a seat in the chair directly by his desk. I'd only been sitting for a minute or two when I was startled by a robust and familiar voice coming from behind me.

"Miss Callahan! How you doin! Long time no see! You are lookin beautiful as eva. I see this guy is ignorin' ya," he says, pointing to Mal. It's the unforgettable, unmistakable Joey G. He's a character, and despite his obnoxious demeanor, he makes me laugh and puts me at ease. "Can I get you a cawfee or somethin? I made it

436

myself," he says proudly. I remember his coffee. He's proud of it, but it's atrocious - like drinking bitter mud.

"It's nice to see you too, Joey. Thank you for the offer, but I'm fine. I won't be here long."

"Sure thing, Miss Callahan, an 'ey – I am sure sorry to hear about the tragedy at your house yesterday. If there's anything I can do, you let me know." He leans in close to my ear and whispers. "I got my feelas out. I'll find out who done it."

"Thank you, Joey," I say with polite cautiousness. Joey's 'feelas' are sometimes questionable. But if he likes you, he'll do anything for you. If not, well… Mal hangs up the phone and flashes me a nervous smile.

"I see ya didn't escape the attention of Joey G," he says nervously, shuffling papers on his desk. "Joey never changes." He's uncomfortable, and his shuffling distraction makes me uncomfortable.

"Mal, I don't mean to be rude, but can we get this over with? I need to take care of the arrangements for Annabelle and notify her parents. Not looking forward to that. I have a lot to do today." He ceases shuffling and sighs seemingly frustrated and on edge by my presence. I'm tired of his immature behavior so I confront him head-on.

"Mal, do I need to talk to another detective? I get the feeling that you are uncomfortable, and I want you to know I understand. I won't be upset if that's what you want." He stops his shuffling again, this time sliding his chair down directly in front of me. He takes my hands.

"I'm sorry, Sam. I'm acting ridiculous, I know. No, I don't want you to go to anyone else. Please forgive me for yesterday. I acted like a fool. I was jealous and… It's been very hard for me since… again, I'm sorry. It won't happen again. I promise."

I accept his apology and move on. I describe the car and the gun I saw – what I could see of it anyway and answer questions about the injuries to Mrs. Lilly and the death of Annabelle. All of this is simply formality – paper. The police can't stop or help in this situation, and Mal knows that. Only Warford, Antonio and I can put an end to this.

"Are you and Anashe alright? Is there anything I can do?" he asks. His sincerity is comforting, but I answer *no.* He hesitates and then says, "Sam, I hope everything works out for you. I want ya to know that you were one of the best things that ever happened to me, and I will never forget it. But I will let it go." He hesitates to deal with the lump in his throat, then says, "I'll take care of everything here, don't worry. You go do what ya need to do."

I think I heard 'goodbye'. He never said goodbye to me, and

while he doesn't say a word, it feels like 'goodbye' final. I never spoke of it, but I always thought of him - always loved him.

He rises from his desk – interview over. He's silent as I turn and walk away, refusing to look back. Never look back. I leave Mal behind in pursuit of what lies ahead. Whatever that may be.

****

The Daughter

Obsession

The 3rd Precinct - Manhattan, NY

Morning – Wednesday, May 23rd, 1928

She sits patiently in her car, far enough down the street from the 3rd precinct to avoid detection. Talking herself into a frenzy and waiting for Sam to appear. She's obsessed, and her mania grows with each passing minute. She knows she must wait. But not for much longer. Not much longer now. She keeps her eyes on Sam, sitting in her car, talking to herself as if she has a demon in her head until Sam is out of sight.

****

"There – you – are. Miss Sam Callahan. What cha doin' at the police station? Talking to your former boyfriend, no doubt. I'm really excited about our newfound friendship. Oh, now shame on me! That's not true! You want the truth? Okay. The truth is that all I want is you dead! That's all I want, really. I mean, everyone is all gaga about that diamond, and yes, I'll take it off your hands – your dead, cold hands, that is, but that is not my true desire. You – on the slab – that's my dream. Has been for a long, long time. You'll join

the others. Yes, yes, I killed them. I did! I killed them all. Idiots! Oh, please excuse me. I shouldn't speak ill of the dead. I'm sorry. I know I shouldn't laugh. Please forgive my rudeness. I'm just so excited! I'll be seeing you. Soon, Miss Callahan, very soon."

****

Sam

Old Friends

The Hotel Suite – Callahan Windsor Hotel, New York City

Late Evening – Wednesday, May 23rd, 1928

Lewis and Anashe are deep in conversation. They are old friends, which makes me feel a bit guilty that I treated him so shabbily this morning. But how was I to know. No one breathed a word to me – not one word -never disclosed that Lewis was an important part of Anashe's life growing up in London. They've spent hours talking. Anashe about her journey from a life of desperation in South Africa to London – medical school, and finally – Tarrytown. Lewis – his life on the streets of London until he was recruited by Mother to drive and protect Anashe. Lewis - another person connected to Mother that I've known for years - Felicity's driver – that was not who they appeared to be. If there's one thing I've learned about Mother and her crew, they are good at their jobs – masters - of keeping secrets.

I get over my snit and join in their conversation, enjoying the story of their history, but I must admit, I rather feel like an outsider. It seems that my life with Mother was rather tame, and I battled an unwanted feeling of jealousy. So many things that others shared with her in her alternate life that I can't possibly understand. Lewis and Anashe have so many stories to share, and I have nothing to offer. I scold myself! *How petty you are! You weren't running for your life and being forced to work in horrid conditions! Alone in the world, being raised by strangers. The present is your time. Now is what's important.* I feel stupid allowing these feelings to even come to mind.

My life with Mother was beautiful – something that had escaped me until recently. It took these extreme circumstances to bring that to light. *No.* I can't be jealous or bitter. My destiny resides in the here and now – taking control of what's at stake and taking care of the people I love whose very lives hang in the balance. That's my purpose. That's what God intended for me. Anashe would be glad that I embraced that.

Anashe is smiling and laughing and engaging and Lewis hangs on her every word, and as I listen to them reminisce, a question comes to mind. I wonder, how long has it been since she felt truly free to really talk about her life? Only with Mother or Sister Mary Agnes, I suspect. How lonely she must have been. I hear her laughter, and the jealousy I felt before seems even more wretched. Could I have survived her life? I don't really want to know the answer to that, and I resolve to never question my purpose in all of this again. Never again…

****

Sam and Anashe

The Death of Captain Grayland

Hotel Suite – Callahan Windsor Hotel, New York City

Late Night - Wednesday, May 23rd, 1928

My watch reads 10:30, and it occurs to me that I haven't spoken to Captain Grayland in quite some time. I want to touch base with him one more time. That way, I'll know whether I can expect to be able to sleep or whether I need to stand vigil with Lewis, awaiting a possible assassination attempt by Fiona Mitchell.

"Anashe – Lewis. I hate to leave this lovely conversation, but I really need to call Captain Grayland, so if you'll excuse me." I'm over-apologetic, probably caused by guilt over my earlier internal jealous fit. I'm relieved that they don't seem to notice.

"Oh, yes," they both reply in unison.

"I would like to speak to him also, Sam," Anashe requests. "I want to make sure he's not overwhelmed with everything I left behind and answer any questions he may have," Anashe adds.

"Sure," I reply, leaving my place of comfort on the sofa and walking to the desk. I take the receiver in hand, request the operator make the call and wait for him to answer.

"River Dell County Police," he says.

"Hello, Captain. Sam Callahan."

"Sam," he replies. His voice sounds remarkably weak. "I was wondering if I was going to hear from you tonight. How are you? How's Dr. Alexander?" He groans in agony, and while he tries to make light of it, there's no doubt he's ill – very ill.

"Captain! Are you alright? You sound sick." Anashe overhears the word 'sick' and immediately asks to speak to him. I motion for her to give me a second.

"Captain, I'm going to put Anashe on the phone. I won't keep you. I just wanted to check on our friend – if there's been any change." The sound of violent heaving and vomiting - moaning is all I can hear. "Captain? Anashe, he's sick!"

He scolds me and lies – tells me everything is fine, and we don't need to worry – then commences to give me a status report. "Sorry about that," he apologizes, his voice stressed and his breathing wheezy and labored. "I think I've got some sort of bug," he groans. "Her car was still in the hotel parking lot about 30 minutes ago when I picked up dinner. I haven't seen her, though. Mona said she hadn't checked out, but no one at the hotel had seen her since earlier today. I've asked Rice to drive by regularly and report. If there's no sign of her by morning, I'll either send an officer to attempt contact with her or do it myself. Hold on a second."

I put my hand over the receiver so that I could talk to Anashe without Captain Grayland hearing. "He's sick, Anashe. He's vomiting and moaning – sounds like he's having trouble breathing. Says he thinks he has a bug, but I don't know. He is very sick!" Alarmed, she grabs the telephone from my hand and starts calling his name.

"Captain! Captain!" she yells, trying desperately to get him to answer. "He's not answering," she says as we both wait for the sound of his voice.

"Dr. Alexander," he finally replies, offering a small wave of relief that is short-lived.

"His voice is so weak I can barely understand him," Anashe whispers to me, her eyes wide with concern.

"Something is wrong - very wrong!" I whisper back. "He said he got food from the hotel about 30 minutes ago!" Anashe calls his name again. Her voice is loud. My stomach tightens as I realize that she's not convinced his condition is due to some bug. The captain is in terrible trouble! She continues to call his name, hoping he'll answer.

"Captain, you need to get to the hospital now. Is there

anyone there with you?" She indicates to me with panicked eyes that there's no answer, but she continues to try. "What did have to eat!" No answer. Anashe is in full-blown panic! "Captain!" She screams. No answer. "Captain!" She screams again. No answer. "Captain! - Sam, he's not answering!" She calls his name over and over. Lewis joins us by the telephone, equally concerned and listening intently.

"Hello! Hello!" Anashe screams. "I hear you! Pick up the telephone! Hello! Who's there? Pick – up the telephone!" My heart is about to burst right out of my chest! "Hello! Who's there!" Anashe demands. "This is Dr. Alexander, who's there!" I wait on pins and needles for some sign from her that everything is alright! "Oh, Lord. Oh, Lord. Okay," she says as her eyes fill with tears and spill over, streaming down her cheeks. She looks straight into my eyes I see her lips move, telling me *he's dead*, but it takes a second to register. My heart sinks. I cover my mouth with both hands and press as if that will hold in the anguish and shock. Anashe takes two deep breaths but struggles to compose herself as she instructs the person on the phone what to do.

"What's your name?" - Anashe demands, her voice cracking under the emotion, her face wet with tears. "Okay, Officer Rice, you need to listen to me carefully and do exactly as I say. Are you ready? *Do not – do not* under any circumstances touch him or anything in that room. I need you to leave *everything* just as you found it. Do not touch anything. Call Chief Tuttle. Tell him that I am on my way.

Where is the captain right now?" Anashe pauses, allowing Rice to answer. "Okay, I want you to seal off his office and restrict access to anyone. Do you hear me? No one comes in there! I know you're upset, and it's hard to see him this way, but we must do everything by the book. Got it? Good. I'm coming! I'm leaving right now! I'm in the city, so I won't be long. I'll be there as soon as I can! You stay with him! Do not leave him alone-!" she demands, crying, her voice trailing off, diminished while she sobs for her friend. She regains her composure quickly, assuring Officer Rice of one final thing. "Let Chief Tuttle know that I'm coming, and I'll see you soon."

Anashe slams the receiver down, doubles over and collapses, sobbing so hard she can barely breathe. Lewis and I feel helpless, but this hits Anashe especially hard.

"I should have never left him!" she sobs, her body shaking violently, wracked with guilt. "I could have helped him! I've got to go, Sam," she cries in anguish. "Another friend, another friend is gone!"

My heart is breaking for her and the captain, and I don't say it, but I'm selfishly relieved she wasn't there. It could have been Anashe, and while I know she believes that her presence there could have saved him, I'm fully aware that had she stayed, I could be driving to Tarrytown to bury her. I'm not the least bit happy about her going up there now, but I know I won't be able to keep her away.

"Okay," I assure her, as Lewis and I help her from the floor. "Don't worry, Darling, I'll take care of it. I promise. Come sit here with Lewis for a minute. I have something I have to do." - We walk her to the sofa, and I get her some water. Lewis sits with her, lovingly patting her arm. - At that instant, the thought of calling Mal leaps to mind. He will want to know, and maybe there's something he can do. But first things first.

Ring – ring, Ring – ring.

C'mon, c'mon answer! I think in my head, not daring to show that my nerves are on fire and my heart is aching. I hear a click.

"Callahan residence," he answers in his usual curt tone. I squeeze the words from my swollen throat – relaying the tragic news about Captain Grayland.

"Warford. Captain Grayland is dead. Yes, you heard me right. He's dead. I don't know. I called him to check on Fiona – he said he got some dinner from the hotel, and he was sick, very sick. I thought of that." "Yes, I think so too. Well – she's distraught, of course. And she's already informed the officer on duty that she's on her way – instructed him to tell Chief Tuttle." "Yes. I know. It doesn't look good." "Very good then, I'll wait to hear from you, Mal." "Yes, I agree. I had the same thought, Lewis?" "Yes, he's here. Right. I'll put him on." "Oh, what about Fiona Mitchell? Is that right?" "I would have never dreamed. You never cease to amaze me,

Warford. And give Antonio my love."

I summon Lewis to the phone to speak with Warford and take my place beside my sister, wanting to comfort her yet knowing that for her, comfort will only come from determining what caused the death of Captain Grayland. I dread the answer, and I think Dr. Olive Alexander won't much like the answer either.

****

Sam and Warford

The Turning of the Screw

En Route to the Callahan Long Island Estate

Early Morning -Thursday, May 24th, 1928

Immediately after receiving his instructions from Warford

last night, Lewis drove Anashe to Tarrytown. Warford arrived at the hotel shortly after, not wanting to leave me alone for very long, knowing danger was close. At 4:00 this morning, Anashe telephoned to inform us that she is certain, beyond doubt, that Captain Grayland was poisoned, along with all the guests at the hotel who ate their dinner after 9:00 p.m. – and sweet Mini who ate her dinner, like she did every evening she worked, was dead at her post – the front desk. Of course, she also said that one of the guests could not be accounted for. A mass murder all to get at one man. I've always considered myself a good and caring person – never crossed my mind to do harm to another.

But if there's one thing I've learned over the last couple of days, it's that sometimes, the only thing that can combat evil and do what is necessary to save lives. I don't like it. In fact, I hate it. But we must stop it, and I don't see any other way. It goes against everything in God's Word, but I know that Mother was faced with these choices in her life. And I'm now reminded of what she meant when she said, "We'll all have to explain our actions to the Creator, my Darling, in doing what we think is right. Our actions are wrong, but our hearts are in the right place. That's all we can do. The rest is up to the Lord. I never knew what she meant by that – until now. I hope you can forgive me, Lord. Praying for that…praying hard."

Speaking of evil, I won't be going to Felicity's funeral today. After Warford's surprise discovery, I don't think I'll be doing that. And if I have my way, her public image will go from victim to murderer in all the social circles she loved - and used - so ripe for the picking. Warford warned me to be discreet, and I will. I'll find a way, I swear, I'll find a way to reveal her as the stain she was. All I need is time.

I notified Mal of the news of Captain Grayland. He didn't hesitate. Anashe told me that he is in Tarrytown, taking charge of everything. Apparently, he told his Captain what had happened and informed him he was going to Tarrytown to help no matter the consequences. His Captain and Chief Tuttle made an agreement that Mal would be on loan to Tarrytown during the duration of the investigation. But I have a sneaking suspicion Mal won't be returning to Manhattan.

The drive to Long Island, which is usually one of my favorite things in the world, is overshadowed by darkness.

"Warford. Are we ready for tomorrow? Do you have it?" I ask.

"Everything is a go," he replies, his tone matter of fact.

"Good," I say, adding nothing else.

Warford – eyes straight ahead, utters only four words in response.

"Yes, Madam. Very good."

****

Fiona Mitchell

The Interview

The Callahan Estate - Long Island, New York

11:00 a.m. – Friday, May 25th, 1928

I park my car at the top of the huge circle drive and scan the

outside of the enormous mansion, remembering entryways and

possible exits. The lavish front doors resemble a barricade,

impenetrable except with permission. I almost blew it the other day

with my slip of the tongue. But no matter. I don't think she caught

it. Still, it's much easier driving through the gate than climbing over

it. I'm glad I came when I did. She's posted two armed guards.

Doubt I'd have such an easy time of it now. I breathe a huge sigh as

I stand before the fortress. I feel like I've prepared for this moment

my entire life, and nothing nor no one is going to stop me now. I've

waited a long time for this. I've dreamed about this opportunity over

and over for as long as I can remember.

I approach the massive doors, admiring the overly large yet

ornate knocker. *Boom, boom, boom.* An echo reverberates inside,

sending a small chill down my spine. A deep breath and the fortress

gate swings open, the gatekeeper before me. Ah, yes. The ever-loyal

Warford. I'm disappointed but not surprised. I planned for this. I planned everything.

I smile my biggest and best smile and burst forth with confidence, saying, "I have an appointment with Miss Callahan at 11:00. My name is Fiona…." He cuts me off! His rudeness lights a tiny flicker of anger - just a little one that I quickly extinguish but won't forget.

"Yes, Miss Fiona," he interrupts, his pompous tone grating and demeaning. "Madam is expecting you. Please come in." He keeps one hand on the door and invites me inside with the other. "Madam is waiting for you in the sunroom. Please follow me."

I follow him as instructed, along with two dogs, panting – faithfully remaining at his heel. Hadn't planned on dogs. Throws me a little, but not earth-shattering. I turn on the grace and charm. "I must mind my manners and be polite," I think sarcastically.

"I hope I'm not too early!" I exclaim in as perky a voice as I can muster. As we walk, I take it all in, making mental notes for later. The open foyer is gorgeous, adorned with polished marble, granite pillars, handcrafted furniture, and a grand staircase covered in rose-colored, plush carpeting. The end of the long hallway opens into a sunlit room, where inside, Sam is peering out the window, holding a cup of coffee. The dogs scurry ahead, excited to see her, spinning and begging for her attention. She responds to them in a very unexpected way.

"How are my good babies this morning? Huh? So good. Yes, you are such good babies!" She speaks to them in baby talk. It's nauseating, and it goes on for what seems to be forever until she commands them to lay down, and they immediately obey. Warford waits patiently for this – display - to end, then promptly announces,

"Miss Fiona Mitchell, Madam." *Am I supposed to bow or something?* I think sarcastically.

She greets me with a smile and sings, "Good morning." Then adds, "I hope you've been well since we last saw each other." My stomach tightens at the sight of her. Her beautiful black satin robe with huge bell sleeves - her hair uncombed and a curly mess – her perfect porcelain complexion. A picture of stunning beauty. No wonder she always gets what she wants. No wonder Mother… she grates on me like a serrated knife cutting meat. I quickly get my expression in check. Don't want my face to give anything away. I force a smile and talk myself into a charming and gracious reporter, just happy to be here. My stomach is churning as she bends down to pet those dogs, still talking to them in that baby voice.

"I'm so glad we ran into each other Tuesday," she says cheerfully. "Felicity had nothing but good things to say about you when we met to talk about…" I'm not in the mood for her emotional dribbling, so I relieve her of her sickening on-and-on about how Felicity revered me.

"Well," I say, faking appreciation. "I'm flattered by her confidence in me. She was a true champion of women, and I'll never forget how supportive she was of my career. She certainly did her best to teach me and guide me. She always spoke very highly of you as well. That's why I was so surprised that you wanted to move the interview to today, considering everything you've been through this week. And with Felicity's funeral yesterday…" *Don't push, keep cool. Keep cool.*

"Well, like I said, we must carry on for Felicity – in her honor," she replies. "And I've decided to take some time away – try to forget all the ugliness. So, it's either today or, who knows – maybe never."

Did she just tell me that she's leaving town and may not come back? Oh, how delicious. This is good news. Perfect.

"Well – I can't say as I blame you," I encourage, sympathy pouring out of me, playing on her sense of loss. "Shall we start the interview? That is, if you're sure." I say, my tone masking the truth. A truth she'll find out soon enough.

"Yes! I'm sure!" she assures, gathering her dressing robe and taking a chair. "Let's begin. Please, sit. – Now, where do we start," she says, arms crossed, looking so eager to talk about herself. But the tap dance will come to an end, Miss Callahan, and then – everyone will be talking about me, the toast of the town.

****

Sam and Fiona

Till Death Do Us Part

The Callahan Estate – Long Island, New York

11:15 a.m. – Friday, May 25th, 1928

There's a hint of anger in Fiona's voice and that fake sympathy. I don't know whether I should be angry or laugh. The fact is, she needs to work on her routine. Her cleverness isn't quite what she thinks it is, and I'm elated that she believes I know nothing. I'm the sitting duck stupidly waiting to be picked off. Nothing like a good surprise. How surprised she'll be.

"Yes, it has been a very difficult week," I say, intentionally going on and on just to grate on her nerves, denying her control. "That's why I'm leaving town for a while tomorrow. I need to get away, you know. So much tragedy. And more bad news! Well, I probably don't have to tell you, being you were staying at the Mayfield." Fiona doesn't answer, her expression instantly stoic, which only gives her away even more. "Captain Grayland and all those poor people at the Mayfield? And the poison of all things!" I'm watching the beast rise before my eyes, and I just keep poking it. "Any idea who would do such a thing, Fiona?" I ask, with a hue of accusatory sarcasm, my words stabbing her at her very core. She avoids my question, but I see that sickening look of pride in her eyes. It's the same look I saw when we met at the Mayfield. Antonio knew. He knew all about her, and he was right.

"Um…My friends call me Mitchy, Miss Callahan," she inappropriately replies, trying to make it personal - trying to regain control.

"Mitchy!" I exclaim, my tone demeaning as if that's the stupidest name I've ever heard. "Well, *Mitchy*…how about some tea before brunch?"

My condescension toward her is chipping away all the layers. She pretends that she doesn't notice it, but I know she does. She can't help but notice. Every fiber of her being forces her to notice. Her smile is forced, and the longer she's made to wait, the more I chip away at her sinister, worthless self.

Time to reverse the tactics. I need her to drink the tea.

"Oh, my word, I don't know what's gotten into me! I just can't believe my rudeness! I really don't know what's wrong with me. I'm so sorry, Mitchy. You see, this is why I need to get away! Please forgive me. Oh, boy. I've done it now, haven't I? Please don't write about my rudeness in the article." I plead. "It's just been a horrible week. Maybe we should reschedule?" I know she'll say no. That's why I'm confident to ask in the first place.

"Of course, I'll forgive you. I understand," Fiona assures. "And no, I wouldn't dream of putting that in the article. Never! I want you to trust me, Sam. Now, we've all been through a lot this week, me included. So, not to worry."

"Thank you, Fiona. Felicity said I could trust you, and now I know I can. I hope I haven't driven you away. I wouldn't blame you if you wanted to leave and just forget it. How rude I was, and again, I'm sorry." Fiona waves it off with her hand, determined that I'm not going to end the interview. The mention of her leaving did rattle her some, though. Of that, I'm sure.

"Oh, yes. The tea. Would you like some tea, Mitchy? You'll love it. It comes from South Africa. It was my mother's favorite, and I've come to love it too." I summon Warford.

"Yes, Warford. Could you bring Mitchy and me some tea while we wait for brunch?"

"Yes, Madam," Warford replies.

I take note of Fiona's reaction. She's agreeable but not long on patience. She's impulsive, and I want her agitated - stepping toward the edge. She's showing signs of distress, tapping her fingers on the table, her expression becoming more and more hateful by the second. Warford returns with the tea.

"Ah! Warford," I greet with excitement. "Is brunch ready?

I'm starving, and I'm sure our guest is too." He pours the tea and exchanges a subtle look, a hint that it's done.

"It is on the way, Madam."

"Wonderful! Thank you, Warford. What would I do without you to take care of me?" Warford doesn't reply. He simply leaves the room in normal fashion. I order the dogs to follow him.

"Go with Warford, now. Go with Warford!" They follow him in obedient bliss. *Mitchy* rolls her eyes in disgust. One more poke.

"I wanted to ask you a question if you don't mind. Something I heard and am curious about," Fiona says bluntly. I smile and discretely glance behind her. Warford and Antonio are now standing guard – watching.

"Of course!" I exclaim, taking a sip of tea.

"Speaking of South Africa, I had read somewhere that your mother, Valentina, had worked in South Africa for a time and during her time there, she acquired an exquisite diamond. The story is sort of a legend, apparently, and I am just wondering if it's true. Just for curiosity's sake."

As she brings the cup to her lips, I see in her eyes the delight she is taking in, letting me know that she's aware of Mother's past and the diamond. I laugh slightly but don't give her the satisfaction of an immediate answer. I want to toy with her just a little. Exploit her inability to deny herself pleasure at the expense of others. There's not much time left.

"Well, *Mitchy*, I think we both know that you didn't read about it anywhere. You heard about it – from Felicity." She can't hide the shock of that statement. "Never expected that, did you? And - you're right. There is a diamond, and it belongs to me now. Has since Mother died. Too bad Felicity wasn't good enough to get her hands on it, even though she tried for years. Mother was just too smart for her, though. She and Foster. Del Ray. And now you."

Her expression is priceless. She didn't expect me to admit it. I push - harder. "And you know what else? It's right here in this house – in the safe. And you can have it. But there's a catch. You have to kill me to get it." There, I issued the challenge. I'm calm, cool and unafraid. She's been completely disarmed, and though her face shows little inside, she's struggling to keep it together.

"Wow!" she exclaims, faking a laugh. "You surprise me! I thought for sure you'd lie and try to say it wasn't true, and then we'd have to have this big argument. How refreshing. I'm impressed. Do you mind if I smoke?" she asks, taking another sip of tea, leering at me over the cup as if she's won. "How did you know?" she demands, taking one puff after the other, nervously tapping her cigarette on the ashtray, her world falling apart and her body and mind beginning to fail. "Mommy was always so careful to keep her secrets. I always hated the way she doted on you and Valentina. I hated it!"

The look on her face says it all. She never intended that to come out of her mouth. But it did, and I intend to use it.

"How did I know what? That Felicity was your *mommy*? Well - I recognized you from a photograph on Morgan and Felicity's mantle. I asked her about you once, and you know what she said. She said you were her niece – Natalie Banes – and you died in a car crash. Imagine that. Warford's the one who discovered who you really are. Don't ask me how he does it. He does have his ways, though. You're the daughter. The one Felicity never loved. She created a psychopath who lives to watch people die. A monster."

Her cigarette has burned down to her fingers, and she's beginning to moan in pain. The poison has begun to do what it does best. Kill. But I want her to admit what she's done, so I step it up a notch. There's not much time left.

"How does it feel, Natalie? How does it feel to know that your life is slipping away and there's nothing you can do about it? Welcome to the world of your victims. Welcome to your own hell!"

"My name's not Natalie," she growls as she doubles over in pain, vomits, hitting the floor, her breathing labored and slow. "I don't have a name!" she screams, her face twisted and wrought with agony. I glance at Warford and Antonio, who are watching everything unfold, prepared if something goes wrong. "I chose the name Fiona Mitchell myself when Mother asked me to do that stupid article! She was always looking for the diamond, you know. She didn't care about anything else. Not you or Valentina…"

"Or you?" I hatefully point out.

She's dripping with sweat, getting weaker. I need to hurry if we are to truly know that this ends with her.

"So, who all have you killed, *Mitchy?* I know you didn't kill Felicity. What happened? Chicken out?"

"Never!" she screams, then gasps, the sharp pains becoming unbearable. "I didn't kill Mommy, that's true. I would have, but someone beat me to it." She sounds disappointed. "But - I did kill Sister Mary Agnes. Get it? I'm *The Butcher.* Del Ray was my mentor on that one," she gloats, which sickens me, but I allow her to go on. I want every detail. "And I did Cooley – Del Ray – Foster - and I poisoned the lettuce for the dinner salad at the hotel, killing your Captain Grayland and all those poor people." Even dying, she manages sarcasm and a laugh, patting herself on the back for her hideousness. "Don't I - do good work? Aren't – I - just the best at this job? Mommy always said I was the best. Taught me - everything I know. I'd – planned on – killing you – with - the same – gun I killed – Foster – with. It's – right here – in my bag. I was going to – set – you up for his murder."

She's getting weaker. I'd feel sorry for her if I wasn't so horrified. Felicity was the true monster. She ruined her own daughter's life – ruined her just like everything else she touched. I look toward Warford and Antonio, patiently waiting. Any second now.

Two more labored and gory gasps and then - she is dead. I can't take my eyes off her, slumped in the chair, head bent back, eyes wide open and empty. I've never watched someone die before, and I've certainly never had a hand in someone's death. My heart sinks a little. I'm conflicted. I'm glad it's over, but Antonio was right when he said that killing a person changes you. The circumstances dictate the degree, but nonetheless – change.

Warford and Antonio slowly walk up behind her. Tears of relief and sorrow fill my eyes, and I can't believe it's finally over. The daughter is dead. They're all dead. The case of the diamond dolls is finished. The living and the dead can now rest in peace. *It's over, Mother. It's finally over. May God have mercy on us all.*

****

Sam and Anashe

Beauty for Ashes

The Museum of Natural History – New York City

10:00 a.m. - Saturday, August 4th, 1928

The museum is packed for the debut of the "Legendary Diamond" Exhibition. Anashe has worked very hard to put together an exhibit that educates about the horrors of the diamond mines of South Africa.

"To Those Who Lost Their Lives, The Story Will Be Told."

Anashe's Momma	*Sister Mary Anna*
Valentina Brandenberger Callahan	*Sister Mary Collette*
Maria De Cordova	*Sister Mary Clarice*
Captain Graff Grayland	*Sister Mary Francis*

And

Sister Mary Agnes, my dear friend and Guardian Angel, who reminded me that God never leaves us,

and He has a purpose for us all.

The story of the legendary diamond, suffered by a child, redeemed for good by God. It brought her pain in the past, and now, it brings joy to the present. Sister Mary Agnes was right. God's purpose will not be outdone, nor will it be forgotten.

"This is what God intended," Anashe says, beaming with pride. "Beauty for ashes. That's what God promised."

It fills me with absolute joy to see her like this, and keeping my promise that the diamond would be used for a good purpose settles my soul. It will be housed here for a long time, the sale of the candy factory footing the bill. But it's a small price to pay. Anashe is what's important. She is financially set, and I have all I could ever need money-wise. And as for love?

Antonio and I married, and he's waiting for me to return to the Florida Keys, where we've been on a two-month honeymoon with no plans to return anytime soon. He sends Anashe his love, but as usual, he doesn't want to face the crowd. I'm only here today to support my sister – help her heal, and to honor those lost. This exhibit and her interaction with the public, children especially, is a perfect start. And Mal is here. He's the new Chief of Police at the River Dell Police Department in Tarrytown. Seems Chief Tuttle decided to retire, and Mal was more than willing to take the position. Captain Grayland's position has yet to be filled.

And last, but not least, there's Warford, who retired and

found himself a beach just as he said. He keeps in regular contact, but I have no idea where he is, and I'm alright with that. He'll turn up one day, and I know if I need him, he'll be on my doorstep in an instant. I haven't decided what the future will bring, but I know God's in control of it. I have faith in that.

Antonio and I are happy, and while I'm not discounting the possibility of using my newfound skills and connections to continue to help others, I'm taking a rest for the moment. But who knows? If there's one thing I've learned, the future is far from set in stone, and the past can blindside you in an instant. I have no idea what tomorrow will bring but,

I'll let you know if something comes up.

About the Author

Hello and God Bless! I'm the author Carolyn McWhorter. And I'd like to share something with you. I needed to know how to write a successful author bio. So – I dove into the internet and read several articles about the particulars of how to write a successful author bio. I gleaned some great information for sure, but I'm here to tell you, I'm not doing that. This fabulous story depicting strong, faithful women breaking glass ceilings, fighting evil and winning spiritual battles, is told in the first person, so that's how my bio reads also.

And while I'm not a famous author (yet), or an author with too many awards to count (yet), and there's not a movie deal (yet), and I don't have any famous authors reviewing my work (yet), can I tell you that you that this tale will lead you through an international journey where you will experience spies, love, danger and evil through the eyes and lives of each and every character. It's truly a unique and exciting experience and it's how I tell a story. I can't wait for you to become a part of the dark and twisted world of The Diamond Dolls, where evil exists, sacrifice foreshadows, love triumphs, and the Godly prevail against all darkness.

So, what are you waiting for? Sam is calling you. Your adventure begins on page one …